God had taken her mother, stolen her. Her death had come during the bitterest days of winter and the cold had taken away her life. Now she was gone. The thought of it still came as a shock. It could not be possible, still so beautiful, now dead. Marsh fever had been the cause. The disease had come on quickly, progressed fast and ended in these unimaginable consequences. Diana could not fathom that her mother died so, taken in the prime of her life by the natural and loving hand of God.

She wiped her eyes. Her breath trembled as she inhaled. Without her mother she felt lost.

A presence loomed behind her, a dark shadow. Diana ignored it. Nothing anyone could want from her would be enough to pull her from this deepest moment of despair. Let them speak with her father, whatever they needed. A moment passed. The figure remained, felt more than seen. Diana remained turned away, forehead against the marble.

A hand gently brushed her shoulder and she tensed. Still she didn't turn to look. Perhaps they'd leave if she didn't respond. Instead, fingers brushed her long hair aside from her right ear. She felt breath, warm and moist against her throat. Diana's fingers gripped the lid of the sarcophagus in surprise. Otherwise she froze, unable to move, unable to turn. She behaved like a child hiding under covers in hopes not to be seen by some imaginary witch. The person, whoever it was, seemed to hesitate. A heartbeat passed. At last came the fateful words, whispered in Diana's ear.

"Your mother was murdered."

Suicide Kings

by

Christopher Ferguson

Suicide Kings

Cover Art by *Diana Carlile*

The Wild Rose Press, Inc.
PO Box 708
Adams Basin, NY 14410-0708
Visit us at www.thewildrosepress.com

Publishing History
First Historical Mainstream Rose Edition, 2013
Print ISBN 978-1-62830-070-3
Digital ISBN 978-1-62830-071-0

Published in the United States of America

Dedication

To my wife and son, who have always been supportive.
And to my parents, Denise and Stuart.

Chapter One
The End at the Beginning

Firenze, February 1497

The sun filled the horizon with angry rays glinting across a thousand lethargic flakes of snow that flurried down from a passing bank of dark clouds. Diana Savrano held a hand over her eyes to shield them from the glare. Her eyes, rimmed with red, already stung. The new flakes made the going treacherous, her black boots unsuitable for the slippery stone streets.

Late as usual. She'd found it difficult to dress herself, to hook the laces of her black dress, to adorn herself in such a dark and depressing garment. For such a complex article, she'd usually count on her mother's help. Though a young woman, she'd never quite managed the dexterity for the most complex formal garb and somehow the designers managed to make things ever more difficult. More hooks, more loops, more layers, more madness. Her mother would not offer her any assistance this evening. Isabella Savrano already waited at the Basilica of Saint Zenobius.

Once, Diana had called out for her mother to help, forgetting her mother was gone. Frustration had reduced her to inaction, and for a while she could only stare at herself in the mirror. Finally she'd summoned up an absolute store of energy, and gotten herself

1

dressed properly. By then the rest of the household had already gone. Her father had left behind one of their Swiss mercenaries as an escort. The young man had kept his eyes averted from her.

Now she scurried along the city streets as quickly as she could. She did not want to keep her mother waiting any more than she already had. Other citizens parted way before her, a fury of black, black dress, black boots, black hair, pounding her way across the crowded streets and piazze. She must have made for quite an odd sight.

Her breath came in rasps, and tears formed at the edge of her eyes, but these only froze into beads of ice, to drop away and mix with the snow. Behind her the Swiss mercenary kept pace easily, silent, watching, assuring she progressed to the Basilica unmolested.

At last the building loomed into view, the great Basilica rising high above the surrounding buildings. The marble and other stones around the outside were designed in such a way the edifice radiated a faint combination of light green and faint crimson hues, particularly in the fading light. The face consisted of so many statues, frescoes, gargoyles, and etchings the building seemed almost coated in spines. Huge wooden doors promised mass inlet for the penitents of Firenze, although in practice only the smaller doors to the sides were ever actually opened.

Diana chose one of those now. She burst into the church, huffing and puffing from exertion, eyes blinded by the oppressive dark within. She stopped short, realizing she'd made too much of an entrance. She wiped her eyes, gave them a moment to adjust.

Candles struggled to light the interior of the

Basilica. At the best of times, with midday sun streaming through the ungenerous stained glass windows, the nave felt cold and oppressive. Sculptures from the finest artistic talents of Firenze did little to assuage this atmosphere, for too often the themes of these sculptures focused on the suffering of martyrs and the ease with which life transitioned to death. Indeed most of the artwork in the church had been commissioned for the many tombs that lined the walls; the exalted dead of Firenze marking their passage with the finest, if morbid, decor.

One of those tombs now sat open, the funerary plaque not yet hoisted into place. Before the black void waited an open casket. As Diana's eyes adjusted to the gloom, she could see a small congregation gathered around that casket. They turned to look as she entered. Most averted their eyes upon seeing who it was, no doubt made uncomfortable by the grief written on Diana's face. Her father watched her without expression. After a moment he turned back to two luminaries with whom he seemed engaged in discussion. The congregants near the tomb milled about, speaking, or sat quietly in prayer in the wooden pews set up near the tomb. Cardinal Michele Lajolo had been asked by her father to officiate at the service and he now stood off to one side, conversing quietly with several mourners.

With a sinking heart, Diana realized she'd missed the service. Fresh tears filled her eyes and spilled over and down her cheeks. Could this day possibly get any worse? She must seem like such a horrible human being to the other mourners. And they were right. Her mother would be so disappointed in her.

She sucked in a deep breath, one arm going defensively across her chest. She couldn't make eye contact with the others present, tried to imagine there were no others in the room besides her. The least she could do was move forward to the sarcophagus and pay her respects. She could spend a little time alone with the dead, ask her forgiveness.

So she proceeded up the little impromptu aisle between the wooden pews, shivering in the cold. A nun stood as she moved past, a thin, sad bird of a woman. Their eyes locked for a moment, but it was the nun who looked away, seeming chastened somehow. Diana focused ahead, one small step after another, making her way forward to greet her mother who awaited her.

When Diana's fingers touched her mother's she found them cold and waxy. They felt unreal. Much unreality needed to be made real tonight. Instead of sitting side-by-side as they always did, fingers entwined as they prayed together for a dead acquaintance, her mother tonight had awaited her with the greatest of patience. For her mother lay in the ornate sarcophagus in quiet repose, her fingers cold because no more warm blood flowed through them. Her mother was dead. And it just could not be so.

"Mother?" Diana pleaded quietly, looking down into the sarcophagus. In death, Isabella Savrano wore the finest deep green dress with a string of diamonds around her neck. Her skin seemed the color of snow, set off against rivulets of dark hair, black with some strands of gray. Diana might have mistaken her for sleeping and hoped even now her quiet entreaty might awaken her from this deep slumber. A drop fell from Diana's cheek down onto Isabella's dress. A last gift from daughter to mother.

Diana collapsed to her knees beside the casket, her legs unable to hold her upright any longer. A great sob burst from her chest, the reality of her mother's death inescapable. Never could Diana have believed this possible, even as Isabella Savrano had sickened with fever, Diana had believed fervently in her mother's immortality. She'd been wrong to believe.

Diana sat arm in arm with death itself. Past marble images of angels, she reached her hand up and over the lid of the sarcophagus to stroke her mother's face. Her other hand held the rosary, fingers ticking off the prayers in deepest grief. Her mother's flesh drew warmth out of her.

Behind her still was most of the funerary procession: the Cardinal Lajolo, her father Signore Savrano, dozens of others who blended together like ghostly strangers through blurry eyes. They gave her time to say goodbye to her mother before the tomb was sealed and Isabella Savrano vanished forever into the wall of the Basilica.

God had taken her mother, stolen her. Her death had come during the bitterest days of winter and the cold had taken away her life. Now she was gone. The thought of it still came as a shock. It could not be possible, still so beautiful, now dead. Marsh fever had been the cause. The disease had come on quickly, progressed fast and ended in these unimaginable consequences. Diana could not fathom that her mother died so, taken in the prime of her life by the natural and loving hand of God.

She wiped her eyes. Her breath trembled as she inhaled. Without her mother she felt lost.

5

A presence loomed behind her, a dark shadow. Diana ignored it. Nothing anyone could want from her would be enough to pull her from this deepest moment of despair. Let them speak with her father, whatever they needed. A moment passed. The figure remained, felt more than seen. Diana remained turned away, forehead against the marble.

A hand gently brushed her shoulder and she tensed. Still she didn't turn to look. Perhaps they'd leave if she didn't respond. Instead, fingers brushed her long hair aside from her right ear. She felt breath, warm and moist against her throat. Diana's fingers gripped the lid of the sarcophagus in surprise. Otherwise she froze, unable to move, unable to turn. She behaved like a child hiding under covers in hopes not to be seen by some imaginary witch. The person, whoever it was, seemed to hesitate. A heartbeat passed. At last came the fateful words, whispered in Diana's ear.

"Your mother was murdered."

Chapter Two
The First Death is the Sweetest

"Your mother was murdered," carried a voice on breath that stank of foul wine and rotten teeth. Diana barely registered the words, and when she did, she thought they must be some horrible seed of her own imagination. She blinked, forcing herself out of her misery. Diana looked up, searched the Basilica of Saint Zenobius for the speaker.

There seemed to be no one standing close. Perhaps it had been her imagination after all. She had not slept well since the death.

She couldn't shake the vividness of the voice, though. Certainly it had been no illusion. If only she had been clear-headed she could have seen who it was. She stood, and stared at the crowd, none of who paid her much mind. The voice had been a hiss; it could have been a man or woman. Not far away stood a man in a green doublet, his back turned to her. She touched his arm. "Did you speak to me?"

He turned and looked at her in sympathy. "No, Lady, I did not."

His was the wrong voice. She turned from him without explaining. Her eyes scanned the others in the Basilica frantically. There! Far away now, across the dark and cold chamber, a nun hurried from the group. Short and thin, she moved past the massive altar at the

7

end of the nave toward a small wooden door studded with iron bolts. As the door creaked open, the nun turned and caught Diana's eye. The woman's wrinkled face quivered but she held Diana's gaze and the rosary dropped unnoticed from Diana's hand.

"Wait!" Diana shouted, her voice echoing endlessly through the cavernous hall. Several dozen pairs of eyes turned to look at her at once, but the nun broke her stare and fled through the door. Shouting had been the wrong thing to do, Diana realized. Picking up the folds of her dress, she hastened to follow the nun. She ignored the looks from the other mourners.

Diana tore open the studded door, finding herself faced with a narrow set of stone stairs winding up. This was the way into the cupola then, the huge dome painted with scenes of heaven and hell. It was a long way up and Diana was poorly dressed for such a climb, but she felt determined. With one hand she held onto the central stone pillar for balance and with the other she held up her dress to keep it from getting under her feet. She looked up, but of course could only see the bottom of the stairs above her. She had no idea how far it might be to the top.

"Sister!" she called up the stairs. "Was it you who spoke to me? I must know!"

No answer came, only the soft retreating sounds of footsteps above. Up, Diana drove herself, higher and higher, round and around until she became dizzy and slightly nauseated. Once she stopped to rest and wobbled on one foot before catching herself in time. She pushed herself onward, ignoring the cramps moving across her diaphragm, ignoring the tightening in her chest as her lungs struggled for breath. Her long black hair billowed out behind her like branches of willow. The stairs seemed endless. Only small windows cut into the stone brought light into the stairwell, and showed her how high she ascended. There must be a thousand stairs, she thought, maybe ten thousand.

At last she came out of the winding stairwell onto a landing. Larger windows paned with clear glass let in better light here, and she could see the landing held supplies for cleaning the dome. The roof displayed an inward facing curve and she knew she must be near the top. Still, the nun was not here as she had hoped. Off to the left, a small door.

Diana ran to the door and opened it, emerging onto a small stone ledge running along the inside of the dome. Down below—it seemed like hundreds of feet— she could see the party of mourners. Her mother's body was just barely visible in its coffin. To the best she could tell, no one saw her emerge on the inside rim of the dome.

Above her were scenes painted on the dome. Domenico di Mechelino had done them, she remembered. At the outside ring, nearest her, were scenes of the damned in Hell, tortured by devils that stripped them of their flesh or rammed fiery spears into their orifices. Closer to the center of the dome, these scenes blended effortlessly into scenes of paradise, of wise men and women engaged in pursuits of learning, or art, or gathered lovingly around Christ on his throne. The message of the dome was not hard to read.

The stone walkway ran around the circumference of the dome. At the opposite side, another little door. Where did this nun think she was going? Diana was resolute. She'd follow the nun to the outside of the cupola itself if need be. Her legs were getting wobbly, and her calves stiffening, but she wouldn't let her body stop her. Through the door greeted another narrow set of stairs, so narrow even her slim body barely fit. She went with her hands in front of her, holding onto the steps in front, pulling herself up. It was dank in here, humidity clinging to the stone. Only the dimmest light seeped in from the open doorway below. If she lost her footing, if she fell, she'd go down twenty feet of the steepest stairs she'd ever climbed, hitting stone after stone.

At the top almost no light reached her, and she groped in the dark against a stone door. At last she found the latch and opened it. A strong wind pulled the door from her grasp and she nearly flew onto her face. Outside, an evening sky beckoned, the last rays of the sun casting a scarlet pallor over the horizon. Even through her thick dress, the night chill cut deep into her. The wind up here blew fierce and dangerous. The landing was not wide, and there was no railing for protection, only the swift curve of the dome that led into the open air. Diana hated to think how far the fall would be.

Here at last, waited the nun. The woman kept her back to Diana and didn't turn as she emerged onto the cupola. The nun's habit billowed in the wind, her body swaying in sudden gusts of cold.

"Sister," Diana called out, taking a few tentative steps onto the landing. She held her dress in tight, both for warmth and to keep it from acting like a sail. She bent her spine low, keeping as squat a profile as she could. "Did you speak to me at the funeral?"

The woman turned, her face haggard. Diana

surmised the nun must have been in her fifth decade. Her eyes were clear and young, but her face wrinkled with age. Her face had a quality that suggested the weathering of experience beyond the cloisters. "I did, lady, but perhaps it was ill-advised."

Diana felt a stab of confusion, whipped into frenzy by the grief of her mother's death. How dare someone claim her mother had been murdered only to later regret making such a claim! "Why would you say such a thing to me?"

"Because I believe it to be true, lady." The wind whipped the nun's habit, flicking the ends of the black robes into the breeze so she appeared like an unholy phantom.

"My mother died of marsh fever!" Diana shouted, although the ferocious winds carried away much of the force of her voice. Awkwardly, Diana crept forward like a well-dressed hermit crab. She constantly peered over the edge of the dome to the darkness beyond. How easily the wind could gust, and push her over the edge. It occurred to her this could all be some elaborate trap, with the nun luring her out here to be pushed to her death. That made even less sense than the accusation of her mother's murder. She could think of no reason anyone would want either of them dead. "How dare you malign my mother's memory by claiming she was murdered!"

Under the assault, the nun lowered her eyes and fell silent. This was not what Diana wanted. She had to get control over her emotions, and so she swallowed and took a step closer. "Do you have proof of what you say?"

The nun looked up, "None that would withstand

inquisition, lady." She looked at her hands that quivered as she spoke. "I am only recently of the veil. Prior to entering the cloister I lived a life that was…unholy." As she said this, Diana assumed she referred to prostitution. It seemed the most likely route for a woman to enter into a life of sin.

The nun continued, "This last week I have seen a man in Firenze I knew from my former life. This man has only one business: to bring death to enemies of his powerful patrons. He did not recognize me under the veil and I kept myself hidden from him, fearing for my own safety."

Diana shook her head, absorbing what the nun told her. "You're saying this man is a hired assassin?"

The nun nodded. "I thought he might have been sent by the Borgia pope to assassinate the mad friar Savonarola. Yet Savonarola lives and your mother has died. Hers has been the only death of a person of note since my former colleague has come to Firenze. That she is said to have died of marsh fever when it is too cold for the disease to take hold in the body has led to my suspicion."

Diana looked away. "Is there more than that?"

The nun nodded. "Just one thing more, although what to make of it I am unsure." She reached into the folds of her habit and produced a parchment. She extended her arm, passing the parchment to Diana. The rough paper flapped in the draft, threatening to be taken away forever if Diana hesitated.

Diana took the proffered parchment. A seal on one side had already broken open. Diana opened it, but between the encroaching darkness and the wind, found she could not read it.

"Keep it safe," advised the nun, "and read it when you can. Perhaps it will make some sense to you."

Diana did as she was told, putting the parchment safely into the folds of her dress. "Who is this man you claim has killed my mother?"

The nun looked down again. Diana sensed her discomfort, although in her urgency to get to the bottom of the nun's claim, it mattered very little. At last the nun said, "He goes by the name of Giuseppe Mancini di Milano."

"Where can I find this man?"

The nun's eyes went wide. "Surely you must understand that approaching such a man is extremely dangerous. I must warn you away from such a course of action."

"I want to know where I can find him!"

"So be it, although you should heed my warning. He was staying at the inn called the Romancier. If his business in Firenze is concluded, he may have moved on from here."

Diana absorbed it, memorized the name. She realized, too, she had been wrong about her guess regarding the nun's former life. "You were in this business with him, weren't you?" she cried. "You murdered people for money."

The nun fell to her knees, hands held out in supplication. "Please do not say such things out loud. I have repented my former life and wish nothing more than to live out the remainder of my days in penance. But when I saw him—" A glint shone in her eyes when she said this, and Diana guessed the two had once been lovers. "—when I learned your mother, always known as a good and generous lady, died suddenly, I could not stand by. In approaching you, I sought only to give your mother an opportunity for justice, but I fear I may have only brought you to danger. Promise me you will not use what I have said to bring trouble onto yourself!"

"Why didn't you go to my father with this?" Diana demanded, as it was the most logical course.

The nun looked tearful and shook her head as if begging forgiveness. She opened her mouth to speak, but she was startled by the sound of grinding metal as the latch on the cupola door worked open. Someone was coming out onto the cupola landing with them.

The nun's eyes glinted in the last rays of the sun. "Quickly, you must get away!" The nun grabbed Diana's arm, and pushed her from the door. "There is another door on the other side of the cupola. The stairway will lead you back down inside. I will stay here so you may escape!"

Escape, Diana wondered. Surely it would only be her father or one of the other funeral attendees coming to check on her after witnessing her sudden flight. The nun remained insistent though, and her fear became infectious. The cupola door squeaked on its rusty hinges. With a flash of panic, Diana picked her way along the landing, careful not to lose her balance. After only a few steps she slinked around the corner and out of sight. Her fear, no longer fueled by the nun, began to ebb. Here she stood, a lady of Firenze, skulking about like a thief on the cupola dome. She still had none of the answers she wanted, only some vague insinuations her mother had been assassinated. Feeling fury welling up inside her, Diana turned back, coming around the corner and back into view of the nun.

What she saw gave her pause. The figure that had

emerged onto the landing had its back to Diana. The entity wore a loose fitting cape with hood, not unlike a Dominican monk's robe. The cape flittered in the strong winds like a specter. The figure loomed over the nun, who gestured frantically and spoke rapidly, although Diana could hear little of what she said.

The caped form spoke in return, and Diana could only pick up pieces of it. It was a man's voice, deep and resonant. Although it must have been a trick of the wind, the voice seemed to harmonize with itself as if two people were speaking at once. Diana had never heard anything quite like it. It was not a pleasant combination such as from a choir, but something that was unnatural and dissonant. The few words Diana could distinguish over the wind were Latin, but she could not hear enough to understand the conversation.

The nun raised her hands, in one of them a small metal cross she held up toward the cloaked figure. The gesture was unmistakable, a rebuke of the unholy. Diana wondered for a moment if the dark figure might dissipate before the power of Christ like the vapors of a ghost.

Either the specter was of a wholly more material nature, or the nun's faith was weak. The figure put one dark hand on the cross and flung it away into the night. The nun screamed then, the sound piercing even from the distance, striking terror into Diana's heart. Diana wished to run forward, to come to the assistance of the nun, but she stood paralyzed with fear and uncertainty. There would be little a young woman such as herself could do against such an imposing figure.

The specter raised one hand high over his head. Diana opened her mouth but her voice refused to come.

The nun put up her arms defensively, but the dark form offered no mercy. The specter brought his hand down against the nun's outstretched arms and he pushed her. Her legs went out from under her and she fell, down to the landing and then over it onto the edge of the cupola. The dark figure kicked the nun's prone body and she went out over the edge of the dome and silently into the blackness below.

Diana's scream now came instinctively, her voice breaking through the barriers of fear. She barely realized the sound was her own until the cloaked figure turned to stare at her, the face lost in the darkness of the hood. To Diana it seemed as if the specter were the Angel of Death himself. Panic now unquenchable, Diana turned and ran for the door the nun told her of. Her dress threatened to get under her feet and trip her. The hands of that specter could only be moments from flinging her off the dome to join the nun below. Diana burst into a flurry of activity. Once she saw the door, she hastened to it, her hands fluttering over the latch. It seemed stuck at first, her terror growing with every second that slipped away futilely trying to work it. At last the rust gave way and the door came open. Without looking back she flung herself through the opening into the darkness beyond. There remained almost no light now, and she felt her way down the stairs as quickly as she could, taking only as much care as necessary not to doom herself to tumbling to certain death.

It occurred to her even if the specter were not directly behind her, he could take the opposing stairway and cut her off at the interior ledge, or the interior landing with the maintenance supplies. There was nothing to be done about that, however. Diana could hardly lurk on the dome indefinitely. No safe hiding place offered itself. She had to trust in herself and in God that she would make it down safely.

At each moment she expected cold hands to lay themselves upon her, to reach around her throat and snuff the life from her. The horror of these thoughts drove her on. She cursed the ridiculous dress that made flight so difficult. She made promise after promise to God, about good behavior, the frequency of her prayers, that she would stop glancing lustily at the Abruzzi's son when she saw him during mass. At last she came out on the interior rim of the dome. Below, far below, she could see her mother's funerary party much as she had left them. They had not moved, evidently unaware of the nun's death.

"Papa!" she called out. From so far above she could not distinguish him from the rest, nor see if they looked up at her. Certainly they could not have failed to hear her voice as it echoed throughout the chamber. There were still so many stairs ahead of her. However, now if she were being followed by the specter at least he would be seen by the funerary party below. Knowing this gave her a measure of comfort. Still, he was nowhere in sight, and she began to suspect her pursuer had quit the chase.

This supposition did not stop her from making haste in her descent down the remaining stone stairs, however many hundreds there must be. At last she emerged back in the nave, exhausted. She bent over her waist, hands on her knees and coughed loudly and violently as she struggled to suck in breath.

Around her the funerary party clustered, anxious. She looked aloft and saw her father staring at her, disapproving. She ignored his look and told the assembled group, "Quickly, we must go outside. There's been a death!"

****

Cardinal Lajolo quickly took control of matters. Priests and church laborers formed a barricade around the body of the nun while several men fetched a bier to carry the corpse away. The funerary attendees added to the little cluster around the body, further obscuring it from view. The crowd served to draw the attention of some passersby however, and a few strangers drew into the circle out of curiosity. They reacted with horror, a few women screamed on seeing the body, although most remained nearby asking questions and discussing the matter solemnly.

The nun's body—Diana realized she had never gotten the woman's name—splayed on the cobblestones, a pool of blood filling the little spaces between the bricks. Her eyes stared vacantly and her mouth held open in a skeletal grin, displaying the remains of a few rotten teeth. One arm bent back around behind her and both legs were twisted like dry twigs. A slimy loop of intestines emerged from within her robes like an umbilicus.

Diana took deep breaths to retain her composure. She'd seen bodies at funerals before, and the relics of saints of course, but nothing like this. She'd been talking to the woman only moments before. Around her, the city of Firenze continued in ignorance. In the distance music played and revelers laughed. Only those few who passed by this street learned of what had happened. Soon the news would pass all over the city. What effect it might have, Diana could only wonder.

The violent death of a nun, even in a modern city like Firenze, could inspire all kinds of superstitious talk. Particularly of late, with the mad friar Savonarola in power, giving wild sermons on witchcraft and heresy. And why shouldn't people be superstitious? After all, Diana herself had seen what looked like a phantom with an inhuman voice. Perhaps evil spirits were at loose in the city.

A gendarme arrived to investigate the disturbance. He asked questions, but from his voice, Diana guessed that he was not sure he had or wanted authority over something that had happened on church property.

"Did she jump?" the gendarme asked, looking to the top of the dome.

"It is a shame," said a man in the crowd, a funerary attendee by the name of Orsini. A business partner of her father's, he'd come with his wife all the way from Roma. Now he clucked his tongue. "Sometimes women don't realize the convent is not the satisfying retreat from real life some think." Beside him, his exquisitely dressed wife shook her head, agreeing with the shame of it all.

"She did not jump. She was pushed," Diana told them. The assembly murmured and the gendarme looked at her without speaking. "I saw it."

"Did you know who pushed the sister?" asked the gendarme.

Diana faltered. "I saw only a figure cloaked in black. When he turned to me I could see no face under his hood." Another excited murmur went through the onlookers. Diana closed her eyes, steeling herself. She knew half the throng spoke of demons loose in the city; the other half asked if she were mad.

"What were you doing up on the dome?" the gendarme asked with a tone that suggested he identified with the latter, more skeptical half.

It occurred to Diana that relaying the entirety of her conversation with the nun to a crowd that increasingly included strangers might not be in her best interest. Fortunately, she was diverted from answering the gendarme's question by Signore Orsini. "The young woman has just lost her mother, with whom she was very close. I think the shock of it has influenced her sensibilities, quite naturally of course." He looked at her with his eyebrows raised, his expression sympathetic and meaning no offense.

"We saw no one go up to or down from the dome besides yourself and the nun," added his bejeweled wife.

"I am having the dome searched as we speak," said Cardinal Lajolo. "There may be places a man could hide." As he spoke several attendants arrived with a thick bier and rolled the nun's body on to it. One used a small spade to move the coil of intestine on as well. This completed, they covered the body with a shroud and hoisted it waist high. The attendants hurried to get the body inside and out of view. The assembled multitude remained standing around the blood pool on the ground. "I wish I had a good sense of what has occurred," Cardinal Lajolo implored. "The disposition of the body is at stake. If she has killed herself, then her soul is damned and she cannot be buried on consecrated ground."

Fury grew in Diana. They really weren't going to take her at her word, preferring to believe instead that she had been stricken mad with grief.

"If my daughter says she saw the nun pushed, then she was pushed," her father said at last, his voice composed, yet commanding. "Is there anyone here who has known my daughter to be prone to lies or flights of imagination?" The chorus of onlookers remained silent. Even if they had thought such a thing, there were few here who would be keen on insulting her father. The Savrano family never enjoyed the kind of power and influence that the Medici family had possessed before being cast out of Firenze. Nonetheless, Signore Savrano conducted lucrative business with many of the assembled men and had their respect. None would want to risk that over the matter of a dead nun. "Very well then," he said at last. To Cardinal Lajolo he suggested, "Given the circumstances, I think it best to offer the nun a consecrated burial. If there's been an error, would not God understand?"

Lajolo nodded. "A wise suggestion, Signore Savrano." The cardinal moved off, intent on seeing the matter put to rest. The gendarme retired as well, without further comment, evidently concluding the nun's death was the cardinal's problem, not his own. The onlookers began murmuring in small clusters, although individuals and groups began breaking away, drifting back into the night.

Diana felt her father's eyes on her, but she could not meet them. She felt humiliated. Her reputation had been secured only because he had put his own on the line, and waited some time in order to do so. Many in the mob certainly still assumed she was delusional with grief over her mother's death. They had only kept silent so as not to offend her father. She sucked in several deep breaths. She did not want to say anything to her father she would later regret. That left her with nothing to say at all. It took her some moments before she could bring her fury and humiliation under control and look at him. His eyes were still watching her, his gaze even and critical. His expression remained difficult to read as it often was.

A moment of silence passed between them. At last he said only, "Come on, it is time to go home."

Chapter Three
The Flame

That night Diana slept horribly. Exhaustion made her eyes weep and her bones ache, but her mind insisted on going over again and again the sadness of her mother's death. That she now had the question of her mother's murder to go over in her mind as well only put sleep further from her grasp. She'd hidden away the parchment the nun had given her...she was too disturbed as it was to try to read it now, and put herself to bed. As the hours went by she tossed and turned, sometimes weeping into her pillow. When she finally drifted off, her dreams turned to the phantom on the dome, who came for her with ghostly arms outstretched. These dreadful images startled her out of her sleep, and she began the cycle again.

The coming of morning radiance brought a new perspective. Nothing could be done about the death of her mother, of course. Yet, if the nun told the truth about her mother's murder, she could do whatever possible to be sure those murderers were brought to justice. As dawn flooded in through her windows, Diana retrieved the parchment and opened it. She recognized her mother's handwriting at once. The parchment read:

"...was a mistake. We must acknowledge now that we have been led astray by false witness. Certainly you must agree with me that the events of last night demonstrate this beyond all debate? I am concerned what would happen if my husband were to find out. As of yet he knows nothing of our secret. Yet I fear that continued secrecy will only make matters worse. My conscience is in turmoil about what must be done. I implore you to meet me soon as we must discuss what to do. Meet me at the church on the Piazza Madonna delle Grazie at dusk tomorrow." It was signed merely, "Isabella Savrano."

Diana flipped the parchment over, then felt for pages stuck together. Nothing. It was the last page of a letter, but missing at least one other page. Diana did not know to whom the letter had been written, or what it was about. Still, she didn't much like what she had read. Her mother had been involved in something she had not wanted her father to know about. The obvious explanation was that her mother indulged in a sordid affair with another man. Yet, the tone of the letter didn't quite seem to match that explanation. And what did she mean about false witness?

Diana sat back in her cushioned chair. She had only moments to herself. If she didn't appear at breakfast, her father might very well send for her, particularly after such an odd evening as last night. Getting a moment alone from then on would prove difficult. She needed some time to think. She had difficulty resolving her feelings for her mother with the secretive woman in the letter. Diana and her mother had always been close, far closer than she had been with her father. Isabella Savrano had been a vibrant, intelligent, cultured woman who treated her daughter with affection. True, now that she thought on it, her mother might have seemed distracted in the last weeks, but there was nothing that would lead Diana to suspect something so serious that could have ended in her murder.

Thinking of her mother she realized once again she would never see her smile, receive a comforting word or piece of sage advice. Her most crucial human bond severed eternally. Diana shook her head to clear it. Weeping and moping were not going to be sufficient to reveal the circumstances of her mother's assassination. Diana needed to summon her strength and her guile. Her mother deserved no less. Fortunately business matters would keep her father distracted, as always they did, so she could begin her investigation without hindrance.

Diana soon dressed and made her way down to breakfast. Her father sat already at the table, but he was silent, looking over papers as he ate. Diana remained quiet as well. Their relationship had never been one of idle chatter and given the previous night's events, she felt even greater distance between them.

Suddenly, as if thinking of it for the first time, he said without meeting her eyes, "I've hired you a new handmaid."

"You've what?"

"It's been more than a month since Silvia left us to get married. The time had come to replace her."

Diana put down her fork. "Am I not to be consulted in the hiring of my own handmaid?"

Her father sipped at some rare Indian coffee without looking at her or matching her raised voice. "An application came in with excellent letters of reference. She worked for the Orsini in Roma, but is eager to make a move to Firenze. I discussed the matter with Signore Orsini, while you were chasing after errant nuns. Besides, I am the master of this household, and employment decisions are mine alone. If you wish to hire your own handmaid, you have been given ample opportunities to start your own household."

So that was the matter at hand. At nineteen, Diana was well past the age most young women married. What was worse, in her father's eyes, was that Diana had turned down several suitors who would have made good matches—one of the Orsini's sons, the elder son of the Borgia pope, a minor count from France who had been quite smitten with her. None of these men interested her. In truth, she wasn't sure the life of marriage and children interested her much at all, but if she was going to doom herself to that kind of servitude, she would be sure it was for a man she dearly loved. Her mother had understood that and intervened with her father on her behalf. The result had been for her father to turn down potentially advantageous marriage proposals to his own embarrassment. From his tone, she guessed he wasn't going to push the issue too far now, but if another good proposal came, he might not refuse it, now that her mother's influence was gone.

Her father finally looked at her, meeting her gaze coolly and without emotion. "You should have married the Comte du Briere. I think he actually loved you."

She matched his gaze without fear or submission. "But I did not love him."

He sighed and put his papers down. "Marriage is not about love. A lucky few might find it, but most of us are content with a passing affection. I've never entertained a proposal from a man I knew to be of poor character or likely to take fists to a woman. You must consider what you are to do with your life. You can't remain in my household forever."

"I could study medicine at Salerno. I've heard that they've taken a few women as students."

Her father drew back in shock, a rare display of emotion. "Certainly not! Even if what you say is true, it is not for women of good moral fiber to enter the trades. You're a Savrano, for the sake of the Virgin Mary, not a common washerwoman."

"Medicine is a trade, true, but it is a trade held in some repute. In our own city, the physician's guild is held in the highest standing. Was not Hippocrates a physician, and Galen—"

"Enough," her father said with a wave of his hand, having regained his composure. "Next you'll say you wish to enter the profession of law."

"Will you at least think on it, Father?"

He looked up at the ceiling as if seeking the hosts of angels painted in elaborate colors there for strength, "If I make you promises you will only get your hopes strengthened for nothing. Medicine is not a woman's work." He went back to his papers, evidently considering the matter closed.

Diana groaned and made a big show of pushing away from the table and stomping out of the room, all of which her father ignored. She huffed her way up the carpeted stairs and threw open the door to her room. Slamming it behind her she let out a scream.

"A poor start to the morning, lady?" inquired a voice from the corner.

Diana spun around to find a young woman off to the side folding linens. Looking the woman over, Diana decided that she needed to improve her powers of observation, for the woman was hardly difficult to perceive. Her age must surely be near to Diana's own, perhaps a year or two younger. She dressed in the formal attire of the household attendees. She would have blended in, had her hair not been a blazing orange-red, cascading down over her shoulders and back without the usual tie or bun the other household women used. Her face was freckled and her skin pale to the point of near transparency, nearly opposite in shade to Diana's own healthy olive sheen. This must be the new handmaid her father had told her about. Clearly, she was not from Roma, as her father had led her to believe.

"You startled me. I wasn't expecting you," Diana explained the obvious, catching her breath.

"I am Siobhan Biern and I am at your service." The girl curtseyed. She couldn't seem to stop smiling though, a disarmingly informal expression that unnerved Diana. She already wasn't sure how the Orsini had recommended her so highly. Perhaps they sought to fob her off on the Savrano family, although that admittedly was not characteristic of them. The girl must have some charms. "I've already seen to organizing your room, lady. I've only a bit more to do. Do you have any other instructions for me?"

Diana edged closer to her, as if observing a potentially threatening and unfamiliar beast. "Where are you from, exactly?"

The girl's knowledge of the Toscana dialect was superb, although the accent grated, like listening to someone pluck the hairs out of a cat's tail. "My father was a sailor from Ireland. When my mum died, he took me with him to Naples, where work could be had. Sadly he died some years back and left me on my own." She shrugged, the silly smile never leaving her lips.

"I'm sorry to hear that. I've just lost my mother."

Finally the smile vanished and the girl's eyes hit the floor. "Yes, your father mentioned so. I'm very sorry to hear about your loss. I know how it is to lose a parent." She touched Diana on the arm. More of that instantaneous familiarity. The girl had no boundaries.

"You've got a very nice home," Siobhan intoned, neck craned, staring at the ceiling.

Although it was her own bedroom, Diana couldn't help herself but to look up as well. On the ceiling was painted a scene from Greek antiquity, women and men gathered around a fountain with one of them apparently lecturing to the crowd on some highly emotional subject while the rest swooned. Both the men and women wore simple bolts of cloth in the Greek fashion although these were often minimal, revealing the grace of the human physique. The painting had been manifest overhead as long as Diana could recall. Some famous dead fellow painted it. Painting really wasn't her thing.

"Do you ever wonder," Siobhan asked, batting her eyes, "how the Greeks ever got anything done when they couldn't keep their clothes fastened? They always have those little bits of cloth but they never stay secure, do they? I mean, the women have always got their breasts out. Don't you think they'd feel silly, walking about like that, everyone staring? And the men, I always wonder how the Greek men had any success with the ladies at all, if they really had to make do with those little…"

Diana cleared her throat.

"What?" Siobhan asked innocently. "It's your

painting."

"Did you say you actually interviewed with my father before he hired you?"

Siobhan nodded. "Oh we had a pleasant little chat, indeed." She looked back up at the ceiling. "It's a queer painting for a child's bedroom, you have to admit."

Diana huffed. "All the ceilings are painted like that."

"So I've noticed. The Romans seemed to prefer more pious and lordly paintings such as popes slaying infidels and Jews, or sinners having their skins stripped away by demons in hell. I think I prefer the taste of you Firenzans to be honest. I thought Italians were supposed to be particularly Catholic folk, but here you are with nude paintings and statues every direction I turn. Why if ever I lack a spot to hang my hat, there'll be some convenient swain with a fig leaf or what not in every corner."

Diana couldn't help herself, a little chuckle welling up in her chest.

"We Irish are quite the opposite. Not a hint of obscenity, but we go about making new servants for the Lord every chance we get."

Diana blurted out a quick laugh, then remembering her dead mother, immediately felt horrible, new tears welling in her eyes. She considered that to enjoy herself was somehow to betray her mother's memory.

Siobhan looked crestfallen. "Oh, look what I've gone and done. I didn't mean to make you cry." She quickly moved to embrace Diana, and Diana, contrary to form and protocol, discovered the gesture comforting. Come to think of it, Siobhan was the first person to show her any real compassion since her mother died. Diana allowed herself a moment to regain her composure before pulling away.

Diana dabbed away the moisture from her eyes. "Well if you're going to be my handmaiden, you couldn't have come at a worse time. My mother has just been murdered and I'm intent on finding out by whom and for what purpose."

Siobhan made a show of looking shocked. "Murder, how horrible!" Whatever else she might be Siobhan was no actress, and Diana could tell she'd heard about the incident last night.

"I see my father already told you."

Siobhan frowned. "He mentioned the falling nun, yes. People tend to like to tell their own stories though; I figured I'd give you the chance."

Reasonable enough, Diana decided. "And my father expects you to report back to him on my activities I presume."

Siobhan shrugged and looked sheepish. "My understanding is that the occasional report is expected under the terms of my employment, yes."

Diana didn't feel terribly bothered. If her father really wanted to impede her, he could have done so far more effectively than by merely assigning her a watch-maid. In an indirect way it seemed a sign at least her father noticed her and cared. Such signs could be rare.

"If you intend to keep by my side at all times, you should know that investigating a murder will be quite dangerous." Diana said this with a tone that implied she knew a thing or two about murder investigations, which she most assuredly did not.

"By definition, most murder investigations are, I would wager."

Diana put her hands on her hips and considered. It took her only a moment to decide. If it would mollify her father, she'd allow this woman into her confidence, at least for now. Besides, it might be just as well to have another mind helping her, if even just to sound ideas. "Very well, then. I've been trying to decide the best place to begin my investigation. It seems that there are several key possibilities. First, there is the man Giuseppe Mancini di Milano whom the nun said may have murdered my mother. He is staying at the Romancier and I would most like to question him."

Siobhan nodded, listening intently.

Diana felt more confident as she spoke, realizing she was not without good ideas about how to proceed. "I would like to find out more information about the nun herself. I never so much as got her name, and I would like to inquire of the Cardinal Lajolo or the local convent about her background. Then there is this note." She passed along the parchment in her mother's handwriting to Siobhan, who looked it over with interest. "We could go to the church mentioned in it, to see if the parish priest noticed anyone meeting with my mother there. And lastly, I should look through my mother's things. My father wouldn't like that, but there could be information there."

Siobhan nodded once more. She looked interested, even excited. "Those all sound like reasonable options. Where do you think that we should begin?"

"I think with Giuseppe Mancini. If he came to Firenze to slay my mother and the job is now done, he could leave at any time. We might already have missed him; my mother has been killed several days prior." Diana noted how she had seized upon the surety of her mother's murder. She still had mainly the nun's word to go by, but this inquiry gave her a sense of purpose. She would hunt the truth no matter how difficult.

Siobhan narrowed one eye. "If this man is truly an assassin, you can't simply walk up to him and ask."

"I realize that." Diana rubbed her chin in thought. "If he is still staying at the Romancier, he might have some information in his room that would be of use. We should search it...that is, if you're sure you wish to come with me?"

"This is the most excitement I've known in years! But I wonder, how will we gain access to his private rooms? We don't know which room is his, and I suspect the innkeeper wouldn't simply let us in."

Diana's brow furrowed. "We need to figure out some way for the innkeeper to show us which room is his. If a package were to be delivered to the room, the innkeeper might very well let us take it up. Once we find out the correct room, we can sneak back in."

Siobhan pulled the edges of her mouth in a gesture of uncertainty. "I'm not sure. He might use a different name."

"I bet he'd use the same first name, perhaps change the last," Diana proclaimed with more confidence than she actually felt. "Otherwise he might be seen not to respond to his own professed name, which certainly would be suspicious."

Siobhan nodded, appearing to think about Diana's rationale. "I have a feeling this is going to prove to be a most unusual position of employment for me."

Diana realized her plans put Siobhan in a difficult position. If they were caught, Diana's father would almost certainly be able to get them out of any legal trouble. Whether he would be inclined to save an employee in the same manner as his own daughter was frankly doubtful. "I should probably do this on my own. You're only a handmaid after all." Indeed it wasn't Siobhan's mother who'd been murdered.

Siobhan shrugged one shoulder. "I'd be in no worse trouble than if I let you face danger alone. Besides, I'm hardly a stranger to adventure, I can tell you that."

Diana felt satisfied and turned, walking crisply from the room without explanation. Siobhan followed quietly. Diana led down a hallway, up one floor to a study with an excellent view of a public plaza below.

Siobhan commented quietly, "Oh look, more naked Greeks on the ceiling. Looks like they're up to something important though, doesn't it?"

Diana ignored her, and from a carved wooden desk, produced a gilded box. She snapped open several clasps and raised the lid. From within she pulled a wooden object, perhaps a foot in length, with a metal tube imbedded across the top, and a thick knob at the back. On top, a complex wheel held a piece of pyrite ready to strike against a metal pan. The body of the device was carved to look like intertwining vines of ivy. It weighted heavy in Diana's hands. To try to lift it and point it with one hand would be very difficult for her. Keeping it in both hands, she held it for Siobhan to see.

Siobhan squinted. "What is it, exactly?"

Diana frowned, disappointed. "It's a wheellock pistol. It was a gift to my father from some painter and inventor. It's one of the first of its kind. My father took me to Milano a few years ago in hopes I might marry one of the cousins of the Sforza family. The painter worked on a consignment for them there. Leonardo showed me how to use it. I think I remember." She looked back into the box and found the small ivory horn with gunpowder, and a dozen or so metal balls.

"Do you think you really could dispatch someone with that?" Siobhan looked skeptical.

"At least I'll have the option, won't I? Is there anything that we're forgetting?"

"A small measure of good sense, I'm beginning to think," Siobhan murmured.

Diana felt her blood rise at the insubordination. "You're welcome to stay here and do laundry if you prefer."

"Forgive me, lady. I just hope we are up to the task."

Diana regarded Siobhan for a moment. "Me too. I don't feel like I have much choice. You do, however. You could very well be killed. Already my mother and the nun were killed. I won't hold it against you if you stay behind."

"I couldn't have that. I'm with you, lady."

Diana nodded, feeling relieved and mildly guilty at the same time. "We should go before my father realizes that we're up to something and tries to stop us." She moved for the door. "I'd hate to see good sense get in the way of our plan."

****

For the delivery, they made up a package sealed with wax and containing several long bricks. These gave the parcel a realistic weight, yet also made carting it across Firenze an unforeseen annoyance. Naturally once this was discovered, the labor largely fell to Siobhan. Diana carried the pistol and a length of good silk rope in her pack.

Once they were outside the Romancier, their final deliberations revealed the weaknesses of their plan. "You can hardly deliver the package." Siobhan pointed at Diana's clothing. "You're dressed for mourning. Mourners don't deliver packages."

"Uggh!" Diana put her hand up to her forehead. "I can be such a fool sometimes."

"Well, you can be forgiven since you've just been through a considerable shock. I'll deliver the package, but you'll have to break into his room once I discover which is his. Can you get through a lock?"

Diana managed a wry smile. "You can't live successfully in my father's house without learning a few skills. If you can determine which room belongs to Giuseppe Mancini, I can get us inside. Don't use his full name though…"

"I remember the plan," Siobhan assured her.

With that the Irishwoman left, disappearing into the Romancier. Diana leaned against the side of the building and waited, which never had been her strongpoint. She fidgeted, sighed, looked beseechingly at the sky. She counted the gold sequin coins sewn into the bosom of her dress, then remarking upon the squalor of this section of town, decided covering them with her black shawl was a better idea. Hours seemed to pass, yet the sun remained stationary. At last Siobhan reemerged from the Romancier, a smile playing on her pale lips.

"Mancini's room is at the top of the stair, down the hall to the right, the last door to the left," Siobhan proclaimed.

"He's still in Firenze then?" Diana remarked,

surprised he hadn't made his escape.

Siobhan raised her hands, palms up in a shrug.

"Huh," Diana said, accepting her good fortune. "Very well, then. I'll get into the room and let you up with the rope."

Siobhan nodded and looked at Diana out of the corner of her eye. "May God grace your fortune."

Diana kept the shawl around her shoulders, trying to look the least out of place as possible. She knew there was no way to truly accomplish this. She was too rich, too young, too beautiful for the Romancier, with or without mourning clothes. She held her head high though, kept her gaze straight, making herself look purposeful as if she had every right to be there, and knew exactly where she was going.

Walking through the door of the Romancier she nearly lost her resolve. It was dark and smelled of alcohol, anger, and urine. She started for a moment, her lungs trying to find breathable air, her eyes blinking out the sting. After a moment she pressed on, stairs visible through the dim light. To her right she perceived a long wooden table with a stack of liquor behind it. A balding man eyed her quietly from behind the stand. There were other men in the room; quiet, unsavory, emitting that stench of failure, resentment, and lust which made the Romancier seem like the first port of stop on an oceanic tour of Hell.

She ignored them, forged ahead. Their ungodly desires would be stoked by her physical features, which were fairer than any of this lot might hope to touch. Yet men such as these feared a woman of power, and she needed to be that woman. She must have succeeded for she reached the stairs and ascended them without molestation, without so much as a comment.

At the top of the stairs she exhaled, realizing only then she had held her breath. She found the door Siobhan had directed her to. With shaking hands she pulled a metal barrette from her hair and used it to disengage the unsophisticated lock that held the door.

The room beyond was small and poorly adorned. It was a corner room with two windows, a small bed with straw mattress, a small desk and a plain wooden armoire. Closing the door, Diana went to the window and found Siobhan waiting below. Using the rope to let her up proved to be easier said than done. Siobhan might not have been a big girl, but she had fifteen pounds on Diana, and there was no piece of furniture to which to tie the rope. Ultimately the door latch had to do, and a moment later a huffing Siobhan tumbled into the small room.

"Doesn't exactly travel in the highest of fashion, does he?" Diana remarked, looking around.

"Oh I don't know. I've had worse. Not everyone needs satyrs and nymphs cavorting on the ceiling above them to sleep at night."

"All right, look around for...I don't know, evidence." A thorough search of the room wouldn't take terribly long. Diana opened the armoire and was greeted by the aroma of clothes long past agreeableness. She pinched her nose. "Is bathing truly so expensive that the poor can so ill afford it?"

Siobhan giggled. "It is said that bathing too regularly may bring upon malevolent humors. If I may say so, it may be of some value to you, lady, to see some of the world beyond Firenze. Try Roma; the whole city stinks. People follow around the pope in hopes that a few puffs of his perfumed grace might alight on themselves."

"Let's not mix our burglary with blasphemy. One sin at a time." A quick look through the wardrobe revealed nothing. She didn't have the heart of desperation yet to go through the clothes that hung there.

"Here, under the bed!" Siobhan called with excitement. She withdrew a small wooden box. "It's locked. I could try to jig the lock."

"Wait!" Diana ordered, a horrid thought crossing her mind. She hefted the box. It was not terribly heavy and as she shifted it, she could feel small objects within sliding back and forth. Coins, she guessed, not terribly many in number. She peered at the lock. Small, intricate, more complex than the box itself. "The lock might contain a trap of some sort."

"Do you think so?" Siobhan sounded dubious. "In that little box? If this man is poor as you say there would be no way he could afford such a lock."

Diana squinted, trying to see inside the dark keyhole from underneath. "Perhaps I've misjudged the man in my initial impression."

"We could always smash the box."

Diana chewed softly on the inside of her cheek. "There will be no hope then of our mission going undiscovered."

"How long do you think that's going to last anyway?"

Diana put the box down, thinking. "Is there anything else of value in this room?"

Siobhan shook her head. "Dirty clothes, half eaten food, unmade bed. Maybe he's got some hidey spot full of clues, but it could take us hours, or never, to find it."

Just the box then. It was all they had. Diana tapped a front tooth with one polished fingernail. With a sigh, she slid the box back under the bed.

Siobhan was aghast. "Are you daft? That's the only thing of value we've found!"

Diana looked up at her. "I won't have you risk a possibly trapped lock. If we take it and we're caught, we'll be thieves. I'll get a lecture; you'll be hanged. I won't take that chance."

Siobhan blinked, apparently experiencing a rare speechless moment.

In the silence, footsteps were audible outside in the hall. Diana met Siobhan's wide eyes. Without a word between them, they simultaneously darted into the small armoire and hid within. Diana took only enough time to slip the ornate pistol from her bag. Together, they were cramped, pushed up together like two rabbits in a warren. The smell of Mancini's clothing seemed to rob the air of whatever sustained life. From the crack between the two doors of the clothespress they could peer out at a sliver of the room beyond, but they had to take turns doing so.

A key turned in the lock and the door opened. A man walked in. Through the crack in the wardrobe, Diana could see he was short in stature, but with considerable musculature and a round belly. Perhaps forty-five years of age were past him, balding with the remains of his hairline shaved close. His clothes were rough-hewn, nondescript. He wouldn't have warranted a second glance under normal circumstances. Now she noticed a certain grace and certainty in his movements. He looked like nothing better than a farmhand, but underneath lingered something more.

He removed a tan overcoat with a tired sigh and burped. He plunked down on the bed and began removing his boots.

"Oh damn," Diana whispered.

"What's going on?" Siobhan hissed. "I can't see."

Diana shook her head wordlessly. She couldn't see as well now that the man, who surely must be Mancini, remained at the edge of the room. A moment later she heard the unmistakable sound of a body stretching out on a mattress. Mancini let out a guttural sound as he relaxed. Mere seconds later, the snoring began.

Diana pursed her lips, resting her head against the arm holding her pistol. A part of her wanted to laugh.

"He's sleeping, isn't he?" Siobhan whispered.

Diana nodded. "What kind of sinister assassin needs a late morning nap?"

"I hope he's a heavy sleeper."

Diana looked at her. "All right, we need to change plans."

Siobhan visibly swallowed. "You're going to shoot him, aren't you?"

Diana only gave her a hard look. As quietly as she could, she pushed open the armoire door and stepped out into the room. She leveled the pistol at the sleeping man's chest, stepping aside enough that Siobhan could exit.

The man lay still on his bed, snoring softly. His round stomach was like a summit rising over the plateau of the bed. Diana figured this particular assassin was no stranger to the pleasures of the dinner table.

"Giuseppe Mancini," she called, her voice firm and commanding. The man on the bed snorted and waved one arm absently, as if flicking away a fly. He did not wake. Diana gave Siobhan an incredulous look. "Giuseppe Mancini, wake up!" She kicked the bed.

The round man on the bed started, and pushed up onto his elbows, looking back and forth at the two women like they were unfathomable creatures. "Who by God are you?" he huffed at last.

Diana held the pistol higher, to emphasize the danger. She had one hand underneath the barrel, for it was too heavy to hold with a single hand. "My name is Diana Savrano. You murdered my mother. I want to know why."

The man squinted at her, breathed heavily in and out for a moment, then shifted his gaze to Siobhan. "Who are you then?"

"I'm just the help," Siobhan answered after a moment's reflection.

He looked back to Diana. "You don't know what you're talking about, girl."

"You were seen and recognized. A woman, cloistered, in her forties. She told me who you were and what would have brought you to Firenze."

"Is that right?" he replied, as his brows knitted. "Where is this woman? Why doesn't she accuse me directly?"

"Because after she told me about you, you threw her from the dome of St. Zenobius."

A look passed across the man's face, his left eye twitching slightly. "If what you say is true, you've found yourself more trouble than you can handle. I didn't throw any woman off the dome, and I didn't murder your mother. Now, put that toy away before one of us comes to harm." He sat straighter, began to push his mass to the edge of the bed.

Diana leaned in toward him with the pistol. "One more movement and I'll blow a hole in your gut wide enough to put a fist through." Her lips quivered as she said it. A part of her hoped he would give her reason to do just that. He stared at her, almost certainly taking her measure. With him watching she told him, "I am a lady of Firenze. What status do you have? Barely more than a slave. If I kill you now, who would care?"

"You might be surprised," he growled. He made no more moves to get up from the bed, however. "What would you have of me?"

"The truth," Diana barked. "Who paid you to kill my mother?"

"I told you the truth. I did not kill your mother." He held one hand over his head, leaning away as she threatened him with the pistol once more. "Listen, listen…it is true that I was hired to kill your mother."

Diana felt a flood of emotion at those words, rage, sadness, disgust. More than anything she felt as if she'd been struck. She could not fathom that anyone would want her mother murdered. "Why? Why would someone wish this on my mother?"

"I don't know," he answered.

"That's not good enough!" she hissed, gripping the pistol with knuckles white as bone.

"I don't know!" he insisted. "I don't ask for such details. I work through an anonymous agent in Milano. I receive a name and an initial sum of money. Once my victim is done, I receive a second sum of money. All communications occur through a secret drop spot. I never know who hired me, nor who works as the go-between. Only the victim."

Diana looked over at Siobhan, who stood unmoving and tight lipped. "What's in the box under your bed?"

His eyes narrowed. "Just a few personal possessions I keep safe from thieves."

"Where's the key?"

"Are you going to rob me now too?" he cried, sounding indignant.

"Give me the key, or robbery will be the least of your concerns."

He motioned with one hand toward the table. "It's in my shirt pocket, over there."

Siobhan found the key and a moment later had the little box open. "A handful of copper pennies, several silver coins and at least seven florins." She whistled. "That's probably more than I'd make in half a year, unless we were to renegotiate the terms of my employment given some unexpected duties."

"Anything else?" Diana asked, her eyes never taken off Mancini.

"There's a small stiletto dagger. Well, this is interesting. He's got a locket on a chain with what looks like a bit of human hair in it."

Mancini's face remained etched in stone through Siobhan's recitation.

Diana thought of the parchment in her mother's writing. She hated to think of her mother lying with this wretched pig, but there was no denying that the note might have referenced an affair. "Is the hair in the locket black?"

"No, looks blonde to me."

Diana was oddly disappointed. The box had given them nothing of value. Certainly he carried more money than most travelers would, confirming he must be up to no good. Aside from substantiating the basics of the nun's story, as much as she was concerned, they had learned nothing. Diana remained quiet for a moment, balancing indecision and frustration. At last she raised the pistol to eye level, taking careful aim at Mancini's crotch. "I'll give you one more chance to tell me why you killed my mother."

Sweat poured down off his nearly bald head. "I told you that it was true I was hired to kill your mother. But I did not complete the assignment. I swear by the Virgin Mary herself that I never did anything to harm your mother."

Diana held her breath. The man seemed sincere…a sincerity brought on by terror. Still she didn't trust him; what he said made no sense. "I don't understand. You said you were hired to kill my mother, and now she is dead."

"Lady Savrano, I came to Firenze to kill your mother. But I swear to you, when I arrived, I had no chance to complete my mission. She was already dead."

Chapter Four
The Anchoress

Diana felt like Mancini had smacked her in the face. Had her mother died of marsh fever after all, or did he insinuate that someone else had killed her? She detected no hint of deception in his voice; indeed her instinct told her to believe him. Nonetheless to him she hissed, "I don't believe you."

He must have detected the note of danger in her voice, for his eyes grew wide and he looked to Siobhan beseechingly. He sat forward, arms outstretched in a desperate gesture. "I swear, good ladies, that I am telling the truth!" Then his expression turned, his look of fear hardening to determination. They'd gotten distracted by his pleas. He'd been allowed to move forward on the bed until he could push himself up. He did this now, standing and launching himself at Diana.

Diana wasn't having it. She steadied the pistol in front of her just as Mancini engulfed her with his corpulent form. At the last moment she couldn't help but blink. Instinctive fear and uncertainty about what the gun might do—about whether she had even loaded it right—gripped her. She turned her face away from the barrel, squeezing her eyes. Only then did she pull the trigger.

The entire room seemed to be pulled apart by the ensuing blast. The explosion was as loud as an angry god. The pistol bucked in her hands, but she managed to keep her hold on it. She didn't realize she had lost her balance until she fell against the far wall and put one hand against it to keep from going down on her rump. Finally she opened her eyes, but this did little good for the room was thick with foul smelling smoke. She could see nothing, but at least Mancini had not landed on her. Her ears rang furiously and hurt, although the worst of the pain quickly subsided.

She looked around disoriented, and saw a writhing form on the bed. Blinking away some of the smoke, she could see Mancini wedged between the bed and the wall where he had fallen. Like a turtle on his back, he struggled to get up, a struggle made worse by a bloody gouge across his shoulder. She'd struck him, but it had been a glancing blow. His face was red and when he set his eyes on her, he looked ready to explode. "You shot me, you whore!" he bellowed and she could hear him even over the ringing. "I'm looking at a dead girl!"

Siobhan emerged out of the cloud of smoke. She'd dropped Mancini's box, but now had his little stiletto in one hand. With the other she tugged Diana's sleeve, "I think we've exhausted our luck, m'lady. Best we be going."

Snapping out of her momentary fog, Diana agreed. As she turned away from the struggling Mancini, Diana opened the door to his room and started down the hall. Here she was, running once again in completely inappropriate attire. This would be much easier in a dress that came up above her ankles, scandalous as that would be. Just along the hall stairs led down. When she came to these she spotted the innkeeper climbing toward them. He scowled when he saw her, "You there, halt!"

She pointed the pistol at him. "Stay back or I'll shoot!" As she said it, a long tendril of gray smoke arose from the barrel, betraying the hollowness of her threat.

The innkeeper grinned and lunged toward Diana. His hands reached for her throat. At that moment, Siobhan appeared at her side. Siobhan slashed the tip of the stiletto across the back of one outstretched hand. The bartender jerked back with a screech, holding his wounded hand. He tottered on the step for a moment. Seeing her opening, Diana lashed with one foot and kicked him firmly in the chest. He went over backward, tumbling like a melon down the wooden stairs.

Diana and Siobhan charged past his plummeting form into the main room and toward freedom. The few other men in the main room cheered, seeming to enjoy the spectacle. Diana ignored them, getting to the door and pushing beyond it to liberty. She turned quickly to be sure Siobhan still followed. Confident she had not left her accomplice behind, she charged into the street. This was an unfamiliar area and she was not sure exactly where she was going, but it hardly mattered. They needed to be away from here.

Along the lane she went, took a random left turn, and followed that street. Other pedestrians watched her and Siobhan rush past with open mouths. The two of them, unescorted young women in formal attire, running at full speed, were hardly inconspicuous. Diana led them on a right turn and there she nearly ran down Cardinal Lajolo.

Hiding the pistol behind her, Diana came to a rapid stop. Siobhan skidded to a halt beside her.

Two bodyguards on either side of the Cardinal began to draw swords, but he waved them down. "Why, Diana Savrano," the Cardinal huffed, brushing himself off. "You nearly knocked me onto my haunches. I should have expected you to be sequestered in mourning. Have you forgotten your mother so quickly?"

The priest's harsh words stung, but Diana was still more concerned about their pursuers. She looked nervously behind them. "No, Your Eminence. I had only an important errand to attend to."

The Cardinal's censorious eyes washed over onto Siobhan. "And who is this with you?"

"This is Siobhan, my handmaid," Diana explained, quickly. There would be no disengaging from the Cardinal until he was ready. Not even if the hounds of Hell were chasing them.

"Irish, I assume from the name," he said with a tone of dissatisfaction. "Have we so few servant girls in Italy now we must hire Celts?"

Diana stuttered, "I-I'm not really sure, Your Eminence." As she turned around this time she saw both Mancini and the innkeeper slide into view. They stopped when they saw the Cardinal and glowered at Diana and Siobhan. Perhaps being cornered by the Cardinal had been fortuitous after all. A moment later, still glaring at her, Mancini and the innkeeper turned and disappeared back around the corner. Evidently, they'd given up for now. Diana breathed a sigh of relief.

"It is unseemly for two young women to be seen about town unescorted. You should return home at once, lest I have a word with your father about your behavior," the Cardinal reproved, never seeming to notice their pursuers.

"Yes, of course," Diana promised. "We'll head right home."

The Cardinal glared and shook his head, but he moved off with his small entourage without further word.

Siobhan leaned in and whispered, "Weren't you going to ask him about that nun?"

Diana shook her head slowly. "Are you mad? I know when not to press my luck." Even as she said it, it seemed an ironic statement. She looked at Siobhan for a moment, and then they both burst out laughing.

"I can't believe we pulled that off," Siobhan said, wiping one arm across her brow. "You would have gotten a better shot off on Mancini if you hadn't closed your eyes!"

"You saw that?" Diana couldn't help but laugh at herself. "Keep quiet about it, would you? You were fantastic with that stiletto. I'm so glad you came along."

"It's my duty to protect my lady when she's in danger. If you don't mind my saying, it might be best to be moving on, should our gentlemen friends double back on us or notice the Cardinal's left."

They moved off quickly, returning back to familiar parts of Firenze.

"What will our next step be?" asked Siobhan once they seemed to clearly be in safer environs.

Diana knew their trouble with Mancini wasn't going to end at the inn. If he'd been willing to kill one Savrano, he'd certainly be willing to go for a second. There would be no backing out now. Only by pressing forward would they find their way out of this mess. "I haven't had a chance yet to puzzle over what he told us about my mother dying before he could kill her. I'm not sure what to make of that. While we still have daylight, I think we should push ahead though. I'd like to inquire about the nun who died last night."

"Very well. Lead on, I'll be with you," Siobhan promised. This time when she touched Diana's arm in a gesture of friendship, Diana didn't mind the impropriety at all. It was good to have an ally.

****

The convent at Saint Cecilia was set on a low hill overlooking the city of Firenze, close enough to set a shadow on the city, yet far enough away to be removed from its worldly concerns. Saint Cecilia cultivated a reputation as a favored repository of charitable donations from the successful merchants of Firenze. Many of the sisters were daughters from those same families, their dowries to the convent enriching its coffers. Looking about the outer walls of the cloister, Diana remarked to herself, the largesse of the Catholic faithful showed in the design. The buildings and acreage were immaculate and well kept. The grounds were beautiful, shaded by mature cypress and smaller almond and olive trees, although these were now largely bare from winter chills. The main hall towered over them, built from sturdy stone imported from the north, near Verona.

Although some of the sisters attended vocations in the city, the convent did not encourage outside visitors. Exceptions were made, however. Diana knew that the Savrano family had donated generously to Saint Cecilia. She suspected her mother's will would contain similar sizable donations in hopes her time in purgatory would be shortened. Of course the family had significant power over the final disputation of a will, particularly that of a woman. Diana felt certain the convent would be disinclined to alienate a member of the family. It didn't hurt that many in Firenze assumed that Diana had her father's ear. Diana knew this was because she enjoyed considerable freedom for a young woman, and many assumed this reflected some influence over her father. That reality did not match the rumors was inconsequential. In moments such as these, Diana found it convenient to profit from them.

As they approached in late afternoon, the convent appeared quiet. Among the trees lining the main walkway, it was easy to remain unobtrusive. Diana felt an atmosphere of calm and tranquility from the place. She could only imagine what horrors the young sisters might endure within those walls, but the cloister was successful in projecting an impression of peaceful contemplation.

"It is like a prison," Siobhan said, apparently missing the correct interpretation.

Diana looked at her. "Signore Orsini implied as much in speaking of the nun thrown from the dome. He suggested some of the sisters might commit suicide because of the treatment they receive."

Siobhan's eyebrows furrowed as she seemed to absorb the words. Diana turned away from her handmaid. Now that they were here she wasn't entirely sure how to proceed. The manicured cypress grove broke against a long open arched walkway that led to a small domed chapel. Diana stepped into the walkway sure this would lead her to some sign of life.

"Have you ever thought about joining a religious

community?" Siobhan asked quietly.

"No, never." She couldn't suppress a shudder.

"Well, why not?" Siobhan asked. "Given your age, I'd assume you haven't been eager to get married."

"Not you too!" Diana stopped and turned round. "Did my father put you up to this?"

Siobhan shook her head, her pale skin turning pink.

Diana put her hands on her hips. "Just because I don't choose to let a man enslave me, doesn't mean I wished to be enslaved by women." Looking at Siobhan, over whom she had enormous control, she suddenly felt awkward. She turned and resumed progress toward the chapel.

Behind her, Siobhan's footsteps followed. After a moment her hushed voice asked, "Don't you like men?"

Diana felt like tearing out her hair. "I like men fine...physically. I just don't see the advantage for a woman in marriage. A wife is no more than a reliable source of progeny for noble families. Meanwhile a husband is free to carouse, womanize, and generally do as he pleases. I for one am worth more than that arrangement can offer." Angry as she was, Diana felt ashamed of her own lack of patience with the Irish girl. Of course her mother was barely a day in her tomb; Diana could be forgiven a lapse of irritability.

A moment later the trail ended at a crossway. To the left, the arched footpath continued around the outside of the chapel; to the right a little corridor ended in an unmarked wooden door. Sensing the latter offered more promise, Diana approached the door and tried the latch. She might as well heave on a latch bolted to a mountain. She looked around, confused and annoyed, "How does one gain entrance to this place?"

As if on cue, a girl in black robes emerged from the wooden door. Her manner seemed hurried, apparently intent on some errand. She was startled at the sight of Diana and Siobhan, and stared at them for a moment. She was youthful, younger than Diana certainly, and thin as a baby bird. From her robes, Diana guessed she must be a novitiate.

Since the juvenile girl didn't speak, Diana began. "I'm Lady Diana Savrano. I should like to speak to someone in a position of authority within the cloister."

The young girl opened her mouth, then closed it again, before finally speaking. "Of course, Lady Savrano. If you'll but linger here, I'll summon one of the elder sisters." Without waiting for a reply, the young girl disappeared back through the wooden door and closed it solidly with a loud thud.

Diana looked at Siobhan, hoping her expression would convey her unbridled impatience. Siobhan met her stare and said nothing.

Sensing her wait would not be short, Diana began walking along the arched path outside of the chapel. It gave her something to focus on, to admire the ancient cypress trees that graced these grounds. After a moment however, she was surprised to hear her name being called.

Diana turned to the wooden door, but found it still closed.

Siobhan pointed. "The voice comes from ahead of us, not behind. The wall of the convent itself speaks to us."

Siobhan was right, in a matter of sorts. The voice, that of a woman, came from a small window set in a brick outlay from the main chapel. Diana approached and saw the face of a young nun in the window, the face ringed by the black and white of a habit. The woman's face appeared familiar somehow, in a distant way, and Diana could not place it.

"Diana Savrano," the woman said again, and her face offered a welcoming smile. "Do you not recognize me?"

As she came up to the window, Diana saw the room beyond was perhaps three feet by eight, not atypical for a nun's cell. However there appeared to be no door whatsoever, only a second window looking in on the chapel. The woman had been trapped in the little room unless she was inclined to try to squeeze through either of the tiny gaps. Only a small cot, table and shelf of books furnished the chamber. A wooden cross hung on one wall.

The woman must be an anchoress, Diana realized, a nun who had taken vows to live in complete isolation, even from the other sisters. In reality, such women were hardly isolated, of course. The other sisters, and even citizens from the city would come to seek the religious, and even practical advice of an anchoress, as such women were considered to be both exceptionally blessed and wise.

Diana regarded the anchoress and studied her face. The woman was a few years older than herself, with an angelic face of red lips and fair skin. Her eyes were blue and the few strands of hair that escaped the headpiece were light brown. Her light features would have been prized in Firenze or Roma, and yet she had chosen to waste them here. Diana did not recognize the woman and told her so.

"We met some years ago," the anchoress persisted.

"Several times, in fact. My father is Signore di Lucca. Your family attended several balls my father held before I entered the convent. You were, as I remember, being pursued by a Frenchmen at the time."

Diana looked at the ground. "That was a long time ago. You've been here since then?"

"I have," she said, no hint of regret in her voice. "My name is Francesca. We didn't know each other well, but I remember you."

Diana mumbled some apology for her own poor recall. In truth, Diana didn't know what to say. Her inclination was to express sympathy for Francesca's imprisonment, but the older woman did not seem distressed by it. Indeed she radiated a certain holy contentment that simultaneously impressed Diana and made her nervous.

"You've come here for guidance?" Francesca asked.

"Of a sort," Diana replied.

"Give me your hand," Francesca commanded, her voice gentle but firm.

Diana hesitated a moment, then allowed her hand to pass through the window of the little cell. She felt like she was reaching into murky water in search of a coin without being sure that some hungry beast awaited her fingers down in the darkness.

Francesca took her hand and turned it palm up, then placed her own across it. Francesca's hand was warm, soft, like a baby's. Yet she gripped Diana's fingers in a firm embrace. Francesca closed her eyes and began to chant, "Oh heavenly father, I beseech you to be with us today as we seek out your grace and your guidance…"

Diana looked over at Siobhan, but found the Irishwoman with her head bowed, hands clasped reverently in front of her. Diana felt both isolated and trapped between the two women, but there was little that she could reasonably do but to allow these events to play out.

Francesca continued her intonations and her voice became faster and softer as if she were barely breathing between the words. Diana thought Francesca had changed to speaking Latin and she could no longer closely follow what was being said. Francesca shook and swayed at her own voice, her hand on Diana's contracting painfully at times, only to release and repeat the cycle. At last she stopped, pulling away from Diana's hand with a gasp. She looked at Diana with wide eyes, breathing in heavily as if she had just run a race. "You will find what you seek," Francesca whispered. "But it won't be what you want."

Diana took a step back, holding her hand against her chest as if it had been burned.

Francesca blinked several times and put out one hand to steady herself in her cell. She was sweating visibly, lines of fluid running down her angelic face despite the frigid February air. She looked up finally, "Diana," she whispered.

"Lady Savrano!" called a voice from what seemed a world away. Diana turned to the sound and saw a tall woman in a black robe had emerged from the wooden door and now motioned toward her. Diana looked back at Francesca who watched her quietly with large eyes. "Thank you for the blessing, Francesca," Diana whispered, averting her eyes. She moved off toward the tall nun without waiting for a reply.

Siobhan fell into step beside her, keeping silent.

Diana had collected herself by the time they reached the tall nun. "I am Lady Savrano," she told the nun, keeping her back straight. "I would like to ask some questions."

The nun held up one hand. "I know why you are here. I am Sister Ophelia the cellarer. You've come to ask about Sister Maria Innocentia." The nun turned her back, motioning with one hand that they should follow.

Diana gave Siobhan a wary look. These nuns were more intimidating and mysterious than Mancini. Still, she followed the sister into a dark and cluttered hallway. She wasn't turning back now.

"Cardinal Lajolo has investigated the matter of Sister Maria Innocentia's death and declared her demise to be an accidental fall," Sister Ophelia informed them. Diana almost sputtered a protest but the sister held up her hand once more. "I know what she told you." They ascended a set of stone stairs, light from a few windows casting away the doom momentarily. "You should know that Sister Maria Innocentia was a deeply disturbed soul. I hope her spirit found some measure of comfort during her time with us, but I cannot be so sure."

"You think she was mad?" Diana asked.

"I know that she was mad," Sister Ophelia responded without a moment's hesitation. "The monk physicians claimed that her madness was a result of an imbalance of her humors and they tried to cure her with bleedings. Sometimes the horrors of this world are enough to drive any person mad, and I have little doubt that Sister Maria Innocentia was well versed in horror." They stopped outside a little wooden door. Sister

Ophelia turned round, facing them with her stern, slightly wrinkled face. Her eyes met Diana's. "Your mother was good to our community. We should have liked to bury her in our chapel had it been her wish."

Diana met the woman's gaze. "Do you believe what Sister Maria Innocentia said about my mother?"

For once the nun didn't answer immediately, but hesitated, her voice quieter when she finally did respond. "Maria Innocentia lived in a world that was haunted by the deepest and most unconquerable evil. I must hope that she was wrong."

"Most women who come to a convent such as this provide a dowry. Did Sister Maria Innocentia pay her own?" Diana asked.

Ophelia's eyes narrowed. "I'm not the treasurer for this community. I wouldn't know." She produced a ring of keys from her belt and unlocked the cell door. "For your mother's memory I'll grant you five minutes." She motioned inside the cell.

Diana nodded in appreciation. As she prepared to step across the threshold the nun touched her shoulder. "If your fears are correct, you should know that no one will help you. You'll be on your own."

Siobhan stepped forward. "I'll help her."

The nun gave her a sympathetic smile and stepped aside, holding open the door to the cell for them.

Diana stepped in, followed by Siobhan. The cell was no bigger than Francesca's although at least Maria Innocentia had been able to leave it. There were essentially the same furnishings, straw mattress, table and chair, small shelf. A tiny window looked down on a field and the nuns' graveyard. As Diana watched, several nuns were even now hacking at the ground, digging a fresh hole, no doubt for none other than Maria Innocentia. At least she would be buried on consecrated ground. Whatever sins she had committed, she deserved at least that much.

Across the walls and ceiling of the room, Maria Innocentia had drawn figures in chalk. Across the lowest levels, men and women danced and frolicked in fields of wheat and sunflowers. The nun had surprising skill at drawing; although the chalk figures were comparatively simple, the anatomy was precise and detailed. The figures were sensuous. A male figure bent a nude female back over his own arm, preparing to place a kiss on her throat. Another male reached out for a woman's long tresses as she ran from him, laughing. Above these scenes, at eye level, kings and dukes sat on their thrones. Around them soldiers made war, gouging out each other's eyes and intestines with military forks and swords. Above these kings and soldiers flew a host of angels with their gossamer wings and beautiful features. Yet if one looked closely one saw that the angels were mockeries. Each had an unholy imperfection; a cloven hoof, crosses instead of circles for pupils, fanged teeth. Above them still, across much of the breadth of the ceiling was drawn a great gaping maw with a dozen rows of sharp, inward facing teeth. A host of dead souls were drawn being sucked into this maw, clawing and screaming for their very survival, but ultimately swallowed into the dark oblivion at the center.

"Oh, dearest God," Siobhan whispered.

"Does it make you think of anything?" Diana asked, staring at the images.

"It makes me think the woman must certainly have

been mad."

Diana shook her head. "It's the inverse of the inferno painted inside the duomo at Saint Zenobius. There, the wicked are tortured in Hell around the base of the dome, but higher up the righteous enjoy the company of the saints until at last there is Christ upon his throne. Here, the contrary. The living enjoy the pleasures of life, disturbed only by the wicked designs of their worldly masters. Up higher the angels promise salvation but, in truth, they are devils and what awaits us is not heaven but oblivion."

There was silence for a moment. Then Siobhan said simply, "Well, I hope she's wrong about that part at least."

Diana glanced around the rest of the room, but there clearly was no more. She had hoped to find a hidden manifesto with a clear explanation for Maria Innocentia's accusations about her mother's death. There was nothing though—only, indeed, the pain of a disturbed woman who had ultimately known too much about the evils of men.

Diana stepped back out into the hall. She glanced at Sister Ophelia. "Thank you for letting me see how she lived. I would like to see that she is offered a proper burial stone. I will make arrangements for payment."

Sister Ophelia dropped her eyes and bowed. "Of course. I am sure she would be touched by your generosity."

With a look to Siobhan, Diana turned back to the stone stairs and found her own way out. Outside the first languid flakes of a late winter snowstorm were making their appearance, lazily drifting down from the sky above.

Diana made her way back over to the anchoress' cell. Francesca opened the little shutters wide when she saw that Diana had returned.

"Diana," she said, softly, "I didn't mean to offend you with my prophesy. You didn't ask for my intervention. I should not have forced it on you." She looked down at her own hands, which quivered slightly.

Diana remained silent for a moment, regarding the other woman. Even through the veil, Diana could see that Francesca was beautiful, she was sweet in demeanor, she was sincere. She would have made an excellent wife and mother. At last Diana asked, "Are you happy here?"

Francesca's eyes lit up. "Oh yes! I am free of the temptations of this world and through my little window—" She pointed back into her cell at the other transom that looked in on the chapel. "—I can see the image of the Virgin, and pray for her intercession on behalf of my immortal soul. There's nothing else that I could want."

Diana thought about that for a moment. She pulled her own dress tight around her, noticing the winter air that seemed to be sweeping in on them. "Don't you feel the cold?" she asked at last, not knowing what else to say.

Francesca smiled broadly and shivered. "Oh yes, I'm freezing."

Diana took Francesca's hand and squeezed it briefly, then she turned back, and began the long walk down the arched path.

Siobhan walked beside her. "Are you all right, lady?"

Outside the arched walkway, the indolent flakes of

snow came down in greater numbers like ash from a volcanic burst. They were beautiful against the backdrop of the bare cypress trees. The earth seemed so naked of life, and still resplendent in its severity. Diana looked up at the arched roof. She felt tears in her eyes, stinging them. "I feel so sad" was all she could say. "I'm not even sure why."

She felt Siobhan's arm around her. "You've just lost your mother. It will take time before you're right again. Come, we've had enough adventures for today. It will be dark soon and your father will be missing us. Let us get home and have some hot food. Things will seem better then."

A wave of exhaustion seemed to overtake Diana. They had so long to walk still. Diana could only nod and let Siobhan lead her back into the city. She longed for hot food and sleep and for things to somehow be very, very different than they were.

Chapter Five
The Prince

By the time they made it back into the city proper, a dusting of snow covered the roads and the roofs. The flakes came down faster, steadier. The sky turned from gray to black, the city punctuating the dark only with the light of candles, lamps, and the glow of fireplaces through paned glass. Diana felt exhausted; her energy drained, her thoughts fuzzy. She wanted nothing more than to settle in back at home, perhaps have a bit of food before getting under the covers and letting sleep overtake her. Her father might inquire where she'd been all day, but he'd have to wait for answers. She didn't want to talk to him. He wouldn't approve. He might even forbid her from continuing down her path, and she'd ignore him of course. What remained between them would crack and what would she do then?

Diana stumbled back inside the Savrano family palazzo. Siobhan took her coat. Lamp light flickered. The smell of meat beckoned to her empty stomach.

Before she could relax, an old family slave, a Byzantine woman named Agathi, approached. "Lady Savrano," she said softly, eyes averted, "a caller has come for you. He insisted on waiting until you returned."

Bewildered, she followed Agathi into the study where a young man lingered. He hovered near the flickering fireplace, examining one of her father's books. He appeared to be in his mid-twenties, slender, wiry with thin black hair. His face was narrow, his nose like a bird's beak, his eyes cool and intelligent. He might have been handsome in a way had his manner communicated a modicum of warmth.

"I present Lady Savrano," Agathi intoned.

Diana blinked. "Agathi, will you see that we are brought some wine and dinner?"

"Of course, lady," the old woman agreed before shuffling off.

The visitor put the book down and took a step toward her, regarding her with his narrow eyes. "Lady Savrano, I did not mean to inconvenience you with the need for food and wine."

In the study, a little table sat to one side for reading and note taking. Diana's legs wobbled and so she took a seat in one of the cushioned chairs. "I'm famished, so it's no bother."

The stranger sat across from her without waiting to be invited. "I am grateful for your hospitality. I should introduce myself. I am Niccolo Machiavelli. I work for the Republic of Firenze."

Diana wrinkled her nose. "You should speak with my father then. If he were to see you dining with me in such an intimate setting as this, he would have his sword at your throat."

Niccolo sat back in his chair, increasing the distance between them. "I meant no impropriety. It is you with whom I have come to speak, however. As for your father, I think that you will find him late coming home this evening. His business experienced an unexpected inspection." His eyes seemed to twinkle in the light from the fireplace.

"Is that so?" Diana regarded the man with a critical eye. In the silence, Agathi returned with a bottle of wine, glasses, and plate of stew for each of them. It took Agathi two trips in quick succession and Diana remained silent until the slave woman left them for good. "Are you here about my mother then?"

"More or less. Specifically I am concerned with the death of the nun called Maria Innocentia outside of Saint Zenobius Basilica, although I have heard it said that there might be some relation to your mother's death."

"I understood the nun's death is a church matter."

"She might have fallen from church property, but she fell onto the streets of Firenze."

Niccolo might be an unreadable wall, but she didn't need terrible insight into his mind to remain skeptical the Republic of Firenze would be eager to grasp a single murder out of the jurisdiction of the church. She considered him silently.

He helped himself to the stew. "Mmm, this is good." He ate carefully, his manners impeccable. Sipping at the wine, he put down his spoon. "Cardinal Lajolo has officially declared the nun's death to be an accident. A merciful gesture as her fall would, on first glance, appear more consistent with suicide."

Diana felt the early tendrils of a headache approaching. She got them when she felt stressed, particularly when she was calming down from a bad moment. There were times when they drove her to darken her room, lest the sun itself drive blades of agony through her skull. She hoped this wouldn't be one of those particularly bad ones. She breathed deeply, which sometimes helped, and continued eating. She decided not to speak yet. He'd asked her no questions, and protesting the nun's murder hadn't gotten her far the previous night.

Niccolo was quiet for a moment, spooning more of the stew into his mouth and chewing with deliberation. They sat in silence. At last he said, "There are some witnesses who say you claimed the nun was murdered."

Diana felt a lurch in her chest as she recalled the memory. How long would it be before that image was pushed to the recesses of her mind? "I saw her pushed from the cupola. Most people seem to feel that I experienced a fanciful vision brought on by grief at my mother's death."

"Your reputation in the city is that of a young woman who sometimes violates the laws against vanity as well as the social norms regarding the conduct of a respectable lady."

Diana felt her cheeks burn. "I permit myself to be seen and heard is what you mean." Even as she spoke, she felt embarrassed she allowed herself to be goaded.

Niccolo nodded once. "Nonetheless, in most circles your name is spoken with respect. No one suggests that you are given to flights of fancy or visions."

Diana regarded Niccolo warily. "You're saying you believe me then."

Niccolo waved his spoon slightly in the air as he spoke. "It's not in my portfolio to examine suicides or accidents."

Diana thought about that for a moment. "I didn't get a good look at the person who pushed her. He was dressed in a dark robe that obscured his face."

"Did you see anything in the nun's manner that

would suggest she knew her attacker?"

"She held a crucifix up to him as if he were a monster. Certainly in the robe he looked like a demon or a ghost. I don't believe he was either."

Niccolo raised an eyebrow. "How can you be so sure?"

"I've never seen a ghost or a demon. I've seen plenty of men who have committed murder. I've been at balls with some, dined with others."

Niccolo's pupils widened at that and he gave her a smile. "Well spoken." He tapped the edge of his spoon with one fingernail. "I assure you I've committed no murders, government sanctioned or otherwise." He leaned in, closer to her. "Your mother though...the sister told you she was murdered, didn't she?"

His mentioning it out loud brought moisture to her eyes. She averted her eyes so he wouldn't see it. It pained her to show him weakness. "Yes, that is what she said."

"Do you know any reason why anyone would want your mother dead?"

"No," she said and met his gaze, "I can't imagine why anyone would. She said a man named Giuseppe Mancini di Milano might have done it. She led me to believe he would have done it for hire. I don't know why anyone would hire him to do so."

Niccolo nodded, spooning more stew as if this were an ordinary dinner conversation. "So, it is reasonable to assume if she knew about this Mancini, he might have known about her and killed her to keep her quiet. Too late though." He pointed at her with the spoon.

All this talk about her mother as a victim of

assassination…it was just so unreal. She could bear it when she kept it in her mind as an investigation, as a puzzle to be solved. When she found herself thinking about her mother, the person who had comforted her when she'd been down, intervened on her behalf with her father, who'd given her unconditional love, it all just seemed so surreal.

"I am sorry about your mother," Niccolo said softly. Diana felt like she snapped out of a trance. She blinked her eyes a few times to bring herself back around. "Especially if she were murdered," Niccolo said. "It must be difficult."

She nibbled at her bottom lip. "Yes, it is."

"I'm going to try to help you."

"Why?" She shook her head. "Why should I trust you? You work for Savonarola."

His pupils narrowed at that. She'd hit an unexpected nerve. Although his expression never changed, she had enough intuition to gauge he cared not at all for the Mad Friar who ruled Firenze. "You're right," he told her, never breaking his gaze. "You've got no good reason to trust me. It's a good impulse to be suspicious of everyone."

"I hope one day I won't have to be."

"There is wisdom and there is trust. You'll find you'll have to pick one."

She stared at him for a moment. "I am not sure I would like to live in the world you seem to inhabit, Signore Machiavelli."

"There is only one world. We may not love it, but we must endure it." His eyes dropped. "Please, call me Niccolo."

"Niccolo," she repeated softly.

He gazed back up at her. "I've heard it said that you have an interest in studying medicine at Salerno."

She felt heat rising in her cheeks once more. "Is there anything that you don't know about me, Niccolo?"

He fell silent for a moment, looking away. His voice was soft as he answered, "I'm only beginning to learn about you." His eyes met hers again. "Does your father approve of your goal?"

She didn't look away, answering simply, "No."

He broke eye contact, silent. She could tell his eyes were on her hair, on her neck. She was used to men looking at her, appraising her as an object of their lust. It gave her pleasure to know she had such power over men, while at the same time her respect for such men inevitably diminished. This was different somehow. His appraisal lacked the lust to which she was accustomed, replaced by something more refined, more respectful. He looked at her like he might a fine painting or classical sculpture. He regarded her with respect and she found she liked his eyes on her in this way.

Her mother though…it was inappropriate for her to have such thoughts at this time. "You should go," she whispered.

His eyes locked on her for a moment, then he stood. "I'll be in touch with you as soon as I learn anything." He moved to let himself out, and then twisted to half face her. "It has been my honor to meet you, Lady Savrano."

She nodded, remained silent.

He turned and left.

****

Blinding lights pulled Diana from sleep like a baby

from the womb. She sat upright in bed startled and alarmed. Tendrils of rapidly fading dreams escaped her mental grasp. She blinked and looked around.

Siobhan tied back one of the heavy curtains. Sunlight poured into Diana's bedroom. Diana fell back against her pillows, hands rubbing her eyes. How dare a servant awaken her when she was not prepared! Grumpily, she mumbled, "Your services in this household are no longer required."

"Begging your pardon, Lady," Siobhan chimed in a tone that suggested she didn't take Diana's comment the least bit seriously. "I thought it best to wake you if you were still intent on investigating the nature of your mother's death. Your father has already left to check on his businesses."

A long yawn stretched across Diana's face. At least her headache had vanished. As Siobhan went along tying back the rest of the curtains, Diana managed to roll lazily out of bed. "What is the time?"

"Nearly midday, lady," Siobhan answered without the slightest hint of reproach.

Diana stood and walked to the window. The city outside, most of which stretched below her window, was dusted with a fine layer of white. Diana's pride in her city swelled a bit at the view. The world seemed so beautiful in a cold and lifeless way. In a different year, she might have been tempted to go outside and enjoy the snowfall. There would be little enjoyment today.

Siobhan helped her get out of her nightclothes and attend to her morning hygiene. For clothing, Diana did her best to learn the lessons of the last two days. She selected a reasonably sturdy woolen dress to wear as well as a good pair of hunting boots. This was the best she could procure as an athletics outfit. At least the dress would be less inclined to bunch up around her feet than her previous choices. Siobhan helped her don the clothes with great consideration.

Offhand, Diana commented, "It always amazes me how the house servants remain awake until the family is asleep and are awake again earlier when the family breakfasts. How do you survive on so little sleep?"

Siobhan, in the process of helping put on a boot, looked up and met her eyes. "The alternative is prostitution or starvation." She went back to sliding the boot up Diana's leg.

Diana mulled that over, rubbing her tongue over one incisor.

Without looking up this time, Siobhan noted, "I saw you had a rather handsome visitor last evening."

"He represents the Republic. He's apparently investigating my mother's murder as well." She paused for a moment. "Did you really find him to be handsome?"

"He was willowy, had unblemished skin and all his teeth. In Ireland, a man such as that is an ideal of beauty."

Diana laughed a little. "I don't know how much he could be trusted. Even if he tells the truth about working for the Republic, there are so many factions…"

"You think he works for Friar Savonarola?" Her tone was clear to Diana. Even if Savanarola wasn't involved in her mother's murder, and there was no evidence he was, he could only be a sinister presence. The Mad Friar's shadow never seemed to bring benefit to those upon whom it fell.

Diana shook her head. "When I mentioned Savonarola's name, I got the impression he disapproved." She stood, tested out her movement in this attire and decided she was satisfied. Overall, she felt rather better than the previous day. Perhaps that was how it was with the loss of a loved one, each day a little better than the last. Undoubtedly a little breakfast would help too.

"Where will we be off to today?" Siobhan asked.

God bless her, Diana thought, the Irish girl was unstoppable. "I would like to visit the church at Piazza Madonna delle Grazie. My mother's note suggested she met someone there who might know something about why she died. Perhaps the priest in attendance might have seen who that is." She thought for a moment, and then said, "I would like to know how the nun received that letter into her possession. I wish I could have spoken to her longer that night."

Siobhan grasped her shoulder in that informal manner of hers. "What is done can't be undone. We can only press forward."

With a moment's hesitation, Diana touched Siobhan's arm and gave her a smile. "Let's get going."

****

At midday the Church at Madonna delle Grazie was only lightly occupied. Though built to hold several hundred, it was small by the standards of Firenze. Nonetheless, it was of exquisite design, the cross behind the altar radiating with gold and silver, a showering display of opulence to backdrop the suffering of Christ. Each of the small chapels lining the nave displayed commissioned paintings by well-regarded Florentine artists. Among them a Madonna by the rising star Michelangelo, now in unofficial exile in Roma. Diana didn't recognize the names of the other artists, although the quality of the paintings was exquisite, even if they tended to focus on themes of suffering, martyrdom, and loss. This church remained darker than the Basilica of Zenobius, the windows too small to let in enough light. The funerary sculptures of rich benefactors loomed like spirits. Marble skulls grinned seemingly at every corner of the church. Upon one chapel altar, a reliquary held the skull of the church's patron saint, one Regina di Lucca who, it was said, had ended the Black Death outbreak of 1348 by absorbing the demons that spread it into her body.

A dozen hunched figures clustered at the front of the nave near the main altar. Each of them radiated years of regret, as if there was little left but a husk of a human being that longed for nothing more than the eternal peace death would soon grant them. One of the penitents, a woman, led the rest in the recitation of psalms in Latin.

"Now this," Siobhan whispered, "is more like the Ireland I remember." She looked up and around admiringly. "Except I don't remember glass windows."

Diana looked at her like she was mad. "I suppose we should find a priest." She actually wasn't entirely sure what she was going to ask when she found one. For the moment, none were in view.

Siobhan fingered the teeth on one marble skull. "What do you have to do to get buried inside a church?"

"Donate lots of florins," Diana answered absently, "or do something particularly noteworthy. If you do something noteworthy your body will draw in countless others who will donate the florins for you."

"Hmm," Siobhan nodded. "What about you? Do you want to be buried inside a church wall, or under the floor where people can walk all over you?" The Irish girl did a small and utterly inappropriate jig.

Diana waved at her to stop. "I really haven't thought about it."

"You should, you know." Siobhan thought out loud. "Women our age die all the time. Childbirth of course, but even if we survive that, there's always plagues, wasting diseases, consumption, poxes, rape during war, beheading if your side gets the worst of some political conflict, and of course the syphilis if you dally with the wrong gentleman caller."

"In what manner is this conversation intended to benefit me?"

"I'm just giving you good advice. Once one of those things finally gets the better of you, you better have your slice of some church set aside." She nodded sagely.

"Oh dear God." Diana ran one hand through her hair. Looking away, she spotted a flash of white. The robes of a priest. "Come on."

Together they ran across the nave, their boots clickety-clacking on the hard stone floor.

The priest turned slowly like a pivot at the sound of their approach. He was old, with wispy white hair and a crooked frame. God surely must call this old soldier back home soon. His eyebrows were raised when he saw them and his mouth opened as if he thought he were being chased by ghosts.

"Father," Diana began, mind racing about how to get the information she wanted, "I am Lady Diana

Savrano and I must ask you some questions."

Rheumy eyes watered as they examined one woman, then the next.

Diana's confidence ebbed. "You *are* the parish priest, aren't you?"

"I am Father Gian," he confirmed in a deliberate, rasping voice.

Diana felt nothing socially inviting about the old man's manner. Initially this deflated her confidence, but she made an effort to rally herself. She wasn't going to be intimidated by some half-dead cleric. She straightened up her back and demanded, "I should like to know if you knew of my mother Isabella Savrano."

"I knew of her," he rasped, "not well. Your father as well, mostly by reputation."

"My mother, did you ever see her here?"

His clouded eyes blinked, and he paused for a moment. A thick tongue ran over his cracked lips. "She had come here from time to time, although I was given to expect that she celebrated mass more often at the larger cathedrals. San Lorenzo, or Saint Zenobius, perhaps."

"But she has been here then? When was the last time that you saw her?"

The priest rolled his eyes up at the ceiling as he thought for a moment, "Oooooh, perhaps a week ago, not much more. I remember because I heard word of her death soon after."

"Do you remember…was she with anyone?" Her heart fluttered in anticipation of the answer. She seemed so close.

He thought for a moment later, then shook his head. "She must have been accompanied. It would be unseemly for a woman of high status to be about town with insufficient escort." His eyes fell languidly on Siobhan. "I do not recall specifically whose company she kept."

"Perhaps there was someone else here that same day? Someone of note who might also remember?"

"Dear Lady, I am nearly eighty years old. One day blends into another."

Her shoulders slumped. Hopes dashed, she could scarcely think of another intelligent question worth asking.

"I must say, the nature of these questions seems highly unusual," the Priest protested, finding his own poise now her hauteur had ebbed.

"Thank you, Father. I have no further questions," she replied, turning away before he could demand an explanation.

Well, this had arrived at a dead end. She'd managed to confirm her mother had indeed come here, probably to meet someone as the letter had intimated. The priest hadn't managed to notice, or remember who it was. On second thought, that in and of itself might be meaningful. If her mother had met with someone else notable from town, wouldn't the priest have remembered that person as well? It could be, if the priest didn't remember the other person, it might be someone unfamiliar altogether. Mancini could fit that bill, for certain, although it was unlikely Mancini had known her mother prior to being hired to kill her. Mancini had also said her mother was already dead by the time he got to Firenze, meaning he would still have been out of the city when she'd met the person she'd addressed the letter to. The person she'd met had to be unfamiliar to the priest, yet staying in town for at least a little while. Plenty of artists would fall in that category, hired on by one wealthy family or another. Her father's friend, Signore Orsini was from Roma, but had been in Firenze for some weeks. Diana knew Orsini reasonably well however, and couldn't imagine him killing her mother.

Siobhan tugged her shoulder, tearing her from her thoughts.

"What is it?" Diana hissed, keeping her voice down in the church.

"We've been followed." Siobhan pointed across the church. There, in a small chapel, knelt a tall thin man in a gray coat, the collar pulled high around his chin. A thick wave of curly black hair spilled around his ears. Only part of his face visible, eyes closed and downcast, a thick bulbous nose peeking out above the collar. Diana didn't recognize him.

"Are you sure?" Diana asked.

"I noticed him as we were walking here. He watched you the entire time with the priest."

A chill went through Diana's heart. So, she'd earned a mark on her head as reward for her inquiries. She supposed she knew it would happen. Still, to think she was being trailed, possibly with the intent to assassinate her left her mouth dry. "It's not Mancini. A henchman?"

"Possibly. What should we do?"

Come what may, Diana was hardly going to cower away in fear. "Let's go speak to him; see what he has to say for himself."

They had only gotten a few steps before the man stood and, barely glancing their way, stepped out of the chapel. He kept his collar up over his mouth, his hair obscuring his face. He moved quickly away from them up the nave.

"He's trying to get away," Siobhan whispered urgently.

"He's going the wrong way." Diana frowned. She picked up her pace, following the man as he moved past the group of chanting figures. Tracing his way along the perimeter of the church, he opened a dark unmarked door that almost blended into the stone walls and vanished through it.

Diana and Siobhan rushed to the door. It comprised a single sheet of metal, lightly embossed with leaves and vines. The handle was a simple metal latch. Diana tried it and found it unlocked. Feeling like a thief, Diana glanced around furtively. No one was watching them. She pulled open the door. Beyond, a simple set of narrow stone stairs lead down into darkness black as death. The sound of feet tip-tapping against the stone faded into the distance.

"What is it with me and narrow stone stairs?" Diana wondered aloud.

"We should fetch a lantern to light our way," Siobhan suggested. "It's far too dark down there to follow him in safety."

"He'll be long gone by then," Diana observed. "Fetch a lantern if you can. I'm going to pursue." She withdrew the long pistol from under her coat.

"You can't seriously be thinking of going down there in the shadows alone?"

"If he's going down there, I assume either he has a light source, or there must be some light down there. Either way if he can see, I can see." Diana used a confident voice although, in truth, she wasn't so sure.

Siobhan stared at her uncertainly, so Diana shooed her off. "Just get a lantern and join me when you can. I'll be fine." Diana turned and began down the stairs. As helpful as a lantern would be, she also wanted Siobhan out of harm's way. She knew as well as Siobhan how dangerous it was to pursue the stranger in the dark. She wasn't about to let him get away though, even if it meant putting her own life at risk.

A little illumination from the dank church helped slightly on her descent. She kept one hand out to steady her balance. The rough stone steps descended steeply with a slight turn to the right. A musty smell rose up from below on a slight breeze.

Along the turn in the stairs the light from above disappeared. However, a similar slight radiance appeared to come from below. She was never entirely without luminosity. Finally she stepped off the stone staircase onto a dirt floor. The room beyond was large and irregular shaped, a rough block-shaped chamber seemingly hewn out of the natural rock. At one point in the past, the room had evidently been used as a storage room. Now the crates and barrels were decayed and rotting. Split open, their contents spilled into the room, little more than undecipherable piles of rags and refuse. A large open crack split the roof above. Through this cut beams of sunlight, giving the chamber its illumination. Diana guessed that this room must be under the alley beside the church. Water from rain and snow had poured through that crack for years, collecting in a half frozen pool in the center of the sunken dirt floor. There were no apparent exits, and no sign of the stranger.

Diana began to think waiting for the lantern would have been the wise course after all, but such was the road untraveled. She held the pistol out in front of her and declared loudly, "Whoever is there, show yourself! I mean only to speak with you."

No answer. If she had to shoot this fellow it would hardly advance her cause very far. She needed to find out who had sent him to trail her.

She took a few more tentative steps into the room, her eyes darting back and forth, scanning everywhere. Above, the sound of the penitents chanting their psalms just barely reached her ears.

From the ceiling a drop of melted snow fell down toward the frigid pool below. In the corner of Diana's eye a shadow moved. It grew, merged with the shadows around it, and became a solid wall moving toward her.

Diana screamed. She spun round, bringing the pistol barrel to bear on the shadowy form. It twisted to one side and she lost sight of it. Then her heart caught in her throat as the shadow materialized next to her. A dark hand rose up into the air above her. A ray of sunlight reflected against something held in that hand. Her breath escaped her. Just inches above her a short serrated blade gleamed. Without a sound, the figure in the shadows swung for her heart. There was only one thing for Diana to do—close her eyes and put her trust in God.

Chapter Six
The Boar

With the assailant's blade only inches from her heart, Diana let her body go limp. She fell backwards, drifting through space without knowing what she might crash up against. She braced for the pain of the knife stabbing through her. Something brushed against her, snagged on the lining of her coat and then tore free. A second later a thousand tiny icy needles pierced her flesh as she splashed into the pool of water in the room's center. She flailed about until her hands and feet found purchase on the cold earth below, but the pool was not deep.

Soaked, she sat up and sucked in a deep breath. A trembling hand pushed frosty water out of her eyes. She expected the man in the dark coat would have pounced on her by now, but instead he stood watching her. She could see him more clearly, his eyes dark and cheerless. The lower half of his face, visible to her now through the opening in his collar, was a monstrosity. The skin looked to have been peeled back away from his jaws, revealing the line of bone below. What teeth he had were thick and jagged, pushing out of his mouth at weird angles. The lower canines were particularly misshapen, large and unwieldy, protruding up and above the thin ragged line of his upper lip. A disease in childhood, she thought, or a mutation of birth…or just a curse from God! She stared at him, open mouthed, able to say nothing at all.

"Diana!" Siobhan's voice calling from above.

The hideous man spun at the sound of the voice. With a last glance at Diana he turned, bolted for the dark corner of the room.

Diana managed to push herself up onto her feet. "Stop! Or I'll shoot you!"

The man ignored her, nearly vanishing into the shadows. Diana raised her pistol, took careful aim, this time keeping her eyes open. With a sense of regret, she pulled the trigger. The hammer clicked home. Nothing happened.

The man vanished, scuttled into the dark corner like a frightened crab. From that corner Diana heard a sound of stone grating against earth. A hidden door! He'd come down here to make a sound escape, of course. Diana did her best to follow, but her sodden dress hung like an anchor and the cold was beginning to pierce through to her joints, making it difficult to move. By the time she reached the corner, she found only solid stone.

A light grew behind her, Siobhan with the promised lantern.

"He's gone through here," Diana insisted. "We have got to follow him."

Siobhan surveyed her closely, looking for injuries. "Diana, you're shivering like a frightened dog. Wherever that goes, you'll be dead of cold before you get to the end. You'll be lucky enough to avoid chilblains as it is. Let's get you upstairs and see if the priest has some robes you can borrow."

Siobhan was right. Diana knew she was declining

fast in these cold, wet clothes. The air in the room wasn't much above freezing and even the main church could hardly be called warm. She'd be fortunate not to catch a cold or worse. "All right, but I want to come back and see where this leads!" she insisted as Siobhan led her to the stairs. She shivered so hard and her joints got so stiff that making it up the stairs proved to be a significant obstacle.

"Did he harm you at all?" Siobhan inquired.

"He tried to stab me, but I cleverly avoided harm by diving headlong into that freezing pool of muck," Diana answered with a sneer at herself. "I tried shooting him, but the gun failed. They call that Leonardo a genius. You think he'd be able to invent a pistol that can shoot when wet."

"You can write him a letter," Siobhan suggested. "For now, let's get you dry."

****

An hour later after a hot tub of boiled water and a roaring fire, feeling returned to Diana's toes and fingers. Siobhan helped her dress in the second outfit for the day. Of her first outfit, her good hunting boots were salvageable. The dress was sadly a lost cause, although it could always be donated to the poor.

"You should have seen his face," Diana told Siobhan as she slipped on a new woolen dress and coat. "The flesh at the margins of his mouth appeared to be eaten away and his teeth were distorted like tusks. I wish I had medical training; I would know what would cause that. I'd wager it was something contracted in youth in order to affect the teeth in that way."

"He could have just been some monster," Siobhan speculated, working on the buttons at the back of the dress. "Or maybe some kind of demon."

"We were in a church, Siobhan."

"Some say the Antichrist himself occupies the Holy See," Siobhan retorted with the air of a wise grandmother.

Diana speculated on that for a moment. It wasn't the first time she'd heard that particular claim. The current pope, Rodrigo Borgia, who'd taken the name Alexander VI, was rumored to hold debased orgies dedicated to the Lord of Darkness. The Mad Friar Savonarola repeatedly condemned the pope in his sermons, although with Savonarola's vicious rule in Firenze, it was difficult to imagine who might be the true Antichrist, he or Borgia. Diana didn't particularly believe the worst of the invective. Certainly Rodrigo Borgia went through life untouched by the Holy Spirit, pope or not. Yet a man did not need to be the Antichrist himself in order to be thoroughly corrupted by power. The world was full of such men.

"I think just a man," Diana said confidently of the attacker at the church. "And I'd wager that he was no Mancini. He could have killed me when I fell into the pool, but he hesitated and lost his chance. Mancini would never have lost his nerve that way."

"You were chasing him with a gun. He might have just been defending himself."

Diana considered that. "You have a good point. His motive seemed to be escape, not homicide. Yet there can be little doubt he was following us. To what end if not to do me harm? No one would send a man such as him to act as a spy. Not with such a notable affliction. He must have been acting alone."

Siobhan frowned. "It has not even been forty-eight

hours since that sister died. How could you have made so many enemies so quickly?"

"There must be multiple parties involved in the nun's death...and my mother's." She went silent. What had her mother gotten involved in? How had neither she nor her father detected any hint of what had been going on?

The Byzantine slave Agathi appeared at her doorway. "I beg your pardon for the intrusion, lady," the old woman intoned, "but there is a gendarme at the door asking for you. He told me that your presence has been requested by Signore Machiavelli." She hovered by the door waiting for instructions.

"Tell him we'll be right down." She gave Siobhan a meaningful look. "You better fetch my warmest coat. I wonder what's gone wrong now."

The gendarme was a tall young lad disinclined to answer questions. From his demeanor, Diana guessed she was not in personal trouble. That was good at least. Silently, he led her and Siobhan south to the banks of the Arno. The wind had picked up, blowing dry flakes of snow into her face. She wrapped her coat tightly around her to keep the worst of the cold away.

At the edge of the Arno she saw a cluster of men gathered, most of them gendarmes. Among them, a frail frame in the midst of the military men, hovered Niccolo, hand ever on his chin. When she drew closer she could see that his expression was grim.

Niccolo looked up at their approach, his eyes locking with Diana's. "Thank you for coming, Lady Savrano. Who is this that accompanies you?"

"This is my handmaid, Siobhan. She can be trusted."

Niccolo's eyes flashed over Siobhan, sizing her up quickly. Diana couldn't miss the briefest look of doubt on his face before he dismissed the girl. He turned to the Arno and led them closer to the waters. "A gentleman's body has washed up on the banks. I would like to see if you recognize him. I should warn you that the sight is disturbing."

Diana instantly thought of her father. Her chest felt like it might split open. When had she last seen him? Not this morning, not since the morning before. She hadn't even thought to ask of him. Whatever his faults, she couldn't bear the possibility of losing him so soon after her mother. One balled fist covered her mouth. Siobhan seemed to sense her mood and put one hand against her back as they edged closer. As they drew near to the ragged form deposited among the dead reeds at the river's edge, Diana breathed a sigh of relief. The form was not that of her father, the frame too short. Whoever it might be, at least it was not he.

The figure lay on his back, splayed open on the ground. No one would have mistaken him for sleeping, even had the weather been pleasant. From the waist up he was bare. His stomach and chest were torn open, the entrails gone, with little remaining of the abdomen but the spine and flaps of skin and gristle. The lungs too were lost, and Diana remarked to herself on the interior structure of the man's ribs with the little muscles running back and forth between the bony cage. A deflated sack of a heart lingered and some other unidentifiable bits of organs. A pair of ragged pants hung just below his pelvic bones, the upper portions of which were visible through the viscera of what remained of his abdomen. His feet were bare, pale, shriveled. His hands were up at the level of his head as if he were surrendering at war. The fingers were limp, scraped and torn. His eyes were closed, head lolling to one side, mouth opened and black tongue protruding. There was a groove in the skin around his neck. Aside from the damage to his gut, his body retained otherwise fair condition. Diana guessed he hadn't been in the water long.

"Do you recognize him?" Niccolo asked.

"Should I?" Diana inquired. It was difficult to tell. The man's flesh sagged, the face battered a bit, perhaps from rocks or debris in the river.

"He was found with a scroll tube tied round his neck. Inside was a note addressed to you."

She looked at Niccolo with wide eyes. He didn't acknowledge her though, staring intently at the body. She looked at the carcass more carefully. It didn't bother her to see the human form in this condition. If anything, the anatomy fascinated her. Still she felt bad for the poor fellow. She stared intently at the face. "I recognize him," she declared at last. "He is the innkeeper of a place called the Romancier. I don't know his name."

"I agree," declared Siobhan beside her. Diana realized the other young woman had never left her side. The sight of the body evidently didn't bother her terribly either, as the Irishwoman didn't look away.

Niccolo pulled at his chin and gave her a long hard stare. "This innkeeper is involved in your mother's death?"

"I don't know," she answered truthfully. More likely, she figured, his death was simply payback for letting them into Mancini's room. She couldn't be sure, though.

"You don't seem entirely surprised to see him here, though, do you?" His voice took a hard edge.

Diana remained quiet, her silence giving him the answer. She didn't look away, meeting his stare until his eyes dropped. She wasn't about to hand over to him every bit of information she had, not knowing his agenda. She doubted he'd tell her everything he knew either. "Can I see the letter?" she asked finally.

One hand reached into his coat and retracted a thin bone scroll case. He passed this to her without a word. She took it in her cold numbed hands, turning it over and over. It was an unremarkable bone case, the sort a courier might use to protect a message from moisture. The ends had been covered and sealed with a kind of hard wax. One of these ends was now open, and Diana slipped the parchment within into her hand.

The scroll was of rough parchment, poor quality. She unfurled it. The script was elegant with looping curves and dramatic flourishes, broad lines crossing through or underlying entire passages. It was the writings of someone well educated. The missive read:

"Diana Savrano:

You are quite clever by half. Will you laugh over this man's fate while you and the Devil dine together on his entrails? Mourn your dead, Diana, no more should die. Your mother's soul already burns in Hell. Seek not comfort in the bosom of the Dark God. An angel watches over your shoulder, ready to guide you to Heaven or to strike you down as your mother was struck down. Persist in consorting with the unwashed souls of sinners and her fate will be yours. Her imperfection runs through you like a crack in marble. I pray, we all pray in unison for your soul. We watch you, we pray for you, and we will be that angel to strike you down if you remain unsaved. Walk down the unholy path no longer, seek solace in the arms of Lucifer and you shall be safe. Alone you must certainly die and burn forever in desolation, lost to God's love.

Blessed in the name of the Lightbringer,

SCA"

Diana folded the parchment in half, and slipped it back into the case. She ran her tongue over her front teeth. She passed the bone case back to Niccolo and he took it without looking at her. "It's not Mancini," she said at last. When Niccolo didn't respond, she added, "We went to see him, confront him. We tricked the innkeeper into showing us his room. Mancini is a cold-blooded killer but he's not—whatever it is that would make someone write a note such as that."

Niccolo looked at her at last. "You didn't tell me you confronted Mancini."

Diana struck a defiant tone. "I figured you would have heard on your own." Her blood raged hard through her veins. She felt a pain in her head as her thoughts pushed out against her skull, threatening to tear her mind apart. She wanted to lash out and Niccolo was the obvious target. "I imagine you have your spies keeping watch on me, don't you?"

"If I had the authority to do so I would, but I do not. My resources are limited, Lady." His tone was unapologetic.

"You want me to trust you, even while you treat me as an enemy of the Republic." Niccolo's face remained calm, though stern. She felt an urge to strike him, if only to make him share some of her agitation.

"My only thought was for your safety, Lady Savrano."

She breathed out a long cone of cold through her teeth. "The words on the page are those of a religious fanatic. I might expect them to be the words of the Mad Friar Savonarola himself, were they not burdened by the name of Satan."

Niccolo blinked at the friar's name. "If it is Savonarola who opposes you, you'll burn in the Piazza delle Signoria before the week is out if you persist. We must both hope that you are wrong in any such suspicion."

She scratched the side of her head with her cold fingers. Looking at him askance, she told him. "There was a man today at the church at Piazza Madonna delle Grazie. He followed me. Disease disfigured his face, the lips damaged, his teeth like the tusks of a boar. Do you know of such a man in Firenze?"

He frowned. "A man with the face of a boar?" He thought for a moment. "Dear Lady, I think I may know the man of whom you speak. I'll go to confront him at once." He called out to several of his gendarmes, who came to his side. He turned to her again, his face softer now. "I truly am on your side, Lady Savrano. I wish you could believe that."

She nodded, eyes averted. She wished she could believe that too.

As he led away the little group, he and two of his gendarmes, with herself and Siobhan in tow, Diana managed to feel a little burst of hope. Niccolo looked to know the man with the diseased mouth. If he was correct about the man's identity, perhaps they would finally make some progress. Perhaps she would finally have some answers on the circumstances of her mother's death. With that hope in mind, she dared to trust Niccolo, if only for this moment.

The home at which they stopped was a modest palazzo not far north of the Arno. The building was old and in need of repair, but it nonetheless spoke to the repute of the family in residence. Two lamps were kept lit outside the main door, above which the family crest of a man's arm holding a holly branch was emblazoned. Aside from this there was little sign of life. Evening fell, the sun having disappeared, and on such a cold night the street stood empty.

Niccolo went to the door and knocked loudly. Within seconds, an attendant answered and exchanged words with Niccolo. The door closed momentarily and more waiting ensued. Niccolo shuffled his feet without a word; the gendarmes stood by silently. Diana kept to the back with Siobhan, not quite sure what her role was in this. Was she expected to accuse the Boar of following her to his face?

A moment later the door opened once more and an elderly man with a skeletal frame and a shock of white hair stood waiting.

"Signore Benedetto," Niccolo demanded. "I am here to speak to your son."

"My s-son?" the old man stammered. "He has done nothing wrong. What would you want with him?"

Diana watched the exchange with curiosity. The old man, frail though he was, spread his body across the threshold, blocking entry. The gesture was defensive, and not that of a man who believed in his son's innocence. Her heart beat fast again, but she was glad for once to let someone else take charge.

"I must insist on having words with him," Niccolo replied. "Stand aside or I will have the gendarmes move you."

Above, the sound of scraping across roof tiles made Diana look up. A shadow disappeared behind a stone chimney. A moment later it reappeared, sailing like a bat across the space between two stone palazzos. "There!" Diana pointed toward the sky. "He flees across the rooftops!"

"Damn!" Niccolo hissed. "Get him!"

The gendarmes rushed off immediately, intent on tracking the dark figure above. Diana could see it would be hopeless. She had already lost track of the shadow herself.

Niccolo pushed the old man aside roughly and entered his home. "You could burn for this," he growled as he moved inside.

Diana followed, moving past the shaking old man. She looked at him from the corner of her eyes. He did not meet her gaze, only staring at the floor, one hand clutched to his heart. The poor old fool worried for his son, she could guess easily enough. Perhaps he might even know that his son was a murderer. An odd sense of sympathy washed over her, yet she pushed it immediately from her mind.

She looked around the entrance hall. Above, a host of anguished painted angels emerged from darkened clouds to do battle with red skinned devils that rose up from a crack in the Earth. A host of nude mortals cowered in fear at the sight of the heavenly war. With Siobhan behind her, Diana felt unusually conscious of the painting, something she would have taken for granted in another time. The entire lives of the

Firenzians were observed by these silent visitors.

Niccolo returned to the old man and took up his collar in one fist. "Where are his rooms?"

The old man shrank back, one armed raised up over his face. "Up the staircase, to the right."

Niccolo tossed the man aside and strode for the broad stone stairs. Diana followed once again, her feet disappearing in the thick carpets that covered the stone. A moment later they had the door opened before them.

The quarters of Benedetto's son were small and, on first glance, unremarkable. The bed, though a four-poster, was small and unmade. The mural on the ceiling showed a scene of the Last Supper, with the apostles gathered around the figure of Christ. Squinting, Diana noted that the paint had been scratched away from all of their eyes aside from Judas. On a table by an open window, a thick candle still burned, its flame resisting the onslaught from the cold night air. A book stood open on the desk, a dull quill cast aside beyond it.

Niccolo looked out the window, head and torso stretching outside. Diana ignored his efforts, turning her attention to the book. The writing was new, as she expected, the page incomplete, a diary. The penmanship was exquisite, loosely flowing and easy to read. She began reading on the open page. "She was there," the words began, "dark, like a fallen angel, beautiful like a peaceful death. I touched her in the dark, her fear a thing more precious than salvation. I could have killed her, it would have been demanded of me, but she is Isabella's daughter and I can destroy no part of my beloved Isabella. Sweetest God, what am I to do? What am I to do?"

"He's mad," Siobhan said, her voice a whisper in

Diana's ear.

Diana jumped, unaware the Irish woman had drawn so close. "Disfigured and maddened. I pity him. He could be no more wretched a creature."

Diana read on. "I reached out to drive a knife home in her breast, but you, my God, stayed my hand. You kept me safe from her wrath. For what purpose have you drawn us together? Could Isabella have been right? Do you bring me her daughter to offer me this chance at redemption? Promise me there will be some relief, that you will end my suffering and bring me to the solace of your exquisite presence." There it ended, the thought no doubt interrupted by their arrival. Before that page in the book were at least a hundred pages of the poor creature's ravings. Among them might be some clue to her mother's fate.

"There's a ladder to the roof." Niccolo closed the open window with a slam. "What do you have there?"

"His diary. He mentions our confrontation at Madonna delle Grazie." She glanced at Niccolo. "Who is this man?"

"Pietro Benedetto. He has shown the curse of God in his features since childhood. His father keeps him well in his charity. Until now he has been a harmless aberration, seen out only at night. I'll need to take the book."

A fire rose up in the flesh of her face. "Are you mad? This diary may contain the information I have been seeking. You expect me to turn it over to you?"

"With respect, you have no choice, lady. It is evidence in an investigation, and thus is the property of the Republic. I will keep you apprised of its contents as they relate to your mother's death. You must trust me."

"A suggestion you offer liberally without providing tangible support," Diana growled, although there was nothing she could do to prevent Niccolo from scooping up the book and taking it from her clutches. He had no more to say evidently and strode from the room, presumably intent on leaving the building. As he left he did not notice that his efforts had stirred a page that had lain under the book, a separate parchment. It was a small page, and floated toward the ground like a feather. With lightning reflexes, Siobhan snatched it from the air and hid it in her coat before Niccolo could turn to notice it.

Once Niccolo was gone, Siobhan retrieved it and gave Diana a glance.

Diana gasped. The page was the first of a two-page letter. The flowing penmanship was more than familiar. Her mother had written the letter.

Chapter Seven
A Sense of Home

Inside her family palazzo, a warmth greeted Diana that seeped into her cold aching bones and began lulling her to sleep. The sutures in her skull felt like they were splitting apart, and a creeping sense of doom fingered its way into her mind. Eyeballs throbbing, she settled into a plush chair and let the heat soak into the frozen joints of her fingers. She ran her fingers through her long hair.

Agathi, always awake, always present, tended to her needs. "A hot cider, if you would." Diana shrugged off her coat. "I don't feel any hunger."

"You should eat," Siobhan protested. "Agathi, bring her some soup at least." She stood over Diana, hands on her hips. "Are you quite all right?"

A quivering hand rubbed tense eyebrows. "Sometimes I just feel my limits. Sometimes I just think we can't succeed. Sometimes I just miss my mother."

Siobhan extended the parchment they recovered from Pietro Benedetto's rooms. "You can read her words."

Diana looked up at her from under tired eyelids. "Would that make me feel any closer to her? I don't know the woman who consorted with Pietro Benedetto. She seems to have lived a whole secret life that I knew nothing about." Still she reached out and took the offered document.

Seeing her mother's handwriting caused her heart to catch in her throat. The note read:

"My Dear Friend Pietro:

I write this letter with the deepest sorrow. I count you among the closest of my friends. You and I have shared a similar desire to learn about the mysteries of our holy nature, a quest that has led us to this same destination. It is my responsibility, for in my enthusiasm regarding the proffered wisdoms regarding these mysteries I have nominated you and championed your indoctrination in the Sacred Council of Apostles in hopes that we would share together in their enlightenment. In so doing I am accountable for whatever fate befalls you, and I can only hope that you will forgive me my foolishness. I hope that you will accept my contrition and believe me now when I say that believing the Council was ever inspired by the goodness of the light and motivated by holiness..."

And so the note ended, the last words blending into the second page already recovered. Not a long note, overall, and obscure at best in meaning. Diana gathered that her mother had joined this Sacred Council of Apostles, and later brought in Pietro Benedetto as well, both actions she later regretted for unspoken reasons. Had this Council then killed her when she sought to leave? What had her mother been thinking? And how had she, Diana, no idea that her mother had involved herself in what...some kind of cult? A heresy perhaps?

Diana felt sickened at the thought of her mother as a heretic. Perhaps it hadn't been the Council who had killed her, but the Papacy or the mad friar Savonarola. Then again, wouldn't either of them have burned her publicly?

Diana's hand dropped, her energy stores no longer sufficient to even hold the paper up. Siobhan slipped the parchment from between her fingers and read it as well. Siobhan's face twisted in thought but she said nothing.

"How did the nun get the second page?" Diana whispered as much to herself as Siobhan. She sighed and rolled onto her left side in the chair. "I can't escape the feeling I am being manipulated, like a pawn in a cruel chess game."

"Perhaps it is true that you are being manipulated," Siobhan offered, "but at the very least you are no pawn. If this is a chess match, then you are the queen, strong and commanding."

"Huh." Diana smiled sadly. "Sometimes queens are sacrificed."

"Then at least know your sacrifice will bring down many of your enemies. Sometimes that is the best we can hope for."

Diana rubbed her head. From down the hall she could hear heavy footsteps, the telltale sound of her father approaching. Her muscles tensed in apprehension. If he knew how she had spent the last two days, he would not approve.

He crossed into the room, still dressed for the working day. He stopped when he saw her, arms folded across his chest. "Diana, where have you been all day?"

"I've been out. There's too much here that reminds me of Mother." It was the truth, and she hoped he'd have enough empathy to accept that as explanation. Diana couldn't help but notice that Siobhan had edged quietly out of view. Probably wise.

Remarkably, her father didn't press her any harder on her whereabouts. "I've wanted to speak with you. The Tornabuoni family is holding a dinner in celebration of their son Bernardo, who has just returned from the French court. It will be tomorrow night and I would like for you to attend."

"Mother has barely been buried for two days. Would it be appropriate for me to be seen dancing and cavorting as if I have already forgotten her?" She felt a vague sense of irritation rising. She could not be sure if she felt irritated because the request was truly unreasonable or simply because it had been made by her father.

Signore Savrano clenched his jaw. "It is for me to dictate how this family will mourn for your mother. I thought this would be a good opportunity for both of us to be distracted. Why, you look like you could use some cause for celebration."

"I don't wish to be distracted from the pain of losing my mother. How can you even suggest that?" She knew how to twist his words apart. It was unfair, but it suited her mood.

Her father visibly squirmed, sought for the upper hand Diana had snatched from him. "I'm merely suggesting retaining some social contacts may be good for us both. This would be a difficult time for anyone, and you always take things so hard."

"How would you know how I take things?" she shot back, picking an unnecessary fight with him. "Do you hear that in the reports from the servants while you count your money at your place of business?"

Her father's face went red and he breathed in deeply before he responded, "I don't know where this discussion will get us. I've made up my mind that we're to attend dinner with the Tornabuoni. The good Lord knows I make few enough requests of you. Let me make this request of you now, that you will attend as well and behave yourself."

"Fine," she snipped, although she was letting the argument go. "I'll pretty myself up in a fine dress and make cordial conversation."

He'd gotten a tacit agreement for what he wanted, but Diana could tell from the crooked set of his jaw that her father was not satisfied. He stood, staring at her for a moment, his mouth opening and closing as if to speak before he thought better of what he might say. At last he spoke, his voice imploring, "Why must you always choose the more difficult path? Why, sometimes, can you just not try to work with the world instead of always against it?"

She looked askance at her father, but did not answer.

He looked down at his hands, which were now clenched in front of him. Looking up he told her, "You are not the only one who misses your mother, you know. I may never have been one much for ostentatious affection, but I loved her in ways that you could never imagine."

He went silent. Diana felt an intense ache across her chest. She could reach out to him, offer him comfort, or accept comfort from him. Somehow though, he could just not fill that abyss in her life where her mother had been. She could not answer him, could not reach across that gulf for her father. Eventually he turned away and left her. With a sense of regret, she watched him go.

****

What dreams she had that night left no memory, yet Diana woke with a vague uneasy sense that they had been unpleasant and better left forgotten. The piercing light of a new morning crept in over the sill of her window. It was early still. She was not accustomed to waking early and her head ached from the lack of familiar rest. Her body was hyper-alert though, her heart already pumping, muscles tense. A few hours of exhausted sleep each night might be the best she could hope for until the mystery of her mother's death was resolved.

She lay for a while, letting the tiredness slowly ebb away. Finally, feeling some energy coursing through her, she turned over onto her back. Her right hand fell back against her pillow, and brushed against something made of paper. Startled, Diana propped herself on one elbow.

A small envelope lay on the pillow not far from where her head had rested during the night. In a loose flowing script it was addressed "Lady Diana Savrano."

With a frown, she sat up and opened the letter. The script read:

"Lady Savrano:

I must plead that you will excuse my intrusion, but I believe the time has come for us to speak. You will be able to find me during sunset at the church at Piazza Madonna delle Grazie, where we met only yesterday. We will be safe of the Sacred Council at that time. Come alone as no one can be trusted.

Sincerest regards,

Pietro Benedetto"

A cold icicle ran down her spine. Who had

delivered this note? How had it gotten on her pillow? It wasn't like her servants to leave a note unannounced in this way.

Now alarmed as much as she was awake she leapt from the bed and marched to the door. Wrenching it open she called for Siobhan and Agathi. Only a moment passed before they both appeared, already dressed for work. They stood silently before her, even Siobhan apparently reluctant to speak.

"Did one of you leave this note for me on my pillow?" She waved the offending article in the air.

Both shook their heads and denied responsibility.

"Do you know what this means?" she asked, voice raised. Her eyes fell on Agathi, who was not in her confidence. If Diana informed her that someone had stolen into her room at night to leave the note, surely Agathi would tell her father about the matter. If her father learned of this she would not be allowed to set foot outside the palazzo again without a ring of guards. "Forget the matter, Agathi," she told the old woman, forcing her voice to lower. "I must have forgotten the letter, myself. I trust you will say nothing of this."

The old woman blinked and nodded. "As you say, lady." She turned and shuffled away, returning to her duties.

Once she was gone, Siobhan whispered, "What is it?"

Diana handed her the note and gave her a moment to read it, watching as her mouth gradually expanded into a larger and larger circle. "He's been in my room," Diana pointed out, once Siobhan looked up with wide eyes.

"Dear sweet Lord," Siobhan exhaled, "how did he

manage that?"

Trying to think through the shock, Diana answered, "Either he is a phantom, or my mother entrusted him with a key to the palazzo." She shook her head, her anger so diffuse she was not sure who was the target. "To imagine him in my room while I slept. He could have slit my throat. Does my father no longer employ armed guards for the palazzo?"

Siobhan shrunk back and swallowed. "If he does have a key and loses it, someone else with more sinister intent could replace him. We must retrieve that key!"

Diana walked back into her bedroom and Siobhan followed. They returned to their normal morning routine, with Siobhan assisting Diana in dressing for the day. "I'll meet Pietro tonight at the church as he requests. I'll insist he return the key."

"It's too dangerous to go alone!" Siobhan protested. "Even if he is innocent of harmful intent, he might unwittingly lead you into a trap by those who wish to see you injury. Mancini in particular. I should come with you."

"No," Diana decided with a shake of her head. "I will go alone."

"What about the dinner at the Tornabuoni residence? You will be expected there at the same time."

"Neither the Tornabuoni palazzo nor the church at Piazza Madonna delle Grazie is so far from here. I can meet with Pietro Benedetto quickly and still arrive at the Tornabuoni palazzo with enough time to avoid arousing the ire of my father." She turned to her servant and friend. "You understand I cannot let a potential source of information such as Pietro Benedetto slip away. Niccolo stole his diary from us, but I might be able to garner the same information from him in person."

"I understand," Siobhan replied, although her brows were still knitted.

Diana took her hands. "If ever there was a time to consider giving up the chase, it has since passed." She broke away, signaling the discussion had ended.

A moment later, while brushing Diana's long hair, Siobhan inquired, "Are you angry with your father for asking you to attend the Tornabuoni dinner?"

Diana looked at Siobhan through the long mirror before them. It was a personal question, but she had allowed Siobhan such personal intimacy in the past. Indeed, she appreciated the feeling of having a friend. "It does not bother me to attend to the Tornabuoni's invitation. Truth is my father could be right. It might be a welcome distraction."

"I'm more than a bit envious. You'll be spending your time in the company of handsome and wealthy Italian men. If that's not to your liking, I'd be more than open to exchanging places. You can have all the scruffy Irish lads you can handle."

Diana said nothing, but gave her friend a smile.

A moment later, Siobhan persisted, "If you were not mad about the dinner tonight, why would you seem so angry with your father?"

Diana's smile vanished. She worked her jaw back and forth, considering the question. At last she answered, "I don't know, to be honest. My father and I have never been entirely close. My mother acted as intermediary between us. With her gone, I don't know what course our relationship might take."

"That is certainly too bad," Siobhan said with a nod. "Granted, my father ripped me from my homeland and marooned me in this land of olive-skinned strangers upon his death, but he will always be the closest person to my heart. I thought it was the same between all fathers and daughters."

"Apparently it is not," Diana murmured.

"I'm told there is a line in the Bible that goes something like 'Pride goes before destruction, and arrogance before a fall', of course I don't read Latin, and so I'm taking others at their word on that. Still, it would seem to apply here."

Diana gave Siobhan a steady gaze. "You think I should apologize to my father."

Siobhan raised on eyebrow. "If you wish to improve your relations with him, it could scarcely harm affairs."

"I'll consider it," Diana answered, although the very thought was anathema to her. Perhaps Siobhan was right though, the Irishwoman had proven herself wise if not book-read on more than one occasion. Perhaps tonight at the dinner with the Tornabuoni she would apologize to her father and give him some reason to feel some pride in her. Assuming of course, that she survived her meeting with Pietro Benedetto.

****

Huddled in the cold church, Diana wrapped her coat around her, holding in tattered ribbons of her own body heat. The building writhed in shadows. Flickering candles provided the only defense against a lifeless darkness that spread like plague. No priest attended. A few dozen penitents skulked in the corners, wallowing in their anonymous guilt. A small cluster hung close to the altar, chanting their novenas. Listening to them made Diana feel infinitely sad. Even the icons hovered like cold and lifeless demons rather than symbols of hope and devotion. Diana wondered why churches sometimes seemed to be amongst the most unholy of places.

Her back faced the door. Leaving herself exposed was a dangerous choice, as she knew very well. She was in God's hands. If He wished her dead, then He could very well take her in His own house. If hands reached for her or a knife went across her neck, the last thing she would do would be to aim her pistol backwards and blow a hole through whoever assaulted her. Hopefully one of these lost souls present would tell Niccolo. She could be buried in the wall of a church just like her mother. Perhaps they could lie side by side for all eternity. 'Here lies Isabella Savrano and her daughter Diana who was too stupid to discover how to avenge her.'

Underneath her coat, Diana wore an elaborate dress of maroon with gold threading embellishments. Small pearls adorned the material making it beautiful to behold and simultaneously uncomfortable. She meant it for the dinner, but it could just as easily serve as a death shroud.

She held her hands before her as she knelt on the cold stone. Rosaries entwined her fingers. She prayed to the Virgin. A shadow slipped into the bench next to her with a sign of the cross. Diana's right hand left the rosary and slipped into her coat, running along the grip of her pistol.

"Hail Mary, full of grace, the Lord is with thee," the shadow intoned beside her. Muffled and flawed, the words came like they were babbled forth by an inhuman mouth. The voice went silent. Without looking, Diana felt the shadow turn to regard her. She sucked in a tight breath between quivering lips. Her hand tightened on the pistol. The shadow whispered, "It is God's grace that I find you well, Diana Savrano."

Diana's eyes flicked to the side, trying to see him without turning her head. "You are the one they call Pietro Benedetto?"

"I am the one they call the Boar," he answered, his breath icy against her throat. "Will you not look upon me? Will you not look upon me like your mother would?"

Mention of her mother stabbed deep in her chest. "And how did my mother look upon you?"

"With kindness," he replied, his voice soft. "As a friend."

She turned then and looked at him, with just the slightest hesitation. She met his eyes first, dark and sad, endless pools of misery. Long dark curls framed his face. He might have been handsome if not for his mouth. Up close she could see the texture of those teeth, the surface smooth and slightly pitted like driftwood. Irregular hunks of flesh flicked against his gums, giving him a horrible inhuman rictus. She felt her brows furrow at the sight of him, her mouth opened, but she said nothing. She did not look away.

"You see a monster," he said.

"I don't know what I see," she replied, her eyes taking in everything. "Your eyes are too sad to be those of a monster. Yet I think God must have loathed you to make you as he did."

His eyes slid over her. His jaws opened once then

closed, the teeth audibly clicking together. "I appreciate your honesty. You are nearly as lovely as your mother."

"You were in love with her." She stated this as a fact.

"Wasn't everyone?"

"Not everyone," she observed.

His eyes dropped to the floor. After a moment he asked, "Do you fear me?"

"You did try to kill me."

"You were waving a pistol at me. I left you alive."

He was right; she had chased him with the pistol. After the run in with Mancini, she reached for that pistol too readily. "I don't fear you any more than anyone else. I don't know who to trust right now."

"Believe in God alone and distrust His children on Earth." Pietro made a sign of the cross. "For we are all deceitful creatures."

"I guess you're going to ask me to trust you all the same."

He looked askance at her. It was difficult to read his expression, distorted as his face was. "I was your mother's friend. I was unable to help her in life. Doing what I can for you is all that I can do to make amends for failing her."

"You can start by giving me the key to the Savrano palazzo."

Pietro's forehead creased with lines. Long fingers reached into a coat pocket and pulled forth an iron key, which he deposited in Diana's outstretched hand.

"My mother gave you the key?"

"She did."

She paused for a moment. The question on her mind was a difficult one in multiple ways. Physically, she couldn't imagine her mother and Pietro together, but she had obviously seen something in the man that bonded her to him. It was even more difficult for her to accept the possibility her mother had deceived her father. Then again, her mother had clearly hid much from her family. There was no point in letting the question fester in her mind as it surely would over time. "Were you and my mother lovers?"

His eyes went wide and after a deep breath he began to chuckle. The sound was harsh, rasping, naked of true joy. After a moment he caught himself. "Even your mother was not devoid of sight. I will not deny that my own thoughts of her went beyond those of spiritual and personal communion. I saw no indication that she returned such thoughts."

Diana felt mildly humiliated, being laughed at. Still, the answer was a relief.

Pietro kept his voice down as he spoke, "Let me tell you some things, Diana Savrano, and hopefully you will understand. When I was but a little boy, I suppose I was as perfect an image of God's own form as any child may expect to be. I was perhaps four or five when I first caught the malady that has so chastened me. How it came to be, I don't know, whether a malady of the air, or an imbalance in the humors, the disease caused horrible sores of the mouth with agonizing pain and festering of the tissue. While the affliction eventually went away, it left me a fiend. When my teeth later came in, they were those of a beast. As you yourself said, it felt as if God himself had shown me great disfavor, a thought I have lived with each day of my life. With my disfigurement there was no question of camaraderie with other children or, as I grew, marriage. I became a prisoner of my parents' home, my shame keeping me shut away from the city.

"At nights I would hear my mother and father speaking. My mother would ask what she had done wrong to have seen me transfigured into such a horrid ogre. My father consoled her as best he could, although I believe her death was, as much as anything, the result of a broken heart. My very existence was a burden for them both, and I continue to be a burden for my poor father. Naturally I understood that if my deformity was not punishment for my mother's sins, than it must be punishment for my own. I could never understand what such a young child might have done to deserve such divine disregard.

"The Church speaks much about suffering on Earth as cleansing for the afterlife. It is, in a sense, a message I am prepared to accept. But if it is true, then I don't understand how God's agents in this world can surround themselves so with servants, and fine clothes and pampered lives. If suffering is the key to holiness, should not God's ministers ravage their own flesh, and tear at their own lives? Instead the Bishop of Roma, who some call the Borgia Pope, presides over unholy orgies, sanctions murder, and is rumored to lie with his own daughter. The prelates of the church are carried forth by slaves in litters, dressed in fine silks and perfumed like Persians."

Diana kept her voice low, "You come close to speaking heresy." It was not a new complaint though. Indeed the Mad Friar Savonarola himself had raised such accusations. His bombast increasingly put him at odds with the Pope, a dangerous situation for him and all of Firenze.

"Let them burn me," he whispered. "Your mother, though perfect in form, and privileged in origin, had come to a similar place in her life. She needed a deeper understanding of the mysteries of life."

"Was she so unhappy?"

"I think her spirit was in need of nurturance."

Diana felt a tug in her chest. "Was it me? Was she disappointed in me? Did I not do enough to please her?"

Pietro put one hand up. "No, that is not what I meant to imply. She spoke of nothing but love for you."

Diana looked down, unconvinced. "What of my father?"

Pietro looked away. "In truth, we did not speak often of him. In my own conceit, I preferred to think of Isabella as my own in whatever limited ways that she would allow. I did not like to think upon how she belonged to another."

Diana stared at her hands, remaining silent.

"We met here one day, your mother and I. In the cold weather I can use a scarf to mask my features. She left the church as I came in. When I slid on a patch of ice, she reached out to help me, and did not pull away even when the scarf came loose and revealed my features. She showed me great kindness. This was a year ago, perhaps. A year as her friend has brought some meaning to my barren existence. Even then she was with the Council. The Council's views on the Church and how far it has strayed from the light of goodness were much like my own, and had influenced Isabella's thoughts greatly. After we spoke on such matters, Isabella invited me to join the Council as my beliefs were already in line with their own."

"You're anti-papists, then?" Diana realized with disbelief. "You want to assassinate the Pope and overthrow the Holy See?" There were many who found the Pope in Roma to be distasteful. Many of these groups of anti-papists were radical and brutal, however, given to the same violent excesses as the Pope or worse. Religion in Italia had become a confusing and disagreeable thing.

Pietro nodded. "There was talk along such lines."

Diana put a hand to her forehead. One of her headaches threatened. Dear God, what had her mother gotten herself involved in? She had been courting death as a heretic with such a group. Criticisms of the Church were certainly not unknown and at times, Diana quietly agreed with many of them. Yet vocal opposition to the Papacy was often a sure invitation to finding oneself tied to the stake with flames licking at one's heels.

"We met in secret," Pietro told her, "in the room you saw downstairs. The priests here are lazy and unwatchful and do not disturb us. It proved a reliable meeting ground and one tinged with an element of irony. When we would meet, we wore masks. Given the delicacy of our mission, it seemed imperative to function in secrecy from even each other, lest anyone of us have the power to destroy the rest."

Diana rolled her eyes. "Sounds lovely. Doesn't anyone meet for dice games anymore?" She shook her head. "In my mother's note to you, she mentioned that something happened to change her mind about the Council. Can you tell me what happened?"

Pietro coughed and looked away for a moment. "Despite our use of masks, our system of anonymity remained imperfect. I knew your mother, of course, and she knew the person who recruited her. A determined effort could conceivably lead quickly up the chain. Rumors began to spread between us that the Republic had a spy amongst us."

"I don't understand. Savonarola is a fervent anti-papist. Why would he work against other anti-papists?" Since taking control of the Republic of Firenze Savonarola, despite being a Catholic friar, more and more criticized the Pope in Roma. Increasingly this seemed to put Firenze on a collision course with the Holy See.

Pietro shrugged. "The Council is outside his control, presumably. That might be enough. There may be forces within the Republic working against Savonarola. I'm not sure, honestly. I wasn't nearly far enough along in initiation with the group to be privy to such information. To continue however, on the night in question, we met at an old graveyard on the far side of the river. One young man by the name of Troilo Ricci was brought forcibly before us and unmasked. The High Apostle declared the man a traitor and spy for the Republic. A death sentence was pronounced upon him. The man swore his innocence. He was held firm, while the High Apostle drew forth a dagger and pressed it to the man's neck.

"Our meetings had been in the main like philosophical discussions before that. Certainly we understood what we discussed was dangerous and heretical in the eyes of the Papacy, but for all our talk of revolution it never went much beyond talk. To see the life of a man, one of our own no less, threatened before us shocked your mother and I, and likely others in the gathering. Before he could be killed however,

Republic gendarmes appeared, weapons drawn. They shouted for us to surrender, but we fled instead. A few men might have drawn weapons on the gendarmes, but most scattered like mice. Your mother and I made it into the woods, then back to the city where we discarded our Council robes, of course. The next morning the body of Troilo Ricci was found hanging over the river from the Ponte Vecchio. His stomach had been cut open and his entrails disgorged into the waters below. I do not know if it was the Republic or the Council who killed him."

Diana absorbed what he told her. It was difficult to imagine her mother involved in such matters. She could see why her mother had become horrified. "When you met with her later, what did my mother tell you?"

Pietro's eyes watered. "Regrettably, she did not make our appointment. I waited for her here alone for some time. I found out she had already taken ill. Soon after, she died."

"Did you think she wanted to leave the Council?"

"It has been my guess this was her intention."

"Would she have been allowed to leave?"

Pietro shrugged again. "She knew details of our discussions and plans. She would have known at least a few members' names." No more needed to be said.

Diana sighed. "So either the Council killed her for trying to leave, or the Republic killed her as a member of a secret society, or the Papacy killed for heresy, depending on who discovered her identity and intensions." She looked up at Pietro. "Whoever did kill her…they may try to kill you as well."

His mouth twisted in an odd facsimile of a smile. "The thought had occurred to me. Won't be much of a loss to anyone, will it?"

Diana stared at him, not sure what to say.

"I don't know the names of the other Council members," Pietro added, softly. "I only knew your mother and one other. A man of little significance whom I recruited in turn. Everyone else wore masks. I was still only a novice."

"How did the nun get half of the letter from my mother to you?"

"That I don't know. It must have been stolen off my person on the night I waited for her. I thought I had lost it, but clearly I did not if it has come into your possession."

Diana wrinkled her nose. She had trouble imagining how the note made its way from Pietro to the nun. The sister had never gotten the chance to explain it herself. Diana wondered if whoever had gotten it from Pietro had used it to learn of her mother's involvement with the Council. Or had inferred her intention to leave? "What will you do now, Pietro? Surely they'll come to kill you. You could make your way to Venezia."

He shrugged again, as if it were little matter. "There will be no more love for the Boar in Venezia than he has found in Firenze. Whether it is the Council or the Papists or the Republic who wishes me dead, I shall make it as difficult for them as I can for as long as I can. In doing so, perhaps I will distract them for a time from your own efforts."

"Here," Diana reached for her purse and pulled out a few florins, "take these. At least you'll be able to keep warm and get some food."

He stared at the coins for a moment, then gently took them from her palm. "Thank you, lady. You have your mother's kindness."

She blushed, feeling she didn't deserve the compliment. "You are mistaken. I am prepared to do things my mother never would to bring her justice."

Pietro smiled. "Then perhaps you will succeed where she could not." He took her hand in his own, the flesh of his hand soft and warm. She watched as he pressed her hand to the ragged remains of his lips. His large teeth felt like cold tusks against her skin. She showed no emotion and when he finished the chaste kiss, she allowed his hand a squeeze. "Keep yourself well, lady," he said, then stood and drew his cape around him. Without looking back he moved quickly from the church.

Diana looked down, thinking. She still wasn't sure how far she could trust Pietro and the story that he told her. Her mother had trusted him that far she believed, but who was to say he hadn't betrayed that trust. Perhaps instead of the note being stolen from him, he had passed it on willingly? Perhaps they had met and he had even slipped her some poison himself? On the other hand, if he told her the truth, at least she understood how her mother had gotten herself in trouble. She still couldn't be sure who was responsible for her mother's death. The Council seemed the most likely culprit, although she didn't know their identities. On the other hand, it could have been the Papacy or even the Republic. A spark lit in her mind. Oh dear God, she thought, if it were the Republic, she'd led them right to Pietro. They could be following her even now. And Niccolo...she had begun to trust him. But could he be responsible for her mother's death?

Chapter Eight
The Two Princes

Dizzying thoughts coursed through Diana's mind as she quickly skirted from the church to the Tornabuoni palazzo. Most of all she was stunned to find that her mother had this whole secret life that she'd known nothing about. She felt a little sense of betrayal her mother had kept such important events from her. She believed herself to be a horrible daughter given she hadn't at all sensed that things had been different in her mother's life.

She glanced around in the piazza outside of the church, one hand kept constantly on the grip of her pistol. Coming to meet with Pietro had been a big risk. Now she had to get back to the dinner with the Tornabuoni family or her father would be angry. She guessed her timing was pretty good and she would only arrive a little late. She'd miss some initial posturing and bragging about whose son had done what, who would receive a Cardinal's hat, who was on a mission to France. Whatever. None of it interested her very much. Her father had little to discuss in those initial stages of a banquet. As a daughter, Diana was not allowed to accomplish much of significance aside from marriage, and that peculiar institution didn't interest her very much. She was just as happy to skip standing around feeling like a disappointment.

Coat pulled tight, Diana moved off, keeping to the shadows. There were a fair number of others in the streets, enough that a public assassination would be unlikely. After a few blocks however, she sensed someone following. She glanced behind. There…a young man, slender and not too tall, long black cape tied round his shoulders. She'd seen him on the way to the church, and here he was once again. His pace matched hers exactly, constantly keeping one block behind, attempting to blend into the other pedestrians.

Diana's heart raced. Could this be a minion of Mancini, waiting for the perfect opportunity to slip a dagger between her ribs? She was not about to have any of that. Still, if she picked up the pace she might lose him, but the gain would only be temporary. Likely as not he knew her destination, and certainly he knew where she lived. He'd only wait for a future opportunity.

No, if she was going to survive this she was going to have to face threats head on. Her grasp tightened on the pistol. Of course she could hardly shoot him in the middle of the street. An alleyway though, dangerous, no doubt about that. All manner of trouble waited down dark alleys. Nonetheless, if she was going to confront him, that was how it would have to be.

She knew this area of town well. After a little thought, she knew where to go. A few turns, and she skirted down a dark and ignored lane. A stack of empty crates provided a perfect point from which to launch an ambush. There, in the darkness, she pulled out her pistol and waited.

She was not left waiting for long. A few minutes after she laid her trap, it was sprung. The young man with the cape rounded the corner. No reason he'd come along this way other than to follow Diana. He looked around the alley, apparently confused as to why she'd come down this way. Before he could realize he was in trouble, Diana leapt out of the shadows and held the gun to his face. "Don't move or I'll kill you." Her arms shook from excitement and cold, and a part of her brain told her to just do it. Shoot him before he could draw his dagger and strike.

The young man's arms flew above his head, eyes white and wide even in the dark passage. "Lady Savrano," he croaked, his voice higher pitched than she'd imagined.

No chance of pretense now, he knew her name.

"Do you have a weapon on you?" she barked.

With his elbow he moved aside his cape until she could see the pommel of a rapier, flecks of reflected light glinting off the metal.

"And a knife in your boot, I'd imagine," she challenged.

Visibly swallowing, he nodded. "Please, mistress, let me explain."

Diana felt that uneasy burning in her brain, the impulse to pull the trigger and be done with it before he could trick her. She suppressed it. Aside from the glancing wound to Mancini, she'd never done anyone harm before. The other day she'd tried to shoot Pietro when it seemed he might be her enemy, but she'd been wrong about that. At very least she needed to hear this man out, lest there indeed be a good explanation. "I think you'd better explain, and fast."

"I'm with the gendarmes."

"You're not dressed in the uniform of the

gendarmes!"

"I know, I know," he flinched, closing his eyes for a moment. "I'm under orders to follow you without drawing attention to myself. My orders are to keep you safe."

"Keep me safe?" she cried, incredulous. "Who has taken it upon themselves to worry about me so?" Even as she asked the question, she guessed the answer.

"Signore Machiavelli has given me my orders, Lady Savrano," the man told her, hurriedly.

She started to relax, figuring the man told her the truth. Still, it could be a trick. "What evidence do you have that you work on Signore Machiavelli's orders?"

The gendarme blinked. "He, uh...told me that if you confronted me and didn't believe my orders, I was to tell you—"

"Yes, out with it!"

"He told me to tell you that you are a stubborn woman who doesn't know what's good for her, and is likely to get herself killed, signorina." He looked like he was ready for the hammer to come down on the pistol at any moment.

Diana sighed. She didn't know him well but somehow that did sound like Machiavelli.

Apparently sensing the danger was ebbing, the young man added, "Signore Machiavelli mentioned you would likely be heading to the Tornabuoni palazzo once you were finished with whatever other mischief you were up to tonight. He wished for me to tell you, under circumstances such as these, that he would eagerly await your arrival there."

She relaxed her grip on the pistol. "Wouldn't it have been easier to inform me that you would be shadowing me?"

"Those weren't my orders, Lady Savrano. I was told only to speak to you if I was confronted."

Of course, Diana reasoned, this wasn't just a matter of protecting her, although that might legitimately be one of Niccolo's concerns. Having her shadowed also gave him an opportunity to spy on her. And here she'd led them to Pietro a second time. She wouldn't have done that if she knew she'd been followed. She hoped he had managed to avoid detection.

Diana's blood boiled. Damn that Niccolo, pretending to be concerned about her, then spying on her instead. Besides she didn't know she could trust him. From the story Pietro had told, it was just as likely his gendarmes had killed her mother on orders from the Republic as it was that the Sacred Council of Apostles had killed her for trying to leave. Either way, she still lacked clear evidence, and had to keep a level head.

"Very well," she said at last. "I won't shoot you."

"You can't imagine what a relief that is to hear, signorina."

"However, we will switch our positions. You are to remain twenty paces ahead of me at all times. If I so much as *think* I see you reaching for your rapier I will blow a hole in you large enough to sail a caravel through."

"I understand, signorina, no twitching."

"If I need assistance I will be sure to scream."

"Yes, Lady Savrano, if you scream, I am allowed to twitch."

"What is your name?"

"Crispino, Lady Savrano."

"All right, Crispino, get walking. You already

know where I'm going."

She watched as Crispino turned without further word and began walking back out into the street. "You can put your hands down now, Crispino!" she called. She sighed and rolled her eyes. If this was the quality of the men watching out for her wellbeing, she was doomed.

****

Warmth greeted her inside the Tornabuoni Palazzo. It felt good to shake the cold out of her bones, rubbing her hands along her arms to warm the flesh. The scent of cooking food hung heavily in the air. Diana's stomach rumbled, and she realized she hadn't been eating well the past few days.

A young female slave, Slavic by the look and sound of her, offered to take Diana's coat. Diana hesitated. Suddenly, with blood rising in her face, she realized she had brought the pistol to the dinner. She could hardly go through the evening with the thing strapped over her shoulder. Handing it over, though…the slave would certainly gossip. Worse, what if someone were to sabotage the pistol? Could she be sure that there were no agents of the Sacred Council of Apostles here at the dinner? She already knew that the Republic would be represented in the person of Niccolo Machiavelli. The pistol was her only defense. It would have been better if she'd left it at home tonight. Neither Pietro nor the gendarme Crispino had been a threat.

There was nothing to be done now. Her only hope was that the slave would keep her mouth shut. Through a half open doorway, Diana could see the banquet in the great hall beyond. Those gathered there hadn't noted her yet. Diana sucked in a deep breath to steady her nerves. The slave girl helped her out of her overcoat. Diana slipped off the satchel that held the pistol and handed it to the girl, pommel visible above the cloth. The young woman looked at it for a moment, hand frozen in the air half way to clutching it. She looked up at Diana with wide eyes.

"Listen to me," Diana told the girl. "Can you tell me your name?"

"Katrianna," the girl answered quietly.

"Katrianna, I need you to help me. I need you to put this someplace safe and to tell no one about it until I retrieve it. My life may depend upon it. Do you think you can do that?"

The girl nodded.

"I know servants talk among themselves. I'm hoping you'll be able to refrain until I leave."

"I'll tell no one, lady." The girl took the pistol, wrapping Diana's coat around it, hiding it from sight. She scurried away into the dark corridors from whence the servants and slaves came and went.

Diana rubbed her hands, cold fingers coming back to feeling. She'd done her best. Either Katrianna would help her or betray her; she could do no more. She stepped through the doorway into the grand hall beyond. She allowed herself a moment to survey the group within. Perhaps two dozen men and women gathered in the hall, clustered in little groups of three or four. They were still talking. That was good. Dinner hadn't been served yet, and she would not seem terribly late.

She spotted her father at once, back to her and speaking with Signore Orsini and his wife as well as the Signore and Signora Tornabuoni. Her father was in his element, holding court with these eminent citizens of Firenze and Roma. Cardinal Lajolo was here as well, as were members of some of the most illustrious families of Firenze: the Riccis, the Strozzis, remnants of the Salviati family, still shattered following their rebellion against Lorenzo of the Medici a generation before. There were younger members of each of these families in addition to their patricians. Young men were dressed up like peacocks, rapiers or daggers at their side as if each of these perfumed dandies needed to prepare for war at any moment. More likely they would draw swords and murder one another over some perceived slight. The young women were bedecked with jewels, eyes scanning the young men, not so much with lasciviousness as with frank appraisal of their worth as husbands.

All the people she expected. Well, except where was that devious little—

A touch at her elbow sent her jumping out of her skin. Niccolo, of course, like a ghost from between flickering shadows. "Christ curses you, Signore Machiavelli," she hissed at him.

He grinned a little. "If only you were the first to say that about me. I'm pleased to see you here tonight."

"Is that so?" she replied, feeling grumpy. "You'll be more pleased I'm sure to learn your man Crispino still breathes, despite I almost fired a lead ball into him when I found him skulking in the shadows."

"Ah, Crispino." He nodded. "I'll have to have words with him about proper surveillance. I hope you understand, I meant only to safeguard your wellbeing."

She regarded him with care. What could she say? If she revealed what Pietro had told her, he'd know she's spoken to the disfigured man, if he didn't already know. She wanted to ask him what his role had been in investigating the Sacred Council of Apostles. Had he or his men killed the accused traitor Troilo Ricci? Had he killed her mother? Certainly the Council themselves made for more likely culprits, but could she be so sure?

On the other hand, she sensed that there was no benefit in coming across to Niccolo as a naïve little waif either. So she replied, "I think you'd like to know if I uncover any information that would do your job for you."

"I would be remiss if I advised you to do anything other than to remain within the safety of your family palazzo."

A clever, non-denial, Diana thought. He hadn't bothered to ask why she'd come late. No doubt he'd get the answer soon enough from Crispino. Together, they stood side by side watching the other guests as if the two of them were empirical observers of some kind of social experiment.

"Do you know the Tornabuoni family well?" Niccolo asked after a few moments of silence.

She shook her head. "They're friends of my father. They have business between them."

Niccolo pointed to one young man at the center of heavy female attention. "That fine young fellow is the guest of honor. Bernardo Tornabuoni, currently holding court with his admirers, is recently returned from Paris and the attention of Charles VIII."

Diana wrinkled her nose, as if noticing an objectionable odor. Charles VIII, King of France, had only recently cut a path of destruction through Italy before retreating back across the Alps in disgrace. His armies had occupied Firenze briefly and, although things could have been worse, had not endeared the French to many of Firenze's citizens.

"He can't be faulted entirely," Niccolo continued, possibly sensing her reaction. "An alliance with France could signal advancement for the entire family. Savonarola favors the French, sees them as agents of God."

"I must have very little understanding of God's ways," Diana commented.

"I as well," Niccolo agreed. "I find it difficult to believe that God should show favor on such a perfumed dandy as Bernardo Tornabuoni."

Diana raised an eyebrow and looked at Niccolo with a grin. "Why, you almost sound envious."

Niccolo shrugged. "It would be pointless to deny he has enjoyed privileges that would be pleasing to most men. I do not mind so much when those privileges have been earned through cleverness or skill. I think that too often they are wasted on a misguided sense of divine anointment. Take the former Medici lords of Firenze, Cosimo the Elder and Lorenzo the Magnificent. Those were men to be admired, not this pampered fool."

"Words of praise for the Medici will find you trouble in Savonarola's Firenze, dear Niccolo."

He seemed unperturbed at that thought. "I have no wish to see the Medici return to Firenze. Yet I can't deny a certain degree of merit among their founding fathers."

People took their places along the banquet table. "It looks like our conversation is to be cut short." She noted that seating was according to rank, a customary observation in Firenze. Given that her father was well-respected and intimately connected to the Tornabuoni, she would be seated with him near the front of the table. Niccolo's family connections and position in the Republic were enough to get him invited tonight, but not enough to position him in a seat of high rank. As she took her place, she decided she'd miss their jousting, if that was what it could be called. Each of his words might be calculated to have some particular effect, but it was a contest she found comforting, as if she had established her stride in it. By contrast, the rich of Firenze, particularly the children of the rich who had known nothing different, she found boring. She might be one of them, but her peers seldom held interest for her. It was one reason among many she didn't marry.

At the head of the table, Signore Tornabuoni and his wife held the position of honor. Their son, Bernardo sat to their right, her father to their left. This arrangement left Diana sitting just diagonally from the young man Niccolo had called perfumed and pampered. Up close there was little doubt Niccolo's words held some merit. The young man was dressed and styled in the latest fashions and held his spine rigid with a slightly irritating aura of self-worth. Still, she couldn't deny that he was handsome, an even blending of his elegant parents. She was surprised more so when he opened his mouth and intelligent words issued forth. Her father commented on the historical difficulties Galilei Galileo experienced in his dealings with the Roman See. Bernardo was quick to note how Galileo's theories and observations unwittingly threatened the Catholic Church's hegemony on celestial and thus heavenly truths.

Impressed though she might be, Diana didn't worry herself overly much so with the sun and the Earth and which revolved around which. She turned away, looking down the table for more interesting conversation but found only the Orsinis and Riccis discussing the finer points of the latest fashions. This was fast becoming the typical sort of banquet her father invited her to. All that went missing was for her to find some way to feel humiliated before the night was over.

"So, you still have not decided to marry, Diana?" The feminine voice jolted her out of her thoughts. She was startled to see all three of the Tornabuonis staring at her, awaiting her reply. Her father coughed and looked at his plate. He would hardly lift a finger to rescue her.

"I, uh…" She cleared her throat. She had forgotten Signora Tornabuoni's penchant for asking embarrassing questions as if they were no more matter than the weather. At least she was right on time to complete the evening. Diana recovered her composure and forced a smile through narrowed eyes and clenched teeth. "I suppose I haven't gotten the right offer yet."

"My dear," Signora Tornabuoni said with a wave of a heavily bejeweled hand, "you have turned down every eligible bachelor in Firenze and beyond. Soon you'll be beyond decent childbearing years."

"She is only nineteen, Giovanna," interjected her husband with an amused tone. "She likely fancies that she has not yet found her prince."

Inwardly Diana groaned. Signore Tornabuoni was partly correct, although his tone of indulgence made her feel like a little girl rather than an adult woman. The implication was difficult to ignore: her whimsical girlish notions had gotten in the way of the practical business of marriage.

"You must pluck the fruit when it is ripe on the vine," suggested Signora Tornabuoni with a tone that implied helpful intent.

"Please, Mother, Father," objected Bernardo, "I am sure Signorina Savrano has her reasons for postponing marital plans. It is none of our business to pry in such matters."

Diana raised her eyebrows at the unexpected defense.

"Well, whatever could be more important than marriage for a young woman?" pried Signora Tornabuoni further.

Her father finally spoke up. "She fancies herself a physician." His tone suggested that this was no better than Signore Tornabuoni's portrayal of her expecting a shining knight on a white charger. The Signore and Signora Tornabuoni giggled and knocked elbows on cue.

Diana resigned herself to a new wave of humiliation.

Once again, Bernardo rose to her defense. "Actually, I have heard that both the universities at Salerno and our own Pisa have accepted a few women among their medical students. Although it is said that the female psyche cannot handle the rigors of such study, or the unpleasantness of human sickness, I have heard that these women have requited themselves quite favorably. Perhaps we should not be so quick to judge."

The giggling died down. "Quite so," said Signore Tornabuoni after a moment. "You might be right. Your time in France has made you worldlier than the rest of us."

What France, which to Diana's knowledge had no female medical students, had to do with it, she did not know. Still, it was enough for her to look out from between her fingers, sensing the wave of humiliation had passed and without its customary fury. She found Bernardo giving her a little grin. She could not help but return it.

It was not lost on her, particularly in her recent paranoid mindset, that the entire exchange might have been a scripted set piece designed to put Bernardo in a good light for her own benefit. The Tornabuonis were one family who had not broached the subject of arranged marriage with her father or herself. Did they now intend to try? If so she had to admit that they had played their parts well, knowing what would impress her. Bernardo might be a dandy, but he was either cleverer or more gallant than Niccolo had given him credit for.

Soon after the dinner started, and this distracted the conversation from anything of value as people stuffed their faces through course after course of the finest and most expensive foods available. Diana, as was customary, became full too soon and could only pick at the later plates.

After dinner the musicians began, and the younger guests began pairing up. Although she enjoyed music, Diana had never been social enough to take much to dancing. As with dress, the styles changed too often for her to keep up with them. This year, the trends were to allow the partners to come into greater contact with each other, to loop arms while performing little twirls and skips. A young man's arm might *accidentally* brush a woman's breast, which was part of the thrill, she supposed. This would be a good time for her to make her escape she figured, but it was not to be.

"Would you care to dance?" Bernardo asked, standing from the table and offering his hand.

Diana stammered for a moment, caught off guard, looking at the older adults around her. The Tornabuonis both smiled, although timidly, as if trying not to push her too hard too quickly. Her father picked at his plate. If he orchestrated this, he knew better than to offer her any encouragement now, which would only inflame her resentment.

Still, Bernardo had been nothing but dignified during dinner, and had impressed her more than once. Diana was not cruel by nature and to turn him down would be to dishonor him after he had come to her aid.

"Very well," she said. "One dance."

As she took to the floor, she warned him, "I don't know the latest dances."

"Don't worry, I will show you," he told her, just the hint of an acquired French accent noticeable in his speech.

He proved an able instructor and in truth the dance was not terribly difficult to learn. Although she felt somewhat like an ox plodding around in a field, she figured that her missteps were at least noticeable only to Bernardo. He remained a perfect gentleman, not taking the liberties with their close proximity that the dance made possible. Envious glances from the other young women in the room only made Diana feel awkward, however.

"So why France?" she asked between twirls, bows, and little jumps.

"My father believes the balance of power in Firenze currently favors the French. He wished that I get experience and connections in the court of King Charles. It was a favorable setting, and I think I learned much."

She smirked. "The last I saw of the French they were fleeing across the Alps." She regretted saying it the moment the words were out of her mouth. She had such a knack for saying the wrong thing whenever in the company of young men.

Bernardo didn't seem to mind however. "Even should the balance of power shift back to the Empire or, Lord help us, England, there will still be value in having seen the inner workings of the French court firsthand."

He was right and she nodded. "Very clever." She glanced over at her father and the Tornabuonis, locked once again in conversation and apparently ignoring them. "I don't suppose our parents orchestrated our meeting, have they? It would be very much like my father."

He laughed. "Not that I am aware of, although I'll admit my parents think themselves quite quick as well."

"It seems that you have no shortage of female admirers."

He rubbed his forehead. "I hope you will not think of me the wrong way. I suspect the attention has more to do with my time in France than anything else. I assure you that I am not accustomed to such notice."

"Spoken like a true Italian man to his betrothed before he ignores her in favor of some concubine." She said it as a jest and, from his smile, she was relieved to see he took it as such.

"I am sorrowed to learn of the death of your mother. I did not know her well, but she is spoken of in the highest terms."

"Thank you," she said. Her heart tugged at the mention of her mother. For a moment, just a moment, she'd been distracted from such matters. "It has been a difficult time."

"I think she would be proud of her daughter to see you now, planning on attending university at Salerno or Pisa."

She felt herself blushing. "That may be little more than a dream. I still lack my father's permission."

"He'll come around with time. The work of a physician holds great prestige."

"My father appears to think differently, at least in my case."

"Too often, our culture has been slow to acknowledge the formidable power of women. Perhaps you will be one of those who change such opinions." He smiled at her.

She felt taken aback. She certainly agreed, yet it was a startlingly enlightened statement to hear a man utter. Either he was possessed of a singular free thinking mind, or he was a theatrical artist. She could not think of what to say in response.

Suddenly the music stopped, and they parted, though standing merely a foot apart. "My Lord," she told him, collecting herself, "I fear I should go. I am still mourning my mother's death and it would not be appropriate for me to be seen engaged in frivolities all night long."

"Of course," he said with a little bow, although his voice was tinged with regret.

She turned to leave, to collect her things and make the walk back to her palazzo, presumably alone save for her guardian Crispino.

He touched her gently on the arm. "Thank you for the dance. I truly enjoyed it."

She looked back at him and heard herself say, "As did I." With that, she turned and left.

Chapter Nine
No Nose and Long Fingers

Bernardo and Niccolo, Niccolo and Bernardo. Her coat on, pistol recovered from the silent uncommenting slave girl, Diana's thoughts bounced from one man to the other. Each intrigued her in different ways. Niccolo intelligent, dark, secretive, both protective and slightly threatening. Bernardo handsome, charismatic, worldly, perhaps too much so in some ways. Diana could scarcely remember the last time her mind had been so occupied with men. Now here she was, in the middle of a quite remarkable and unpleasant time, her mind drifting between two. Diana had never been one to fawn foolishly over the male of the species. Yet she would be lying to herself not to acknowledge finding a certain attraction to each of them. Of course there remained the possibility that Niccolo might have something to do with her mother's death, although she judged this possibility as quite remote.

Diana pinched herself to break her thoughts. Such concerns were neither here nor there at the moment. She could hardly start courting either of them in the midst of her investigation. Avoiding assassination loomed as a much more pressing concern. At very least she could wait until she got home and safely in her bed before ruminating over the two men. No doubt Siobhan would delight in comparing their merits.

Diana gauged the time as after midnight; the streets now were much quieter. Ahead of her Crispino resumed his patrol keeping his distance as she requested. Despite that she didn't fully trust him or his boss Niccolo, his footsteps ahead of her were reassuring.

Not a long walk, fortunately. Diana huddled her coat tightly, and kept her head down, ignoring a few wispy flakes of snow that wafted down. Ahead, Crispino turned a corner, leading the way through the dark. Watching her own feet, Diana paid him little mind. In a moment however, she realized his footsteps had stopped.

She paused, listening. No footsteps. For a second she thought she heard a muffled voice, more a gurgle than anything coherent. It was enough for her to guess that all was not well. A course of fear flowed through her veins and her hand at once seized the pommel of her pistol. She looked around, forward and backward. She still remained the only person on the street that she could see. All else was deserted, barely a candle showing in the windows of nearby houses. Up ahead, perhaps thirty paces was the corner where Crispino had vanished. Back just a few paces a dark alley offered a dubious shelter in which to hide.

Diana considered calling out for Crispino. Perhaps there was some simple explanation. He might have stopped to wait for her, or fallen ill. Instinctively she rejected such facile rationalizations. Trouble waited around that corner. She was certain of that. She could turn and flee, go back the way she came. The safest course, yet it would mean abandoning Crispino. What if he were still alive, in need of assistance? No, she wouldn't leave him behind.

She drew the pistol, cocked forward the hammer. The thought of it being out of her care during the banquet returned to her. Paranoia gripped her. What if someone had tampered with it? Nothing she could do about that now, if so. Looked like she was on course to find out.

Since she couldn't move forward, and wasn't about to run away, she ducked into the darkened alley. It was black as coal within, and smelled of urine and filth. No doubt the denizens of the buildings on either side pitched out the contents of their chamber pots into the alley. Lovely. Diana begged God that whatever else happened, nothing knocked her to the ground.

She really had no plan. She could double back around through the alley, approach the point she had last seen Crispino from the opposing direction. Then what? She had only one shot in the event that hostile forces awaited her. At least it was a course of action. Maybe something cleverer would come to her once she had more information.

As she prepared to move off, she heard footsteps in the main street, walking slowly toward the alley. She peered around the corner, hoping it might be Crispino. It wasn't. The figure, barely visible in the dark, was short, round, similar to Mancini, although not as well-muscled. The glint of a dagger shone in one hand.

Diana stepped backward, hoping she hadn't been seen. She trod lightly, trying not to make a sound. She looked back behind her, to the other exit from the alleyway. Her breath came fast. The alley had been a good place to hide, but it also might prove to be a trap. If more than one assailant hunted her, she could be caught in this narrow, dark chamber.

So she made for her only escape route. A moment later a glowing orb appeared in the opening, blocking her escape. The glow of a lantern. In its yellow light she saw the image of a tall lanky man with oily hair and fingers long and slender like those of a skeleton. He grinned at her and smiled a smile full of crooked and blackened teeth. Turning around she found the other entrance to the alley now framed the round figure she'd seen in the street. Damn them, she was trapped! Slowly, the two figures converged on her. She swung the pistol back and forth between them, deciding which to shoot. Which of the survivors would be quick enough to catch her when she ran for it?

"Diana Savrano," the round figure hissed. He came into the glow from the lantern so she could see him better. What she found was a hideous, repulsive man indeed. Squat and squalid, with skin the pallor of a corpse and a gaping skull-like orifice where his nose should have been. She thought at first he might be a leper, although the rest of his face, unhealthy though it might be, showed no other sign of that horrid disease. Instead she guessed he'd lost his nose due to violence. A fight perhaps, or he might have fought as a mercenary at war. He grinned at her and wiped his crusty lips with a blackened tongue. He held up his left hand for her to see. His fingers entwined the hair of young Crispino, whose head dropped below that hand, the face caught in a last expression of suffering. The eyes were rolled back, the mouth twisted open as if trying to scream. A few drops of blood visibly fell from the slight stalk of a neck that remained beneath that head.

Diana's stomach twisted in a knot at the sight, but

she held firm, keeping the pistol trained on No-nose. Staying put had been a waste then. Crispino never had a chance. She should have run.

"Mancini sends his regards," the leering noseless man sneered. "You seem to have particularly raised his ire. You must have been a rather naughty girl."

Long-fingers with the lamp laughed, making a hacking sound that sounded of consumption.

"You diseased lot are the best he could find to send after me?" she asked with bravado. "Couldn't find the balls to come himself?"

No-nose giggled, the sound high pitched and grating. "Well, this signorina certainly can talk. Not knowing your place is likely what got you into this trouble. Come on now, girl. Put that thing down, and we'll be sure things go for you quick and easy, like with your friend here." With that he tossed Crispino's head at her feet. It landed with a sickening thud and rolled a few inches away.

Diana forced herself not to look at it. She tried to swallow but found her mouth to be entirely dry.

"I wouldn't go waving that firestick around," No-nose sneered. "Let's have you put that thing down now before you go hurting yourself." The fat man kept his distance, no doubt hoping the pistol would be too inaccurate to hit him at a distance. Behind her though, she sensed Long-fingers edging closer.

She met No-nose's gaze. "You seem like a man who enjoys the pleasures of the table."

His grin faltered at the unexpected comment. "I'm not sure insulting me is going to do you much good at a moment like this," he growled.

"It will if it means you can't run fast." As she said

that she spun and faced Long-fingers. The tall gaunt fellow was still grinning at some comment he'd found funny. His face was beautifully illuminated by the lantern he held in one hand. She aimed her pistol for his face and squeezed the trigger. She prayed the most morbid sacrilegious prayer of her life: that God would help her take a life. Within the workings of the pistol, she felt the internal wheel spin. Would it work? Had the gun been sabotaged? An eternity seemed to go by since she pulled the trigger. She felt a moment of despair. Then a spark caught and the pistol discharged a burst of fury. A round black hole appeared between Long-finger's eyes. The back of his skull came loose in several messy, hairy globs. The lantern spun out of his long grasp, and his corpse dropped to its knees. Before he fell further, Diana was already past him, darting out of the alley.

"Foul bitch!" No-nose screamed. Behind her she could hear his heavy footsteps. She dared not turn, but she guessed her estimate had been correct and he'd not be capable of catching her. A minute later she didn't hear the footsteps anymore. No doubt it was too risky for him to follow in a city that had likely been woken by the gunshot. She finally turned and saw she was alone. Coming to a rest, she put one hand against a brick building and collected her breath. Her side stung with the effort of running, and the cold air tore at her lungs as she sucked in deep breaths.

Dear God, she'd killed a man! She waited for the realization to truly hit her. She wondered if she would be ill, would feel herself forever changed. Nothing happened immediately. She felt herself to be the same Diana as before. Was she so heartless a woman that she could shoot a man down and feel so little? Of course Long-fingers had obviously been a particularly vile specimen of man, with clear intent to do her harm. Still, she could not help but wonder how much the last few days had hardened her. Then, she wanted nothing more than to learn how to save lives. Now she'd taken one. Perhaps it wouldn't be the last. Perhaps her own would be taken as well before all were over.

She should go back. Gendarmes would come to investigate the violence that had been done in the alleyway. They'd come to her with questions. Perhaps it would be Niccolo, inquiring as to the nature of the death of his man Crispino. She wiped her forehead with the hand that still grasped the emptied pistol. Let them come find her. She was done with them all for tonight. She turned her back and walked home where she hoped to find sleep and dreams untroubled by murder.

****

She went straight to her bedroom without speaking to anyone. With candles lit, she took off her dress, and let down her hair, and looked at herself in the mirror for a long while. She pulled down the lid of one eye and looked at the white ball. Still the same Diana. It felt like the world around her had gone all wrong. For better or worse she as of yet felt unchanged.

Staying away from open flame, she reloaded the pistol. At least it hadn't been sabotaged. It now had at least one human life to its record. So did she. There was little concern about legal ramifications. The clear status differential between herself and Long-fingers, the fact she was a woman...no one would bat an eyelash other than to remark she had taken care of herself so well. Enforcement of homicides in Firenze tended to be sporadic during even the best of times anyway. Killing Long-fingers wouldn't find her any more trouble she didn't already have.

She slipped the pistol under her pillow, hammer uncocked so she didn't blow her own head off during a restless moment in her sleep. She kept the candles lit, allowing them to burn down during the night. The flickering glow soothed her. As she lay down, her mind replayed the events of the evening, but she cast these thoughts out, and forced herself to think instead of pleasant moments. Inevitably she remembered her mother and time they spent together. Warm, comfortable moments, now lost forever to the past. Soon she fell into an easy, peaceful sleep, indeed the best that she rested since her mother died.

When she woke in the morning she felt well, confidence reinforced by success in fending off Mancini's effort to have her killed. Siobhan came to attend to her, the Irish girl's mood curious and expectant.

"Has anyone called on me this morning?" Diana asked first thing, without offering any explanation.

"No, lady," Siobhan answered, sounding unusually formal.

Diana felt a twinge of disappointment and surprise. Given the death of Crispino, in particular, she had expected Niccolo to inquire from her what had happened.

"You were home late last night, lady," Siobhan observed.

Diana slumped her shoulders. "You can cease with the 'ladies'. If you have something that you want to know, just ask."

Siobhan grinned. "It had occurred to me that perhaps you might have met a gentleman of interest last night." She got out a comb and began working on Diana's hair.

"Several in fact. Let's see...I met with Pietro Benedetto, the Boar, who kindly informed me that my mother had joined an anti-Papist cult prior to her death. Next, Niccolo was at the banquet where he acknowledged having me followed by Republic gendarmes. I also met the gentleman Bernardo Tornabuoni, who was all face and fluff, and you would have liked him very much I think. I suspect my father would like for me to fall in love with him, and it might not be entirely out of the question. Lastly, two rather unpleasant denizens of the worst side of town managed to behead the gendarme following me and accosted me as well before I blew the head off one and made good my escape back here. I think that covers my evening in the main."

Siobhan stared at her through the mirror before them for a moment. "So basically an average evening in the life of Diana Savrano."

"Of late, yes, so it would seem." She sighed. "In truth, I don't know where to begin to explain it all."

"We'll have to talk seriously about the assault on your person last night. But start with this Bernardo," Siobhan offered, "the man with the face and the fluff. You said you might love him?"

"I said it wasn't out of the question. It's a bit hard to focus on that at the moment with all else that's going on. Still, he was handsome and intelligent and gallant. It would have been better to have met him at a more convenient time. He is entirely Niccolo's opposite in most respects."

"Niccolo? So you care for Signore Machiavelli as well?" Siobhan remarked, with surprise in her tone.

Diana shrugged. "He's interesting, intellectual, mysterious. He might also very well be responsible for my mother's death for all I know."

"Anyone might be responsible for your mother's death for all that you know. You can hardly use that to rule out any men at this point."

Diana frowned. "You're really not known for giving good advice on men, are you?"

Siobhan shook her head. "No, not really."

"Why are we even discussing this? Did you not hear me? I told you I killed a man."

"Oh. Well it was bound to happen, wasn't it? You came very close to killing Mancini not a few days ago, and would have done it too, had you not closed your eyes. It sounds like you have learned that lesson at least."

Diana shook her head. "You are amazing, Siobhan. Any other woman I have ever known would be horrified to learn what I have done."

"No other woman you have met is from Ireland. Besides, from what you've told me, the bloke had it coming to him. Should we feel sympathy for a man who accosts young women in the middle of the night and murders gendarmes? My only concern is for your own safety. I'm impressed to learn how successfully you defeated these villains. Nonetheless, I would insist on accompanying you on any further excursions."

Diana looked at herself in the mirror. "Had someone told me a few days past what my life would become, I would have laughed. Until last night I fixed myself upon the goal of saving lives, not taking them! What vexes me most of all is that I am not more bothered by killing a man than I am. Uhh. I make no sense."

"You make perfect sense." Siobhan eyed her in the glass. "You're coming to adjust to a difficult new reality. That you have adapted so well is astonishing, and you have surprised yourself. Take some gladness from this. Were you doubled over in grief at your own actions, it would bode ill for the course you have selected."

Diana stood. Siobhan was right; she had done nothing but defend herself. Her steeled nerves were a positive sign. How many others might have given up where she had persevered? She felt ready for any adversity that might come.

Diana touched Siobhan's shoulder, remembering that the other woman seemed to take comfort from such physical gestures. "Siobhan, you might not know much about men, but your counsel in these other matters has been invaluable to me." The other woman smiled with evident gladness. "Come, let us breakfast. We must discuss our next move."

Sitting beside Siobhan at breakfast was a breach of convention, but Diana no longer cared. Agathi served them without commenting on the unexpected lapse of protocol. Strawberries with cream sauce were on order for the morning. A tall Moorish slave, Maslamah, came through the hall on business elsewhere in the palazzo. Maslamah's purview focused on grounds keeping and repair, talents for which his skilled hands and mind were well suited. As he passed through, Diana inquired of her father's whereabouts.

"He has left for the day, lady," Maslamah replied with a small bow. "Business interests demanded his attention as I am given to understand, Signorina Savrano."

"Hmmmph," Diana murmured, despite that his absence was hardly unusual.

"Still haven't made peace with your father?" Siobhan inquired before burying her teeth deep in a plump strawberry. "Where do they even get these in the middle of winter?"

"I put on a decent show for him last night I suspect," Diana replied, dodging the question somewhat. Siobhan appeared to be too enamored of fresh fruit to press the issue. A moment later Maslamah returned.

"Lady Savrano," he intoned, his face passive as ever, "two Republic gendarmes have called for you at the front door."

Diana looked at Siobhan, who merely stared back, the plump strawberry obscuring the lower portions of her face. Diana put down her napkin and stood. "Very well." Indeed, she had been expecting some manner of attention, given events of the previous night. Niccolo was sure to desire an account of what had happened.

She followed Maslamah back to the door where, sure enough, two young gendarmes awaited her. "I am Diana Savrano. Are you here on orders of Signore Machiavelli?"

"No, Lady Savrano," replied the taller of the two, a young fellow with dark hair and skin, "Friar Savonarola has requested we deliver you for an audience with him."

The bottom fell out of Diana's stomach. Dear God,

what did the mad friar want with her? Momentarily, she found herself rendered speechless. Finally she found her voice. "Friar Savonarola...am I under arrest?"

"No, lady," the gendarme replied, although he did not seem shocked by her question, "we were not led to believe such steps were in order. However, my understanding is that your attendance at his request is urgently desired." So, she was not under arrest, but it could be easily arranged if she proved uncooperative.

"Leave me a moment to retrieve my coat, if you would." Stepping back inside, Diana asked Agathi to fetch her coat. To Siobhan she briefly explained, "Friar Savonarola wishes to speak with me."

"Oh my!" Siobhan exclaimed. "Whatever for?"

"Well, I assume it's not for tips on managing the latest dances. If I'm not back by nightfall, you'll have to inform my father. Say nothing until then."

"The household slaves are likely to tell him if he returns before you," Siobhan observed.

"True. Do what you think most appropriate then, and wish me luck." Diana slipped into her coat. No point in fetching the pistol. The gendarmes would merely take it off her, perhaps confiscate it for good. With a last look at Siobhan, she left the palazzo and turned herself over to the mercy of Savonarola.

Without word, the gendarmes led her through the streets of Firenze. She kept her coat huddled close against the cold, a fold of the cloth covering her mouth. Being led in such a way, she felt like a criminal taken to trial. How many others had been brought before Savonarola in much the same fashion, only later to hang from the stake burning? She decided it would be in her best interest to play submissive with the likes of

Savonarola. If only she could keep her mouth shut. If only…

The guards brought her not to the Palazzo Vecchio, the traditional seat of the Firenze Republic as expected, but rather to the Basilica of Saint Zenobius, where her mother was buried. The great nave was empty, despite that it was mid-morning. Sunlight streamed in through the stained glass windows, illuminating the generous hall as was rarely possible at any other time of day. Cavernous though it was, the room felt warm and inviting, perhaps not least because her mother rested here.

Diana's eyes were drawn to her mother's tomb, just to the left of the main doors. A stab of guilt flooded through her. She had not been once to visit the tomb, although perhaps she might be forgiven for that, given that her time had been spent trying to identify her mother's murderer.

For a moment Diana believed she was alone in the Basilica. Then, across the nave she spotted a prostrate form before the altar, a blur of plain robes against the marble. Unmoving, it might very well have been a corpse.

Slowly she approached the altar, her footsteps echoing across the nave. The robed form against the cold floor did not turn to greet her or otherwise acknowledge her presence. Diana felt increasingly awkward, even as she guessed that might be the intent. She resisted the urge to clear her throat. Her attendance was known, of that she was sure. Patience would be the better virtue for the moment.

At last, like a creature rising up out of the gloom, the figure on the floor rose up to a kneeling position, although he faced away, looking up at the figure of Christ impaled on the cross like a lover toward his lost love. "Upon to us our bleeding angel has fallen," the figure whispered, even the whisper carrying like a shout on the cold air in the empty chamber. "Love is a colder thing than death."

Diana said nothing, tried very hard not to make a sound.

"You are Lady Diana Savrano," the figure said with full voice, turning toward her. The grizzled features and hawk-like nose could only be those of Savonarola. His eyes, joyless and stern, pierced through her.

She met his gaze, refusing to look away. Probably she should look down, be a properly demure female, but she couldn't bring herself to do it. Still, she could be respectful at least. She had no reason to call Savonarola an enemy. "I am she, Friar Savonarola."

He nodded as if satisfied, and pushed himself up to a standing position. He was in his mid-forties perhaps, unhandsome by any standard, skin stretched taut over his bones. "It is your mother, Isabella Savrano, so recently buried in this very cathedral?" He waved his hand over in the general direction of the tomb.

"That is true, Friar."

"Death is so often a cause for grief among the living. Yet the dead are that much nearer to communion with God. It is the dead who should grieve for the living." He took two awkward steps down the altar to come closer to her. "I have been hearing something of the death of your mother and your own actions in response to her untimely demise."

"May I ask what it is that you have heard, Friar?"

He looked at her with something akin to a fatherly smile, although his face could not quite seem to manage such a gentle expression. "The priests who officiate here at the Basilica complain that your mother's ghost haunts this place. They claim they can hear her sorrowed cries at night, crying out for vengeance. It is rumored that your mother's death was brought about by man rather than God and you intend to see your mother's spirit put to rest."

She paused, thinking over her words carefully. "I don't much believe in ghosts. Do you think that God allows spirits to haunt this world, spared of their eternal judgment?"

One eye narrowed as he peered more closely at her. "Only Satan's unholy angels haunt this world in violation of God's law." He seemed satisfied by her answer, though. "If you wish to ease your mother's soul, that goal would be more easily met through prayer for intercession on her behalf, to speed her progress through Purgatory."

At least Savonarola didn't think her mother condemned to Hell. Such was a positive reflection on her own self, at least she so hoped. "I will remember to redouble my efforts in the spiritual realm. But I assume you wish to speak to me regarding my efforts to answer for her death in this mortal world."

Savonarola nodded. "The actions of a young woman, unmarried beyond appropriate years, seen in public with only another young girl in attendance...brandishing a firearm with intent to do harm. To say that these actions are unbecoming a young woman of your stature would be a serious understatement. A woman of beauty such as yours would in the best of times arouse impure desires in men allowed to view her. At a time so troubled as this, you place yourself at greater risk for harm." His eyes traveled over her body in a manner that seemed oddly indifferent as it appraised her form. "Even if you find the answers for which you seek, I doubt you will find satisfaction in them."

Diana swallowed. "You're not the first person to tell me that."

The Friar's eyelids closed for a moment. "Perhaps you should listen."

"Forgive me, Friar, but I can't," she insisted, aware she was now going out clearly on a limb. "I find that the world I understood has been shattered by my mother's death. I must understand why it happened. I must understand what happened."

The Friar appeared to lose his strength for standing and settled down on the altar steps. He crossed his fingers in front of his face, watching her through them. "You know already your mother was involved with the physical degenerate called the Boar."

"Pietro Benedetto, yes, I know of him."

"Then you know that together, they became involved with the cult that calls itself the Sacred Council of Apostles. Their involvement with the Council naturally provides one thread for your inquiry. There is another you might consider."

Diana's brows furrowed. "What would that be?"

"The relationship between your mother, Isabella Savrano, and Pietro Benedetto may have extended beyond the spiritual."

Diana pulled a face. "That's absurd."

"Because of his visage, you mean." Savonarola

nodded. "I agree that lust of the flesh is unlikely for a soul such as Pietro Benedetto. However, there can be little doubt the Boar and your mother were of like minds. They spent time together, they spoke like intimates do. Who can say where there is such a meeting of minds between man and woman, whether the heart will follow? Whether or not this is even true, there is only the appearance of such infatuation to be considered."

Diana thought for a moment. Her mother met regularly with Pietro, both as part of the Council, then later according to her own letter, alone with him. Her relationship with him remained secret, as part of her larger involvement with the Council. However, could their relationship have seemed something more than two friends conjoined on a spiritual quest? Could they have appeared to be lovers, despite Pietro's obvious physical abnormalities? Could someone prone to jealousy have read the signs in such a way? The implication dawned on Diana with horror and revulsion. "You dare to accuse my father?" she barked at Savonarola, no longer watching her tone.

If the Friar took offense at her impudence, he gave no sign of it. "I merely open a line of inquiry that would be obvious to most investigators. Is it not true in the case of murder, that the victim most often has been betrayed by those closest to their hearts? We seldom have more to fear than from those who mask their hate in the guise of love."

Diana took a step back, unbalanced by his words. Could it be that her own father was involved in her mother's death? Did she dare to even think such thoughts? She wished she could think it absurd, but how well did she know her own father after all? Could his distance from his own wife and daughter extend to murder? She looked at the stone floor in shame.

"Consider fully the costs you may pay, before you continue your quest for answers," Savonarola intoned.

Diana let out a long slow breath. Her composure returned as she did so. She managed to look up and meet Savonarola's gaze once again. "What of you, Friar? With due respect, I am certain that you did not invite me here to give me a fatherly lecture. What is your interest in the death of my mother?"

Savonarola's grin widened, appearing quite satisfied once again. Diana got the sensation that she was being put to...and thus far passing, certain tests. "My interest is in the Sacred Council of Apostles, to which your mother was privy."

"I don't understand. As anti-papists, do you not share their views?"

Savonarola's grin curled into a sneer. "Though it is true the Papacy has lost its way and come to rest in the hands of a defiler, Rodrigo Borgia, I find no common cause with the Sacred Council of Apostles. I seek to restore the throne of St. Peter to the humility and grace of the Mother Church of Christ. The Council seeks to place upon the throne of the Holy See, one who is legion with God's most favored and most despised angel."

Diana absorbed his words, thinking for a moment. "Lucifer? You claim the Council are Satanists?" If true, Pietro had left out a considerable detail to his narrative.

"They are, although that information is known only to their more trusted members. It is a secret unlocked through advancement in their ranks. Their belief is that

Lucifer was wronged by God, and that he is deserving of the throne of heaven as a good and righteous leader of men. They have been fooled by his charm and his lies. Your mother, entrusted into their upper echelon, learned their secret. She came to me in horror and confessed her sins. Absolved, she sought only to undo the damage that she had wrought."

Diana's mind reeled with the revelation. Pietro might not have known about the Council's darker motives. Isabella Savrano had convinced him to join the cult. She must have been trying to get him to leave the cult before...before what? Diana exhaled sharply and put a hand to her mouth. "The young man Troilo Ricci who the Council accused of spying for the Republic...it was not he who had betrayed them, but my mother!"

Savonarola nodded. "The raid on their abhorrent coven failed, scattering them like frightened rats. Had it but succeeded this entire episode would be behind us, and your mother a hero of the Republic."

"Then you do think it was the Council who killed my mother. My father is innocent!"

For once, Savonarola looked disappointed. "You cling to the narrative you wish to be true. I have no evidence that the Council discovered her cooperation with the Republic, so all alternatives remain possible. We must each consider further, it may well have been your father who introduced your mother to the Council in the first place, and he placed higher than her within their hierarchy of power."

Diana considered Savonarola's words. It all seemed too farfetched, her parents members of a Satanic guild. Yet even what she knew to be true thus far, her mother involved, yet perhaps working as a spy for the Republic, that was farfetched enough. Her entire world seemed turned upside down. She wasn't sure she really knew anyone anymore. "I cannot believe I knew of none of this. How could I have not seen what occurred in my own household? I was so content to remain alone in my rooms with my books and my things, and I did nothing to help my mother when she needed me most."

Savonarola looked up at the ceiling with its elaborate paintings. His face revealed not adoration but repulsion. "Silly books and pretty baubles, are they not at the heart of all vanity? And is not vanity at the heart of all sin?" He looked back down at Diana. "What matters is that your current actions do honor to your mother's memory. Go now, in peace."

Chapter Ten
Snow and Ash

Duties for the gendarmes apparently did not extend to escorting Diana home. Just as well, perhaps; it gave Diana time to think, and she had much to think over. Granted, like all the players in this increasingly complex drama, she had to wonder about Savonarola's motives and, thus, the quality of his information. If he were blatantly against her interests, interfering with her quest would be of little difficulty. He could accuse her of witchcraft and have her burned in the Piazza della Signoria. She'd hardly be the first. Nonetheless, if his interference was limited to toying with her in the Basilica in which her mother was buried, she felt safe in ruling him out as a major opponent, at least for a time. Was his information good though? Her mother involved with a Satanic cult...ultimately spying on behalf of the Republic? And Savonarola's suggestion that her father might have played a role in her mother's death, could she dare to consider the unthinkable? She set that thought aside for the moment. At best, it was idle speculation on Savonarola's part. The rest he had told at least had the vestige of being informed fact. It fit she supposed, even with Pietro's story, assuming her mother hadn't gotten the chance to warn him to leave the group. Or perhaps he hadn't believed her...or perhaps he hadn't cared.

Diana walked with her head down, thinking and ignoring the other pedestrians. She realized her boots were crunching new-fallen snow and looked up at the light gray sky while icy flakes fell onto her face. Snowing again, and looking like it would be a significant amount. Would this winter never end?

It was curious, what Savonarola had said about potentially finding answers to her questions that she wouldn't like. He had used that to lead into insinuations about her father. What troubled her now was that Savonarola hadn't been the only one to warn her. If he knew something more, he appeared disinclined to tell her. The other had been the anchoress, Francesca di Lucca, who'd made the same warning as part of a prophesy. Perhaps the theatrics about divine inspiration had merely been that—theatrics. Or perhaps a girl foolish enough to barricade herself in a cold cell, would be impressionable enough to interpret a bit of overheard gossip as a holy prophesy. No doubt the anchoress overheard immeasurable amounts of tittle-tattle as townspeople came to her for prayers and intercessions. Maybe she'd even received a confession or partial confession that had influenced her. Anchoress or not, what she heard from others was not bound by the sanctity of priestly privilege. Whatever the girl knew, Diana would find some way to wrench it out of her.

Determined, Diana turned to the South, across the Arno for the walk to the convent at Sant Cecilia. She crossed the Ponte Vecchio and headed up into the foothills, reaching the convent by midday. The grounds were quiet, only a few of the sisters out and these ignored her. She moved quickly to the little alcove of the anchoress, which she blessedly found free of other penitents. In fact, the stone shelter seemed so quiet she irrationally thought that the anchoress might have left the structure for some form of holiday.

Peering in through the window, she found Francesca di Lucca resting on the simple cot within. To announce herself, Diana tapped her fingers against the stone wall. The sound was disappointing, but it sufficed to stir Francesca. The anchoress' face lit up. "Diana Savrano, I am surprised to see you here again. It is a pleasure that you would visit me. How have you been?"

Diana put her hands on the sill, startled by the cold stone. How could the poor foolish girl survive like this? "Things are a little unbalanced, as you might imagine."

"I've been thinking of you much since you came last. I hope I did not upset you greatly."

The forlorn expression on Francesca's face touched Diana. "You didn't upset me," she assured her, struggling to place a smile on her face. "In fact I hoped to speak with you a bit about that day." She found it hard to think of the words. At last she burst out with a little self-conscious laughter. "Oh my, you know I should have brought you something, some fresh bread or some good wine."

Francesca smiled. "I didn't ask to be secluded behind these walls to be given offerings. I appreciate the thought. Have you come to pray with me?"

Diana looked down. "Not exactly, I'm afraid. I've come to ask you about the other day when you gave me the…prophecy. You told me something to the effect that I would be troubled by what I might find."

Francesca watched her without saying a word.

Diana continued on, "I've just met with Friar Savonarola and he told me much the same thing."

159

"Friar Savonarola," Francesca repeated with raised eyebrows, although her thoughts were otherwise unfathomable.

"Yes. Obviously it occurs to me that he might know something, although I have little means to persuade him to tell me anything he does not wish. As an alternative, I hoped perhaps the words you said to me might have been influenced by something you might have heard. People speak to you of many things, town gossip, confessions…"

Francesca looked confused. "My words to you were influenced only by God."

Diana winced. How would she get what she wanted from the girl without offending her religious sensibilities, nonsense though they might be? "Yes, but sometimes God works in odd ways, does he not? Perhaps if you think back there might be something, a past meeting with a penitent that planted the seed of some suspicion."

Francesca shook her head after only a moment of thought. "Nothing I can recollect. Besides, even if someone had told me something, I'm not sure I would be allowed to repeat it to you. If it were said in confidence between them and God, that is."

A hot wellspring of frustration rose up in her. "You're no priest," she accused with unintended venom, "you do not intercede on behalf of God. What people say to you and you to them has no special meaning."

The words spent, Diana's frustration eased, yet she immediately regretted her lack of tact. Francesca looked stunned, deeply wounded. The older girl's eyes darted up and down as if in confusion.

"Oh, Francesca," Diana sighed, "I'm sorry. I didn't mean that. I only hoped you might be able to tell me something."

Like a snake, Francesca's hands darted out and seized Diana's from the windowsill. The older girl's fingers seemed if anything, colder than the stone. They held Diana firm, like wires. Diana could only stare back in shock.

"I know you need answers," Francesca whispered, eyes like deep pools. Then she closed her eyes, and held Diana's hands only tighter. "Dearest father, hear our prayers. We come to you with deepest humility and pray for your heavenly guidance..."

A repeat of the previous prophecy, only this time Diana decided she had nothing to lose. Closing her eyes, she hoped something of value would come of this. After a moment of listening to Francesca's prayers she became aware of feeling lightheaded. She opened her eyes, watching Francesca swaying back and forth in her holy ecstasy. Still her equilibrium seemed to fail her and increasingly she felt like she might collapse to one side. Her stomach began to rebel, nausea bubbling up from inside. She tried to pull away but Francesca held her firm.

Francesca's breath seemed ragged, coming in unpleasant spurts. Between those breaths, Francesca intoned, "As I will be tomorrow, so has Isabella been. Your face is above mine, and you look frightened. The moon above you frames your features as your hair falls downward onto my own face. You lean down to kiss me. I am so cold." She sucked in a breath that quivered, sounding cold and terrified at once. "Later you sit alone in an unfamiliar place. On a bed, you sit and beside you

161

a pistol loaded with your own hand. A great despondency washes over you, I cannot see what it is that has you so fractured, and…oh!" Francesca suddenly leaned over and wretched, great dry heaves wracking her frail body.

Their connection cut, Diana's hands no longer held in that crushing grip. Diana's balance did not return and, no longer rooted to the anchoress' room by Francesca's grip, she slipped off to one side into a row of low bushes beside the convent walls. Splitting pains coursed through her skull and her vision swam as though a most horrible intoxication overtook her. She struggled to remain upright, a part of her brain thinking the safest thing would be simply to lie down until the feeling passed. Gravity decided the matter for her in the end, and the very ground seemed to rush up toward her. In the last moment she realized that her angle was bad, she was too close to the edge of the convent. Nothing to be done for it now though, not in her state. When her head collided with the impenetrable stone of the convent walls, it brought the blessed relief of darkness and oblivion.

****

"Don't try to sit up too quickly, or you'll faint again." The words pierced through a haze of confusion and pain. Diana's eyes opened, but her vision blurred. Over her bent a form of black, long arms reaching toward her like those of the phantom who had thrown Sister Maria Innocentia to her death. She tried to sit up but, as promised by the voice, waves of nausea and lightheadedness quickly made such efforts perilous. Diana eased back down where she lay, having confidence that God would not have led her to her doom through the anchoress' visions. Through even her corrupted sight she could tell she was in a cramped and dark room, walls of stone, few windows. She lay on a simple straw mattress. Probably the convent then, with the black figure another of the nuns.

"I'm fine," Diana murmured, more from embarrassment than from any genuine sense of well-being.

"Nonsense," her savior insisted, the voice female and older, authoritative. A few blinks later and Diana could make out enough detail to see it was Sister Ophelia, the nun who'd shown her Sister Maria Innocentia's room earlier. "Here is a cup of wine. It will make you feel better."

"Since when did wine help either dizziness or nausea?" Diana griped, though she still sipped from the proffered cup. The wine within was thin and bitter, barely better than the stuff they tried to grow in Spain. She felt her face pull into a horrified expression. "Ugh, you call this wine?"

Laughter from the fuzzy image of Ophelia. "Well, you seem to be coming around well enough."

"How is Francesca...Sister Francesca?" Diana pushed herself back up into a sitting position. Her symptoms were slowly abating.

"Sister Francesca is resting, but is otherwise fine. Her visions at times can be quite powerful. Tell me, did you share in them?"

Diana rubbed her head. "Thankfully no, merely standing next to her sent me into apoplexy. If that is what the contemplative life offers, I can achieve much the same effect with good wine and still enjoy the company of men." Grumpy and sore, she did not even care if she shocked the older nun.

Ophelia, far from taking offense, chuckled at her comments. "It suits some and less so others. I take it that you are less than enamored with religion?"

Diana raised an eyebrow, sipped at her cup of wine, each time hoping that the contents would miraculously improve in taste. "I have no quarrel with God; it is his representatives on Earth who manage to irk me." She paused and looked up. "Please forget I said that."

"I'm not an instrument of the inquisition, Lady Diana. Within reason, you may speak your mind."

Gradually feeling more herself, Diana sat fully upright, no longer needing to support herself on one arm. "I don't think there's much else to say about it." She shrugged.

"And yet you sought out audience with our own Sister Francesca, who has nothing to her name but her close relationship with Christ. Tell me, did she manage to give you the succor that you sought?"

Diana shook her head. "Not much more than gibberish. That is the secret to prophesies, isn't it? Be sure that they're vague enough they can be creatively made to fit any eventual outcome."

"I wouldn't know," Ophelia responded with a tolerant smirk. "I've never been blessed with the gift of foresight. You must have believed in her to come seek her out."

Diana felt foolish at the implication she had come to have her future read. "I thought only that she might have known something about my mother's death. I thought perhaps someone might have told her something that influenced her prophesies."

Ophelia frowned, looking skeptical. "Why would you think that?"

"She basically told me, last time I came here, that I would regret investigating my mother's death. Today I met with Savonarola and he told me much the same thing."

"Did he?"

Some of Diana's wits began to return to her. She was prattling on without much thought to someone she knew little enough about. She should keep her mouth closed, say less and listen more. So she only nodded in response and changed the topic. "Can you tell me if the figures Sister Maria Innocentia drew in her cell still remain?"

"They were drawn in chalk, dear, and as you might imagine, we were not terribly eager for them to linger. We indulged her visions in life, but in death her cell must be prepared for a new novitiate."

Too bad, Diana thought. She would have liked a fresh look at them. The reversal of heaven into a demonic maw...those drawings were not merely the random musings of a disturbed mind, although Maria Innocentia had certainly been troubled. Something began to come together in Diana's intellect. Maria Innocentia, former assassin by admission, surely had not come by happenstance on the secrets of her mother's murder. Diana began to suspect the poor nun had been more intimately involved from the start. The drawings...heaven as a secret cover for a very real Hell ruled by a tyrant God, that image seemed consistent with the beliefs of the Sacred Council of Apostles as Savonarola described them to her. If he told her the truth—and of course that could hardly be taken for granted—might Maria Innocentia herself have been involved with the Council? Such a revelation cast troubling light on her own disclosures to Diana that night on the dome. Had she truly cast light on a sinister scheme or was she too, only part in a larger machination?

"Oh dear," Diana said at last, snapping out of her thoughts. "Do you know what hour it is?"

"I'm afraid it's near dark, dear," Ophelia responded.

"I must be going!" Diana stood, wobbled a bit at first, but decided she was on as sure a footing as could be hoped. She set down her near finished cup of poor wine.

"Are you sure, dear?" Ophelia pressed. "You should not unduly strain yourself after such a spell. I could send a messenger to your family if you like, have them send a carriage for you."

"No, that won't be necessary," Diana insisted. "I'm feeling infinitely better. Thank you for your time, and I am sorry to have put you out." Before Ophelia could attempt to stop her, Diana whisked herself out of the room, wrapping her coat tightly around her. She saw herself out, directing herself as best she could through the dark and senseless passageways of the convent.

Outside the cold hit her like a cruel stone wall, yet it served also to restore her senses to their fullest capacity. The sun was low on the horizon, feebly resisting the onslaught of night. Before beginning the long walk home, she peeked in to Francesca's little stone room. Little sunlight made its way in through the small windows and Diana could barely see. A form huddled motionless on the simple cot, wrapped tight in a blanket.

"Francesca?" Diana whispered, but the form didn't move. Sleeping, Diana decided, and didn't want to wake the older girl. With a sense of regret, she turned and walked away.

****

Sleep came harder and harder each night, Diana's thoughts ruminating over each new encounter, puzzling over each new bit of information. She knew she needed to sleep, and tried to distract herself, but to no avail. Growing frustration over her insomnia only made things worse.

So she tossed and turned and tossed some more. Even the moon seemed to go away, leaving her isolated in her sleepless misery. Yet it meant she was wide awake to hear as a pebble struck the glass of her window.

Diana sat bolt upright. Could it be someone from the Sacred Council of Apostles come to do her harm? Immediately, Diana recognized that as an irrational thought. No assassin threw pebbles at the windows of their targets.

She dashed to the window. Then only did she realize that the pebble could very well have been an assassin's plot, for she must have made a striking target in her white nightgown standing in front of the window. She half expected to hear the shot of a harquebus at any moment. All she saw though was a cloaked figure standing in the street outside her family palazzo. The figure glanced furtively from side to side, no doubt keeping an eye out for the family guard. Apparently satisfied he was unwatched, the figure waved up at her window.

Could it be Pietro? That would be awfully daring to show up at her palazzo once again, knowing that Niccolo must be keeping a watch on her. Then again, breaking into the palazzo and leaving a note on her pillow revealed he was nothing if not daring. She opened the window and recoiled from the blast of cold that struck her. She could feel flakes of snow against her skin. So it was still coming down. She peered down at the figure below, too far away for her to clearly recognize immediately.

"Who are you?" she hissed, trying to whisper so she wouldn't wake the household, yet be heard by the figure.

The figure drew back the hood of his cape. "It is I, Bernardo Tornabuoni!" the young man proclaimed a little too loudly, as if it were the most natural thing he should appear outside her window in the middle of the night.

Her heart skipped a beat upon recognizing his face. She must look ghastly. "What are you doing here?" she hissed back at him, hoping he might catch the hint to keep his voice down.

"I've come to see you, of course," he replied, still too loudly. His tone teased along the frigid air, "Can't you come out and play?"

She felt her cheeks burn, glad the distance would prevent him from noticing. "It's the middle of the night. If my father finds you here, he'll run you through."

"Then you should come down before he finds me!" Even from the distance she could see his smile, wide and bright. Damn him, it was like finding a small naïve dog on the threshold. She turned away, thinking. "Don't force me to serenade you!" he called out.

This kind of thing was not an unheard of gesture. At another time, she might have been deeply flattered by the effort. Bernardo clearly underestimated the likelihood of her father cutting him down in the street. Still, despite all she'd become involved in, she couldn't deny a certain attraction toward Bernardo, at least from their first meeting. Fine, she'd meet with him. Perhaps the distraction would do her some good.

"All right," she called, motioning with her hand for silence. "If you'll be quiet, I'll come down. Give me a few moments."

Closing the window, she looked around for something appropriate to wear. She wouldn't wake Siobhan to help her. That would take too long anyway. She found a rather simple red dress she could put on without assistance, then her boots and overcoat. Glancing in the mirror she found her hair in disarray, and did her best to put it in some kind of order. All in all, she looked precisely like someone who just leapt out of bed. Hopefully Bernardo wouldn't be expecting too much.

Diana thought about her pistol, hid under the pillow. She decided against taking it. How could she explain it should he notice? Besides, in his care she should be safe enough.

Satisfied things were as good as they could get on such terribly short notice, she hurried downstairs, being as quiet as possible. The household was dark, only a few candles illuminating the halls. The palazzo never entirely slept. Always, two or three guards remained awake, patrolling for intruders even in the quietest of times. She knew their habits though, and avoided them with ease.

Outside she shivered, but steeled herself and hurried through the dark until she found Bernardo. "You're mad, you know!" Diana swatted him on the arm.

"I wanted to see you," he explained, grin wide.

"Couldn't you see me during the day when it would be more proper?"

"Actually I did stop by in the afternoon, but apparently you were out gallivanting. Didn't you get my message?"

She closed her eyes. Upon return from the convent, she'd avoided most everyone, getting to bed before anyone noticed her and asked questions. "No, I missed it. My fault. I've kept to myself a bit more than usual lately."

"Yes, about that, I think it's time you had a chance to unwind and have some fun."

"What, now?" she laughed, incredulous.

"Of course, now," he insisted, never losing his smile. "I know a tavern that stays open nearly until dawn. It's frequented by artists, revolutionaries, infidels and anti-papists. I thought it might be just your sort of place."

She cocked her head at him. "Do you think so?"

"Come see for yourself." He extended a hand to her.

With a little glow alight inside her, she took it.

Mere moments later she found herself inside a small, warm tavern alive with the sounds of music and the smells of food, wine, and warm bodies. Altogether too many people were crammed into the small space, most of them far below her standing or that of Bernardo. Not that any of them might have noticed, the way she'd had to throw herself together so quickly. Women and men both frequented the tavern and they associated together freely in a manner that would not have been easily permitted in higher society. Laughter, flirtation, close physical proximity, and alcohol were the orders of the evening.

Seated at a small table by a window, she and Bernardo had to lean in to hear one another. "My sort of place, eh?" Diana smirked. "Does this inform me of what you must think of my character?"

"What?" He looked innocent. "This place is fun, exciting, unconventional." He motioned for a male attendant who was busy rushing from one table to another fetching food and drinks. "What would you like, Diana?"

"Wine, of course. Whichever is their best. Perhaps a pot of stew with it."

Bernardo repeated her requests and added some of his own that she could not hear over the din. In one corner of the room, a small group with a young female singer pounded out a folk song called "Ragazza stupida" to the delight of the crowd. Several young women danced on tables, shoes off, dresses pulled up to reveal their calves. Their male companions, each of them wiry young rakes, got up with them, grinding their bodies together to the music. One table gave way under a young couple, sending them spilling to the hilarity of the crowd.

Diana caught herself smiling at it. These people lived far outside the grace of God, but for all of it they lived a joyous life unburdened by the rituals and rigors of nobility. Something could be said for that.

Bernardo watched her over his cup of wine. "It is

good to see you smile. It's even better to think I might have something to do with it."

She thanked the attendant as he placed a cup of wine before her. "You flatter yourself, Bernardo Tornabuoni," she replied, unable to hide a grin, fixing him with a mischievous look.

The attendant placed a third cup before them and left. Diana looked at it with crossed eyebrows. "What is this?"

"Brandy. If you haven't tried it before, the taste is a bit more powerful than wine. Have a sip."

Suspicious, Diana held the cup under her nose and sniffed. The aroma was vaguely similar to a strong wine, although indeed it held the promise of greater potency. Narrowing her eyes, she put her lips to the cup and swallowed a small mouthful. Her throat immediately erupted in flame. It was all she could do to avoid spraying the amber liquid on Bernardo. She forced it down, roaring with heat all the way to her stomach where it burned like a furnace. Her lungs began to spasm, sending her into fits of coughing. She sat like that, fist over her mouth, tears streaming down her cheeks, unable to speak a word between uncontrollable coughs for what seemed an endless stretch of time.

"So, do you like it?" Bernardo asked at last with a straight face.

Laughter coursed through her between diaphragmatic spasms.

"I guess I don't need to worry about sharing," Bernardo added with a twinkle in his eye.

Diana shook her head, her fits calming at last. "All yours."

"I'm glad you came with me," Bernardo observed, sipping intermittently from his wine and brandy cups. "I feared you might refuse me."

Diana gave him a sideways look, regarding him curiously. The wine and lack of sleep loosened her tongue. "Do you fancy me then?"

He met her gaze evenly, with confidence. "I do. Does it bother you terribly?"

Diana pretended to think for a few seconds, then shook her head.

"Good. I feared you might have had a lover."

Diana raised an eyebrow in surprise at his comment.

"The young Republic official, perhaps?" Bernardo prodded.

"Niccolo?" she gasped, hoping her voice sounded incredulous rather than the stunned surprise she actually felt. He'd seen them talking at his parents' palazzo, and managed to surmise much. "No, we don't know each other very well at all."

"Your father wouldn't approve of you falling in love below your station," Bernardo observed, "which is exactly what it takes to make many young women fall in love."

"Is love so cynical that it must be used as a weapon by women against their fathers?"

Bernardo shrugged. "Love is a weapon. If you are fortunate enough, you entrust it to someone who will treat it with kindness and care. If fortune frowns upon you, a lover can drive that weapon through your heart."

A serious turn to the conversation, but Diana enjoyed the philosophical talk. "Which kind of lover would you be?"

He smiled and looked down into his cup, bashful for once. "That is an answer that must be judged from action, not words."

The band switched to a song called "Amore di Numero Uno", a slower number with a grinding percussion. The young couples dancing pressed their bodies ever closer, their writhing ever more approximate to carnal intercourse than would ever be allowed in polite society.

Bernardo stood, cup of wine in one hand and offered her his other.

She looked at him, incredulous. "You don't think one sip of brandy is going to get me rutting with you atop a table, do you?"

He smiled, ever confident. "I won't lay a hand on you if you wish. Dance with me. You'll enjoy it. Your beauty will put every other woman in this place to shame."

She gave him a piercing look, yet she smiled. Throwing caution to the wind, she took his hand and he helped her atop their table, which fortunately proved reasonably sturdy. Their cup of brandy soon went spinning away into the crowd. True to his word, Bernardo never put his hands on her. This became a sensual game of its own however, their bodies moving to the music, ever closer, teasing one another, never touching, yet never far apart. Diana felt incredibly self-conscious at first, although soon began to come into her own, and take pleasure at the very forbidden nature of her behavior. Like Bernardo, she held a glass in one hand, with the other she pulled up the hem of her dress revealing her slim, firm calf. This was nearly a pornographic gesture, and it electrified her. When she heard whistles of appreciation, she knew these were for her, but pretended not to notice, as if above such conceits. She let go of the edge of her dress. Her hand found Bernardo's and their fingers entwined. She didn't look at him though; the very primitive nature of the atmosphere demanded an eroticized anonymity. She felt her sexuality struggling for freedom and it thrilled her.

Only a taste though. She prized her honor too greatly to give her body to him after just one dance. Bernardo seemed clever enough to know not to push his success. With the song over, the musical group returned for a more festive number. Bernardo helped her down from the table by one hand. He didn't gloat over his success in convincing her to behave in such a scandalous fashion. Ever the gentleman.

Dawn had nearly broken by the time he returned her to her family palazzo. They didn't share another moment as intimate as their dance atop the table at the tavern. Still, the night had passed in pleasant conversation. Though thoroughly exhausted by the end of their evening, Diana enjoyed herself, forgot her miseries for some hours.

"I've got to get inside before my father wakes," Diana insisted with a giggle as they stood in the snow.

"Of course, my dearest," Bernardo replied with a bow, pressing his lips against her hand. "I hope we will dance again soon."

She grinned but refused to answer his question directly. "Until we meet again, Bernardo."

"Until we meet again," he returned, and spun round and walked back into the night from which he had emerged hours earlier to whisk her from her bed.

As she watched him go, she spotted a shadow in an

alleyway, a boot, the edge of a cloak. Her joy filtered away like water on the sand. One of Niccolo's men, no doubt. Niccolo, oh dear, Niccolo. So different from Bernardo. Thoughts of him returned her to confusion. Perhaps it was for naught. She had no idea what Niccolo thought of her, after all. He'd never come to her window, never taken her on such an adventure as Bernardo had. Perhaps to him, she was nothing more than part of some investigation. A means to an end. Well, he'd hear about Bernardo now, wouldn't he? Perhaps that would stir something up.

She sighed. Something to figure out on the morrow. Dear God, she drowned in fatigue now. Her regular headaches, held at bay with excitement and wine, threatened to return. She wanted to sleep…sleep until all her troubles were gone. If God loved her, she'd wake to find the murderers of her mother dead, Bernardo and Niccolo having sorted out among themselves which would love her, and her father resigned to have her attend the medical school at Salerno. Diana supposed that God more likely slept soundly, as ever he seemed to, and only dimly aware of her if at all. He would snore through her prayers, and she would awake to find the world as ever it was, cruel, confusing, and profoundly lonely.

Chapter Eleven
The Virgin Death

Diana slept well into midday and would have stayed in bed longer had Siobhan not finally shaken her awake. There was much to tell the Irish girl: about her meeting with Savonarola, about yet another strange interaction with Francesca di Lucca, about her realization that Sister Maria Innocentia had herself been part of the Sacred Council, about her night with Bernardo.

Siobhan seemed to be in awe of all that happened, yet also in something of a tiff. Once Diana finished her narrative, Siobhan stood with hands on her hips and remarked, "Well you certainly had an interesting day for yourself while I've been stuck here folding your unmentionables."

The back of her dress fully laced, by Siobhan of course, Diana stood and regarded herself in the mirror. "Then don't mention them. What should I have done? When the Mad Friar who enjoys burning people at the stake for dressing too cheerily invites me for an audience, should I ask if I can bring a companion?"

"You could have picked me up before you went off to the nunnery, couldn't you? What if the old biddies had it in for you? Who would have protected you while you were busy having your fit?"

Siobhan did have something of a point. Diana had

taken considerable chances yesterday, acting alone, no weapon. She'd behaved with risk, even in relation to the past few days. "I'd like to look in on Francesca today. I want to be sure that she is well."

"Admit it; her prophesies have got you thinking."

Diana waved her off. "Nonsense. Francesca is a foolish girl." She put her hands down on the vanity and looked into her own eyes. "But she's sweet in her own way. Even if she is mad."

"You don't know that to be true!" Siobhan protested. "For all you know, God may really be speaking through that girl."

Diana remained silent, watching her reflection.

Siobhan shook her head in frustration. "One day you'll learn to have faith in something."

"As I had faith in my mother?" Diana looked down. "While she joined a Luciferian cult? While she plotted to assassinate the pope? While she cavorted with a man not her husband? Where does my faith begin if it cannot begin with her? With my father, who makes me feel like a stranger in my own home? With a God who deals out fortune and famine with capricious randomness? Or with you, whom I have known but a few short days?"

Diana regretted the words as soon as they were uttered. Siobhan looked wretched as she cried, "When have I wavered in my support of you? It may be only a few days, but how long do you need to see into a person's heart? Francesca too. Be it miracle or madness, she has reached out a hand to help you. Your condescension sullies her effort."

Diana turned to face her. "I meant only to express concern for her. As for the rest, faith has never come easy for me. What little I had has been taken from me. Still, it is no excuse for how I have spoken of Francesca, or of you."

Siobhan nodded, her temerity visibly draining away in response to the apology. "Very well. Our words get away from us at times."

A knock at the door interrupted them. Agathi, eyes averted. "Signore Savrano asks to see you, Lady."

"Does he?" Diana chewed on the words, thinking. "Tell him I'll be right there."

The slave woman shuffled away with the message.

Diana gave Siobhan a sideways look. "I have a feeling this won't be a pleasant conversation. I know you give him reports about me. Perhaps you could return the favor. Do you know anything about what he's thinking?"

Siobhan looked at her feet. "To be honest, Lady, I've glossed over some of the rougher patches of your adventures. Suffice it to say though, that he knows you're inquiring into the death of your mother."

"And now he's going to try to stop me," Diana thought out loud with certitude. Friar Savonarola's words returned to her. Could it be that Diana approached the answers, too closely for her father's own comfort?

Siobhan looked empathetic, a half frown creasing her face. "Best of wishes to you."

Diana nodded and left her bedroom, walking down the long halls and upstairs to her father's reading room. If he wasn't at one of his businesses, this would be where she would find him during the day. She walked slowly, dragging out the experience. Part of her felt like a little girl walking toward punishment. The rest of her though, felt far worse, dreading what truth might lie behind that door.

She knocked. Her father's voice gruffly invited her to enter. He hunched over his table, accounts spread over it. His back faced her, and he did not turn when she entered. This was hardly atypical, but given her nerves, it could only seem like a worse sign still. Without waiting to be invited, she took a seat in a plush velvet chair. Minutes ticked by. A spring-loaded single armed clock standing against one wall tallied them for her. She rolled her eyes up at the ceiling, then down to a bookcase where she read through titles she'd read plenty of times before. Hands wrung in her lap. She sighed. Again, louder.

Finally, her father turned round toward her. His eyes bored into her as they always did, but his expression ever impassive, showed the slightest hints of empathy. "How have you been feeling, Diana?"

She pulled her face muscles up dismissively and shrugged with one shoulder.

"These have been difficult times in this household," her father continued. "With strength and unity we will persevere. There are a few things over which I would like to speak with you. I understand you slipped away with Bernardo Tornabuoni last night."

Heat seared her cheeks, and Diana closed her eyes. Dear God, this hadn't been the line of questioning she'd expected. Her father always had some means to get her to look away first, to gain the upper hand. She could never win with him.

Her father didn't wait for her to answer. "I'm not so foolish as to be unaware that the young today are accustomed to slipping away for trysts. Yet you must understand that you have a reputation to protect and your reputation as a young woman of the Savrano family reflects on the family itself." By which he meant him.

"Father, I didn't *lie* with him! We merely talked."

He nodded, seeming satisfied. "I am pleased to hear that. Nonetheless, people will natter about a young woman who slips away unescorted with a young man not of blood relations in the middle of the night. It is not so much what you have done as what people think you have done which has the power to ruin you."

He was right, of course. She could have been seen with him. Especially how she had behaved, dancing with him on the table, their bodies mere inches apart, people would assume they were intimate. She nodded, accepting his words. What else could she do? Inwardly she fumed; fully on the defensive right from the start of this conversation, it would be impossible to extract anything good from it.

"Are you fond of Bernardo Tornabuoni?"

"I am discovering some fondness for him," she replied with an edge to her voice.

"It would be well for you to find fondness for some young man, given your age. Although I would have preferred something more prestigious, the Tornabuoni family is well respected and longtime friends. A match between you and their son would be desirable for the family."

Oh dear Lord, things hadn't progressed that far! "Father, I've only met him twice. I'm hardly prepared to marry him on that basis! Besides, what good would it do for the family? If I marry, I'll become a Tornabuoni, and the Savrano line would die out." Unless her father remarried, she realized a moment later. "You're already thinking of remarrying, aren't you?" The disgust in her voice shocked even herself.

Her father visibly blanched, a rare moment where she'd managed to catch him off guard and wound him. "I have no immediate plans, of course. Naturally, I would wait an appropriate mourning period for your mother. But it is true, I would need to remarry one day, for the very reason you mention."

Diana drew back, horrified, even if it were irrational, at the thought. "Did you not care for my mother at all?"

"You have no right to question the affection I had for your mother. Why must you always make it so difficult for me to speak with you? I try to talk with you openly about the facts of the world in which we live, yet you do nothing but search for something to be hysterical about."

"Why should I not have such questions?" Diana demanded. "What evidence do I have for your affection for her? When did I ever see you hold her hand, or grace her with a loving glance? And here she is barely in her grave with you ready to plan your next wedding."

Her father's face reddened, his jaw set. "You forget your place, Diana."

"As you have forgotten your place as husband to my mother! You have been too stuck in your books even to notice that she died of a summer disease during February. The circumstance of her death might not interest you very much, but I for one am going to do everything to avenge her memory."

Her father's face went ashen. "I'm well aware of your little investigation. In fact I wished to speak with you about that as well. I've tolerated it so long as I figured it might be a harmless outpouring of grief. Now though, I've been hearing whispers you may be putting yourself at very real risk for harm. Some people do not like others digging in their business."

Well, here it came at last. "I don't care what you say. I'm not going to stop until I discover who murdered my mother."

"Murder!" her father sputtered, putting a hand over his eyes. "You impudent fool. It's true your mother did not die of malaria, but neither did she succumb to murder. She took her own life! There, I wished to shield you from the knowledge, but you push everything past natural limits."

Diana's heart coated with ice and she gasped for some moments like a fish on the dock. Even her eyes felt like frost had coated them. At last she managed to whisper, "You lie."

Her father turned round and plucked a parchment from a drawer in his desk. He extended this to Diana with a trembling hand. "Take it. The proof you need."

Diana stared at it for a minute, paralyzed. Then, like she were watching but not controlling it, her hand reached out and took the parchment. She didn't read it, not yet. Without another word, not trusting what she might say, she turned and walked for the door."

"Diana!" he called from behind her, then again, more softly, "Diana?"

She passed through the threshold and closed the door behind her.

****

"My heart is heavy with the deepest sadness I have ever known. All that I have come to believe has been revealed as a lie. Those mountebanks on the Council who seduce the lost and unfortunate have taken me for all that I had. In giving sway to the influence of those scoundrels I have put to risk all I hold dear. At what cost will come my actions? I have exhausted every means for extricating myself from the Council, and each effort has come to naught.

"The fault, ultimately, is mine alone. I have put my family, my daughter, at great risk. And poor Pietro, I have introduced him to such horrors he did not deserve, as if he has not seen enough already in his poor wretched life. The grief is more than I can bear. I have no more energy, no more plans, no more hope for the future. I am done in. There is nothing left to be done but for to lay back and invite death to take me. Perhaps then, with the sacrifice of my own life, shall those I hold dear be able to continue their own with safety. Perhaps that is the sacrifice God wants from me. That is it, then. The price for this endeavor will be my own life. So be it."

Written in her mother's hand, the letters looped and flowed across the single page. On the last few letters were smudged; ink ran under the weight of Diana's tear. She folded the document once she had finished. She could not draw a breath out of fear such a simple action would shatter her heart.

Siobhan's breath was warm on her neck. The Irish girl perched over her shoulder, where she had read the note with her. Silence hung between. Diana couldn't so much as look at her, so deep was her grief, mixed now with the deepest sense of shame. Her poor mother, life taken by her own hand!

"It's not exactly a suicide letter," Siobhan

whispered gently a moment later.

Diana wiped her arm across her face. Had she heard Siobhan correctly? "What?"

"I understand how it reads as such, but it's not entirely clear, is it? Obviously, your mother is despondent, hopeless even. And she may believe she has to sacrifice herself, presumably for your benefit, but look at how she words her letter. It's passive. She's talking about no longer resisting death, not bringing it on herself."

"Even I know that's grasping for false hope!" Diana sputtered, rising to her feet and walking away from the bed.

"Listen to me for a moment, won't you?" Siobhan insisted. "I'm not saying suicide isn't a hypothesis we must regrettably entertain henceforth. But I don't think it's yet a certitude. She doesn't speak about killing herself, not directly. She does not apologize for her imminent actions. She speaks about her sacrifice being something God may want, when of course suicide is prohibited by God under any condition. The note is neither addressed nor signed. I think this might be a chronicle, not a goodbye epistle. Probably a good many women facing moments of hopelessness might write something like this, at least those who can afford paper. I think she may be talking about martyrdom, not suicide."

"Martyrdom," Diana repeated with a sniffle. "Do you really think so?" She did not want to allow herself to be caught up in nostrums. However, nothing could be so dismal as the thought of her mother's suicide.

"I think we must explore all possibilities. Just as we should not cling to belief in the best of possible outcomes, nor should we be quick to grasp hold of the worst. Even if it were true that your mother took her own life, it would not change the fact that she would have been driven to it by some outside source—presumably the Council. We know an assassin had been hired to kill her. And if Isabella Savrano took her own life, she certainly did not take those of Maria Innocentia or the innkeeper at the Romancier."

"Or Niccolo's man, Crispino," Diana finished the thought. "On a practical level, it changes nothing." Emotionally, it mattered much. She hated the thought of her mother lost forever to Hell having ended her life with a cardinal sin. Nonetheless, the Irish girl gave her some hope. "Thank you, Siobhan. You're a good friend." She gave Siobhan a tight hug, a gesture violating conventions of status unthinkable mere days ago.

"We're going to root out the villains who did this to your mother," Siobhan promised. "I won't let you down."

A knock at the door, Agathi once again.

"Oh dear God, Agathi," Diana moaned, wiping away a few last tears, "what is it now?"

Agathi looked chagrinned. "There is a gentleman here to see you. Signore Machiavelli. He awaits you in the aventurine sitting room."

"Thank you, Agathi. Tell him I'll be right down." Diana looked at Siobhan without saying anything.

"It's about time that man called on you since you nearly were killed," Siobhan observed with displeasure.

Diana agreed. She'd felt profoundly disappointed he hadn't seen to her wellbeing following the death of Crispino. Then again, she'd been gone from home most of the day, and hadn't given him much of a chance. Friar Savonarola may have kept him at bay in the morning. She supposed she should at least hear him out.

Siobhan must have seen something in her face. "You're actually going to speak with him then?"

"Don't you think I should?"

"I suppose I won't be able to talk you out of it, will I? Don't tell me, despite catching the eye of a gentleman such as Bernardo Tornabuoni, you still have fancy for a common clerk? One who's been little help and more than a little hindrance I might add."

Diana rubbed her eyes. "I'm still not sure how I feel about either one of them. And I have no idea how Niccolo feels about me. I might be no more than an investigation to him. I don't claim to be immune to the flights of fancy common to members of our sex. At least I try to be practical about them."

"Which is why you're still a spinster," Siobhan quipped. "Go on, see what he wants."

This meeting couldn't possibly be worse than that with her father, Diana reasoned. She found Niccolo downstairs, composed as ever he was, apparently immune to the boredom of waiting. His eyes casually scanned his environment, casting over the architectural features of the room to the ever-present murals painted above.

"Signore Machiavelli," Diana said.

He stood when she entered, and sat only when she took a chair across from him. "I am pleased to see you well, Lady Savrano."

"Are you?" Diana responded with a twinge of irritation. "I would have thought you might have called on me yesterday."

Niccolo regarded her without revealing any emotion. "In fact, I tried to do just that. Unfortunately, in the morning you had business with Friar Savonarola, and much of the rest of the day you spent at the convent at Saint Cecilia. Perhaps I might have waited until nightfall and then thrown pebbles at your window."

Diana let the quip pass. "I'm very sorry about Crispino."

Niccolo nodded. "I am as well. He was a good man. I expect there must have been another culprit besides the one you dispatched? Perhaps you could describe him?"

"It wouldn't be difficult to spot him as he lacked a nose. I don't suppose you know of such a character in Firenze." After all, Niccolo had known how to find Pietro.

Niccolo frowned. "I am not aware of anyone with such a description. Likely an associate of Giuseppe Mancini from Milano. You are fortunate to have escaped with your life."

"Fortune smiles on me," Diana said without smiling.

"So she does." A moment passed in silence. "I understand you're courting Bernardo Tornabuoni?"

Diana tapped her fingers against her knee. "I think he would like to court me, but I haven't yet made up my mind. Of course I already know your opinion of him."

"Yes, I suppose there is not much more for me to say." Niccolo looked away. A moment later he added, "Although I don't mind saying I'm surprised you'd find much interest in such a fop."

Diana couldn't help but smile. If Niccolo weren't

personally interested in the matter he could have simply kept his mouth shut. For once, Diana found herself on comfortable ground with him. "Oh, I don't know, Niccolo. I'll grant you there is some truth to your accusations regarding his background. I've found him to have his charming and gentlemanly qualities as well."

Niccolo glanced at her out of the corner of his eye. "I'd warn you about charming men such as he. Some men learn the skill of honeyed language they use to seduce young women. There is a particular skill at play in making the recipient feel special. Naturally, in making every woman feel special, in truth none are special at all."

"You needn't worry over me, Niccolo. If I were so susceptible to sugared words I would have surrendered my virtue long ago." She giggled a bit, but Niccolo only gave her a disapproving glance. "Besides, what's got you so concerned with my honor?"

"I only wish to speak as one who would call you a friend."

"Surely I am gladdened you would call me a friend, but I must wonder if your interest in my virtue extends beyond that of friendship."

Niccolo drew back. "Whatever could you mean?"

"It occurred to me that your comments might be borne from a jealous instinct?" She raised her eyebrows at him.

His eyes traveled over her body in a quick, instinctive gesture he probably barely noticed himself. So many men made what they thought were furtive glances, which in truth were nakedly obvious to the observant woman. "I don't deny your features are agreeable and you possess a certain wit that makes for stimulating company. I don't need to point out to you though, that you are a principal in a sensitive investigation of primary importance to the Republic, and I am commissioned in charge of that investigation. I don't see that this should preclude cordial affiliation but anything more would certainly be inappropriate."

A flare of impatience fired down her spine. Why did some men insist on placing rules and restrictions around their passions? "Our emotions cannot be lit then snuffed out like a candle. Can you say you have no affection for me?"

"As you have interest in Bernardo Tornabuoni?"

Dangerous territory now. Balancing honesty with pragmatics. "I do have some affection for Bernardo Tornabuoni. But I discover I have some fondness for you as well. If you have no affection for me in return, then it is misplaced and my course becomes clearer." Strictly speaking, this was not entirely true. Her evaluation of Bernardo Tornabuoni did not hinge entirely upon Niccolo Machiavelli. She might ultimately conclude Bernardo didn't interest her solely on his own merits. She didn't feel the need to have another man to fall back on to make such deliberations. Still, putting pressure on Niccolo in this event had its advantages.

Niccolo squirmed in his seat, could only meet her eyes for a few seconds at a time. "I won't deny my thoughts stray to your welfare more than they ought. So too, I can't deny I would rest easier were you not seen in the company of Bernardo Tornabuoni. It is unrealistic for me to have such expectations. Any affection for you would, by necessity, carry the stigma of impropriety so long as this investigation is underway." He stood and smoothed out his doublet. His jaw set, stern. "I am satisfied to find you well. I think it best I should go."

Diana slumped in her seat. She had her answer sure enough, but she'd pushed him too hard on the matter. Of course he had matters of propriety to keep in mind. She hadn't given enough thought to his position. Whatever feelings he might have for her, he could do nothing about them, not now in the middle of this investigation. Trying to convince him otherwise would lead nowhere. Niccolo would never be the sort to act in such a risky, careless manner. No, that would be Bernardo.

She ran her tongue over her teeth as she watched him go. Hmmph. Now what? Breakfast, for the first thing. Food in her stomach would give her the presence of mind to know what to do next.

Diana enjoyed a breakfast of strawberries freshly imported from Egypt. She dipped the fruits in a cream made from beans the Spaniards found during their New World explorations. Being alone, save the servants, gave her an opportunity to clear her head. She pushed her father and Niccolo from her mind. Complicated men, the both of them. She wouldn't countenance the idea her mother killed herself until she had further proof one way or another. Until she actually had evidence to support one hypothesis or the other, ruminating on the matter would serve no purpose.

The first thing for today would be to check on Francesca. She'd left the young nun in a questionable state. Her unease would only be given succor by seeing for herself that the older girl retained her health.

She'd only just decided her course with certainty when the matter concluded without her. Agathi escorted in a young novitiate, the same girl Diana had first seen at the convent. The girl huffed, struggling to breathe air into strained lungs, leaning on Agathi for support.

Diana stood, gawking at them. "What's the meaning of this?" Deep in her heart, she already knew the dreadful answer.

The novitiate looked at her with red-rimmed eyes. "Sister Ophelia sent me to fetch you, for she thought you would want to know. Sister Francesca di Lucca, your friend, has gone to her heavenly embrace during the middle of last night.

Diana could only stare. How much strain could her heart take in one day?

The novitiate took her silence for confusion. "Francesca the anchoress...she's dead, Lady Diana!"

Chapter Twelve
Breath of the Dead

For the second time in barely a week, Diana ran her fingers along the cold arm of a corpse. Francesca occupied a simple wood coffin. Her arms had been positioned at her sides, a crucifix clutched in one hand, a rosary in the other. Eyes closed, lips slightly open, she appeared deep in sleep. Only her pallor, ghastly and nearly gray, revealed her true status among the dead. Running her hand along the top of Francesca's arm, she could feel the soft fine hairs. Under these the skin was cool.

The body lay in the main convent chapel, just under the image of the Virgin Francesca adored. Nuns, like bees, tittered in and out, differentiated from each other only by age and height. No others were here to be in attendance for Francesca. Her parents, it seemed, were away in Naples, fleeing the cold. The people of Firenze for whom she had offered intercessions, prayers, and even worldly advice, by and large did not see fit to come out and attend to her as she left this world. Granted, today must be the coldest day in years and snow piled thick on the streets. Nonetheless, the absence of gratitude saddened Diana. So be it. She would be family for Francesca tonight. She'd sit in vigil for her friend, if they had even been that much to each other, until the nuns lowered her body in the frozen ground.

"They won't bury her tonight," Siobhan informed her, rejoining Diana following a conversation with a few of the nuns. "The workmen broke a pick axe on the frozen ground. Darkness approaches. They'll pick up the work in the morning. Francesca will lie here tonight." Siobhan peered into the wooden box. "One night won't make a difference."

Her body won't begin to stink, Siobhan meant. The chapel held too much heat to stave off decomposition. If the burial party couldn't hammer through the winter ground soon though, they'd have to toss the body into the snow to thaw out in spring with the ground. Assuming animals didn't get at it first.

"Don't act so forlorn," Siobhan said.

Diana couldn't look at her. "I should have known Francesca was unwell. I spoke to her yesterday when I left here, but she did not answer. Rather than help her I just left her in her cell. What manner of friend was I to Francesca?"

"I admit in retrospect it seems bad," Siobhan stammered. "All errors are clear looking behind us. I am sure you just thought she slept."

Which had been exactly the case. Still, a little extra effort could have made the difference. Call it apathy or lack of wisdom, either way the result was the same. Diana had contributed to Francesca's undoing. Diana let out a long sigh in hopes it might relieve some of the pressure on her heart. It didn't.

A hand came to rest on Diana's shoulder. Sister Ophelia.

"Thank you for letting me know," Diana whispered, glancing away.

"She regarded you as a friend." Ophelia withdrew her hand. "I can give you only a few minutes more. It will be nearly time for vespers, and none from outside our community are permitted. You are welcome to attend the burial proper if you wish. We expect it will be undertaken tomorrow in the late morning, once the grave may be dug."

Diana nodded, blinking away moisture. Sister Ophelia turned and walked off.

Poor Francesca, thought Diana. Stupid girl for choosing a life walled off from proper shelter. Mad too, what with those visions of hers. She'd meant well in her eccentric way. Certainly she didn't deserve to die. She deserved better protection than she'd gotten. She deserved better friends than Diana herself had been.

Diana wrapped her fingers around Francesca's, cold and lifeless. She felt the hard rosary beads in her own hand. She'd have to remember to replace them properly. She lifted up Francesca's hand as if coaxing the girl out of her coffin. Underneath her arm the skin was pale and unblemished. Francesca might as well have been a perfect porcelain doll. Even in death her cool, light beauty was unmistakable. She'd chosen to secret it away here in this chaste jail. Then again, had Diana done much different? Rejecting one man after another in fear of the prison of marriage. One prison or another. Only death offered freedom. Perhaps Francesca was better off now.

"What are you doing?" Siobhan hissed, noticing her tampering with the body. "I'm sure that's sacrilege, or ill fortune or something!"

"Don't be a fool," Diana murmured. Chastised though, she let the arm fall back, and replaced the rosary beads in a rough approximation of how she had found them.

Siobhan put her arm around Diana's shoulder. "We should go. There's nothing more to be done here tonight."

"I'll arrange for the finest cenotaph for her at the Basilica no matter what the cost. She deserves nothing less. She deserves much better than the anonymous grave she'll have here."

"Of course. I'm sure she would appreciate that very much." Siobhan guided her for the door.

Diana looked back, her vision blurred. "What am I to do now?"

Outside the sun lay a sliver on the horizon. Feeble rays cast purple, pink and orange against the dark winter clouds moving in for the kill. The vision was astonishing and so remarkably transient.

****

At home, Diana determined to be left alone. It was not a difficult matter. Her father could not be found. Siobhan had already done her best to console Diana, and now kept her distance. The other servants and slaves had no wish to intrude upon the moods of an unhappy mistress. Diana secluded herself in the palazzo library, candles lit, surrounded by books. She always felt comforted by them. She'd spent enough time immersed in them rather than interacting with the real world outside the palazzo. The fireplace was already going. Wrapped in a blanket, she stared at the blackness outside the plated glass window.

A deep hurt suffocated her heart. The death of her mother was bad enough. Now her indifferent reaction to Francesca's silence had led to her death. A mistake that could not be undone.

A tear ran down her cheek, but she didn't wipe it away. She deserved to be miserable. To allow herself any comfort would be an abomination. Better to let the pain fester, to wallow in it, to explore it thoroughly. Perhaps it would never end.

Diana couldn't stop picturing Francesca's body laid out in the coffin, an exquisitely beautiful corpse. Crucifix in one hand, rosary in the other in that unnatural pose of holy slumber preferred for the dead. She had seemed perfect, unblemished. Unless one felt the coolness of her skin, it might have seemed she were sleeping.

Tomorrow they'd put her into the ground. That would be that. How long would it take for her body to freeze solid? Somewhere in an ancient text she'd read that frozen bodies bounced if dropped rather than shattered. Of course, you could never be entirely sure if what the Greeks or Romans said was true. Ancient wisdom could turn out to be obsolete.

Diana tapped her chin. With the coming of spring, the ground would warm and Francesca's body would putrefy. Diana had read an account of the process, the experimentation done with pigs of course, not humans. A physician at Salerno detailed the process. Diana ruminated on it, imagining Francesca's body as the veins ran green, the abdomen bloated with fetid vapors and finally split wide. Her tongue would protrude, the eyes sink away to nothing. Noxious fluids would soak her burial clothes. The skin would peel back from the nails and teeth, and a bloody seepage would ooze from her orifices. Some ignorant fools, digging up decaying bodies, mistook this as evidence of vampirism, the bodies bloated from feeding, and still dripping with a recent meal. Eventually Francesca would dry out, turn black, leaving little more than dried skin, bones and ruined garments.

Thinking of things in such a clinical way helped her get some distance. No matter what, king or madman, everyone eventually came to the same end. Someday it would be Diana herself in the same state. Perhaps not so far away.

Bodies didn't keep long. Even in the cold, they didn't stay perfect for long. Francesca still looked perfect though, didn't she? Maybe eight, nine hours dead when Diana had seen the body? She tapped her chin some more. She stood. Scanned the bookcase. What was that physician's name? On faculty with Salerno, not a terribly well known author. Books about dead pigs got you only so much readership. Diana's voracious interest in medicine was all that had drawn her to the tome, although the details of death were fascinating in their own way.

Diana's eyes darted from one book spine to another. Regrettably the books were in no particular order. Some were not labeled. She hoped she might recognize it. Otherwise there were hundreds of books here to go through. Her mother and father had both added to the expansive collection. Diana had as well, when she'd come of an age. Books had been one appetite they all shared.

Diana took a few down that looked familiar. Medical books, but the wrong ones. Finally a small, leather bound tome fell into her arms. Cover unlabelled, the book still in good condition. Inside the author, Centuri Pagoria di Caccamo of the University of

Salerno. All right, she had to admit, she would never have remembered the name without seeing it. She flipped through, page after page of script punctuated by rough anatomical drawings.

Okay, this was the part that got stuck in her mind. According to Pagoria, several hours after death, the body began to show dark discoloration on whichever portion sat lowest to the ground. The stain became most noticeable by ten to fourteen hours following death. Pagoria suggested that the extent of the discoloration could indicate the time of death, although no conclusive guidelines were offered. Pagoria also didn't know what caused the discoloration. Several postulations included the possibility that contact with the ground sped up the process of decay, or, citing Ibn al-Nafis, blood settled to the lowest portions of the body following death, although why this should be, he offered no explanation.

Pagoria could very well be an idiot. That alone never seemed to preclude anyone from writing a book. If he was right, though...

Diana snapped the book shut. The flesh of Francesca's arm had shown no discoloration.

Her mother's death had appeared originally as malaria. Perhaps Francesca's apparent demise at the hands of exhaustion and the elements had little to do with the forces of nature or the hand of God. Easy enough to believe that a girl daft enough to live nearly exposed to the worst of winter would succumb to illness. Perhaps, as with her mother, the hand of man brought about Francesca's fate. More to the point, perhaps they had botched the job. Were there not poisons that could mimic the symptoms of death if taken in the right dose, without actually killing the imbiber? What if Francesca had been given some of just such a poison, and ingested just enough to render her into catatonia, but not yet death? Would that not explain the lack of discoloration on her arm?

No doubt, a dose of wishful thinking played a part in this line of inquiry. Still, Diana felt a stab of excitement...and hope. She searched the bookcase one more time, more certain this time. Xenophon's *Ephesiaca,* wherein the heroine imbibes a potion willingly to enter a deathlike trance. Mythology, to be certain, but perhaps an element of truth? Diana tossed this tome aside, indifferent to any harm that might come to such a valuable book. Her hands flew over the dusty librams, agitated now. A book on herbology and potions. Arsenic, belladonna, rare seeds of the *nux vomica* tree, hemlock, oleander, mushrooms... nightshade. Most of the rest brought on vicious and painful deaths, but the nightshades brought on delirium, catatonia and death in high enough doses. A good way to mask a death as due to the elements.

Believing she had found the answer, Diana read on, excited. The antidote for nightshade poisoning consisted of crushed calabar beans, hardly something she had on hand. The book warned the beans themselves could be toxic if too many were administered. Wonderful. She closed the book, and stared at the blackness outside the window. Could Francesca still be alive? She wouldn't be for much longer. Once they put her in the cold ground, she'd die.

Diana couldn't sit by again. True, she might make a fool of herself if she was wrong about Francesca living. Yet, the cost of inaction meant consigning Francesca to death a second time. Diana cared for her reputation no longer. She'd do whatever she could for Francesca, whatever the cost.

A worse concern involved her diagnosis of nightshade poisoning. What if she guessed the wrong poison? Calabar beans would only worsen her condition then. Doubtless other drugs she had not considered might produce similar effects.

She had to pick a path and go with it. She kept the herbology book with her and darted from the room. Downstairs she found Agathi. "I need you to run an errand for me," she told the slave woman. "I need you to go to the apothecary on the via de'Tosinghi. Wake him if you must. Tell him I need calabar beans, crushed and dissolved in a saltwater solution." She thought for a moment. "And two pipettes, one just smaller than the next in diameter. The largest should be no more in diameter than the width of a common brass ring. Can you remember that?"

Never one to ask questions, Agathi merely nodded.

"Pay whatever is the cost." Diana handed the slave woman a handful of florins, which she suspected would be more than enough. "When you have these, meet me with them at the Convent at Saint Cecilia."

Just the slightest raised eyebrow. Then Agathi left.

Next, Diana found Agon von Landau, commander of her father's small force of palazzo guards. Diana rarely crossed paths with him. Typically she remained content merely noting that he and his small company of Swiss mercenaries kept their palazzo safe from intrusion. That Pietro had gotten past them even with a key spoke to his skills at stealth and subterfuge. Agon had spent many years as a condottiere in the service of various Italian republics. His Swiss mercenaries had a reputation for ferocity, unlike too many of the Italian companies who ran for the comforts of home at the first sight of conflict. Now past his prime, palazzo guard essentially functioned as a retirement occupation. Nonetheless, in his fourth decade, Agon cut an imposing figure. Well over six feet in height, he rippled with muscles and possessed cold blue eyes that held no fear of violence. With a long scar running down the length of his face, Agon couldn't lay claim to male beauty. He was loyal to her father though, and Diana didn't doubt his competence. For perhaps the first time she could remember, Diana had reason to call on him.

"Agon, I need your services," she told him.

If he was surprised, he hid it well. "Yes, m'lady. What do you need?"

"I must rescue a friend from difficult circumstances and I expect there may be resistance. I'd like to request an escort from yourself and several of your men."

"I am pleased to be of service. May I ask the destination?"

"The Convent at Sant Cecilia. My friend is the anchoress there, and someone has tried to poison her. I intend to take her out of there, by force if it must be so."

If Agon found anything distasteful in the notion of roughing up a bevy of old nuns, he didn't show it. Of course it was possible that Republic gendarmes or even Cardinal Lajolo's guards might be called in to intervene against her effort to remove the anchoress. She needed protection.

"I'll fetch Leuenberger and Calmy-Rey and we'll don blades. We should be prepared in five minutes if that would serve."

"Excellent, Agon, thank you." If Diana's suspicions about Francesca being alive came to nothing, she would look like a fool in front of an increasingly larger pool of individuals. She fetched Siobhan and updated her on the night's plans.

"Do you really think she might still be alive?" Siobhan asked, jaw and eyes wide open.

"I'm not sure, but it's possible. It's like the woman in Xenophon's *Ephesiaca* who drinks a potion that makes her appear to be dead, though she only sleeps."

Siobhan's brows knitted. "Why on earth would she do such a foolish thing?"

"Well, you see, she thought that her lover must be dead and feared being forced to marry another man whom she didn't love...oh by God, I don't have time to explain all this now. We must meet Agon and his men and be quickly on our way."

The two men Agon selected were tall and muscular like himself, though younger by at least a decade each. On their hips they all wore spadone longswords. Under her coat, Diana hid her pistol.

Agon led them outside. Immediately it became evident that something was amiss in the city. A strong odor of ash carried on the crisp air. To the north, in the direction of the Piazza della Signoria, a deep orange glow rose above the buildings. As she watched, flickers of flames rose above the city line. The flames must be at least five stories high! Was the city on fire? She wouldn't have thought it possible on such a cold night as this.

A cacophony could be heard from the direction of the fire, shouting, cavorting, laughter and screaming, all in an anarchic mix. The noise was not appropriate for people fleeing a fire. In truth, Diana thought it sounded more like a cross between a carnival and a riot.

"Agon, what's going on?" she asked.

He looked in the direction of the orange glow, but with several blocks of buildings between them and whatever was occurring, no sense could be made of it. "I don't know, lady. I could send one of the men to investigate, but that would cost us time."

"No, we must make haste. We'll take our chances." Onward they pressed, heading south toward the Arno, away from the conflagration. Despite the late hour and the cold, many others were out on the streets. Most of these were citizens, pointing to the fire and speaking amongst themselves with evident confusion and alarm. Up and down the street, bands of children and youth caroused. At times, these would waylay the citizens, verbally accosting them and in the case of the older youths, openly threatening them. To what end was unclear.

"Your city has gone mad," Siobhan said, eyes narrowed.

Diana didn't reply, yet she couldn't help but to agree. She couldn't remember any precedent for the chaos on the streets tonight. What terrible timing, whatever was going on. Any other night, she could have easily barricaded herself in the family palazzo. Tonight, she had no choice. Fortunately, with the three heavily armed Swiss leading the way, most of the youth kept their distance. Inevitably though, a large gaggle of young men surrounded them, preventing them from moving on. Catcalls and hoots from the throng of young men got her heart beating faster. Perhaps ten of them hemmed in her little party. Mostly poor, judging by their dress, although they carried clubs and knives.

"Where do you lot think you're going?" demanded one tall wiry youth, brandishing a butcher's knife.

Agon drew his sword with a swoosh. "No business of yours, child. Step aside or I'll cut you down where you stand."

The group of youth tittered nervously. Longswords or not, at ten to three the youth could hardly back down without losing face.

"We wish no confrontation," Diana spoke up, hoping women's words might stave off inevitable male conflict. "Can you tell us why you accost us so?"

Another youth, smaller and younger answered her. "It's Friar Savonarola's orders. All vanities are to be burned. Books, jewels, nice clothes, anything that distracts us from our prayers as we await the End of Times. All must be consumed in flame. Beyond is our holy furnace." He pointed to the glow from the north. His manner seemed less aggressive than the first rogue.

So it was a bonfire. And they were destroying anything of beauty. Of course Savonarola would be behind it. She didn't need to be distracted by these matters, not tonight! "I have an accord with Friar Savonarola. If you so much as touch me, you will regret it."

The taller youth laughed. "One such as you in league with the Friar? A lady powdered, perfumed, and bejeweled such as yourself. And under your arm a book, no doubt containing all manner of blasphemies. Give us the book and your fine coats and jewels and we will be satisfied as to your righteous intentions."

"No doubt the wine you buy with those spoils will satisfy you more than the Holy Spirit," Agon growled.

"Now stand aside!"

"Gentlemen, I hope you could trust that our mission is a righteous one, for we are intent on saving the life of a holy sister. No good is served by bloodshed tonight. When did Christ ever compel his disciples to lift a sword for him?" As she spoke, she noted that the three Swiss had moved to form a protective semicircle around her, with a building wall forming the rear boundary. To her surprise, Siobhan joined them as the fourth member of the semicircle, stiletto drawn. The Swiss didn't seem to think it odd a young girl would be left to guard their flanks. Diana thought her handmaid should be cowering inside the circle with her.

Sadly the youth all had weapons drawn and moved in on their little group. She drew her pistol with sadness in her heart. "Siobhan," Diana implored, "step back where it is safe. There are too many of them."

"Don't you worry about me, Lady," Siobhan responded, never looking back. "My da showed me a thing or two with the blade, he did. Each of us here is paid to see you home safely and that's the end of it."

No time to puzzle that over more. Confident fools, the youth moved in like jackals on an easy kill. Their hoots and laughter would haunt Diana's dreams for nights to come. Instead of effortless prey, the youths were met by a barrier of steel. Blades swirled in the night, glinting echoes of the distant bonfire catching on the steel. Laughter turned to screams. Blood sprayed in wide arcs and slicked the street. Seconds passed like hours. At the center of it all, Diana could barely keep track of all that happened. For a moment she could not tell if her guards were being overwhelmed, or if they held their line.

At one moment Agon drove his sword into the stomach of the tall, wiry lad who had done most of the speaking for the ruffians. Another scoundrel leapt in, intent on driving a blade into the back of Agon's neck while he looked away. Diana raised her pistol and, for the third time in only a short while, discharged it with the intent on taking a life. The thunderous noise, the blast of fire and smoke. Over it all, a man yelped and fell. Agon, startled, looked back at her and gave her a smile like she had swatted a mosquito off his arm.

To her right, Siobhan stepped in front of another youth, ducked a club as if doing so were the most natural thing, and drove her stiletto into the man's pubis. Not even stopping to see the harm she had done, she moved past the squealing villain, rolled back under another club, and drove the stiletto deep into the eye socket of a second rogue.

Only seconds had passed. Three Swiss mercenaries and an Irishwoman stood, all unscathed, over seven dead or dying Italians, while three others made haste in all directions. Diana felt like a stallion trapped in a burning barn. How could these four be so cool in the midst of such violence? How could Siobhan in particular?

Diana stepped to the youth she had shot. A gaping hole in his neck discharged fluid like a fountain. He yet lived, eyes rolling madly, each desperate breath sucking its way past his own leaking essences. He looked up at her, wordlessly pleading for her to somehow fix the damage she'd done. It was the smaller youth. As she watched, his life slipped away and his hopeless struggle finally ended in silence.

"Lady," Agon said. "I did not know you were

armed."

Taking a deep breath, she nodded, not trusting her voice to remain steady just yet.

"You did well." He nodded in appreciation. "I owe you my life. I suggest we continue moving lest the few escapees return with more of their sort. I don't want to have to fight off waves of these idiots all across Firenze."

Diana blinked and breathed deeply again. She'd killed a second man. The first had been a hardened criminal. The second, little more than a misguided boy. True, it would have been worse to let Agon die. Her life increasingly became one of such difficult options.

Siobhan slipped her hand in Diana's. "We are ready to move on."

"Excellent," Agon answered and, with his compatriots, moved off to the South. They left behind them the few pitiful pleas of the young men not yet dead.

Siobhan pulled her after the Swiss, orienting her.

Finally getting her wits together, Diana asked, "You fought like one of the Swiss. How did you manage that?"

Siobhan gave her a funny look. "I told you that I learned much from my father. What did you expect? It's what your father hired me for after all, to keep you safe."

"What? My father hired you as a handmaid!"

"Well, yes, that. I am your handmaid, and always at your service. But my specialty is a peculiar one. That was the service that I performed for the Orsini, mainly serving as protection for the Signorina Zaira Orsini before she married. Did your father not tell you?"

"No, he managed to forget that detail." A lot of pieces certainly fit into place regarding the Irish girl. No wonder she'd been so willing to follow her around the city, putting herself in danger right along with Diana. For her, it was second nature. Diana felt humbled. "Forgive me, Siobhan, I've underestimated you many times."

"I don't know what you mean. From the first you have made me feel as a friend. We can discuss this in detail later. For now we must make haste for the sake of another friend!"

Chapter Thirteen
Nightshade

Across the Arno, Diana returned to the Convent at Saint Cecilia for the second time that night. Before she had come invited in the company of a friend. Now she invaded the convent in the company of soldiers.

Agon rapped the pommel of his sword against the sturdy wooden door. Minutes passed before a fat young novitiate answered. She glared at them with a slack jaw.

"Stand aside for Lady Savrano!" he commanded.

"What's the meaning of this?" she managed to stammer, sounding more dazed than defiant. "What business do you have with us?"

"Move or I will move you," he answered and she stepped aside.

They filed past her, the Swiss first, then Diana with Siobhan taking up the vanguard. Diana couldn't help but stare at the novitiate. Could this seemingly innocent girl have been the one to slip the poison to Francesca? More and more it seemed as if enemies were everywhere in Firenze. No way to tell friend from foe, innocent from guilty. No one could be trusted.

A hall to the left led to the main chapel, where Francesca awaited burial. A few candles on the altar held a lonely rear-guard action against the frost. No fire here, the only heat radiating in from the rest of the building. Winter held the room firmly in its grasp. Even without being buried, Francesca might have frozen to death overnight.

The coffin, lid placed over the body, rose above the shadows on a small table before the altar. Around it the sculpted figures of Saints leered down, as if mocking the poor girl. Diana thought it amazing how easily the beauty of a chapel could change to a flickering doorway to Hell in the abyssal light of a few candles.

She stood beside the coffin, her breath forming clouds in the air. Now she experienced a moment of dread. If she were wrong... With both hands she pushed the lid off the coffin. Not being nailed down yet, it fell away with ease, clattering to the floor with a great bang. Within Francesca lay much as before, rosary in one hand, crucifix in the other crossed hand, eyes closed, expression tranquil. The beautiful dead, maybe not quite so dead.

She reached out her hand, caressed Francesca's cheek. "Dear Francesca, forgive me. This is not the world we prayed for, but come back to it for my sake." She looked up. The others watched her. The Swiss impassive, leaning against the wall, Siobhan expectant, hoping against all hope. "I need more light," she told them. "I can't see to do what I need to do."

"They must have a lantern here somewhere," Agon said. "Go, fetch what you can find." The other two Swiss left them. Soon the unmistakable sounds of an aggressive search put Diana's nerves on further edge.

"What's the meaning of this!" a woman's voice cried. A dark form slid into the room like a ghost. Moving into the feeble candlelight, Sister Ophelia's features became visible. Behind her, another ghost, the young novitiate. "You are intruders here! Would you defile our sanctuary?"

Diana looked down sadly at Francesca's face. "Whatever you have here, I would defile it to save a life."

"Lady Savrano? I would have expected better from Isabella's daughter. Who do you mean to save? Surely you see Sister Francesca is as dead as a sinner's soul. Do you fancy yourself a necromancer? Or do you think Christ has given you the power to steal back souls from Heaven as he did with Lazarus?"

Diana looked up at her, squinting in the dark. Just then, the two Swiss returned with several lanterns. These they quickly filled with oil and lit, hoisting them up to hooks hanging down from the ceiling on chains.

Sister Ophelia pointed her finger at the men. "Why do you help her? Each of you will be damned for what you do here tonight."

Agon looked askance at her. "Sister, after all else we three have done, I think God will forgive us for stirring old women from their snug beds. Now shut it or I may become tempted to do something that will be worth damnation."

Sister Ophelia took two steps back at that. She turned to the novitiate. "Fetch the gendarmes!"

Agon snorted and turned his back on her.

"Help me get her out of the coffin," Diana commanded.

The two younger Swiss sheathed their swords. One took Francesca's shoulders, the other her feet. Diana cradled Francesca's head as they lifted the body from the coffin, and placed it gently on the ground beside the table. Then they took two steps back.

Agathi appeared then, mercifully. Diana thanked

God the woman had made it through on the chaotic streets. "Blessed Jesus, Agathi, I feared you would not get here."

"I am sorry, lady." Agathi bowed her head. "The streets were filled with violence. I would have been here sooner, but I kept to the shadows and took a safer route."

"Do you have what I asked for?"

"I do, lady. I got exactly what you requested." The woman handed over a vial sealed with wax and two small pipettes. In this darkest moment Diana felt a little thrill. This must be the delight a gambler felt on rolling the dice, the rake on bedding another man's wife. She might tonight take back Francesca from God's embrace. She hoped he might forgive her for snatching a soul from heaven.

Diana knelt beside Francesca's motionless form. Above them the lanterns burned, giving her the best lighting she could hope for. She leaned over, her hair forming a protective curtain around Francesca's face. She put her hand against Francesca's cheek. Cold. She sighed.

No one spoke, not even Sister Ophelia.

With a trembling hand she parted Francesca's black robes, exposing her sternum. Diana pressed her ear against Francesca's cold chest. Nothing. She squeezed her eyes shut, held her breath and listened...and listened... There! The slightest murmur, fluttering like a bat trapped in a sealed cave. Could it be her imagination? Her own heartbeat pulsing through the flesh of her ear?

Diana ran her tongue along her lips. She pressed them to the stone floor, so cold it hurt. She licked them again, this time pressing them against Francesca's forehead. The flesh felt warmer, much warmer than the stone. Colder than a healthy person, no mistake, but warmer than should be a corpse dead now nearly twenty-four hours and stored in this coldest of rooms. The body generated heat as only living bodies did. Probably she'd been saved being placed in that sealed coffin, her own body heat keeping herself warm enough to survive.

Diana sat back. "I think she's alive," she whispered.

No one replied. She stared at them, five statues in the dark.

"She's alive!" Diana pronounced with certainty.

Siobhan rushed forward, the first of them to move. "What must we do?" she asked, nearly breathless.

"It's impossible!" Ophelia hissed. "She's dead, I checked her myself."

"Silence, woman," Agon growled.

"She is in a deathlike stupor brought on by poisoning. It would have been easy to miss unless you knew to be suspicious."

"Poison?" Ophelia repeated, jaw slack.

Diana ignored the nun. She held the calabar bean serum vial up to the light of a lantern. "Siobhan, you must help me. I cannot do this alone."

"What must I do, Lady?"

Diana took the larger of the pipettes. With two fingers she snapped off the very end, leaving a jagged edge. This she inserted down through the wax sealing the serum vial like a needle through cloth. As the tip pushed down through the fluid within, the pipette filled with the solution. "Bring me some wax, still warm and malleable, from one of those candles." She pointed toward the altar.

Siobhan did as beckoned and returned quickly. Diana used a small amount to seal the end of the larger pipette jutting out of the vial. Then she handed the smaller pipette to Siobhan. "Hold this in the flame until both ends are sealed shut."

Once again, Siobhan went to the candles and returned with a finished product. The heat had melted the glass until now it resembled a simple thin glass rod.

Diana didn't take it yet. Holding the vial back up to the lantern light, she held her breath. She hoped this would work the way she thought it should. Slowly, she pulled the larger pipette out of the vial. As she anticipated, the pipette remained filled with serum, despite being open at the bottom, jagged end. The wax seal on the back end prevented the liquid from draining back out of the pipette's tip as she extruded it.

"Let me see the smaller pipette."

Siobhan handed it over.

Diana took a deep breath. "Extend Francesca's arm for me. Hold it steady."

Siobhan pulled Francesca's arm over into a pool of lantern light. Diana examined its underside. According to the medical books she'd read, a vein should run through the crook of the elbow, but in such poor illumination, Diana could not find it. A pulse of desperation surged through her. She'd be damned if she found Francesca alive, only to be helpless to save her. She turned the limb over. Here on the back of the hand, vessels ran over the wrist and back, toward the fingers. "Hold her hand very still."

"What are you going to do?"

Diana didn't answer her, and no one else spoke. She bent over, careful not to spoil what lighting she had. She rubbed the jagged edge of the larger pipette against the flesh covering the largest of those vessels. Holding her breath once again, she gently pierced the tissue with the point, slowly driving the tip of the pipette into the back of Francesca's hand. Holding it in place, where she thought the tip ought to be in the middle of the vein, she took the smaller, sealed pipette and eased it through the wax covering on the back of the larger pipette. The fit between the two pipettes was not ideal, the smaller one being too small, really. Better that than too large to fit, though. As she eased the smaller pipette down into the larger one it forced most of the fluid within the larger pipette out and into the vein.

The deed done, she pulled the contraption free of Francesca's arm. A moment passed. Nothing.

"Did we use enough?" Siobhan whispered.

"I don't know."

"Should we try more?"

"If we give her too much it will kill her as certainly as the nightshade would. If I even am right about this being nightshade."

"How did you know to use the pipettes like that?"

"I don't know."

"Are you sure it worked right?"

"Damn you, Siobhan, do you plan to spend the entire night asking questions I cannot answer?"

"I don't know," Siobhan replied. A moment later she whispered, "What if it's not nightshade?"

Diana could only glare at her.

Seconds later, Francesca coughed. The sound of it

made Diana's heart stop cold. Francesca lurched suddenly, her back arching violently before she turned to the side and vomited up her guts in a thin violent stream. Diana held Francesca's head, keeping it from slamming against the stone, and holding her hair back from the foul smelling mass. Francesca curled in a fetal position, never opening her eyes but beginning to shiver violently.

Behind them whispers. One of the Swiss said, "It's a miracle!"

"Is she dying?" Siobhan asked.

Diana shook her head. "Shivering means her muscles are functioning once more. She's weak though. We'll need to return her to warmth. She'll need fluids too once her stomach settles down. You there!" She pointed to the largest of the Swiss. "Can you carry her all the way back to the palazzo?"

The man responded with a curt nod.

Sister Ophelia stepped forward, her face twisted. "Francesca is a sister of our order. You can't remove her from our care!"

Diana turned on the nun. "Someone within these walls tried to kill her. I won't abandon her again. The only place I know that she'll be safe is at my palazzo."

"How can you know that?" Ophelia insisted.

"Because I'm not dead yet."

The biggest Swiss hefted Francesca in his arms. Instinctively she turned in toward the warmth of his body. Agon pulled the coverlet from the altar and wrapped Francesca in it like a blanket. An act of sacrilege, but not even Ophelia complained. The older nun stood, open mouthed and watched.

Finally Ophelia managed a protest. "Cardinal

Lajolo will hear of this, I promise you."

Diana stared at her as her entourage filed back out into the cold. "So be it."

****

Wrapped in the thick blankets of Diana's own bed, Francesca settled down to continuous but mild tremors. Several times her eyes opened and she looked around dully. Never did they register recognition, and she didn't speak. Time, Diana hoped. A little more time would see her made right. Agathi got the fireplace going in the room. Siobhan managed to get Francesca to take a little broth. Promising signs.

"You saved her life," Siobhan told her once Francesca drifted off to uneasy sleep.

Diana nodded. "I know." She cocked her head, looking at the sleeping girl and nibbling her lower lip.

"What's wrong?" Siobhan asked.

"I don't know." She shook her head. "Get some sleep. We've all had a long evening."

Siobhan put her hand tenderly on Diana's shoulder. "If you need anything, don't hesitate to wake me." She left, closing the door gently behind her.

Francesca didn't need a guardian watching her all night. The Swiss mercenaries had already adopted the little nun and would cut down anyone who so much as spoke ill of her. Diana had done as much as she possibly could.

This should be a moment of triumph. She'd plucked Francesca from certain death. So why was she standing here moping? Something bothered her. Something was wrong. What was it?

The memory of Francesca lying cold and still in her coffin, for all appearances dead. How easy it would have been to have closed the lid on the coffin and put her in the ground. How close they had come to doing just that.

The poisoner employed nightshade.

Friar Savonarola's face came to Diana's mind suddenly. His lips twisted in an unnatural grimace, his approximation of kindness. His lips opened and whispered to her, "The priests who officiate here at the Basilica complain that your mother's ghost haunts this place." His eyes twinkled in the glow of countless candles. "They claim they can hear her sorrowed cries at night."

Ice shot through her veins. She turned away from Francesca, lip quivering. "Mother..."

Downstairs she flew. She hurried past Siobhan without explanation.

"Diana, what's wrong?" Siobhan called after her.

Diana burst into the kitchen, where the Swiss were still gathered, shaking off the cold by the fire. Already tears flooded her eyes. "Agon. I need you again!"

He stood at once, stepping toward her. "What is wrong?" he asked with a frown. As he spoke, Siobhan plunged into the room.

"We must get to the Basilica of Saint Zenobius. My mother." She couldn't manage another word, breath catching in her throat.

"Oh dear," Siobhan gasped.

Agon set his jaw. "The basilica isn't as isolated as the convent." He turned to the other two Swiss. "Leuenberger, fetch four more men and bring pry bars."

Minutes later Diana was back in the cold, escorted by Siobhan and a ring of Swiss mercenaries. Now they walked toward the great conflagration in the center of the city, flames licking up and beyond the rooftops. Thousands of hours of ideas and writing destroyed in a single night. The air stank with the acrid smell. Catcalls and cries cut into her ears. Still she cast it all out of her mind. She could only think of her mother. She imagined her waking, the nightshade wearing off finally, cold in the dark box that wouldn't open.

She shuddered. Could it be possible...could there still be time?

This time they passed unhindered through the city. Seven heavily armed Swiss was enough to dissuade even the largest gangs. Siobhan held her hand tightly as they walked, saying nothing. Diana couldn't so much as meet her eyes.

The torched books cast their shadows long against the basilica doors. Embers flew about like fireflies. Somewhere in the crowd a woman screamed.

Agon climbed the stone steps to the basilica door, tried the handle, banged on the solid wood with a mailed fist. He turned to one of his men. "Crack it open."

Silent, like a zombie, the Swiss broke apart the door lock and pulled open the big doors. Into the cold void they shuffled leaving the fiery mass behind them. One of the Swiss set about lighting candles inside the nave. Just left of the entrance stood the tomb of Isabella Savrano. A stone plate marked the spot where her coffin recessed into the wall. Entwined with it, two female angels stared with cold marble eyes, wings unfurled, daring the onlooker to defile the sepulcher.

Diana stood before it, nails driving grooves into her palms. "Mother," she whispered.

"Get it open," Siobhan ordered stepping in front of

her, nearer to the sarcophagus.

Agon's men moved past her, pry bars ready. They went at the stone face without hesitation. With all they must have done and seen in their lives, the mere act of desecrating a grave must have been a minor matter indeed. They groaned and grimaced as they heaved and pushed their weight against the metal bars. Screams split the frigid air as stone ground against metal. At last the stone plate broke free and collapsed to the ground, shattering into several big pieces.

Siobhan gasped and leapt back. Diana stood her ground, ignoring the pain as flecks of granite pierced her ankles.

"Hold, in the name of the Republic!" Swords were drawn. Shouts were raised. Diana turned. Republic gendarmes, a half dozen or more. As she watched one got too close and a Swiss blade lunged. The gendarme managed to block it and retreated back to the circle of his comrades. Half a dozen gendarmes would never be a match for an equal number of her Swiss. Yet behind the first half dozen would be another and another.

"Our business is none of yours!" Agon shouted back at them.

Diana opened her mouth, but no words came.

"You are defiling sacred ground," responded a shadow at the door, a silhouette against the inferno in the square. Weaponless, the figure strode in through the gendarmes with a cool confidence that put even the Swiss to hesitation. Finally, he moved into the light of the candles.

"Niccolo," Diana gasped.

His eyes went wide. "Lady Savrano, how have you come to be at the center of this madness?"

Siobhan stepped in front of him. "We've just this night taken the nun Sister Francesca from death's grip. We've come to do the same for Isabella Savrano."

Niccolo frowned at her words. He looked to Diana.

"My mother," she pleaded. "Nightshade."

Niccolo looked to the tomb, already half opened. After a heartbeat he motioned to the Swiss. "Proceed."

The threat of battle eased, they turned back to the open tomb. Two of them reached in, arms and torsos into the gaping maw of the mausoleum. They heaved and hauled out the front half of Isabella's heavy coffin. As they pulled it free, more of the Swiss moved to take up the middle section and the end.

A smell like forgotten wet clothes hung heavy in the cold air. It could be just the natural smell of the dank tomb, couldn't it?

Niccolo looked at her, his expression tight and difficult to read.

Diana didn't know what to expect. Her mother had lain in the tomb for days. Even if she had been paralyzed by nightshade as Francesca had been, did any hope remain that she might live? The basilica grew cold, especially at night. Could her mother survive in such conditions for so long? Perhaps it hadn't been nightshade at all. If her mother had killed herself, certainly she wouldn't have chosen such an uncertain method. If it had been someone else, what purpose was served in such a torturous death?

Niccolo motioned with his fingers. "Open it."

Diana held her breath. Inside could be her mother, still alive, rescued like Francesca. Nothing could bring greater joy to Diana's heart. A remote hope to be sure, but she dared to think it might be possible. If God had any love for her at all, could he not grant her just this one thing...that she was not too late to save her mother?

Agon put a pry bar between the coffin lid and body and pushed down, forcing the nails loose. He knelt, fingers under the now loosened lid. Lifting from his legs, he heaved, pulled the lid open. From the top of the lid, tatters of lining hung down, torn apart as if by some animal. Lines were gored into the wood of the coffin lid itself. The odor of mildew became pervasive, stinging Diana's nose. She stepped forward.

Siobhan, closer to the casket, gasped, a hand coming up to her mouth. She turned and gaped at Diana. Past her, rising up just past the lid, fingers stretched out, flesh emaciated and clinging to the bone. Like claws, they hung frozen, immobile in the cold. A glint from a lantern reflected something embedded in the coffin lid. Stuck in a tract of brown, a fingernail.

Siobhan moved to block Diana's way. "Don't," she said. "There's nothing to be done."

Diana shoved her aside. All eyes were on her, the Swiss, the gendarmes, Niccolo. There could be no mistaking the collective look, sorrow, uncertainty, horror. It didn't matter, she had to see for herself.

Forward she moved, until the clawed fingers revealed arms like the wings of a baby bird. A jolt of a memory—Diana stroking the cold flesh on the night of her mother's burial. The flesh hadn't been blemished. She'd taken notice of it on Francesca, why not with her own mother?

Diana could see her mother's burial dress now, already staining from the process of decay. Above them her mother's arms reached up, skeletal, as if to embrace her. Her mother stared at her, face sunken in, the flesh mottled and gray. Her eyes were open; lifeless orbs covered with milky glaze. Around her face, her long dark hair still framed the process of death in a kind of ironic beauty. Her mother's mouth hung open, teeth bared like an angry dog, lips pulled back in the unmistakable rictus of a terrified death scream.

A touch on her arm. Diana shrugged it away violently. Her hands covered her mouth, eyes strained open so wide that the corners hurt. A sound in her ears like the rushing of a vicious ocean deafened her. When she opened her mouth, it felt as if her soul came rushing out in one long breath. If she screamed, she could not hear it.

She stared up at the others, at her Swiss guardians. Where so recently they had looked upon her as a miracle, now their eyes quivered. Agon, could only gape at her. The gendarmes collectively skitted back as if she were some form of haunting. Niccolo stepped forward, his mouth moved. She couldn't hear what he said. He reached out with one hand but Diana recoiled. She could not bear human touch.

Through the mass of bodies she rushed. Where she moved, each of them stepped away, giving her easy access to the open door. The sound in her ears pounded, throbbed, and became louder still. She ran as if to escape it, but it followed her endlessly. Out into the night she burst, and the cold served to contrast cruelly with her fervor. The bonfire raged ever higher, and for a moment she thought to fling herself on the conflagration. Instead she turned, turned to the right for no particular reason and ran as fast as she could. Away from Siobhan, away from Niccolo and the other men in the church, away from the accusing glare of her mother's body.

She had failed, failed to save her mother when she might have done so. There would be no excuses, no forgiveness, no redemption. She could only run, ignoring the others on the street, ignoring the burning behind her, ignoring the crippling pains in her lungs as she sucked in lifeless air. At last her body could take no more and she collapsed against the corner of a building. Bereft of energy, she found herself immersed in the most painful and unimaginable void ever.

Chapter Fourteen
The Unkindest Cut of All

On and on, round and round, Diana walked the streets of Firenze. Around her in the dark the city still tittered. Ash and snow mixed in the sky. Forms gathered together in the streets or lurked in doorways. They stared at Diana as she passed, watching, sometimes whispering together, but none of them approached her. She, in turn, took little enough notice of them.

Black, hateful emotions swirled within her chest, tearing at her organs like a ravenous beast. Should she have taken someone into her confidence and attempted to relay her feelings, she could never have done them justice. Losing her mother was bad enough. Knowing she had failed to save her defied comfort.

Cold and tired she found herself outside an inn, a weary old place that catered to traveling merchants of modest means. Here the streets were reasonably quiet. Savonarola's bonfire glowed in the distance, orienting her to where she had wandered. Most of the excitement in Firenze centered closer to the flames. Here, she stood alone in a remote corner of Hell.

Her joints hurt and she could no longer feel her fingers. She looked up at the plain wooden door. She couldn't go back home...face her father. She couldn't bear the thought of anyone's eyes on her. She'd crack open.

Placing one cold hand on the rickety wooden railing, she ascended the stairs to the doorway in fatigue. An unsteady hand worked the knob and her shoulder nudged the thin door aside. Wearily, she shuffled in.

A small blaze glowed in a simple fireplace in one corner, the only illumination in the room beyond. Still it offered a fragile reprieve from the frost. Diana's eyes scanned the room. Behind a simple wooden desk an old man lingered. Probably the bonfire had kept him awake, a spot of luck for her given the hour. He eyed her suspiciously, as if she might have been a ghost passing immaterial through the wooden door.

She couldn't manage to look him in the eye. "I'd like a room."

He cleared his throat, an unpleasant sound rich in fluids. "You'll be wanting a fire and warm water for bathing?"

"Just the fire," Diana said, her voice barely a whisper. "No amount of water can cleanse me tonight."

"So be it." He produced a simple iron key and crossed out from behind his desk. His body wobbled from one side to another as he walked. He passed in front of her toward a narrow flight of stairs leading up into pitch black. Diana could only guess she was meant to follow. Up they went, Diana feeling her way by the railing. A hallway on the floor above blessedly shown with the light of a single candle protected by glass. Rows of unmarked doors lined the narrow hall. Diana might easily have been in a mausoleum.

The old man went to one door and opened it with the key. He left the door open for her, continuing down the hall to light an ember with the candle. Moments later, he returned, using the ember to light kindling in a small fireplace. As the wood sprang to flame, Diana could see her accommodations. The room was of moderate size, bigger than she might have expected. The bed also was larger than she guessed, an old four-poster with thick mattress. True the covers were worn and the wood scratched, but it promised comfort. A small table and chair were unremarkable, as was a tin tub for bathing. A long mirror hung against one wall, and Diana's pale reflection flickered in the light. She looked away.

Next to the bed a chamber pot, still smelling faintly of urine. Two big windows looked out over the street. As fortune would have it, she could see Savonarola's bonfire perfectly. If the old man had thoughts about the conflagration, he kept them to himself. Instead he turned to her and said merely, "You've got the copper?"

She produced a silver coin and held it aloft between two fingers. Its reflection glimmered in the old man's eyes. Slowly he reached out and took it from her like some kind of exotic beast. She could feel his eyes on her, appraising her. She stared at the floor.

"If you need anything," he grunted.

She nodded and he left, closing the door softly.

As the fire took life, the worst of the cold receded. It was enough for her to shrug off her coat, pull the awkward holster off her shoulder. She withdrew the pistol and placed it gingerly on the simple table. Then she sat on the edge of the bed and sank her face in her hands.

Dear God, how things had gone so horribly wrong. Now, alone in this alien room, her grief poured out of her like from an arterial wound. Her body shuddered, and tears poured from her eyes, blocked only by feeble fingers. Her mother, her poor mother, how she had failed her. She'd gone on her hunt for murderers, picking her way mindlessly around the city…whilst all the while her mother lay trapped and terrified in her coffin. How things might have been different had she taken a moment to visit her mother's grave.

Savonarola had even given her a clue, telling her about the cries the priests had ascribed to ghosts. If only she'd taken a moment to think about what Savonarola had said. Could she have saved her mother?

Now her mother was dead for sure. No mistaking it this time. The image of her mother, skin mottled, clawed fingers reaching out for salvation that never came. That image she could never forget. It was her responsibility. Might as well have been her that slipped poison to her mother.

She could have saved her. She could have saved her…could have saved her.

A flare from outside caught Diana's attention. Through the window a column of flame shot up from the bonfire as something shifted within the burning mass. A wall of sound quickly followed this as the crowd hooted and hollered their appreciation of the burning. Individual pages rose up into the air on drafts of warm air, their edges glowing with flame. Each returned to the ground only as cold ashes. There, before her eyes, ideas burned. It seemed like the world itself no longer made any sense. The city itself slid toward Hell, with Diana one of its trapped denizens.

She rubbed her temple. Her head throbbed with one of her worst headaches. For once she thought the pain well deserved. She'd become such an utter failure. Her mother dead due to her own incompetence, the mission to find her killers going nowhere, her own life in constant danger. No longer could she bear it. Some other person could take all of this—someone stronger than herself. Every person had their breaking point, and she had reached hers. It would be so much easier if it had been her who had taken the poison. She could be resting quietly in her own grave rather than wallowing in this misery. It happened all the time, didn't it? God called people back, even those still in their youth. Why not her? Couldn't it just as easily be her? If God willed it, he could take her life.

Who would even miss her? Not her father who paid her barely any mind; Siobhan might be a friend, but she'd find lucrative employ elsewhere with her particular set of skills. Truth be told, Diana had never been adept at cultivating a close cabal of friends and colleagues. Her mark upon this Earth, were she to leave it suddenly, would amount to nothing at all.

Her eyes alighted upon her father's pistol, her loyal companion in all of this. Her fingers trembled as she reached out for it. In her hands the heavy wood felt good, an anchor of reality for such a surreal night. She'd taken lives with this instrument. The first had deserved it; a murderous degenerate unmissed by the world. The second, though…only a youth caught up in an unfortunate moment. What might his life had been had their paths not intersected? This pistol had blood on it, blood that flowed over onto her hands in copious amounts. What would one more matter?

Hands shaking, she cocked forward the hammer and put the barrel against her temple. What would it feel like, the hard ball going through her brain? Would there be a moment of intense pain before the darkness came? Would her life just snuff out like a candle? The old man downstairs would find her, fetch the gendarmes perhaps or simply call the gravemen to take her body away. That would be it, just another soul lost on the bonfire night.

Diana thought of the priestly warnings about suicide. An eternity in Hell, unforgiven by God. Where was God though on a night like this? She didn't know if she ever really felt his presence. Tonight the city of man seemed orphaned of any God. Only this rock of a world, with men and women rutting, killing, cowering in fear like any animal. No matter the course of their lives, each of them ended in a miserable, painful death. Could there be any sense left in prolonging that pain? If God lived, he'd simply have to forgive her...or not.

Still, this was a decidedly final decision. Once the trigger pulled, no second thoughts, quite literally. The steel against her skin cold, repellant. Her hand tensed and released over and over, in time with her shallow breathing. A dozen times she made a decision—pull the trigger, no, don't, do it, don't!

Her mind flashed to that image of her mother, hands raised up desperately, that last look of terror frozen on her face for as long as it took for the flesh to melt away to bone. That face—that accusation—would be with her for always...for as long as she lived. How long could she endure a life like that?

She would just have to take her chances with God's wrath. "Lord God," she whispered, "If you even exist. If this is not your will, then I ask for your intercession." She doubted that little prayer would buy her much sympathy if this ultimately proved to be a spiritually horrible decision, but at least it was something.

She sucked in a deep breath, then another. Her free hand rubbed her left temple. Her head seared with pain. Very well, it was now or never.

She squeezed her eyes together tightly. Her finger trembled on the trigger. She hoisted the heavy pistol up so it was perpendicular to the floor. The ball would go straight through her skull, no glancing shots. She hoped this wouldn't hurt too much.

The decision made, it was still so hard to choose the exact second. Much like diving into a cold pond. Though the course of action was set, every moment seemed precious. Enough of this. With a surge of adrenaline and determination, she pulled the trigger.

She felt the concussion as the hammer slammed down, felt the wheel inside the pistol grind as it threw off sparks. Then nothing. Just the empty echo of the hammer against steel dying away.

Diana released her breath and opened her eyes wide. She was still alive. She jumped up and threw the pistol onto the table like it was a snake. Disbelieving, she stared at it, her mind struggling to comprehend. Breath came fast and shallow. She could still feel the cold circle of steel against the side of her head.

The pistol sat motionless on the table where she had thrown it. Though it seemed somehow alive to her now, another entity, it gave no signs of life.

Diana looked down at her hands, stretched her fingers. Still alive, despite her best intentions. Had her prayer been answered? Was it God's intercession on her behalf? Slowly it dawned on her what had happened. She'd fired the gun earlier when she'd killed the youth who accosted their group on the way to the convent. In the ensuing chaos, rescuing Francesca, finding her mother, she'd never reloaded it. Stupid really. Not a miracle. Just her own ineptitude.

Nonetheless, that itself could have been the Lord's method, couldn't it? She'd never forgotten to reload it before. If she simply tried again, would that be a more flagrant disregard for God's will? Surely he wouldn't rescue her twice.

If it were the case he wanted her alive, for what purpose? To find her mother's killer? She'd proven herself far from competent at such a task. She doubted it could be simple love. He treated his creations with too much contempt and cruelty to understand love.

Either way, what did it matter? What God wants, God gets. Fine then, she'd leave matters more fully in His hands.

She approached the table, reaching gingerly for the gun. It didn't burn her fingers when she touched it, didn't bite.

She hefted it in her hand, regarding it like a mischievous child. More deep breaths to steady her nerves. Carefully, her hands still quivering, she took out the powder and shot, reloaded the weapon. No more errors. It would be just God's decision this time.

With the pistol fully loaded, she cocked forward the hammer once again. She approached the bed, laid out waiting for her. The bed was generous in size, large enough for two people. Two straw filled pillows provided comfort for the sleepers' heads. Nothing remotely like the comforts of her own bed at home, but not terrible for an inn. Gently she placed the pistol on the left pillow, barrel pointed inward to the right side of the bed, hammer free to swing. She took care to be sure the barrel faced the middle of the right pillow.

She moved around the outside of her bed, fingers lightly tracing along the blanket. She pushed down once gently to test the mattress. Filled with straw. Scratchy. Even in her present state, her mind protested the unpleasant accommodations. Exhaustion threatened to overwhelm her. Even if she could bear to return to her own home, which she could not, her body could take no more exertions. Her calf muscles ached with each step; her feet felt like they were on fire. The grinding pain in her head simply wouldn't stop. Her brain had no energy left to work on either; all she could contemplate was sleep, whether she woke or not.

Once, she turned and stared for a moment outside the window. Burning pages rose up in drafts of hot air, only to flutter down to Earth again like fallen angels. So many ideas, so much knowledge. Beyond the fire, Firenze, her beloved city stretched out, mere shadows in the deep darkness.

With a sigh, she turned away and finished her circumnavigation of the bed moving over to the right side. With a tired hand, she pushed back the blankets. At very least it was too cold for insects. She saw none of the bedbugs or lice she might have expected. She sat on the edge of the bed and pulled off her boots. Her toes felt like they had been holding their breath and were finally allowed to breath. She wiggled them in the cold air, before swinging her legs up and over into the bed. She pulled the blanket over onto herself before the cold could get at her too badly.

Gently, she eased her torso down. As she had feared, jagged bits of straw poked at her. How anyone managed to sleep like this, day in and day out, she could never guess. For tonight, she'd manage. Fatigue would help her see past the discomfort. Her head settled into the straw pillow. With bones aching, she turned onto her right side.

The open barrel of the pistol stared her down, like a lover, or like a mortal enemy, she couldn't quite decide which. Together they had taken lives, the first well-deserved certainly, the second an unfortunate victim of circumstance, although still beyond her control. The third, well...Diana had no doubt this pistol would take a third life. The only question was whether that would prove to be her own. God would decide that. If He wished her to live...to press on, to endure, well she'd know that by tomorrow morning. If He preferred to end her misery tonight, so be it.

Diana wondered how much she tended to toss and turn at night. Just the right bump could be enough to loosen the hammer, send the wheel inside the pistol spinning, spraying sparks against the powder within. She'd never hear the shot, never wake to realize what had been done. It would be God's hand, not her own. Surely, He couldn't fault her that.

She blinked, eyes feeling languid. They closed for a moment, burning with the need to remain closed. Still, she forced them open for one more look at the pistol, her most steadfast companion. What would her dreams be like tonight? What kinds of horrors could she expect?

Sleep could not be put off forever. Her eyes demanded to close. Perhaps just for a moment. She'd let them rest. Rest quickly turned to sleep and sleep to dreaming.

The dreams that came were, in their way, a surprise. No horrors visited her in her sleep, only memories of her mother in better days, years gone by. Long before her death, long before the Sacred Council of Apostles, Diana herself merely a girl, they walked hand in hand in gardens above the city. The air was warm, the weather serene, and when her mother turned and smiled at her all felt right with the world.

Outside her mind, in the real world, Diana's mouth stretched into a smile, only inches from the gun barrel. Inside, within Diana's mind, she knew a moment of peace, of real peace. The first she had known in days. With time this faded, and only a dark empty oblivion replaced it.

Chapter Fifteen
Phoenix

Light streamed through the windows, irritating Diana's eyes as she blinked away her sloth. Remnants of some dream scattered from her consciousness, slipping away like shadows with the darkness. She couldn't even recall if the dreams had been pleasant or dreadful.

Momentary confusion overtook her. The unfamiliar surroundings gave her a surreal sensation, as if she might be trapped in one more dream. Gradually her memories returned. Her mother, the burning pyre, her own flirtation with death. One long lurid nightmare that didn't recede with morning.

She arched her back, the muscles stretching as blood flowed more freely within them. Then she twisted over onto her side and glanced back down the barrel of her pistol. For a moment she just stared into the blackness. So, perhaps God didn't want her dead after all. At least not by her own hand. True, there was hardly clear proof of divine intervention, but twice down the road of self-destruction had been enough for one twenty-four hour period. Besides, although she could hardly consider herself happy or optimistic or pleased with herself, at least the crushing weight of despair had lifted. Hope, true hope, remained a fleeting fantasy, but in its place she found the steadfastness of someone with nothing left to lose. She'd found the bottom, found herself ready for death. If she were meant to die, then let Mancini do it, or one of the Council themselves. What need was there to do their work for them. Perhaps she might even yet do them some damage in the process.

She took the gun from where it had rested overnight. Carefully, she eased the hammer back down so the weapon was safe. It would do no good for her to blow a hole in her hip while walking. She swung her feet over the edge of the bed and, pistol still in one hand, stretched out her limbs like a cat.

"So now what?" she asked the pistol, hoping her madness had descended far enough that it might respond, perchance with good advice. Only silence answered her though and she returned the pistol to its fashioned holster. She took care of her morning hygiene and collected her few things.

A moment to regard herself in the mirror left her shaking her head. She looked terrible. Her dress was dirty from gallivanting all over the city and rumpled from sleeping in it. Her hair tangled in an abyssal mess. What cosmetics remained from the previous day were hopelessly compromised by tear marks. Had she wished to pass for a whiskey-starved prostitute only her good teeth would have spoiled the disguise.

Sluggish, she struggled with the holster and slid on her coat. Few enough the things she had with her. The clothes on her body, the pistol, some florins in her purse. She might flee to Venezia or Napoli and survive with some thrift for a few months off those coins. She'd hardly be the first Firenzian to flee in such a manner. She could even plead her case to the King of Napoli;

her standing was high enough he might grant her an audience and besides, he was ever eager to stir mischief in Firenze.

Perhaps she needn't go so far. Might there not be a power more locally to whom she could turn? There was only one man whom she could be confident had told her a grim kind of truth. Watching the books burn the night before, she knew with no doubt that if Savonarola wanted her death, she would have been cast onto the flames alongside those despised volumes. Savonarola would not have slipped poison to Isabella Savrano or to Francesca di Lucca. With a word, he would simply have sent either woman to burn upon the stake. Savonarola was a man of grand statements, not slick intrigues. In realizing this, she could be sure that he was one person who was not against her. Whatever else he might be, and Diana saw more than a little of the Devil in him, he was not her avowed enemy, not at this moment. It was time to turn to him and see what succor he might offer.

Down the stairs and through the entrance hall she slinked like a thief. An old woman now watched the inn, and Diana barely glanced at her. Shame burned in her, as if the woman would guess her self-destructive plans for the night before. It would not be possible to be out of the inn too quickly, and if she never returned there it would be for the best.

Diana breathed deeply once she was out the door and back on the streets of Firenze. The air felt much warmer than the day before, and melted snow ran in little streams down the street. Above, gray clouds still loomed, and it was unlikely that this temperate respite would last very long.

Across town, Diana set off, keeping her head low and avoiding eye contact. People were out on the streets and an air of normalcy seemed to return to the city. Still, people could be seen to speak in hushed tones about the night's events, and if Diana looked carefully, she found she could spot bits of ash that had landed like snow. The closer to the center of town, the more this was true, and here even the remains of the great bonfire scented the air with the odor of spent flame.

Diana's goal was the Palazzo Vecchio, where the government of Firenze historically housed. She had no way to be certain that Savonarola would be there, but she could think of no better place to search for him. She remained uncertain of what she would say to him, and could only trust that the God who had intervened to spare her the night before would inspire in her the proper words.

The palazzo itself was a tall, imposing building, managing to somehow capture terror and beauty at once in its architecture. A solid stone structure, the palazzo did not radiate warmth and its single off-center tower angled toward heaven not in adulation but like a dagger stabbing for the heart of God. People came and went from the palazzo on their business and gendarmes stood guard outside the main door.

Waiting in the line outside the door, Diana let her eyes close and tried to relax. What was the worst that could happen? Well, the worst was that Savonarola might suddenly turn on her and have her burned at the stake. Nonetheless, she had to believe that this would be unlikely even if he did not look favorably on her requests. Standing in line to see a priest always brought forth such anxiety in her, whether for confession, communion or whatnot. The majority of them always seemed both unhappy and disapproving. She wondered sometimes how the men entrusted to guide God's flock onto the path of righteousness could display such contempt for that flock at times. Once in confession a young priest had made sexual advances toward her; although his advances had been cordial enough and not vicious, and he had taken her rebuff well, the event had left a mark. Never again had she viewed the vestments as separating priests from other men who too often were prone to aggression and rapaciousness.

Lost in her thoughts, she did not notice that the line had parted for her. Only the silence startled her from her reflections. She looked up and swallowed. The petitioners had stood aside from her, giving a clear path to the door. There stood a young man all in black, his eyes locked on her own.

"Niccolo!" she gasped.

His expression was unreadable, his manner stiff and formal as always. "You have been expected," he told her in his even tone.

God, how must I look? A silly and girlish thought if ever there was one. She stepped forward, looking him in the eye, waiting without word for explanation.

None came. "Follow me," he told her and returned to the dark interior of the palazzo without waiting to see if she obeyed.

Feeling as if this were all some surreal dream, she stepped over the threshold and into the palazzo. She looked from left to right at the gendarmes, but neither of them seemed to pay her much mind. Neither did they see fit to remove her pistol from her, though surely the grip was visible, for she had not securely fastened her coat.

The palazzo had few windows and so the interior was lit with candles that flickered and threatened to die in the drafts. Diana felt as if she had been plunged back into night. Niccolo, in his black costume, presented a difficult figure to track in the dark, and he never once turned to face her or to speak of what had happened since she had fled from her mother's grave.

She longed to converse with him, but felt a gulf between them. So she kept her silence until at last Niccolo brought her to a small dining room in the darkest recesses of the palazzo. Here Savonarola awaited her, hunched over a simple breakfast of plain bread, a bit of fruit and water. The contrast between the striking opulence of the palazzo and the meager form of Savonarola's diet, as well as the wooden plate and cup from which he consumed it felt difficult to reconcile.

Niccolo extended one arm to indicate she should enter. With some hesitance, she did so. Then, silent as ever, he turned and left them alone in the dining room.

Savonarola looked up at her, one eye squinting. He chewed half-heartedly on a crust of bread as he regarded her. In turn she stood straight and unapologetic in the face of his scrutiny. Best to remain silent though, to allow Savonarola control over their exchange.

At last he spoke, his voice strained and tired. "I am pleased to find you well, Lady Savrano. Won't you sit to breakfast, and talk with me?"

She raised an eyebrow. "You want me to dine with you?" For a priest to maintain such contact with an unmarried woman was unusual.

"...and talk with me," Savonarola confirmed. As

he spoke figures emerged from darkened halls, wait staff who held out a chair for her and quickly brought her a meal of wine, quails' eggs, eel, and fine bread. The figures might have been ghosts for all Diana could see of them in the dim room, lit only by a lonely candle.

With a last suspicious look at Savonarola, Diana tore into her breakfast. When had she last eaten? She could barely remember. Even now she hadn't realized how much hunger weakened her body until the food lay before her. Savonarola watched her with a look of interest, even amusement.

"I feel sorrow about your mother," he told her after some minutes of silence. His voice echoed through the room, deep and foreboding.

Diana hesitated, her fork hovering over a plate still half full with food. "I appreciate your words," she replied, her own voice crisp, high, contrasting his own. "My efforts proved insufficient to see to her best welfare."

Savonarola plucked a grape from his plate and popped it into his mouth, chewing with deliberation. "When I began as a novice with the order, my master bade me to inscribe a copy of the Gospels. I was never one who had talent with pen or paint, but I labored at this task with devotion sometimes twenty hours a day. My mistakes were frequent, and when made required that the task be abandoned and started anew. So much paper, valuable paper wasted on my pitiful attempts. My master chastised me with his words and with his fists. Finally, my skills improved so with the most Herculean of efforts, I scribed a magnificent set of the gospels." Savonarola's lips twisted into a grimace of a smile. "Each page lovingly crafted, engraved with the finest drawings my hand had ever made before or since. It was the most beautiful thing I have ever created."

Diana watched him, chewing on a boiled egg.

Savonarola's eyes slid sideways, locking on her own, his voice dropping an octave. "When I had finished, my master looked over what I had done. Without a word, without an explanation, he threw the completed work into the fire and left me alone with the embers of months of painstaking effort."

Savonarola sipped from his wooden cup, swallowed loudly. "How I hated him—hated him as Satan must hate Christ."

Diana stopped eating, staring at Savonarola without knowing how to respond. At last she asked, "Have you forgiven him now?"

Savonarola chuckled. "A year after this event he suffered apoplexy and died. But on his deathbed I came to him. I don't know if he could hear me in his last moments, but I spoke of what he had done. And then I asked him to forgive me."

Diana put down her fork, appetite slipping away.

"Your mother is now with God," Savonarola said simply.

"With how she sinned, with the Council, won't she spend time in Purgatory?"

Savonarola regarded her with his watery eyes. "Don't you see, girl? We are already in Purgatory. Destined to repeat out our sins over and over, until at last we see through them and mend the tears in our soul. Then, and only then, shall we be prepared to enter into the grace of God. Your mother saw her own sins, suffered and died for them. Her time with us has come to its end. I feel great joy for her."

She watched him quietly. Her body remained too exhausted to allow her much emotional reaction to his words. She didn't know what to think really. What could he know about the fate of her mother's soul? Pondering it offered nothing of value. The afterlife...her mother's afterlife was too remote. All that mattered now was in this life her body moldered in the grave.

Savonarola must have sensed that her thoughts wandered for his eyes glinted in the way that they did and he changed topics saying, "I'm sure you haven't come to me this morning to receive a homily."

Diana straightened in her chair with a deep intake of breath. "You know that I've been trying to discover who has killed my mother. In truth I have not yet been very successful in my efforts."

He nodded, "I am well aware of the course you've set for yourself. I'd suggest that perhaps you have been more successful than you give yourself credit for. A little girl floundering in the dark could easily be ignored and you certainly have not been ignored."

She looked down for a second. She had difficulty remaining focused and confident around Savonarola. Each new statement required her to summon up her courage. "It seems to me that our goals in this case are as mutual as we might expect. For different reasons we each want to get at the heart of the Sacred Council of Apostles. I would like you to help me. I would like you to grant me authority to conduct my investigation in the name of the Republic of Firenze."

Savonarola regarded her silently for a long, uncomfortable moment. "You understand that what you ask for is unprecedented. For a woman to involve herself in the work of men to such a degree, you will anger many who are not your enemy simply for flaunting the rules of society. Under different circumstances I would condemn you myself."

She met his gaze, unwavering. "I understand that for which I ask. I am willing to accept whatever costs may come."

Savonarola puckered his lips, thinking. He then gestured to the lurking shadow servants, calling for one of them to bring him parchment, pen, and ink. These were quickly delivered and without word, Savonarola set himself to scribbling on the parchment. Several minutes passed in this manner, and Diana remained quiet, sensing this was no time to interrupt.

His work completed, Savonarola pushed the parchment across the table to her. "This is a warrant that grants you authoritative powers on behalf of the Republic of Firenze. With this writ, citizens of Firenze are compelled to answer your questions subject to seizure and criminal penalties on failure to comply."

She picked up the writ. The parchment felt heavy in her hands. Now that it was done, now that she had gotten what she'd come for, she no longer felt certain that she wanted this.

"You'll find it won't open every door in Firenze," Savonarola murmured, one hand holding his face partially obscuring his words. "Nonetheless, you are now in a position of power, real power, however temporarily. The enemies you make will be permanent."

She tucked the writ into her dress. She stood up, her legs still wobbly from the stresses of the past day. "I thank you, Friar, for entrusting me with this authority."

He nodded. "I hope I will not be proven wrong about you. You are a very brave and determined young woman. The ranks of the saints are filled with such brave and determined young women. It is an unfortunate fact most of them died violently."

Diana swallowed and bowed her head in respect. Then, feeling that further words could gain her no more than she'd already gotten, she turned and left back the way she had come, through dark corridors until finally greeted by the light of day.

****

The stone fortress of her family palazzo seemed like an alien structure when finally it came into view. She stopped in the street and regarded it for a moment. Columns of stone rose up toward the sky, the artifice interrupted at ground level only by the family coat of arms. On a brass plaque, three roses intertwined reaching up together for the sky. She approached the coat of arms and ran her fingers along the cold metal. When she was a child she had imagined that the three roses signified her family: mother, father, herself, an inseparable unit. Silly of course. The coat of arms predated any of them. Now such flights of imagination seemed all that much more foolish. Her hand dropped to her side.

"Lady Diana?" a voice hesitantly called.

She turned. One of the Swiss mercenaries watching the door drew near to her. Tall, red-haired, rugged, he came carefully as if in fear that a careless move might cause her to explode. "We've been scouring the city for you."

She knew the tone in his voice: fear. What could a man such as him have to fear of her? "I'm here now,"

247

she told him, disinclined to explain herself. "I'm sorry if I've inconvenienced you." She brushed past him, through the door, coming home.

Inside warm air crept into her cold skin, reaching her aching bones. Standing in the entrance hall, looking up at the ceiling. As a little girl she must have once stood like this and looked up at the images there, the half-nude woman futilely fleeing from the unwanted embrace of a satyr. The fleeting tendrils of a memory eluded her.

A hand on her shoulder. Siobhan scrutinized her with concern. "I feared the worst," the Irish girl told her.

So she had guessed the depths of Diana's misery. Diana opened her mouth to speak, to say something, to apologize perhaps, but no words suited. She met Siobhan's eyes, unsure of what to say.

Siobhan lowered her own glance, taking Diana into her arms and holding her there for a moment. Warmth passed between them, a welcome change from the cold outside. Still there was a barrier even Siobhan could not penetrate. "Come." Siobhan pulled away from the embrace. "There is someone you must see."

Siobhan took her by the hand, and without a further word, led her upstairs. Diana followed, too tired and drained to resist. The girl brought her to a guest bedroom, spacious and lavishly designed. Light poured in through a wide window, illuminating a woman's figure sitting by a writing desk wrapped in a thick blanket. Golden hair cascaded down the woman's shoulders. A flash of green underneath the blanket. The woman wore one of her mother's dresses.

Siobhan stepped aside at the door, allowing Diana

to enter. This she did without a word.

The woman at the desk turned at the sound of their entrance. Francesca. She arose, dropping the blanket. There she stood, still weak, her legs quivering with even this effort. Isabella Savrano's green dress gleamed with magnificence in the late morning sun. Francesca di Lucca seemed like a seraph basked in God's radiance.

Diana locked eyes with the other woman, unable to speak. At last, Francesca approached, her steps like those of a newborn fawn. She stopped a few feet from Diana. "In my death I saw many faces. I thought that they were angels, but when I woke the only face I saw was you. You were my angel."

Diana raised her hands just up from her sides a bit, palms out helplessly. She tried to respond, found no words, and then at last blurted, "That doesn't make any sense!" She burst out laughing as she said those words, but even as she laughed she knew it was fragile and that somehow, Francesca standing there in her mother's dress, incoherent as ever, had been the one to pierce her.

Even before she felt Francesca's thin arms around her the tears began to come. She collapsed into Francesca's embrace, unmindful of the other woman's weakened state. Sobbing turned to shudders and she clenched up handfuls of her mother's dress in angry fists. The two of them slowly collapsed to their knees. Francesca rocked her back and forth, like she was a frightened child. Diana buried her face into Francesca's neck as the tears flowed unstoppable and raw, burning her eyes.

Siobhan joined them, kneeling down and wrapping her own arms around the two of them, lending her strength to their fragile embrace.

"It's all right, Diana," Francesca whispered over and over. "We three are bound together. We three will surely prevail."

****

A good while later when there were no tears left to be spent, the three of them sent for a bowl of fruit and sequestered themselves into a forgotten upper floor room. With a bottle of fine wine between them, and the requested plate of figs, they tried to make some sense of their predicament.

"Besides ourselves," Siobhan asked, "who can we trust?"

"Friar Savonarola," Diana pronounced, "for only so long as our interests coincide." She already had explained to them her reasoning—that her mother would have died in flames had Savonarola wished her dead. The other two agreed and it was decided.

"It's like a rabbit kit finding concordance with a bear working together to dig up roots," Siobhan observed with a somber voice. "So long as there are enough roots, they remain fast friends. Once the roots run out, the rabbit kit starts looking tasty to the bear."

"What about your father," Francesca offered meekly. "Could we turn to him?"

Diana shrugged sadly. "He has been less than supportive. For what I know, he might very well have killed my mother himself."

"I doubt that, but she won't listen to me," Siobhan added.

"Perhaps we could take this matter to Cardinal Lajolo?" suggested Francesca.

"With the luck you've had in a Catholic convent,

I'd just prefer to keep the religiously inclined authorities at bay," Siobhan groused. "Bad enough we've got Savonarola watching over our shoulders."

"Perhaps I could confide in Bernardo?" Diana thought out loud.

"Just because you fancy him," Siobhan replied, "doesn't mean you can trust him. You've spent time with him twice. Besides, your other paramour, Niccolo, has been less than helpful, despite being well advised on current matters."

Diana nodded. Siobhan was right.

"Wait, you have *two* suitors?" Francesca looked at her with wide eyes.

"It's a bit more complex than that." Diana looked down at her hands.

"It would be a deliciously romantic tale if one or both of them mightn't have murdered her mother," Siobhan clarified rather bluntly.

"Oh," Francesca said, still looking amazed.

Diana looked sideways at the older girl. "You'll have more than your share of suitors now that you're out of that convent." At once, she realized she'd misspoken, assumed too much. "You're not going back, are you?"

Francesca stared down at her hands. "I don't think I'm welcome. They haven't even inquired after me."

"Odd about that, don't you think?" Siobhan piped in. "Here they have a nun returned from the dead, as good a miracle as any. If that wouldn't bring in the gold I don't know what would. That they don't show any interest speaks of guilt to me." She nodded as if her opinion was the surest thing ever.

Diana looked up, watched her friend for a moment.

It was odd.

Francesca twisted a little ring around on her finger. "I'm not sure what direction my life takes now. If they don't take me back, I'll be a scandal to my family." She sighed. "And even if they don't, I don't feel released from the vows I made to God."

Diana's heart sank. "I'm very sorry that my situation has brought harm to you, Francesca."

Francesca reached out and patted her hand. "It's nothing you could help. Whatever is happening, it is part of God's plan. His plan for us may not always be pleasant, but it always has purpose."

"I wish I could always be as sure of that," Diana said.

"So," observed Siobhan, "it seems that, aside from the dubious exception of the Mad Friar, we can trust no one?"

A minute of silence underscored her comment.

"Then it will be just the three of us," Francesca concluded softly, at last.

"That's two good friends more than I had when I started," Diana said with a smile for them both. "We'll begin with you Francesca. I'm reasonably certain the same poison was used on you as on my mother."

Francesca turned paler than before. "I can't think of why someone would want to kill me. As I told you before, no one has imparted any knowledge about the death of your mother unto me."

"You don't know who might've slipped you the poison?" Siobhan pressed. "Someone who might have brought food the day Diana visited you?"

Diana chewed on her tongue a bit at that. Thinking, thinking…

Francesca shook her head. "I can't remember much of that night, past when I prophesied for Diana. I wish that I could!"

Siobhan looked visibly disappointed, but Diana said, "It's all right. Probably a side effect of the poison. Nothing you could do about it."

"Why that particular poison with such an odd effect?" Siobhan wondered aloud. "Why not something like arsenic to get the job done without error?"

"Arsenic brings on a bloody agonizing death. It could easily raise suspicions of poisoning. Nightshade brings a quicker, less messy semblance of death, consistent with apoplexy, which comes on all the time. By the time the drug wears off, it is too late. As we saw." Diana squeezed her eyes shut, trying to blot out the memory of her mother's corpse, grasping desperately for freedom.

"I was fortunate that the ground was too frozen, and the gravedigger's spade broke," Francesca said with wonder. "And that you were clever enough to figure out what they did to me, Diana."

Diana looked at her and nodded. Who, though, were *they*? She was beginning to have a suspicion as to one of those involved. "I'm not sure how much you should thank me. I believe it is my fault that you were poisoned in the first place."

"Why?" Francesca asked, clearly disbelieving.

"Because you had prophesied to me about my investigation. Prophesies that began to come true." She looked up and met Francesca's gaze. "And I told someone about that."

Chapter Sixteen
Fire on Babylon

Seeing the convent at Saint Cecilia always filled Diana with wonder. Even in the depth of winter, God's hand seemed to brush against the place. Every stone, every tree, every pane of glass seemed in the perfect spot. Only today were the cracks in the edifice becoming apparent. A pile of rubble toppled unattended where the wall of Francesca's cell had been torn down to remove what had then been believed to be her dead body. The livelihood of the place, the frenetic energy of the sisters who did so many good works in the city bled out of that wound in the convent wall. Those few sisters who stood outside the place watched Diana with a helpless wonder as she approached, no longer a mere penitent, but increasingly the woman who would undo them. Diana felt their eyes on her and in their gaze felt a flare of real power swell within her. Flanked by two of Agon's tall Swiss, and wielding Savonarola's writ, she was now as powerful a force as she could ever hope to be. A fleeting moment, she reminded herself. With her mother's death avenged, she'd cast it away herself if Savonarola didn't wrench it from her. She could only hope to flirt with such darkness for so long without becoming afflicted by it. She had enough gloom of her own to contend with for the foreseeable future.

Diana rapped her hand against the thick wooden

door. The young and plump novitiate who answered, watched her with doe eyes. "I'm here to see Sister Ophelia," Diana stated.

"I'll fetch her at once," the novitiate promised, beginning to close the door.

One of the Swiss mercenaries put his paw of a hand against the door, and pushed it fully open instead. The young novitiate stepped back with a gasp.

"Best that we come with you," Diana told her.

The novitiate dropped her eyes and nodded, acquiescing meekly. So was this how it was to wield power, Diana wondered, to leave the teaming masses quivering before you? Did people only seem to love you out of fear? Who could live like this for any length of time, separated so fully from one's fellow man?

The novitiate led them to the main chapel where Sister Ophelia knelt before the altar. The sight of her, back turned, the very image of humility before the image of Christ filled Diana with burning. The hypocrisy of it... She gritted her teeth though, sucked in a deep breath. "Sister," she called at last, her voice echoing across the cavernous room.

Ophelia turned her head, slowly pushed herself up. She coughed once, a loose watery rattle filling her chest. Her eyes looked Diana up and down. "The other sisters speak of you as if you are a saint. They say you have brought Sister Francesca back from the dead."

"But we both know that isn't true, don't we?"

Ophelia's eyes dropped and she turned back toward the altar.

"Which God do you pray to?" Diana asked accusingly. "Do you whisper to Christ, or to Lucifer, as your wronged and fallen God?"

Ophelia looked back out of the corner of her eye. "I was sixteen when my father exiled me to this convent. I'd made the error of falling in love with a man of little promise, you see. I gave that man my virtue, and my father discovered my sin. Here I have been ever since. I can no longer remember the appearance of either of their faces. You can't imagine what pure Hell is here in God's service."

"I *can* imagine it," Diana replied. "I see it in the look of loss and fear I see in the faces of the girls. I acknowledge that I don't envy you your life course."

"Nor I yours," Ophelia said, with words that surprised and stung.

"You didn't need to kill Francesca over her prophecies. They've brought me no closer to answering my quest."

"They will," Ophelia said, her voice barely a whisper. "They will."

Diana frowned, finding a well of pity for the older woman. "Savonarola will have you burned for what you've done."

"So you're in his league now. Some saint."

Diana bristled. "I could speak on your behalf."

"For a price, of course. You'd have me betray all that I've come to believe." Ophelia stepped forward into the nave, her head held high. Not an ounce of shame in her manner. A heretic, a murderer, all a source of pride. "What else have I got? I'd rather die on the stake, than live as a hollow shell of a person in one of Savonarola's dungeons."

"Who brought you into the Sacred Council of Apostles?"

Ophelia's expression soured and she stomped her

foot. "I'll never tell you that! Your cleverness has brought you to me, but the trail ends here."

"But Sister Maria Innocentia, you brought her into the Council, didn't you?"

Ophelia ground her teeth for a moment, regarding Diana coldly. At last she deigned to speak. "Maria Innocentia came to us as a lost and troubled soul. The church of Christ could offer her nothing but the promise of damnation, so great were her sins, so deep her misery. The Lightbringer...he could promise her true redemption in a Heaven meant for the glory of everything humanity could achieve. It was he who brought wisdom to man, where God would keep us forever in ignorance. What was his reward for this act of generosity? An eternity of pain and suffering, Prometheus on the rock, Lucifer in Hell, the parable across faiths is consistent. He who reached out to us with the greatest love was made to suffer the most." Ophelia wiped her mouth with her sleeve. "Maria Innocentia found one brief moment of comfort in the promises of the Lightbringer."

"Promises." Diana spat the word. "What good are they?"

Ophelia frowned. "What more does your faith offer you? Look around and see what the reign of your God has wrought. His ministers on Earth...the Borgia Pope, consorting with his own daughter, murdering the good people of Rome to steal homes he finds beautiful, sending his assassins against any who speak against him, but you prefer the Mad Friar with his burning stakes and bonfires."

"I have no love for either man."

"Careful what you say," Ophelia observed with a

grin. "It will be you who is the heretic."

"You mistake the failings of man for the failings of God. If we have made this world a wretched place we are all that much more wretched for placing the blame on a remote deity when we should take it for ourselves."

"What use is a remote deity," Ophelia said. "A God who lets wars ravage the land, disease shroud us in pain and fear, and who allows rape and violence to take seed in the hearts of men."

"You are ignorant to expect this world to be the Paradise of the next life. Much as a mother must allow her child to take his own steps, make his own mistakes, should not God expect the same of us? If this life is meant to prepare us for the next, why should we expect more than pain and suffering and loss?" Diana's lip trembled as she spoke these last words, her thoughts on her mother. "Do we not become stronger for the pain we endure?"

"God's gifts have brought me only pain, not strength."

"That failure is your own. You say you suffer because you were sent here. Why? Because you suffered under the blows of another woman? Because you were denied the comforts of a man's embrace? How many suffer in the cold, without food, without shelter, and yet speak God's name with love and grace. Are they not the ones who are truly strong?"

"Are you truly prepared to lecture me on suffering, with your perfumed hair and your painted lips, wearing a dress with a value in gold florins that would feed a peasant family for years."

Diana felt blood steam the flesh of her cheeks. "At

least I do not presume to think my suffering gives me license to murder innocent people who have done me no harm."

Ophelia's shoulders sagged, as if the fight went out of her. "We could spend all afternoon skirmishing but what good would it do either of us? I won't do what you want. I won't tell you who killed your mother. You can't spare me Savonarola's fires even if you were so inclined." Ophelia looked down, reached into the folds of her black habit and produced from within a thick but short bladed knife.

At once the two Swiss drew their swords, the sound of metal sliding against leather becoming all too familiar to Diana. Diana stood still, watching. She knew Ophelia meant no threat. She understood only too well the other woman's intentions.

Ophelia waved away the sword blades. "I mean your mistress no harm. It is my own path that has come to its natural end." She placed the tip of the knife against her own breast. Her eyes fell on Diana, weary, sad. "I didn't feel glad about slipping the nightshade into the food I brought Sister Francesca. Sometimes we must make hard choices that lead us to do things that are unsavory, wouldn't you agree Lady Diana?"

Diana only shook her head, whether in disbelief or denial, she couldn't be sure. "Why Francesca? Why not kill me when you had the chance?"

Ophelia grinned, although her eyes held no joy. "You're not the first to ask me the very same thing. Suffice to say I am just an old woman, not an assassin. Surprise, indecision...I have nothing against you, nor your mother, misguided as she came to be. Besides, your attempts to avenge your mother were leading you in circles. What to gain by killing you? It was only after you mentioned Francesca's visions I knew she could make you truly dangerous."

Diana closed her eyes for a moment. "You tried to kill a poor frail girl over her delusions."

"Best you think them so. She will only lead you down a path of darkness."

"I am already on a path of darkness." Diana experienced terrible sadness grip her. In mere moments Ophelia would make her watch her die. Diana had not the strength to try to stop her. For what purpose anyway—to spare her life now so she might face a more dreadful death at Savonarola's hand? True, Savonarola might force names from Ophelia, but Diana felt she couldn't quite go that far. She wouldn't let herself become like Savonarola, even if it meant she would never discover who killed her mother. But suicide…what of its eternal cost? "Don't do this. Better to let Savonarola burn you than risk your immortal soul." Her own decision spoken aloud. Ophelia could not understand how personal those words were.

Ophelia laughed nervously and looked down at her own chest. "Could you tell me," she muttered without looking up, "do I have the dagger placed properly? I'll have only one chance to get it right."

Diana ran one hand through her hair. She paused, and then said, "Move the blade down an inch. The heart is lower than where most people think it is."

Ophelia looked up, her smile warm and genuine. "Thank you, Lady Diana for that small kindness. We might be enemies in this life, but I hope we will bask together in the Lightbringer's warmth in the next." She thrust the dagger into her own breast with both hands.

A gush of magenta spurted across her fingers. She coughed, "Oh," and then fell to the ground without a further sound. She hit the floor face first, her bloodied right hand quivering a bit.

The Swiss mercenaries sheathed their blades. Diana watched Sister Ophelia die for a few minutes, unsure what emotion she should expect to have.

With the help of the Swiss, Diana turned Ophelia's cell inside out looking for anything of value. Unlike Maria Innocentia, Diana found no arcane drawings across the wall and ceilings, no signs of cancerous madness. The trappings were simple, miserable, pathetic, the possessions of an imprisoned soul. A Bible figured among the belongings, the spine still fairly crisp, the pages undamaged. Little else of value could be found, even tearing apart the bedding, and searching for loose stones in the walls and floor.

Not even personal effects, no letters from family, no treasured reminders of a life she'd left behind her long ago. Ophelia had been a vacant soul. Unmissed, unmourned, sure to be quickly forgotten. Diana leaned against one wall of her cell as the mercenaries made their last futile efforts to find anything of importance. "She was unloved," Diana observed. "It's no wonder she felt God had turned his gaze from her." She cast her eyes downward, entwining her fingers together before her lap.

The Swiss stood straight and together they shrugged. Nothing. Without further word, Diana turned and left the convent behind her for what she hoped would be forever.

****

A roaring fire kept them warm. Diana, Francesca,

and Siobhan clustered beside it, blankets wrapped round them, keeping out the winter chill. Though no nearer her goal, Diana took comfort in their little cabal. She felt less alone than she had even the day before. More, she felt an odd surge in confidence, despite Ophelia's taking her own life rather than divulging the name of the person who had ordered Francesca's death. To think, if she'd been successful the night before, if she had reloaded the gun after taking the youth's life…

Agathi brought them hot drinks, sweet with cinnamon, and the hot fluids helped them warm their bones. Outside snow came down once again. It seemed the winter would never end.

"Was it really so bad to live in a convent?" Siobhan asked, sipping at her drink.

Francesca looked down. She rarely met either of their eyes. Diana could tell her friend would take time to adjust to life outside the cloister. She couldn't go back now. Diana hoped she never would. She was selfish to think that way. Francesca had been at peace as an anchoress. Diana couldn't understand it, but that didn't give her the right to wish her friend unable to return to that life. Nonetheless, Diana hoped Francesca's days behind those walls were over. She couldn't shake the opinion Francesca was wasted on such a life.

"It wasn't so bad for me," Francesca replied softly. "Sometimes the older sisters could be cruel. Not all of them, but some of them lost their way in Christ. Ophelia wasn't one of those though, she always performed her obligations dutifully. I would never have imagined her a part of such a heresy." She kept her eyes on the warm cup in her hands. "I always felt comforted in the embrace of God. Outside of that, I'm…lost."

"I don't think God lives only in a convent," Diana said, "or a church. I don't think he blesses you any less because you are here with us rather than in that place. I don't feel you are any less holy than before."

Francesca looked up, eyes sparkling in the fire, but said nothing.

"Diana's right," Siobhan added. "We're all in very different places than we could have imagined even two weeks ago. Certainly things have been difficult at times, but you must imagine God has brought us together in a manner He intended. If not He could have let you die in the convent, couldn't He?"

Francesca nodded. "What you say is true. Diana's insights, which led to my rescue, bear the mark of God's inspiration. His light shines brightly in you." She smiled at Diana.

Greater warmth spread through Diana than made possible by warm drinks or fire or blankets. She had no doubt Francesca remained the prime source of God's inspiration if any of them enjoyed such a blessing.

Siobhan apparently thought the same way. "Diana, Ophelia said that Francesca was poisoned because of the visions she saw on your behalf."

Diana nodded, watching the other girl.

"Clearly your visions are making the Sacred Council nervous, Francesca. Perhaps you've been approaching closer to the truth than is comfortable for them."

Francesca looked down again. "My visions seem to have brought more trouble than guidance."

"That's my fault," Diana chimed in. "It was I who opened my mouth to Ophelia like a fool, nearly sending you to the grave."

"And it was you," Francesca reminded her, "who brought me back from the grave in an act the whole city is speaking of as a miracle."

Diana blushed. "No miracle. I used good medical science."

"Whatever your methods, I believe you were guided by God. I see no reason why God must work around science when science would do just as well," Francesca observed.

"I think you should try another prophecy," Siobhan suggested.

Diana felt a pit form in her stomach. Even if there was some truth to the notion that Francesca's visions were inspired by God, and increasingly Diana thought there might indeed be some truth, she never found them pleasant. Francesca's visions mainly foretold horrible things to come. The physical effects on Diana had also been unpleasant…dizzying, nauseating, finally knocking her unconscious the last time. Diana wasn't sure she felt up for another round.

Siobhan's eyes were wide, animated. Clearly she thought this would be a good idea.

Francesca looked over at Diana. "Before I had performed them when I felt inspiration. I'm not sure what might result if we ask…"

Diana sucked in a deep breath. "I won't deny feeling some trepidation. I don't seem to take them well. And I can never seem to riddle out their puzzles. Still, I suppose it is better to have information than not to have it. Between the three of us, perhaps we could figure out their meaning better than I have been able to do alone."

"Great!" Siobhan exclaimed as if Diana had given a full endorsement. "How do we do this, then?"

Diana looked to Francesca for guidance. The older girl drew into herself a bit like a spring flower in a late frost. "Well, before the prophecies came at God's behest, on his time. This time we're asking Him for one. He tells us only what He wants to tell us, when He wants to tell us. We may certainly pray for more, but it is within His right to deny our request." Francesca met Diana's eyes, "You should prepare yourself for the possibility that you were never meant to succeed in finding who killed your mother. Sometimes we can learn much more from failure than from success if we open ourselves to learning life's hardest lessons."

"I can't let myself believe that." Diana closed her eyes for a moment. "I must try with every fiber of my being until I have nothing left to give this quest."

Francesca nodded. "Very well. Give me your hand."

Diana reached out hesitantly. Whenever she touched Francesca in this context it brought her pain of one sort or another. This felt like trying to force herself to touch a hot stove. Francesca took her hand before Diana could pull back. No jolt of pain surged through her. Francesca's hand was cold, the fingers little more than bones. Francesca closed her other hand over the top of Diana's. The older girl closed her eyes.

Before, a trance had overtaken Francesca almost immediately. Now Francesca seemed to be doing little more than meditating.

"Anything?" Siobhan pleaded after a moment of silence.

"Siobhan, please!" Diana barked as much from

frustration as irritation with Siobhan.

"All right, the more impatient we get, the less likely this is to work," Francesca observed. "Let us try to clear our minds of anything negative, any fear, any worries, any doubts. We must be receptive to whatever message God is willing to deliver."

"I don't suppose we could put forward our questions in advance?" Siobhan asked.

"Siobhan, we're not playing animal, vegetable, mineral with God!" Diana hissed.

Siobhan closed her mouth tightly.

"You two, please," Francesca chastised. She tightened her grip on Diana's hand and returned to her quiet meditation. Diana tried the same, closing her eyes, trying to excise all the dark thoughts from her mind. Be receptive, be receptive to the voice of God. Please, oh please, God, tell me what to do—how to find my mother's killer.

A moment later Francesca let out a sharp exhale. "I'm sorry, Diana. I just don't think we can call upon God's visions at will. If He wanted to impart particular knowledge on us, He would do so without our prompting."

Diana nodded, shoulders slumped. She couldn't deny a profound disappointment. It must be irrational to find disappointment in God. Everything that happened did so at His beckoning, didn't it? It was silly to hope that some prophecy would miraculously turn everything around for them.

Siobhan patted Francesca on the shoulder. "You did your best."

Diana stared at the fire. "The truth is, I'm at an impasse. If the Council is clever, they could simply disburse for the moment, go underground. It won't be long before Savonarola tires of me, withdraws his support. The Council could reemerge later, stronger, and I'd just be none the wiser. I have no other good ideas."

Minutes passed in silence, each of them lost in their own thoughts. Only the crackling of the fire cut through that silence.

A gentle rap at the door interrupted their contemplation. Agathi poked her head into the room. "A gentleman here to call on you, lady," she whispered.

Diana's eyebrows shot up at the announcement. Rather late for a caller. Niccolo perhaps? Unlikely…he'd seemed rather cool toward her not long ago. Wait. Could it be… "Is it Bernardo?" she asked.

Agathi nodded. "The young Don Tornabuoni, indeed lady." She withdrew from sight, her message delivered.

Diana looked over at her two friends. Francesca was uncomprehending, but Siobhan gave her a little smirk. "Diana has a male admirer," Siobhan explained. "Well, two really!"

Francesca smiled shyly, looking down.

Diana shook her head. "I think Niccolo is done with me. He's been a witness to too much negativity between my mother's tomb and my deal with Savonarola."

Siobhan looked down with a slight nod. "Well at least you've still got Bernardo," she observed brightly.

Diana rolled her eyes. "With all that's going on, let's see how long this will last. Come with me, won't you? I'd like to introduce you to him."

The three of them hurried downstairs. Their

excitement wasn't quite what it might have been in more pleasant times, but Diana still felt nervous for her friends to meet Bernardo. She wished her courtship, if that was even what she could call it, had come at a different time. Just as she had lost the interest of Niccolo, it would be easy to lose the attention of Bernardo.

They found Bernardo in the same study where she had first met Niccolo. Bernardo looked splendid as he always did, dressed formally in rich decorative clothes. The rapier at his side was gilded and shone in the flicking light of the fireplace. He smiled broadly when he saw Diana and held out his hands to her.

She took his offered hands and they exchanged kisses on the cheek.

Bernardo's look turned concerned. "I wanted to come to see you to make sure that you were well. I heard about what happened last night at the Basilica."

Diana nodded. She hoped he wouldn't ask her for a detailed rehash of all that occurred. "Thank you, Bernardo. I appreciate your concern. It is comforting to have you here." It occurred to her she would have to introduce him to her father. Having suitors arriving unannounced simply would push the limits of his patience, particularly after their last discussion. Diana stepped to the side and motioned toward her friends. "Bernardo, I would like you to meet two of my closest friends."

Siobhan stepped forward and greeted him first, giving him a curtsey. "It is a pleasure to meet you, my lord."

"The pleasure is mine." He took her hand and kissed it gently. He turned to Francesca, who shuffled forward with far greater hesitation than Siobhan. Her eyes remained downcast.

"This is Francesca di Lucca," Diana explained, "a childhood friend with whom I've recently become reacquainted." She hoped he wouldn't ask for an elaboration, although apparently he'd already heard about everything that took place at the convent.

Bernardo reached out to take Francesca's hand. The minute they touched, Francesca grabbed his hand in a tight grip. Her head snapped up and her eyes seemed to glaze over. Bernardo recoiled like he'd been slapped, but couldn't let go of Francesca's hand.

"Uh-oh," Siobhan whispered.

Diana could only watch in horror.

Francesca swayed. "Pain courses through you, fire burning all about. Above you a cloaked figure, hand outstretched in menace." Bernardo's face turned white and he staggered. Francesca's eyes rolled like a panicked horse, but onward she continued. "Someone who holds you in great affection stands above you, weapon leveled at your heart. And then…"

Bernardo fell backward, breaking their embrace. His head hit a bookshelf, sending several tomes spilling. Siobhan rushed in and caught his head before he hit the floor.

Francesca held her hand up to her head, steadying herself against one wall. "I'm sorry, Diana," she moaned. "I didn't mean to. I didn't see it coming."

Diana put her hand on Francesca's arm. "It's all right, are you well?"

Francesca nodded, eyes averted.

Diana looked down at Bernardo. Siobhan tended to him.

He breathed, but his eyes were closed, clearly unconscious.

Siobhan looked up and frowned. "Well, I think we certainly made an impression."

Chapter Seventeen
Matchmaker

Bernardo reclined on a couch, a cold rag across his forehead. His skin maintained a sickly pallor, but at least now he was awake and speaking. Francesca, mortified, sequestered herself away in an upstairs bedroom with Siobhan accompanying her, while Diana attended to their felled guest, bringing hot soup and wine.

Bernardo held the cloth to his head as if his brains might fall out. He managed a weak smile for Diana. "Your friends certainly are unique."

Diana nodded. "I've been on the receiving end of Francesca's visions myself. I know how it feels. You should recover quickly enough if your experience is like my last."

Bernardo's eyebrows rose. "She's done this for you more than once then? Do the visions ever come true?"

Diana shrugged. "To some extent, I suppose some have. They don't always make a lot of sense in the moment until you can look back at them. The visions would be a lot more useful if Francesca could just say, 'I see exactly who murdered your mother and that person is…'" Diana held her arms out as if waiting for the answer.

Bernardo gave a cynical laugh, but then flinched, the effort apparently hurting his head. "The vision she gave me is frightening. I hope she is wrong about this one."

"She claims they are from God. If she is correct, I imagine they are quite accurate."

"Do you believe her claims?"

Diana looked away. "I didn't think much of them at first. More and more, I don't know what to think. The Bible is full of prophets to whom God spoke directly. I never expected to meet one, but perhaps Francesca has better acuity to hear God than the rest of us. I'm trying to keep an open mind."

"As you say it would be helpful if her visions were clearer. Nonetheless, perhaps it is for the best. In light of all that has happened I have to ask if pursuing your mother's death in the manner you have is the wisest course."

A surge of resentment rose in her chest. "What are you trying to say?"

Bernardo looked down, apparently reading the tone in her voice. "Diana, I care about you, and I'm not trying to say investigating your mother's death is an unworthy cause. There are others looking into it. Would it not be better to leave this investigation to the authorities of the Republic? I have no doubt Savonarola will have those responsible burning in the Piazza della Signoria before a fortnight is out."

Diana felt her cheeks grow hot. "I am fond of you as well. But if it were your mother, what would you do?"

Bernardo's features fell. "I agree, the urge to seek vengeance would be overwhelming but..." He stopped and gave her a weak smile. "Is there anything I can do to help at least?"

Diana took his hand. "Sweet Bernardo, I am touched you would think to offer, but I could never ask such a thing of you. I have already involved Siobhan and Francesca into my own travails far more than I had any right to do. I won't be responsible for any harm coming to you. I must ask for patience. I wish that we had met under more pleasant circumstances. I hope that I will be able to resolve the matter of my mother's death soon. Perhaps then I will be able to turn my attention to more positive matters?"

Bernardo nodded, squeezing her hand. "You are a most remarkable woman, Diana. I hope your father appreciates your efforts on your mother's behalf."

Diana's eyes darted away from his. "I think my father would prefer a daughter in a more traditional mien. Still, he has not interfered, and for that I suppose I must be thankful." Instead her father had become a recluse in his own home, and they barely crossed paths. In this time of her mother's death, they only drew further apart. Perhaps by the time this was over, if she still lived, she'd have lost him too. Strangers living together under one roof...perhaps not even that if he grew angry enough with her.

She watched Bernardo, their eyes locked for a long silent moment. She wished their meeting had come at a different time. How much different things might have been. She hoped it would be possible to salvage something with him whenever her life returned to normal. "I can have one of the Swiss guards see you make it home," she offered. She hoped he would accept, but knew he would not. Even sickened, it would not be masculine enough for a young man such as Bernardo to accept an escort, particularly at a lady's behest. If only she could assure him she'd think no less of him; yet the more she insisted, she knew the more resistant he would become.

He didn't surprise her, demurring on her offer. "I am feeling much better. I should be able to make my own way home." He stood, brushing himself off as if he had been on campaign. "Perhaps once you have settled the matter of your mother's death, you might have time to spare for a gentleman's attention?" He grinned.

A smile widened across her cheeks. "I would like that very much."

"Good. I will take my leave of you then, and wish you the very best of luck. You will be in my thoughts." A moment later he was gone. From a second story window, Diana watched him walk away, heaviness in her heart. She wondered if ever she would see him again. She hoped she would, that fate would see fit to reunite them once again.

****

With heavy steps, Diana trudged upstairs to where she knew Francesca and Siobhan waited. With a sympathetic look Siobhan patted her arm. "Don't worry overmuch so. If he's worth much at all, he'll desire you still once this business of ours is completed."

Diana could only sigh. What could there be to say?

Francesca shuffled over, holding a little piece of paper in her hand. She kept her eyes averted and her manner remained subdued.

"Francesca, it's not your fault," Diana assured her.

Francesca looked up, long lashes nearly obscuring her sorrowful eyes. "My vision couldn't have come at a worse time, nor been more worrisome in content."

Diana agreed with Francesca's assessment but

remained silent.

Siobhan spoke up, ever the optimist. "Perhaps the meaning of the vision is different from what first appears. Was that not the case with the last vision?"

Both Diana and Francesca nodded, but neither added any more to the vain hope.

Francesca held out the note. "This arrived for you while you were with your suitor."

Diana took the note. "I don't think we can think of Bernardo as my suitor, not for the moment." She held the note up where she could read the address. Her name in flowing script crossed the front of the parchment. The handwriting looked familiar, but she could not place it. She opened the note and read aloud from it.

"Dearest Diana:

We must speak at once. Your efforts have brought you closer than you might think to the identities of your mother's murderers. In their fear of you they plot your undoing. Even now they conspire with one of your household for your final ruin. Let us meet in person, so I can tell you more. Meet me early this evening at the Church of Santa Trinita. Come as a penitent to the confessional booth and we will be able to speak there in privacy.

Yours always,

Pietro Benedetto"

"Is it his script?" Siobhan asked.

"I'm not sure," Diana admitted. "Let us check." The three of them retired to Diana's bedchambers and found Pietro's previous note. Comparing the handwriting, they found it to be similar to the recent note. "I can see little difference between the two. I must assume this is Pietro's handwriting." Nonetheless a stitch of apprehension remained in her chest. "Last time he brought the note to me personally, slipping past guard and servant to leave it beside my sleeping form. How was this note delivered?"

Francesca told her, "Agathi brought it to us while you spoke to Bernardo. She told us only that it was delivered to the door, not by whom."

"She would have mentioned the Boar," Siobhan added. "So it must have been on some other personage."

Diana frowned. "I have difficulty imagining Pietro hiring the services of a courier."

Siobhan raised an eyebrow. "You took away his key and exacted a promise that he would no longer burgle your home. Do you expect foul play with this missive?"

"I do," Diana nodded. "The note speaks at once about mysterious danger within my own home and simultaneously draws me from its safety. At the destination I could not confirm that Pietro summoned me until I am sequestered in the privacy of the confessional. I see the hand of Mancini in this and suspect the most vile ambush."

"What shall we do then?" Francesca asked.

Diana smiled at her friend. "You must stay here for certain in order to rest and return to your full health. For now, it will be for myself and Siobhan to attend to these matters. An ambush may be afoot, yet a treachery discovered can be turned against those who lay the trap, can it not, Siobhan?"

The Irish girl answered with a wry smile. The die had been cast.

****

The last embers of the setting sun played across the horizon spilling rays of pink and orange against a tapestry of clouds. The harshest of the cold had eased somewhat, a relative burst of warmth moving through the streets, turning snow and ice into streams of running water. The people of Firenze were also out in great numbers, enjoying the turn in the weather and perhaps also sensing that the worst excesses of Savonarola's bonfire were over, at least for now.

Diana and Siobhan picked their way through the unexpected masses, attempting to look as inconspicuous as possible. They could not help but obtain some strange looks for, underneath Siobhan's heavy coat a rapier blade in its scabbard protruded like a leathery tail. Siobhan did her best to keep the weapon as obscured under her coat as possible, but some sightings were inevitable and the spectacle of a woman with such a weapon was enough to entice more than a few stares. Diana had no similar sword, only her usual pistol which could be easily concealed under a heavy fleece. She displayed no skill or training in swordplay, unlike Siobhan whose talents in military matters continued to amaze Diana, and so bringing along such a weapon of her own would be a waste of time.

Diana thought over their plan, which didn't extend much beyond the obvious. The main assassin would most likely be found in the confessional, whom Diana would confront with the pistol. Siobhan would keep any other assassins at bay with the rapier, and both hoped that the throng of congregants in the church would keep the confrontation from spilling beyond a brief altercation.

With a look passed between them, the two women

 Christopher Ferguson

crossed the threshold into the church. Inside, its confines were as dark and gray as any other, the musty precincts broken by great columns of stone and lit only by the flickering efforts of a multitude of candles. As expected, though no priest currently said mass, a considerable crowd of penitents assembled in the wooden pews, seeking healing, solace, absolution, and whatever else. To Diana, people seemed at their least human in moments such as these, chanting, swaying, mimicking one another like a herd of insane beasts. To follow along with a mass was one thing, but this primal worship felt like a hopeless desperation to her, the devotion of these masses filling otherwise empty holes in the lives of these people. Diana felt compassion for them and at the same time guilt for looking down on them so.

Both sides of the church were covered in wooden and iron scaffolding, towering up from floor to ceiling. Behind each of these platforms, workmen erected elaborate cenotaphs of marble and bronze, commemorating the important dead of the Church in Firenze. Now the workmen were gone, but the scaffolding remained. Behind the iron frame and wooden boards, Diana could see the faces of angels staring back at her from stone. The designs were beautiful and yet frighteningly morbid as always they seemed to be.

Among these masses, Diana could spot none who appeared unduly suspicious or unusual. There were men aplenty and any might be among the assassins laying in wait. None seemed to watch the entrance overly much so however, and most were still too wrapped in coats to see clearly. She would just have to wait until they

278

showed themselves.

Along the left stood the confessional, currently unattended for no priests were officially in audience to provide forgiveness to the sinners. This was their target then, where surely danger awaited her. She nodded to Siobhan, who maintained her post just left of the entrance where she could guard Diana from threats coming from the congregation. Diana held in a deep breath and moved with a brisk pace toward the confessional. The box was an elaborate wooden thing, carved with scenes of heaven on the side for the priest and of hell on the side for the petitioner. Subtlety in message had not been the intent of the designer. Two doors awaited, the closest one for the priest, the furthest for the sinner, the entire contraption meaning to shield those within from view or overhearing.

Diana approached the confessional. She became deaf to the sounds of the penitents around her, their woeful chanting, the recitation of prayers and dirges. She forgot about Siobhan, who stood behind her, hand no doubt on the hilt of her rapier. How many times in a box such as this had she sat in the dark, confessing her sins to an old man who knew her not at all? Could such old men truly impart God's forgiveness upon her, or had she merely confessed her sins of pride and vanity, deceit and envy upon the voyeuristic inclinations of men isolated from the normal vigor of human life? It had been years now since she had stepped inside such a box. For a while, her mother had beseeched her to return to the fold of the Lord's confession, then had stopped. The end of her mother's entreaties must have marked the date of the beginning of her mother's accord with the Sacred Council.

Her hand reached out, instinctively for the handle that opened upon the penitent's bench. The fingers trembled, the wrist cramped. If she entered here, what awaited her? A sword thrust through the thin wood of the confessional? A pistol shot to the face as she turned to see her interlocutor? Behind her, how many innocent looking faces in the crowd watched as she stood there, themselves ready to plunge a dagger in her back if she hesitated a moment too long?

Enough! She turned from the penitent door, right hand drawing the pistol from under her coat. She spun to the left and yanked hard on the priest's door. As it came open, she thrust her pistol into the darkened recess within. Within a figure hunted, intent on the latticed opening between both the priest and penitent's seats. A corpulent form in the robes of a priest, he looked up in surprise as she pulled free the door. She didn't recognize him at first, fixating instead on the odd admixture of pigment between the skin on his nose and the rest of his face. In a second, she realized she gazed down on No Nose, Mancini's henchman who murdered Crispino. Now he held a matchlock pistol against the latticework between the confessional spaces. So it was intended to be a pistol shot to the face!

He grimaced on seeing her and tried to pull his pistol round. Diana didn't hesitate and fired her own point-blank into the scoundrel's heart. The shot thundered in her ears, setting them ringing and polluted the confessional with a thick smoke. No Nose coughed up a single spatter of blood and slumped, the pistol clattering to the floor of the confessional.

Even with the ringing in her ears, Diana heard the screams from the congregation. The mass of penitents rose from their seats like a flock of frightened birds and mobbed for the exits. From amidst this mass, several youths emerged, blades pulled from underneath coats and came for her. Siobhan intercepted these men with her own blade and the shimmering and clanging of steel mesmerized Diana for a moment. Diana did not doubt Siobhan's skill with a sword, but against three of these assassins, she could not hope to hold out for long. Diana reached into the confessional and retrieved No Nose's pistol.

"Siobhan!" she shouted, and when the other girl turned, hurled the pistol through the air on a careful arc, grip down. Siobhan swiped at one youth who lunged in clumsily and caught him across the jaw. As he yelped and leapt back, Siobhan snatched the pistol from the air and spun round just as a second youth moved in, blade intent on her heart. Siobhan discharged the pistol into the ruffian's face, his visage disappearing into a mask of gristle and blood. The odds thusly evened, Siobhan set herself to using the church pews to her advantage, keeping the remaining two assassins from surrounding her.

If she could just keep them at bay, Diana could reload her pistol and pick them off one by one. She set to this task at once, shaking hands attending to the delicate task. She just completed it and began her aim when movement in the corner of her eye caught her attention. Upon the scaffolding across the church a man stood, dressed in black, a long object cradled in his arms. A smoldering ember, lit like a match, glowed near his ear. Diana realized the danger just as that match came down and the harquebus he aimed for her head fired forth a funnel of flame. Diana retreated behind the confessional just as an immense chunk of its fine wood came apart, the splinters stinging her face and catching in her hair.

His shot missed, and he was disarmed now! Diana returned to her former spot, pistol at the ready, but found that the man in black had retreated slightly, taking refuge behind a marble angel from which to reload his gun. From her position, only the luckiest of shots had any hope to hit him. So be it. Diana would mount the scaffolding on her own side of the church, from which her aim would be better, so long as he didn't reload his own weapon first!

Diana sped past the clanging and ringing forms of Siobhan and the two assassins, and pulled herself up the small iron ladder to the first level of the scaffolding. Here a great bronze sarcophagus presumably held the mortal remains of some unfortunate soul long since moved on to the hereafter. Of better value, the sarcophagus afforded her some protection from gunshots. Here she steadied herself and took her aim. The man in black rammed home the metal rod down into his gun, finishing the reload of his weapon. As of yet, he seemed unaware she had changed her position. Diana lined up the barrel of her pistol on the struggling form and fired, temporarily blinded by the cloud of fire and smoke. She heard the shot strike home however, the wet sound of lead sinking into flesh.

A moment of elation swept through her and she strained forward through the smoke, better to see how her shot had taken its mark. As it cleared she saw the man still stood, the harquebus leveled, match glowing aside his ear. With a scream she retreated back behind the sarcophagus, all but falling into place. The harquebus erupted, and instantaneously her left hand felt split asunder in the most shocking pain. Like a fool, she had left it supporting herself atop the tomb. Now, too late, she pulled it back and regarded the damage done. The last finger looked like little more than a mound of ground meat, the tip shot clean away, the rest coated in blood. For a warrior, a most insignificant wound, she tried to tell herself, but, oh God, how it hurt! And all that much worse for being too much the fool to remember to hide all of herself behind the bronze.

She pulled her left hand into a fist, the only thing that eased the pain. Rivulets of blood ran out from between her fingers onto her coat. She breathed through her teeth, trying to control the worst of the agony. She didn't have time to indulge the hurt; more would soon follow if she didn't return to action.

Now the figure in black clamored up a ladder, seeming to move higher up the scaffolding. He favored his left leg, and she could see that her own shot had taken him in the thigh. Better to lose a finger than take a shot such as that, she reasoned. Diana could guess whoever held the higher spot, seized the advantage. Still, now they were both disarmed and Diana decided to reload her weapon first before seeking a higher spot from which to shoot. Reloading was made harder by her injured hand. She curled the last two fingers of her left hand into the palm as the torment would not allow her to use them. The rest of the hand ran slick with blood, her grip now both clumsy and slippery. Still, she worked with care and diligence. As she put powder and lead into her gun, she hazarded to look down to assess the status of her comrade. Below, Siobhan remained a vortex of steel and rage, at once the measure of her two opponents, but unable to quite get the advantage.

Diana took a calculated risk and, with the gun reloaded, maintained her current spot, steadying her pistol over her left arm. She studied the two youths accosting Siobhan, tried to judge the patterns of their movements. Finally as one lunged in toward Siobhan's back, she discharged her weapon just as the scoundrel moved into her sights, and by such divine fortune scattered the man's brains about the floor of the church. Siobhan glanced up with a grin and a brief wave before setting upon the last youth; that contest now so much more in her favor.

Diana chanced to look up toward the man in black just as the match came down on the harquebus. With a squeal of fear she dove back behind the bronze tomb, remembering to bring all of her this time. A shot rang against the bronze, but this time no searing pain followed it. Diana worked furiously to reload her weapon. Her wounded hand dropped the shot and it threatened to roll away before she caught it and rammed it home in the barrel. Then she peered up above her cover, pistol held steady over her left forearm.

The man in black pulled the long rod out of his barrel, having completed his own reload. Now he hoisted the long harquebus against his shoulder. He had the advantage of height. Diana would find it harder to hide now behind the bronze sarcophagus. She closed her left eye and took careful aim. She might not get another chance. She put pressure on the trigger, careful not to yank too hard and throw off her aim. She fought against the urge to close her eyes. Better to get some stinging powder in them than take another shot. She pulled the trigger back against the pistol and felt the hammer slam home, the wheellock spinning within and sending sparks flying into the pan.

The gun fired, Diana's vision once again obscured by the resultant cloud of acrid smoke. She flinched, squeezing her eyes tight against the shot she expected to greet her soon if her aim had been errant. No shot came and a second later, she heard the unmistakable sound of a body hitting the floor of the cathedral after a substantial fall.

By God's grace, she'd got him. She waved her hand in front of her face, dispelling the fumes from the gun and saw below the man in black spread-eagled on the floor, twitching ever so slightly. The sight of his fall distracted the last swordsman so Siobhan found her opening and ran him through the heart. Their enemies vanquished, all fell silent and, for the moment they were alone in the church with their fallen opponents.

Diana hurried down the scaffolding, a difficult task with her wounded hand.

"Diana," Siobhan exclaimed upon seeing her, "you've been hurt!"

"Bastard shot my finger off!" she cursed, and felt shame at the tears of pain running down both cheeks. She paid Siobhan little mind though and quickened to the man in black. Now that he lay in clearer light she could see his face and as expected, found him to be none other than Mancini. The last moments of life slipped through his fingers. Though his eyes were open and he watched her, he appeared unable to move his limbs, and with each intake of breath he coughed back up a spray of crimson blood. A hole in the right side of his chest made a sucking sound as he tried to breathe. Diana speculated she'd gotten him in the lung. Death would come soon.

As he saw her he smiled, blood spreading across his teeth and collecting against his gums. "How many dead you have behind you, lady?" he wheezed, his voice barely a whisper. "I should be proud to call you my daughter, were you my own."

"Tell me who hired you to kill my mother. You've nothing to lose now, and I've earned the right to know."

His eyes glimmered. "That you have, but I have never once lied to you. I never knew who hired me to kill her, or later to kill you." He hacked up a sorrowed laugh, spraying blood through his lips as he did so. "I'll see you soon enough in Hell. We'll share a toast together then, won't we?" And with that last his eyes went gray, the sucking sound in his chest ceased and Mancini, who seemed for so long to be the shadow around every corner, went on to his final judgment. May God have mercy on his black soul.

"Damn!" Diana exclaimed, feeling yet another door slam shut in her face. "Even in death, Mancini is useless to me."

"At least he is dead," Siobhan observed. "The Sacred Council will have to act on their own now. Made up of fattened citizens as I am sure they are, I fear them far less than a veteran such as Mancini."

A cohort of gendarmes rushed in through the door of the church, swords drawn. "You there!" shouted their leader, a youth of fair complexion and build. "What manner of calamity has struck this church?"

Diana placed her pistol in its holster lest miscommunications do their worst. She withdrew instead the warrant given her by Savonarola and passed it to the youth. "We have struck down these assassins of Milano by the authority of Friar Savonarola," Diana explained wearily.

The youth read the warrant with raised eyebrows before handing it back. "You've slain five scoundrels? Two women?"

From the tone of his voice she guessed she might well have told him she'd just reached up into the sky and plucked down the moon as if it were an apple from a tree.

"Do not underestimate these women," called a familiar voice from the door, "for these five are not the only victims of their wrath." Niccolo, of course. He stepped into the nave, the gendarmes immediately giving way in deference to him. He surveyed the damage done with an impassive eye. "How fortunate you have Savonarola's warrant, though no matter how unassailable your legal position, a scandal will be unavoidable."

Two women killing five men? Niccolo was right; they'd be the talk of the town for months. "What do I care for scandals? My path has been unalterable long before now."

Niccolo approached her, regarding her with care. "I have some authority in spreading the news of this incident. I will take care that the story is told so as to portray you two in the most favorable of lights. There are enough people in this city who like the tale of virtuous maidens defending their honor against foreign brigands that you will soon find yourself heroines."

Diana met his gaze. "Thank you, Niccolo," she said more softly this time. She could not help but notice

Siobhan move away from them discreetly.

"You're injured," he observed with a pained expression.

She held up her left hand, spreading the fingers so he could see that the last remained only in part.

"Come, I can bind it for you." He ripped a bandage from his own shirt, and bound her destroyed finger in the gentlest manner. As he tied the bandage round her palm he inquired coolly, "How fares Bernardo Tornabuoni?"

She laughed at that. "I don't think he'd care much for a nine-fingered wife who's killed more men than he."

His lips pulled to one side as he thought over his comment. "When I first met you, I worried greatly for your safety. More and more, I see how greatly I underestimated you. Any man of wisdom would consider himself fortunate to find a wife of such strength as yourself." He looked directly into her eyes.

"Oh Niccolo," she sighed, "how did I get to this place? All my life I fantasized about saving lives. Instead I find myself most adept at taking them!"

He touched her arm, gently and quickly, an uncharacteristic gesture of affection. "Go home, Diana. Get some rest; take care of your wound."

She nodded, wiping away the drying remains of her tears from her cheeks. She began walking away, exhausted and ready for the rest Niccolo recommended.

"Oh," Niccolo called after her as if remembering something, "I've found the man called the Boar. He languishes in Savonarola's prison and his fate rests in the friar's judgment. If you have any final words for a poor suffering penitent such as he, I wouldn't wait long past the morning."

Diana considered his words quietly. "Thank you, Niccolo," she replied at last and, with Siobhan at her side, left behind the slaughter they had wrought.

Chapter Eighteen
The Hunt

Diana gritted her teeth as Siobhan and Francesca argued over how to treat her severed finger.

"We need to heat up a blade to cauterize the wound," Siobhan insisted, a long kitchen knife already procured for the job.

"Are you mad?!" Francesca scoffed. "Can you even imagine the pain of that? And it will leave what remains of the finger a horrid ball of tissue. We must stitch the wound to stop the bleeding."

Diana liked seeing Francesca coming round a bit and sticking up for her ideas. Unfortunately she knew neither of the other girls' plans were optimal. No best path for treating a wound like this offered itself. Cauterization was too brutal and dangerous, and there wasn't enough free tissue to adequately stitch closed the tattered remains of a partially severed finger. "Enough, both of you!" Diana snapped. "Someone bring me some spirits, quickly!"

Siobhan left on her orders, leaving Diana and Francesca alone for a moment in the kitchen. Diana trailed a pattern of blood drops wherever she moved. Her right hand remained firmly clamped on her left, the strip of cloth between them soaked through. "For the love of God, I never imagined one finger would bleed so much." The blood loss worried her. It wasn't much compared to a head wound, but it didn't seem to want to stop. Eventually it would become a problem.

Siobhan returned with a bottle of brandy. "Strongest I could find."

Diana held her hand over a pail. "When I take away the cloth, pour the brandy over my finger liberally. Once it's done, Francesca, I'll need you to pass me those strips of cloth."

Francesca nodded, beside her the torn remains of one of Diana's father's freshly laundered shirts. It would have been best to boil the cloth, but Diana was impatient for a fresh bandage and this would have to do.

"All right." Diana peeled away the soaked cloth to reveal the miniature remains of her left little finger. It looked terrible, a black and purple center infused with blood. Without waiting for instructions, Siobhan let the brandy pour. Diana saw white before her eyes, arrows of agony shooting up through her elbow toward her shoulder. "Sweet Mary, mother of Christ," she hissed.

Francesca passed her long strips of the white cloth. These were lengthy enough that Diana could secure them in place by wrapping them round her wrist. She applied them liberally, one after the other, until blood no longer soaked immediately through the outermost layer of wrappings. The result looked very awkward but appeared to do the intended job, and the pain ebbed to a constant roar. Twice daily, once in the morning and once in the evening, she'd have to tap the bandaged stump hard against a solid surface to encourage the proper formation of scar tissue, and reduce the potential for chronic pain. All because she didn't know how to duck properly.

Siobhan and Francesca watched her apprehensively.

"I'll be fine," Diana assured them, finally breathing easier. "No one dies from losing a finger."

A figure appeared in the doorway—her father.

"Perhaps I spoke too soon," she whispered to herself.

Her father surveyed the scene quietly for a moment, the blood on the floor, the blood on her coat and dress, the wrapped hand. "Would you young ladies kindly leave us for a moment?" he asked at last, his voice steady and calm.

Siobhan and Francesca obeyed without a word. Diana watched them go with a sinking feeling. She ran the fingers of her good hand through her hair, forgetting they were matted with blood.

"The servants told me you'd been injured. I've heard as well about the incident at the church," her father explained, his face unreadable. "Is the injury bad?"

She put her good hand against an unused stove to steady herself. "I lost most of a finger. Could have been much worse though I suppose."

He nodded, made no move to come closer to her. "You left five dead behind you I've understood." She nodded. "These men were involved in your mother's death?" he asked after a moment's pause.

Diana nodded again, finally looking him in the eye.

"Then it's over?"

She shook her head. "These men were only hired by others. I still don't know who wished her dead."

"Well, at least we can be sure her death was not a suicide now." He nodded to himself, "That's something at least."

Her soul would be in heaven, not trapped forever in Hell is what he meant, Diana figured.

He looked at her evenly. "I would prefer not to lose a daughter as well as a wife. Can what you've accomplished thus far not be enough? Let Savonarola take care of the rest. He has as much reason as you to destroy this...Sacred Council." So, her father had been brought fully up to speed, no doubt by friends within the government.

His statement retained some truth. If she stepped aside now, Savonarola might very well press ahead where she left off, rooting out the Sacred Council once and for all. She could stop now, resume some semblance of a regular life.

Her father sighed, looking at his feet, probably guessing before even she did she would never turn back. "I could never imagine the little girl I once held in my arms would leave half a dozen dead in her wake."

His words broke her heart. She looked down at the floor, eyes remaining transfixed on a droplet of her own blood.

A moment passed. Her father sounded so weary when at last he spoke. "I always relied on your mother to act as an intermediary for us. She seemed always to know what to do, what to say to you. I suppose I never allowed myself a proper chance to understand you. I haven't been much of a father to you. For that I am sorry."

Diana looked up at him, watched him for a moment. "Perhaps neither of us have come to understand the other. If you haven't been much of a father to me, I haven't been much of a daughter for you."

Her father pursed his lips. "I don't suppose it's the same thing, do you? I should have known long ago you weren't meant for the typical course of a woman from Firenze. I just don't know how to support you on whatever course you are on."

Diana's eyes burned and she sucked in a deep breath to keep her emotions under control. In his way, he was trying to apologize, she knew. Still, within the apology she couldn't help miss the note of despondency; that she could never be the daughter he expected…the daughter he wanted.

"Whatever I have that you need," he said softly. "Money, the Swiss Guards, whatever it takes for you to finish this safely, you take it. You needn't ask."

"I haven't been…" she replied, unable to stop from breaking into a wide but fragile smile. He smiled back at her as well, a rare moment of warmth and connection passing between them. "Thank you, Father," she said at last.

He nodded. "Be safe."

****

The prisons of Firenze were much as Diana expected, and worse. True to her imagination, the cells were dank and dark, a central corridor between the bars running with a thin turgid stream of water, leaked down through a cracked ceiling from melted snow in the streets above. Diana hadn't anticipated the stink, the stinging smell of fermenting urine and worse. She nearly gagged as the first wall of this smell hit her when the jailer opened the main door. The inmates receded into the corners of their cell, visible only by the flash of lantern light against a scuffed boot, or scab of flesh.

These were a quiet lot, paying a woman in their midst no mind at all. Death awaited these men and women, enemies of Savonarola to a name. Some had been prominent in former lives, others scoundrels through and through. Most had spent their time on the rack and now merely awaited the Mad Friar's final decision on their fate. No hope emanated from any of the cells.

The jailer, a stiff young gendarme practiced in the arts of suppressing compassion pointed out the cell of the Boar to Diana. She thanked the jailer and went to the bars at once calling out the Boar's name. "Pietro. It is Diana. Are you there?"

From the darkened recesses came a stirring and a shadow emerged. In the dim light she saw his teeth first, the great tusks rising up from his lower jaw. Then she saw the bruises that covered the remainder of his face, evidence of the beating he assuredly took at the hands of his captors. "Lady Savrano, it is the greatest of pleasures to receive your company," he said, the words struggling to form properly around his massive teeth.

She felt a tingle in her spine and a heaviness in her heart at the sight of him. Always a pitiable creature, to have fallen to such a depth. Could God have smiled on poor Pietro any less? "Pietro, I must confess I never expected you would be captured. So wily and clever you always seemed."

The corners of his mouth, torn from abuse, nonetheless curled upward into a kind smile. "Unfortunately all things must come to an end. No matter how clever you are, there is always luck to work against you. Fear not for my fate; all will happen as it should." He gripped the bars between them to support his weight. "I have heard much about your travails, and what I hear impresses me greatly. You are truly from your mother's blood."

A pronouncement no doubt containing both good and bad implications. "Niccolo Machiavelli told me you were here. Have they treated you with any decency at all?"

"Firenze is not known for the clemency of its courts nor the mercy of its inquisitors," he answered with a wry smile. "What time we are allowed together will not be well spent lamenting over my inalterable fate. You've come to ask some last questions."

She didn't know to what degree she could trust Pietro, but he had been her mother's friend. To hear him speak with such finality troubled her. This affair had brought death to so many. "Mancini is dead. In his last moments he still insisted he hadn't been the one to slip my mother the poison. Nor that he knew who hired him to try. He had no reason to dissemble in those last moments."

"Nor any incentive to tell the truth. Still, I suspect one would hire the sort as Mancini when one wants an assassination known to the public, not disguised as natural death."

"It's frustrating. Even as I progress forward it seems I know nothing more than I did at the start. I understand in your own dire circumstances, helping me must seem a trivial matter."

"I assure you, it is not. My difficulties in the end, were brought on only by myself—allowing my own seduction by this mystery cult as a salve for loneliness. Better by far had I kept to my rooms and the shadows. I might have contented myself with the life of a monster rather than the death of a heretic." He regarded her with sorrowful eyes for a moment. "If Mancini speaks the truth, it would seem two individuals, likely both within the Sacred Council, wished death upon the Lady Isabella, your mother and my friend. Her first error, shared with myself, came in seeking solace with the Council, her second error in vocalizing her intent to leave perhaps not only to myself, who ranked below her in the Council, but perchance also to that person above her, whoever had recruited her to the membership and whose identity, like my own, would be known to her. In leaving the Council, she presumably raised fears she might go to Savonarola with what she knew about the group. Those in the leadership position presumably were those to hire Mancini. However, whoever recruited Lady Isabella for the cult, his or her identity would be known by your mother and have particularly much to fear. In some impatience, they may have taken matters into their own hands."

Diana felt the familiar pain growing behind her forehead. "So the Council raced itself to kill my mother."

Pietro offered a sad smile. "Unfortunately that is one weakness of a masked mystery cult. Membership at differing levels don't always communicate well. One element of the group did not know what the other planned. The lesser plan...that of the singular individual to poison your mother might have worked well, had not the greater plan already been in motion. Unnecessary though he might have been, Mancini nonetheless arrived in Firenze. He soon was recognized by his former paramour, the nun you knew as Sister Maria Innocentia, probably one of the most poorly named of all nuns."

Diana furrowed her brows. "Was not Maria Innocentia herself part of the Council?"

Pietro half shrugged. "A recent addition, low ranked, and quite addled besides. A shadow of whatever murderous assassin she had once been when at the side of Mancini. No doubt Ophelia brought her into the fold of the Council, and likely regretted it soon after. It was unwise to bring one such as she into the Council, although she might have done the damage that she wrought, regardless. Mourning the death of your mother, of whom she was fond due to your mother's charity to the sisterly order, and seeing the arrival of her former lover Mancini, she cleverly connected the two. My relationship with your mother was not very secret, and she managed to steal from me part of the note your mother had written to me detailing her concerns. It must have come as a shock to poor demented Maria Innocentia who had found some comfort in the mysteries of the Council."

"But she was fond of my mother and her memory and, hoping to find my mother some justice, spoke to me at my mother's funeral."

Pietro nodded. "By then however, the Council had caught on to her and one of them chose to eliminate her. Again, whether a solitary choice, or the action of the leadership, it is difficult to say."

"So this entire plot is founded on foolishness and fear."

Pietro's eyebrows raised a bit. "Fear of the stake. Fear of Savonarola. Fear of the fate that even now awaits me."

She shook her head. "People are so idiotic." Even as she said it she wondered what she truly meant. Were the Council foolish for following their errant beliefs down a disastrous road to its inevitable conclusion? Or were men like Savonarola and the Borgia Pope imprudent for turning the love of God into such a bloody business? How was it that men with such ease twisted the love of God for their own cruel instincts? Or perhaps she herself was simply naïve and God truly was the vindictive and jealous entity the priests sometimes made Him sound.

"You look despondent," Pietro observed.

"I never managed to get any closer to the Council themselves. Even with Mancini dead, I still have no idea who killed my mother."

Pietro smiled at her kindly. "Your accomplishments have been wondrous. You have the Council on the defensive. You've done so much more than Savonarola ever managed on his own."

She cringed at his name. "It does not bother you at all to find I have become his pawn?"

"You each use the other for a mutual purpose. Predictable and I imagine, temporary."

"Let us hope." Diana went silent for a moment. "I would never have imagined how deeply mired in death I would become. I suppose I understood it might be necessary to use violence from the moment I took my father's pistol. Even then it seemed such a fantastical idea. At first I worried I wouldn't have the stomach for violence. Now I worry it has bothered me so little. Perhaps I am no better than the men I hunt."

"You didn't begin this," he reminded her. "And many people would be surprised by what they are capable of when put to the test." He licked his tongue along the outside of one of his tusks, an absentminded gesture. "I may be able to help you bring an end to the Council."

She raised her eyebrows, listening.

He went on. "I've told you recruitment into the Council is hierarchical. As your mother recruited me, so I recruited a colleague as well. Aside from your mother, the only individual I ever considered a friend. Some way I have returned that favor, is it not? Assuming the Council still meet, following him could lead you to the rest. He's only a low-level member, undoubtedly innocent of your mother's death. I'll give you his name under the condition you do not pass it on to Savonarola. He does not deserve this fate." He motioned to his jail cell.

Diana nodded. "I agree to your condition. I will protect the identity of your friend to the best of my abilities."

"That will suffice. His name is Rogelio Bercuoli. He is a cobbler of some repute, of average physique but possessed of mannerisms that alienate him from his fellow man. As with my physical afflictions, the result has been to isolate him from those who would be his companions. The Council offered him a social congress unavailable to him through more typical channels. I suppose this to be the case for many who joined, myself no exception."

Diana consigned the name to memory. "Thank you, Pietro. I wish I could do something to alter your own fate. A word with Friar Savonarola, perhaps?"

Pietro chuckled. "Do not mistake a piece of paper with your name and his signature for real influence. To associate yourself in his eyes with one such as me even in the name of mercy would only be detrimental to your own self. Savonarola has no mercy in his soul."

He was right of course. Diana felt helpless, a perpetually familiar sensation. "Very well. I'll wish you a miracle then."

"They do occasionally happen," he smiled.

"Best wishes, Pietro." She turned slowly away from him, feeling there was more she could say to him but no words came. When finally she emerged back into the light she realized she had held her breath, not against the foul odors of the jail, but against the stench of hopelessness and of death.

Chapter Nineteen
Foretold

Finding and tracking the youth Rogelio Bercuoli proved an easy enough task. The young man lived alone above his cobbler's shop, which, as Pietro had indicated, enjoyed a fine reputation despite the social limitations of the proprietor. From what Diana could observe in several days of watching him, Rogelio lived a solitary existence, had few friends, rarely smiled. He seemed little more than an accidental interruption in the normal flow of entropy with his living cells merely waiting for their eventual release back to the natural chaos of things. He worked hard during the day and at night, though he refused to become a shut in, his nightly outings were solitary and he dined alone in a regular circuit of fine establishments in the city. Diana felt sorry for him. Such a bleak and lonely existence, his seemed. What confidants he did have appeared to be cut from much the same cloth as himself and Pietro, the undesirables of Firenze.

For their expeditions to track him, Diana hired a carriage at her father's considerable expense. Hardly the least conspicuous method of surveillance but Diana could not stomach lingering on street corners for endless hours in the cold. At least in the carriage, Diana and her compatriots could share warmth. Diana decided it had been a wise decision. Several days of scrutiny led them no closer to the Council. At least Rogelio appeared to take no particular notice of them. They began watching him from the time he closed his shop each day until after midnight when he appeared most likely to have retired for the night. Diana reasoned he wouldn't be able to leave his shop during the day, and it would be difficult to coordinate meetings later at night when few people would be sure of the exact time. This plan left most of the day uncovered. Yet they were not professional gendarmes. It wouldn't be safe to watch him alone, and they had to sleep.

By the third night, they began to wonder if this effort wasted their time.

"Are we sure we can even trust your friend Pietro?" Siobhan whined, visibly becoming increasingly uncomfortable cooped up in the carriage hour after hour, night after night. "Maybe he's still working for the Council and leading us off on a wild chase."

"If so, they would have ambushed us in the carriage by now if they're smart. It's what I would do." Diana looked up to see two pairs of eyes watching her in the dark. "What?"

"Those who live by the sword, die by the sword, Diana," Francesca chided.

"Lots of people who don't live by the sword still die by the sword. At least having a sword gives you a fighting chance," Diana replied.

Francesca actually groaned, causing Diana to give her a scowl.

"Maybe the Council figured out Rogelio is a weak link, recruited by Pietro, and didn't invite him to any more of their meetings," Francesca added.

Diana kept silent, but inwardly admitted it could be possible. What a waste of time this would be. "Even if it's true, we've got no other alternatives. No other information."

"It's fine, Diana. I'll be out here with you as long as you need," Francesca assured her.

"Yeah, me too," Siobhan added with a downward inflection. "I'd just rather be doing something active, like strangling one of them." She shifted in her seat. She wore the same rapier as during the fight in the church, and now added No-Nose's former pistol to her arsenal. From her constant fidgeting, the weapons made it hard for her to get comfortable.

"Maybe their plan is to just let us freeze to death out here in the cold," Diana groused.

"It's not so bad," Francesca offered with a shrug.

"You've been living in a cave carved into the side of a convent the last few years," Siobhan observed. "This must be luxury for you by contrast."

Francesca gave her a cool glare. Diana felt a surge of pride for Francesca. Slowly the girl seemed to be heating up a bit, not just recovering physically, but throwing off the freeze in her development set in during years spent in near isolation as the anchoress. Seeing a little spunk in the woman seemed right. Then again, it was a matter of perspective perhaps, and Diana couldn't be sure that her perspective on things made much sense at all.

"Our fellow is leaving," Siobhan announced. Indeed Rogelio closed the door to his store and apartments, dressed in a heavy robe, arms kept close to his side. He didn't look around as he set out and, as best they could tell, took no notice of them. He kept his eyes down on the street, and looked no one in the eye as he passed them.

"Another night of dinner alone?" Francesca wondered.

Diana tapped on the roof of their cab, but their driver already knew the routine. Giving Rogelio a little space so their trailing him would be less prominent, they set out. One little horse drew the carriage so a relatively slow pace for them would not be unexpected. He ate at a different establishment each night, or attended the theater or opera, always alone. True to form this night he dined in a little hole in the wall while they waited in the carriage, unappeased hunger creeping upon them.

There he remained for an hour or so. Rather than return home, he set out toward the north, to sections of the city in recent disrepair. As before he kept his head down, walking at a crisp pace.

"He's not heading home," Francesca observed.

Diana felt a quickening of her pulse. "We know he doesn't have friends or family to visit. Maybe this is finally going to lead to something."

Rogelio brought them into a part of the city once amongst the most illustrious but which had been scoured and particularly oppressed under the occupation of the French armies a few years prior. Too far away from the city center to benefit from the essential lifeblood of enterprise, these frivolous mansions remained ghostly shells, their former owners dead, occupying apartments closer to the city center, or fled to safer parts of Italy, if such places existed. The hulks that stood dark and empty were a sad reminder of a happier time in the city when the cruel but steady hand of the Medici held sway. Now they were like tombs.

Only one of them glowed with an internal light that flickered as if from candles or lanterns. Rogelio clearly intended that house as his destination. They had to follow from a greater distance now, for the traffic here was much lighter than in the city center. Yet unmistakably he approached the house and disappeared into the shadows surrounding it.

With him inside, they brought the carriage closer. Like the others here, this house once would have been beautiful. Now the grounds were overgrown, the building itself beginning to groan under the oppressive weight of nature trying to reclaim its bounty. The signs of life from within flickered obscenely, like positioning a corpse to appear alive. Diana watched the house for a moment, and took in a deep breath. When she looked down at her hand, she found it shaking.

"Well, this is it then," Siobhan observed. "What's the plan?"

Diana looked at her with a raised eyebrow. "I thought you might come up with one."

"This is your mission. Besides your plan at the church worked well enough."

"Did it?" Diana asked with irritation holding up her bandaged hand with missing finger.

"Compared to five dead assassins, I'd say we came out rather well."

"Easy for you to say, you ten-fingered whore."

"Whore?" Siobhan repeated with raised tone and looked intent on saying more, but Francesca interrupted her.

"I think it looked like he just went through the

front door," Francesca observed, moving between the other women to look out the carriage window. "I bet the Council guard the door, but perhaps we could get in another way. Don't you think?"

Diana nodded. "It's got plenty of windows and we've climbed in through second story windows before."

"No rope this time," Siobhan said, her tone still clipped.

Diana rubbed her face. "We've got half the arsenal of the Firenze gendarmes with us and no one thought to bring rope?"

"Well, anything can look obvious in retrospect, can't it?" Siobhan complained.

"We may not need rope," Francesca observed. "The Council can't possibly guard every window and still have a meeting inside. And there are plenty of overhangs and abutments. If we help each other we might still find a higher window we can reach."

Diana considered it. "It might be wise for you to stay here in the carriage. You could fetch help if things seem to go awry."

Francesca's brows furrowed, the first time Diana had ever seen her irritated. "I haven't been accompanying you in this carriage night after night just to be left behind when we finally get somewhere."

"Are you willing to take a pistol?" Siobhan asked.

Francesca recoiled. "I'll have no part in killing. I understand you must do what you must do, but I can't take another life, no matter what the value of that life."

"So what are you going to do?" Siobhan asked. "Pray over them? Or perhaps you can knock them out by telling them their fortune."

"Siobhan!" Diana snapped and the Irish girl went silent with a sullen frown.

"I can't take the life of another, but I can help you two keep yours. I can keep watch for guards while you two do whatever it is you plan to do."

"Fair enough. I just wish I knew what it is we two plan to do. Perhaps we'll know more once we get inside. I suppose we should get moving unless either of you have any last insights?"

Only silence from the other two.

"Very well then. Let's go." Diana threw open the carriage door before she lost her courage. The cold hit her like a hammer, but she pulled her coat closer and did her best to endure it. The ground crunched beneath her feet. Behind her the others followed.

Hunched down, she approached the forgotten home. From what she could see, no guards were evident. Always possible someone watched from the dark, from behind an upper window perhaps. She'd just have to take her chances.

The long run across the grounds to the side of the house seemed to go on for half an hour. Only minimal cover presented itself, and Diana had to hope the darkness would be enough. She took a circuitous route to avoid passing in front of the home, where guards were most likely to be posted. At any moment she expected to hear someone shout, her approach discovered. Yet, she made it to a side wall of the home without incident, Siobhan and Francesca joining her immediately. Didn't mean they hadn't been seen, of course. Perhaps the Council preferred to surround them quietly before striking. They'd have to press on and hope that wasn't the case.

Diana kept her body pressed against the wall. The shadows here were thick, sheltering them from the ambient light of the moon and city. The face of the wall was irregular in nature, jutting in and out as rooms came and went, probably added on from the original structure when this area thrived. Fortunately, this meant it would be possible to climb up onto one of these extensions and get into a two-story window.

Siobhan seemed to have much the same idea. She looked to the roof of one of the extensions. "I can hoist myself atop this; lend you two a hand up."

Diana nodded. "Up you go then." She watched as Siobhan scrambled up the surface of the wall, fingers finding holds in the cracks of the surface. A moment later she peered down from the roof, extending a hand. "All right, who's next?"

Francesca motioned toward her. "You go next. You can step in my hands."

"Thank you." She thought to protest and suggest Francesca go next instead, but the woman was right. With her hand, Diana would have the harder time climbing. Francesca might not be as strong as Siobhan, but she had at least recovered from her poisoning and had proper use of both her hands.

Francesca hunched down and made a step out of her crisscrossed fingers. "I've seen men do this. I hope I don't drop you."

Diana stepped onto Francesca's hand and with the other woman's help, tried to propel herself up to where Siobhan could reach her and pull her up the rest of the way. She didn't quite make it, scrambling to keep hold. Her injured finger slammed against the wood and she bit her lip to keep from screaming. Her good fingers found niches in the stone wall, though to her they seemed barely enough to hold on, let alone climb with. She couldn't see how Siobhan had made it look so easy.

"What's taking so long?" Siobhan demanded, her head a silhouette in the dark blue sky.

"I only have nine fingers!" Diana hissed back. A moment later though, she managed to pull herself high enough that Siobhan got her under the arms and pulled her the rest of the way. Thereafter, Francesca made a leap upward and Diana and Siobhan caught her and pulled her up as well.

Now ten feet off the ground, Diana felt horribly exposed. From within the house she could now hear talking, singing, chanting; she couldn't be sure and without certainty, her imagination began to run away from her. They needed to get inside. Up here, they faced two second-story windows, both broken and easy points of entry. They led into the same darkened and empty room.

"If the Council are at all clever, they'll have a couple gentlemen patrolling the house for uninvited guests such as ourselves," Siobhan observed.

Diana nodded. "It's a big house. They can't all be patrolling, or it wouldn't be much of a meeting."

"I'll be responsible for watching for guards," Francesca offered. "You two do what you must."

Using her elbow and feet Siobhan kicked out some of the remaining glass, allowing enough room for them to crawl through safely inside. The room within felt no warmer than the outside despite at least offering shelter from the breeze. Only limited light presented itself here, and details were difficult to make out, but the room appeared to be rather large, a bedroom perhaps. A large stone fireplace sat cold and empty in one corner. Most of the furniture had been taken away long ago, and what pieces remained were broken apart. The floor crunched with shards of mirror and flecks of wood. Even after French troops left behind a damaged shell, wave after wave of vandals and vagabonds further reduced this mansion to a hellish crust. Their marks showed their passage through here, whether crude graffiti upon the walls, or the dried stains of human excrement in the corners. The memories of the people who had owned this luxurious home by contrast, were no more than ghosts; faint outlines where once a picture or mirror had hung on the wall, grooves in the floorboards where once had stood a bed. Holes had been knocked in many of the walls, and the rotting influence of nature had worked on these further, giving the walls an ulcerated look. Diana felt sad and an odd sense of adventure at the same time. Under different circumstances, exploring these old husks might have been a great adventure. For tonight, they had more to fear than vandals and vagabonds.

"The darkness will get worse further in," Diana realized. "We should have brought a lantern."

"Too dangerous. We'd be spotted. Besides, look under the door." Siobhan pointed to the closed door, which presumably led outward into the hall. Underneath, a faint flickering glow could be seen. Someone had thoughtfully left the corridors of this place illuminated. Siobhan drew both her pistol and rapier, and Diana did the same with her own pistol.

"Francesca, stay behind us, and run for it if there is any trouble," Diana said.

"You'll get no argument from me on that,"

Francesca nodded.

Diana went to the door and worked the latch. It moved easily under her touch, feeling loose if anything. Carefully, she eased the door open, dreading a telltale squeak or groan that would reveal their whereabouts. As she opened the door, Siobhan carefully poked her head out and looked both ways.

"Candle in a wall sconce," Siobhan told the others. "Must be for the guards. No one is here at the moment though. It's safe."

With the door open they could hear sounds from within the house much better now. A myriad of voices at times, both male and female, at others a single male voice intoning. Sometimes they sang, sometimes they chanted, sometimes they merely spoke. To Diana it sounded like nothing so much as a Catholic mass. She stepped out into the hall, keeping as quiet as she could. Inside her chest, her heart intoned its own crazy beat. This seemed crazy. No warrant from Savonarola would help her here. "Sounds like the meeting is coming from downstairs. Probably in the main reception hall. I'd like to get a look at it from above if we could."

"If there is a central reception hall like you say," said Siobhan, "it could have an open area above it, which would explain the excellent acoustics of their little meeting. Perhaps the rooms adjacent will have holes knocked in the walls like the first. We could observe reasonably safely through there."

Diana nodded and motioned for Siobhan to lead the way. The Irish girl did as instructed, pistol held out before her, rapier at her side. Diana looked back to give Francesca an encouraging smile, and felt gladdened to see the third member of their trio appeared resolute.

Silently they crept down the first hall, then turned to the left, moving into the center of the building. Each time one of their feet crunched on a piece of glass or creaked on an old floorboard a wave of terror swept over Diana. Nothing leapt out at them however, and their progress went on uninterrupted.

Each of the hallways glimmered with light from one or two candles held in wall sconces. These made the going much easier, but reminded them that patrols could be expected. Doorways lined the halls, and Diana wondered what might lie behind each, what the rooms might reveal of their former occupants. Probably, like the first, they would be found too heavily damaged to reveal much at all. The wood demonstrated streaks and lines of damage from unintended exposure to the elements.

The second hallway led to a third, wider, with the remains of carpeting. This led out onto a grand open area. A domed ceiling held the wire relics of what once must have been a grand chandelier. This spidery skeleton hovered over a wide curved staircase covered with thick stained carpet. From a central landing, two other hallways radiated off into the darkness. They were at the heart of the house. More light radiated from this area and the voices from below were much louder now. They must be just above the main reception hall in which the Council service was being held.

Siobhan held up her pistol for them to stop. She looked back. "Guard," she mouthed silently.

Diana peered around Siobhan's shoulder. Indeed, a corpulent balding man sat on a stool just above the winding staircase on the landing. Across his lap a matchlock harquebus lay, although Diana noted he had not lit the wick. At the moment he stared lazily down the stairs, not overly attentive, nor concerned with the activities below. Probably a hired thug, Diana reasoned, and bored from too many hours sitting in the dark.

Circumstances were less than ideal. Diana reasoned the best rooms for viewing the reception area—assuming there were holes in the walls as in the first room—would be just across the landing in the next hallway. As languid as this gentleman seemed to be, it would be quite impossible for him to miss them slipping across the landing to the next hall. Siobhan might rush him with the rapier. He'd never get the match on his gun lit and fired before she'd cut him down, but he might manage a shout to the throng below. They could wait for him to patrol the corridors, if he ever bothered, and for the moment he seemed quite content with his thoughts.

Siobhan looked back and shrugged, apparently going through about the same calculus.

Diana chewed on her bottom lip, dismayed no good ideas came readily to her. As she watched, the man stood and stretched. He scratched his scalp through what remained of his hair. Of course the bastard was bored. He'd look for anything to attract his attention, get up, walk around—if they could just time their own movements with his distraction, they could potentially get across the landing and into the next hall. Whispering, Diana conveyed this to Siobhan and Francesca.

A minute passed and the man slung the harquebus over one shoulder and stared up at a spot on the wall where once a painting had hung. He seemed to try to discern its image from the lightened rectangle it had left behind. This would be as good a moment as they could expect, his back partially turned in their direction.

Diana motioned to Siobhan and quietly, almost tiptoeing, the Irish girl slunk across the landing, in full view had the man been watching. Her blade glinted in the lantern light, a dead giveaway. Diana thought she might faint, and she could feel Francesca's hand on her own, gripping her painfully.

After what seemed an eternity, Siobhan slipped past the landing and into the secure darkness of the hall.

"Go ahead," Diana whispered to Francesca. "I won't let him hurt you." She steadied her pistol across her forearm, keeping it trained on the guard.

Francesca nodded grimly and like Siobhan, stepped out into the landing. Her movements were slower, less graceful than the Irishwoman's and for a moment Diana feared she would make some noise to alert the guard. At last though, she too slipped into the darkened hall across the landing.

Now however, the guard apparently decided his efforts to discern the long-lost painting were futile. He turned back with a grunt, sitting down once more with the harquebus across his lap, now more intent to investigate the contents of his nostrils than anything else. Just perfect. Now they were divided.

Minutes passed, which Diana spent biting her lower lip. If another guard patrolled these halls, eventually he'd come upon either her or Siobhan and Francesca. She could only hope that boredom would overcome the guard once again and he'd allow his surveillance to lapse. Finally after an eternity he stood once more, harquebus over his shoulder, and descended the stairs leaving the lantern behind. He disappeared from view.

Diana shook her head; if only they had waited they could all have crossed the landing easily with no risk. Diana hurried across now and found her comrades waiting. They led her down a short corridor and took a turn to the left, where a door stood open.

"While we waited for you, we found a room which suits our needs." Francesca led Diana in through the open door, and closed it behind them.

This space was a bit smaller than the first room, but just as devoid of life. One moldering, but mostly intact chair sat to one side of the room. Otherwise little more than debris and rubble remained. A good size hole in one wall, perhaps two feet in diameter, glowed fiercely with light from below, and voices rose together as a chorus through that opening. Diana went to the opening and peered down below.

The congregation of heretics milled in a rough circle in the hollowed out remains of the main reception area. Lanterns and torches provided good illumination for the three dozen or so men and women dressed in long hooded robes, with Venetian masks to cover their faces. Most of the robes were brown or gray, although toward the front of the cluster, a half dozen or so individuals, all men by Diana's guess, wore robes of pure white. Two of these men sat just to the side of a makeshift altar, while a third man in white appeared to lead the ceremony. At the moment he held aloft some dusty tome and proclaimed something loudly in Latin. Diana struggled to translate in her head.

"What's he saying?" Siobhan whispered.

Diana shook her head. "Something about the book being some kind of true gospel of Lucifer. I can't make it all out, and don't think it matters too much anyway. Typical heretical rubbish."

"Might be the robes, but this lot seems a bit paunchier than I imagined. Don't seem quite so intimidating now I lay eyes on them," Siobhan said.

"Well, there are nearly forty of them, and three of us." As Diana said it she noted several more men at the periphery, unmasked and each armed with a harquebus. "A couple of them at least are armed. Besides I suspect the men and women in this room have been plucked from the top echelon of Firenze society. Merchants, politicians, lawyers...on the whole, much more dangerous for the long-term than oafish soldiers."

"Robes and masks—" Francesca looked over Diana's shoulder. "—they look plenty spooky to me. I'll keep an eye on the hallway, unless you have something you'd prefer me to do?"

Diana shook her head. They needed someone to keep an eye out. Francesca quietly left through the door behind them.

"So now what?" Siobhan asked.

"That, I don't really know. Can't very well kill all forty of them, can we? Even if it were possible, not all of them are involved in my mother's murder."

"I can't imagine any of them are pure and innocent either. If not your mother's murder, then the murder of someone."

"Either way, unless you've learned how to reload a firearm a lot faster than I can, it's just not possible."

Siobhan frowned, having no real answer to that.

Behind them, the door opened once more. Francesca hurried to them, breathing quickly. "Someone is coming down the hall," she whispered urgently.

The three of them hushed, even holding their breath. Two pistols remained trained on the door. Even with the heretical service droning on behind them, they could hear the soft footfalls as someone approached, a guard patrolling most likely. One footfall after another, creaking on a floorboard. At one point they stopped just on the other side of the dividing wall, and a loud thump startled them. Diana realized a moment later that it must have been the sound of a harquebus being rested on the ground.

Following this a soft thump against the wall likely announced someone leaning to take a break. Moments passed, stretching on until at last the footsteps resumed down the hall and out of earshot.

Only then did Diana allow herself sufficient breath. "I think we are unwise to have approached this situation without an established plan." She massaged her aching temples.

"Are we at an impasse?" Francesca asked.

Diana nodded. "There's so many of them, and no way to tell who is responsible for my mother's death. I would imagine one or more of the men in white may have ordered her death, but I can't decide which of them may be the leader—the priest leading the prayers or one of the men sitting just to the side."

"Ah, their masks hide their identity," Francesca observed. "Would it help your decision to know who they are?"

"I suppose we might be able to make a more informed decision if we knew who those men were. It's not as if we can ask them to remove their masks so we can decide who to shoot."

"We could summon the hounds of your friend Savonarola," Siobhan suggested. "He'd happily see this whole lot burn."

Tempting thought. "It would take hours to get back into town, inform Savonarola, for him to assemble enough gendarmes and return to raid this establishment. By then this heretical meeting might be over. Besides the last Republic botched raid led, if indirectly, to my mother's murder."

"I had better resume my watch on the hall." Francesca turned away. "Another guard might come by."

Diana waved her acquiescence absentmindedly, lost in thought. Francesca disappeared once again into the hall.

"We have two shots between us. Say one for the officiating priest, another for one of the other men in white. Make our best guess and hope that God guides our shot," Siobhan suggested, twitching a bit with energy.

"And if we chose wrong and hit someone with no involvement in my mother's death we become no better than murderers ourselves."

"These people, from low to high are all heretics and hardly deserve any better. Whatever they knew or did not know about your mother's death, the blood of someone is on each of their hands, you can be sure of that. Besides the men in white are all clearly of high status. Is it unreasonable to suspect each of them consented in your mother's assassination?"

"Without evidence? I am wary of such a random killing. I do not think God would guide the hand of violence."

"Well, we can hardly go down and interrogate them one by one, can we?"

Diana shook her head angrily. "I was wrong to bring you both here. We've gone to great risk for nothing. The best we can do is return to the city center and alert Savonarola."

"You yourself said that won't work!" Siobhan protested, a bit too loudly.

"I've made up my mind," Diana replied firmly. "We're leaving. Would you kindly fetch Francesca?"

With a dejected look, Siobhan nodded. She moved quickly to the door and opened it. Diana could hear her voice whisper, "Francesca?" A moment passed and Siobhan repeated the whispered call a bit louder. Finally Siobhan entered the hall, the door closing behind her. Diana watched the congregation below, now slipping into a group chorus that sounded vaguely similar to the droning of monks, only with mixed sex voices. They seemed a reasonably devout lot; she had to give them as much. And against her expectations, she saw no evidence of human sacrifice or sexual orgies or consorting with winged demons. This apostasy consisted of a more mundane composition, that of ideas gone hopelessly astray from the canon of the Christian church. The penitents below had been led off course, not by an inclination toward evil, but by their own search for answers to the greater mysteries of life and death, perhaps fueled by a natural repugnance toward the behavior of Christ's recent representatives in Rome. Hatred of others, fear of death, is that what it all came down to? Is that what ultimately fueled what had become of Christ's message? If these heretics should burn for eternity for their specious beliefs in a benevolent Lucifer, should not Christ's representatives on Earth burn with them for pushing them toward such fallacious ideas?

Her musings were interrupted by Siobhan's return. "I can't find Francesca!" the Irish girl whispered urgently.

"What?" Diana immediately panicked that Francesca had been apprehended by the guard. Yet she reasoned, if that were the case there would be a general outcry. Even now guards should have been pounding on their door. "Oh dear. What has the anchoress gotten herself up to?"

"We can't very well leave now, can we?" Siobhan observed. She settled down near the hole in the wall once more, pistol back at the ready.

Diana shook her head, agreeing. The poor nun wanted to be helpful. Diana began to think she knew what Francesca might try. The woman's questions had not been idle. "There." Diana pointed to a new figure, robed as the others, making her way through the congregation. The person had pulled the hood of the robe low, hiding the face, which undoubtedly lacked a proper Venetian mask to conceal Francesca's visage.

Siobhan coughed out a laugh. "By all the gods of wood and stream, she's got a pair of brass ones on her, doesn't she?"

Diana didn't share in her amusement. Francesca would be more likely to get herself killed than anything else. "Keep your aim ready. Our first priority has got to be to get her out of there safely."

Siobhan cocked her head to one side with a raised eyebrow in response. Not terribly encouraging.

Diana swallowed. "Nothing good can come of

this."

Francesca, for certainly it was she beneath the robe, moved through the crowd and up to the front. She stepped forward among the men in the white robes. No longer part of the natural choreography of the cult, Francesca would not be able to retreat. They'd notice her, see she had no mask, see she didn't belong. Bravely the young girl stepped forward, right up to the priest who stared at her, no doubt startled.

Diana trained her pistol on the priest, resting the barrel over her left forearm. "Siobhan, I need you to protect Francesca as best you can."

In a dramatic swoop, Francesca reached out and snapped away the priest's mask. A horrified gasp went up among the throng at such a sacrilegious behavior. The men in white sitting to the side of the priest struggled to their feet.

Diana's finger twitched on the trigger. She squinted to make out the priest's face from the distance, in the flickering light. His mouth dropped open, and stood like a statue at the uninvited interruption. An older man, in his fifties with a scraggly beard. Not someone Diana recognized. Not a member of Firenze's elite. Which meant, priestly duties aside, he might not have been responsible for deciding to end her mother's life.

Ignoring the agitated murmurs of the heretical parishioners, Francesca spun to her left, and snatched the mask away from one of the men in white who had been sitting, then the second. Then, one of the guards reached her and grabbed her hand in his own meaty grasp and pulled her away struggling.

Siobhan's pistol erupted just to Diana's left. The

guard took the shot in the head, his brains erupting like a geyser onto the huddled throng behind him. The gasps turned to screams, and the mass of brown and gray robes turned as one, crushing each other to get toward the door. Francesca used this moment wisely herself, to disappear into that sea of brown and gray, Diana could only hope to make her own escape.

Diana remained focused though. Of the men in white robes, three had been unmasked. The priest she had already dismissed. Of the two men who had been seated and now were unmasked, one she did not recognize. The other—dear God it was Cardinal Michele Lajolo, the very man who had officiated at her mother's funeral. He stood now, apparently stunned by this unexpected turn in events, his jaw slack, his eyes vacant.

True rage surged to her temples and threatened to burst her arteries. With no doubt she knew, she just knew, this man had played a significant role in ordering the death of her mother. It was enough for her. She squeezed her trigger and found a most unholy delight, a flare of evil satisfaction of a sort she hoped never to feel again, as a burst of red marred the breast of his white robe and he toppled backward over his chair. His flailing arms knocked aside a burning lantern and this spilled its flammable contents across the floor of the home. The resultant blaze was meager in form; a determined effort could have doused it easily, but the Council and their flock were now well beyond such an endeavor The remaining men in white joined their lesser brethren in fleeing the scene, pushing for the door like a herd of sheep.

"Satisfying?" Siobhan asked, as she coolly

reloaded her pistol.

"I hope never again to find such satisfaction in taking the life of another human being," Diana replied tending to her own weapon. In truth, part of her felt such a relief at the death of Lajolo like a weight had been lifted. Her mother's death had been avenged, at least in part. Another part of her remained sickened, and saddened, to find her mother's death had left behind a dark ember in her own soul.

"Since no one is bothering to put it out, that fire is perking up fast," Siobhan said. "We've got to get out of here."

"Agreed!" Diana turned just in time to see the door to their room burst open. A tall, lanky man in a leather jerkin barreled in, match on his harquebus smoking. He brought the barrel down, drawing his aim on Diana. She could only stare at the barrel in surprise, waiting for the shot to hit her like a hammer.

Siobhan moved quickly though, lunging in and striking the man's left hand with her rapier. The bones in his wrist snapped and the barrel went up, the round discharging uselessly into the roof. Small slivers of wood rained down on Diana, snapping her out of her freeze.

The guard cried out briefly, staring at his shattered hand before Siobhan put an end to him, driving her rapier hard through his chest until the blade came out his back. "Come on," she told Diana as the man toppled.

Into the hall they ran. From down below they could still hear the screams of the multitude seeking to escape the gunfire and the flames. Their easiest egress would be the way they came in. But Diana wished to be sure

Francesca got out safely. She couldn't leave her friend behind.

They returned to the stairway landing. The bald man hadn't returned to his post. Diana moved to descend the stairs. Siobhan grabbed her sleeve. "Don't be a fool, there are thirty or forty of them down there!"

"All of them intent on escape. I have to be sure Francesca got out all right."

Siobhan opened her mouth to speak, but at that moment a harquebus shot ran out and Siobhan's spine arched in pain. She swore and spun round on her heels, pistol leveled. There down the hall, the bald man, his harquebus discharged. Seeing his shot hadn't killed Siobhan he tried to turn and run, but she shot him down as he fled.

With her assailant down, Siobhan collapsed against the wall, one hand clutching her lower back, mouth twisted in a rictus of pain.

"Siobhan!" Diana cried in terror. "Where are you shot?" She moved to inspect her friend's injuries, her medical mind already wondering about how serious the shot might be.

"He shot me in the arse!" Siobhan told her through gritted teeth. "Can you believe that? Of all the places to get wounded." She pulled her hand away from her buttocks, found it covered with crimson, and replaced it.

Diana's mind went through the medical texts she had read in a flash. If one had to get shot, getting shot in the buttocks was about the best place one could choose. The muscle would likely absorb the worst of the blast, a general absence of exposed organs. There might be some chance of hemorrhage, but no more than elsewhere. Diana decided Siobhan's chances were good, and allowed herself a moment of relief. "You should be fine once we get you out of here and to a surgeon."

"Fine?" Siobhan repeated, outraged. "Do realize with a shot to the arse, people will think I got hit running away?"

Diana blinked. "Well, technically we were running away."

"Not specifically from him!" Siobhan snapped. "Oh God, it hurts! You can't even imagine!"

Diana frowned and wiggled her nine fingers for her friend. "Can you walk?" Diana asked, changing the topic to something more critical.

Siobhan nodded. "I can, just not so quickly as before. I can see myself out all right. I won't be much use to you down below, though. I urge you to come out the window with me."

Diana shook her head. "I can't leave Francesca. Are you sure you can get out by yourself? I won't leave you either."

Siobhan nodded. "I'll meet you outside. I think this lot will all be running home. No need to hide any longer."

Diana gave her a quick embrace. "Be safe, Siobhan."

"You too, Diana. Be careful."

With a sense of apprehension, Diana turned and began her fateful descent into the flames. She hoped she did the right thing, leaving Siobhan alone. If she aided Siobhan, she abandoned Francesca, and by aiding Francesca she abandoned Siobhan. Either choice was fraught with risk. If in the end, she chose wrong, and one of her friends came to harm, she'd never forgive herself.

By now the scent of smoke stung her nostrils. As she took the steps down, the Council members were fleeing for the door, trampling over each other, pushing each other, cascading over each other. Any sense of shared purpose they might once have had disappeared in the urgency of self-preservation.

She plowed into their mass without any thought for her own well-being. Her eyes searched about desperately for her anchoress friend. "Francesca!" she called out, her voice drowned out by the screams of the terrified throng. From one brown or gray robe to another, she could barely tell the difference in this mass of arms and masks. These people jostled and pushed her, not because she had slain one of their own, but because she stood between them and the door. At last, she pushed her way through them and their whirling gathering slid past her like a rough winter wind. She turned back to watch them for a moment, pressing each other to get toward the door and safety. She didn't see Francesca among them.

Just through an archway, the reception area burned. The flames had gone up and across the far wall now, spreading easily through the rotted wood despite the cold. Heat flowed copiously through the doorway. She could still see the outlines of the two dead men, Lajolo and the guard, flames coating their bodies now like a blanket. No sign of Francesca.

"Diana," hissed a male voice from behind.

She spun to find herself face to face with one of the figures in brown, a serenely smiling Venetian mask hiding whatever emotion might lay behind. Lowered against one leg he held a wheelock pistol much like her own.

Diana brought her own pistol up, resting it across her left forearm. She hesitated to fire. Dressed in brown, he wouldn't be one of the important leaders.

"I'm the one you want," the man said, his voice low, raspy, unidentifiable.

"What do you mean?" she shouted, conscious of the growing inferno behind her, crackling wildly now with the sounds of splintering wood.

"I'm the one you've searched for. Let the others go back to their lives. I killed your mother."

Diana sobbed instantly, blinking away tears at the words. "Why?"

"I'm sure the Boar told you. Only he didn't know she told one other of her intentions. Me. She trusted me and I poisoned her so as to protect my own future. I didn't mean for it to be the way it was for her. I had no idea nightshade would have the effect on her it did. I intended her death to be peaceful. Believe that at least." She could see his eyes only through the mask, and beheld in them something like true sorrow.

The voice was impossible to register. Could it be her father? The sorrow in his voice—who else could it be? Tears came down her face. "How could you do such a thing?" she begged to know.

"I could offer any number of excuses, but ultimately it is a matter that I valued my own life over hers, isn't it?" he said coolly. A moment passed. Diana felt like her heart might split in two. "If it matters at all to you, I've come to regret what I've done."

Diana let forth a raw primal scream. For a moment she could not look at him, whatever the risks; despite he might shoot her, she could not stand to look in his direction, mask or no mask. Only with great revulsion could she bring her eyes back toward him, staring at him over the barrel of her gun. Her hand trembled on the pistol. The pain in her finger throbbed with every pulse of blood through her body.

"Would you not shoot me down, knowing it was I who killed your mother?" the figure asked quietly.

Behind her, the flames roared higher, stronger, sending gusts of heat rolling through the front hall. Minutes…seconds…the fire would spread through the hall. If they remained standing here it would engulf them. Yet she could not move, could not pull the trigger, could not murder a man, even if he had murdered her mother. Her instinctive rage had been spent on Lajolo. It angered her—a dark part of her she'd never known before—to learn she had such a weakness.

"I thought not," he whispered, his voice almost sad. Slowly, he raised his pistol.

Diana fired at last. Her shot took him in the sternum with a snap, and knocked him to the ground. His pistol scattered away and his head clunked against the rotted wood floor. He lay there, arms outstretched, gravely wounded.

Diana rushed to his side and knelt. He breathed still, although the breaths came shallow and quick. Through the mask, his eyes rolled over to her, wide and afraid. She reached down for the mask. She had to know, even if it were her father, even if she committed patricide, she had to know.

Her fingers hesitated.

"Do it," he whispered.

She snatched away the mask, flinging it into the shadows. She held her breath as she stared down at the face beneath. Not her father. Bernardo Tornabuoni. "Oh, God!" she said, horrified. "You?"

"I'm sorry," he whispered, his breath raspy. "I was afraid of the Mad Friar. I was just afraid." He reached one hand toward her, but she wrenched her arm away, moved out of reach. She stared at him, speechless, dizzy, nauseated. "The flames. I don't want to die in the flames. The pistol…"

She gaped a moment, not comprehending. Then she followed the direction of his shaking fingers to his own pistol, cast aside when he fell. She stood and hurried to it, taking it from the spot where it had flown. Her own pistol she tucked into its holster and now this one she braced over her forearm as she had learned to do. The barrel, she directed toward his skull.

He looked up at her, weakening now beyond words. Her body shuddered, and tears came furiously from her eyes. She hesitated, caught between an act of murder and an act of mercy, the desire to see him die painlessly or to let him twist in the agonies of a cleansing fire. Could she be like Savonarola, finding pleasure in consigning others to the most horrible of deaths? Gritting her teeth she forced herself to concentrate, to take careful aim as she slowly squeezed the trigger.

****

She found Siobhan and Francesca sitting together outside. Well, Siobhan lay on her stomach on the cold ground. The rest of the Council had scattered into the night. Diana could still see a few of them disappearing into the darkness, returning to their normal lives, perhaps now never to return to the heresies of the Council. Who knew, it didn't matter. The Council would be Savonarola's problem from now on. Diana had her satisfaction. If only it left her satisfied. At the end of it all, her mother still moldered in the grave, and Diana only accomplished adding a list of dead to her own reckoning.

Siobhan and Francesca at least were safe. Siobhan, not surprisingly, remained in obvious discomfort, although her bleeding did not seem bad. "Damn carriage of yours took off at the first sight of trouble. Can you believe that? I've got to walk all the way into town with a lead ball in my arse."

Diana sat next to Francesca. The older girl still wore the brown robe she'd gotten for her ruse. She watched Diana without speaking.

When she felt she'd gotten enough control over her voice to keep it from degenerating into bawling hysterics, she said, "Quite brave of you, what you did, Francesca."

"I sought to end your impasse." Francesca cocked her head to one side. "I hope that it was the right thing."

Several heartbeats passed in silence. Then Siobhan said, "You've found who killed your mother, haven't you?"

Looking away, Diana muttered, "Bernardo," and her resolve broke, her shoulders unable to hold back their shudders, nor her eyes a flood of tears. She wept for her mother, whom she'd been unable to save, and for Bernardo whom she'd begun to love despite that horrible secret he kept from her. She wept for her father, whom she'd accused of murder. She admitted that no small part wept for herself, who had been so stupid, too sheltered to stop this evil before it occurred, and unable to do anything but kill in response.

Heat from the conflagration behind them swept over her and with it came the comforting arms of her friends, Francesca and Siobhan.

Chapter Twenty
Denouement

Diana sat on a set of stone steps across from the Basilica of Saint Zenobius. With a parchment and piece of charcoal, Diana sketched its outlines. She'd never done much drawing before, never really had the inclination. Suddenly this morning, she'd decided to see if she had any talent for it. Given the result so far, it looked more like a barn than a basilica; she guessed she would not be ranking as the first female Great Master of Firenze. Still, it provided good distraction. Drawing the Basilica also made her feel close to her mother, despite that she had not set foot in the cathedral since the fateful night of Savonarola's Bonfire. A month had since passed.

She didn't notice she had company until the figure blocked out the sun and cast her in shade. She looked up, one hand shielding her eyes. With surprise, she found Niccolo standing above her. A pang of guilt swept across her chest. Somehow she lingered on the thought she'd managed to wrong him. She felt certain she had, even if she could not exactly pin down what she'd done wrong. "Niccolo, such a pleasure," she told him.

He sat next to her, returning her to the warmth of the sun. "It is good to see you. I'm glad I found you here. How do you fare, Diana?"

She used her cheek muscles to make a facial shrug. "As well as might be expected I suppose. My finger only aches when it rains. The headaches have mostly gone away. My father still treats me like I'm made of glass, though. That's actually kind of nice, in a way."

He smiled, a gesture for him that never quite managed to look kind. "And your comrades?"

"Siobhan finally manages to walk without bitching and moaning about it. Francesca has recovered her health completely."

"She hasn't gone back to the convent then."

Diana shook her head. "Francesca tends to look for Godly messages in events. Nothing like being poisoned and buried alive to give you a message it's time to move on, I suppose. She still doles out the occasional brain-numbing prophecy though. God is not about to leave that girl alone." She flashed him a tired smile.

He chuckled, politely.

"It's good to see you, Niccolo. I wondered how you were."

He held his hands to the air. "The same as before. I am but a loyal servant of the Republic." He looked over at her and smiled. "In fact I come to you bearing an unusual message on behalf of the Republic."

"Oh? I returned the Friar's warrant."

"Not that. A compendium of thoughts and issues has coalesced in a way which might advantage you, although I'll spare you the details." From his tone, he wouldn't tell her those details if she asked. "The short version of it is that the Republic has paid a full tuition for you at the Medical College at the University of Pisa."

Diana stared at him as if he'd told her she could

now flap her arms and fly. Finally she managed to cough out an incredulous laugh. "That's a cruel joke to play, Niccolo. You know my thoughts on this matter."

"I'm not joking." He produced a parchment from inside his doublet and held it out for her. "This is your letter of appointment. We don't have any sway with the University of Salerno, as I know that is your first choice, so the University of Pisa will have to do."

She snatched the parchment from his hands, unrolled it and read, disbelieving. The contents of the letter were as he said. She now was a medical student at the University of Pisa, should she choose to act on the letter. "This is very generous. I don't understand." But she did of course. In part it would be Savonarola—and Niccolo's—appreciation for helping to splinter the Council. But it also rid the city of a strange and monstrous woman who took lives like a man. She had no future here anyway. Better she go to one of the few places where women who acted like men might be accepted.

Niccolo waved off her protest. "An account has been taken out at the Fuggers' Bank branch in Roma in your name. Held in trust, the account will pay out enough to cover modest living expenses for the duration of your studies. You'll have to present this parchment to the bank officer in Roma"—he passed her another scroll—"and regular disbursements will be sent to you at Pisa."

She held the two parchments like they might erupt into flame in her hands if she were not careful. "Dear Niccolo. I don't know what to say!" She flung her arms around him, hugging him like a true friend. At last she let him go and looked down. "Niccolo, I am sorry that our paths did not cross more resolutely. At a different time…"

"At a different time we would not have met at all and your father would never have consented for a mere clerk to court you anyway." He smiled at her. "And I would not keep you from your dream…your destiny. Perhaps we will meet again one day."

Her face softened into a grin, warm at the fantasy of it, yet quietly knowing it was only fantasy. "I would like that very much. I suppose you will know how to find me."

"I do at that," he agreed. "I do at that."

****

With her few things packed and a heavy heart, Diana searched out her father. She found him as always in his study, poring over his accounts. She knocked on the door, waiting for his soft but firm voice giving her permission to enter. She stood nervously by the open entry waiting for his acknowledgement.

He turned halfway to face her. "You're prepared to go then?" he asked softly.

She nodded. "I am, Father."

His mouth twitched and a moment passed. "You are certain you don't wish me to rent a carriage for you? You'll find it a long walk to Roma."

"It's not fair for me to ask anything more from you." He already provided her with an immeasurable support in insisting on maintaining Siobhan's wage for the duration that she remained in Diana's company. An odd way to maintain a friendship to be sure, but it did mean her own stipend would need only be shared with Francesca, rather than between three women. "Besides I look forward to the journey."

"You may change your mind when you are several days out. There are all manner of dangers on the road for young women traveling alone." He chuckled softly a moment later. "Why do I worry? Between you and Siobhan you'll be armed better than any brigands you might meet."

She smirked and said. "I will miss you, Father."

He looked over at her, out of the corner of his eye true, but it was a rare moment in which their gazes met. "Probably far less than either of us would wish. Truth be told, I've never been much of a father to you. If you stayed, I don't think I'd be able to change that. We both relied on your mother so much just to maintain the peace between us."

Diana nodded. "I will miss you. I'll write you from Roma."

"Do that." He chuckled once more. "Avoid the pope if you can. I hear it told that he likes young women of your sort altogether too much."

She smiled. "I will."

"Francesca is certain about joining you? She is welcome to stay here until such time as she reconciles with her family."

"Thank you, Father, but they seem disinclined to recognize an ex-nun among their daughters. I'm not sure reconciliation is coming. Besides, I like having her with me for my own selfish reasons. I have only two real friends in the world."

"Then it is decided." He nodded. "Be well, Diana."

****

One moment she would never tell her father, would not share even with Siobhan and Francesca. Days earlier, when she had first told him her intention to leave for Roma then Pisa, her father invited her to take anything among her mother's things that she wished. It was a lovely gesture and though she had nothing in mind, she hoped for a small memento she could keep with her.

The rooms Isabella Savrano inhabited in life had not yet been gone through and cleaned out. No doubt most of the items would eventually go to charity. The valuables would stay with the family. Isabella had several rooms to her own and, as with any lady of means, they contained many things.

A necklace or ring were the most likely objects to serve as a memento, Diana figured. No way would she haul some elaborate dress all the way to Roma and then Pisa. So she searched through her mother's vanity drawers for something suitable. She found it there, not a keepsake, but the unexpected.

A vial of the sort an apothecary might use. Within, powder. A sniff, a slight taste with the tongue, enough to suggest it might be nightshade. And the vial was not full.

Diana thought of how she'd imagined her mother's death, that her mother had written to Bernardo expressing her intentions. That he must have ridden back from France himself to dispatch her, masking his return as a triumphant completion of his apprenticeship at the French court. Later he had poisoned Francesca, expecting her visions might eventually lead to him.

It all fit.

Except for this vial. Could the link between Francesca's poisoning and her mother's have been mere coincidence? Could Bernardo have confessed to her mother's death in addition to Francesca's poisoning as a final act of repentance? The final page of a sad, but clear story cast into doubt by one vial.

If there must be doubt, it would be her own. Her father had been through enough. Her mother's memory restored. What was done could not be undone.

Diana selected her token, a gold and emerald necklace she had always favored. She took the vial as well, and destroyed it and its contents the very same day.

****

Diana stood between Francesca and Siobhan on the outskirts of Firenze. Before them the road stretched out long and cold toward Roma.

"You're sure we couldn't take up your father's offer of a carriage," Siobhan groused. She affected an exaggerated limp whenever the subject came up.

"I am no longer of the household Savrano. I must make my own way in the world." She grinned at Siobhan. "Besides, I think the journey will be fun."

"I agree," piped in Francesca, whose spirits had risen immeasurably at the thought of visiting the Holy City. "I've never really been much outside of Firenze, and Lucca when I was a baby."

"Roma is big and filthy and filled with verminous men whose only leisure is to despoil the virtues of young women and sometimes young men," Siobhan intoned, "beginning from the pope and working down." With a look at the other two she rolled her eyes. "But yes it will be an adventure. To his credit the pope has begun to employ some fabulous artists. I've heard it told that Roma might rival Firenze someday soon as a center point of the arts."

"I doubt that very much," Diana scoffed. "What

city could be more beautiful than Firenze?" Even as she said the words, she found them bittersweet and melancholy. As much as she loved it, she could not say that Firenze had been good to her. Perhaps Roma and Pisa would be different.

"Let us go then." Francesca took the first step. "I doubt your stories of the evils of Roma, Siobhan. Nonetheless, with all we have been through in Firenze, how much worse could things possibly get?"

A word about the author...

Aside from being an author, Christopher J. Ferguson is an associate professor of psychology specializing in forensics, an occupation which helps inform his writing.

He has worked with a wide range of offender populations, from murderers to sex offenders to child abusers. His works include several published short stories in *Orion's Child, Nefarious, Midnight Horror, Blazing! Adventures, Stories That Lift* and *Fantasy Gazetteer*. He is also a contributor to Time.com and CNN.com.

He lives in Winter Springs FL with his wife and young son.

Visit Christopher Ferguson at his website.

http://www.christopherjferguson.com